Praise for Andrew Kane's first novel, *RABBI, RABBI*

"Andrew Kane writes with keen wit and well crafted insight . . . a must read, literary and spiritual journey." *Faye Kellerman, Novelist*

"Kane delivers some stunning portraits . . . this first novel is a warm, richly colored story that will move readers of any faith." *Booklist*

"In true potboiler fashion . . . walks us through his characters' journeys with insight, sensitivity, and fine attention to detail that are rare." *Hadassah Magazine*

"An enjoyably lightweight page-turner . . . exotic fun." *The Jerusalem Report*

"Kane has a penchant for scandal . . . he has written a first novel that is likely to be enjoyed by religious enthusiasts, heretics, and most people who are undoubtedly somewhere in between." *Long Island Jewish World*

"Beautifully constructed . . . hard to put down . . . fast paced story that sustains suspense and holds the interest." *Catskill-Hudson Jewish Star*

"A moving story of the power of love and faith . . . a richly textured tapestry." *Bayside Tribune*

"An unusual and original novel . . . absorbing tale . . . filled with impressive learning . . . wrapped around by a touching romance." *South Shore Record*

"Andrew Kane paints a wonderful picture . . . a poignant examination . . . a must-read piece of Jewish-American literature." *Steven J. Bernstein, Former Hebraica Librarian, Yale University*

"A worthy edition . . . provides us with an understanding that profundity and complexity are not the same thing." *Great Neck Record*

"Kane brings in numerous characters who are well drawn . . . insightful commentary on the contemporary Jewish scene which is well worthy of note." *Dade Jewish Journal*

Joshua

A Brooklyn Tale

Andrew Kane

abbott press®
A DIVISION OF WRITER'S DIGEST

Joshua
A Brooklyn Tale

Copyright © 2011 Andrew Kane.

Abbott Press books may be ordered through booksellers or by contacting:

Abbott Press
1663 Liberty Drive
Bloomington, IN 47403
www.abbottpress.com
Phone: 1-866-697-5310

Because of the dynamic nature of the Internet, any web addresses or links contained in this book may have changed since publication and may no longer be valid. The views expressed in this work are solely those of the author and do not necessarily reflect the views of the publisher, and the publisher hereby disclaims any responsibility for them.

Any people depicted in stock imagery provided by Thinkstock are models, and such images are being used for illustrative purposes only.

Certain stock imagery © Thinkstock.

ISBN: 978-1-4582-0074-7 (sc)
ISBN: 978-1-4582-0073-0 (e)
ISBN: 978-1-4582-0075-4 (hc)

Library of Congress Control Number: 2011917247

Printed in the United States of America

Abbott Press rev. date: 12/02/2011

ALSO BY ANDREW KANE

Rabbi, Rabbi

AUTHOR'S NOTE

While set in real places, this book is a work of fiction. The characters, events, and dialogue are all products of the author's imagination. In instances where known names or events are employed, the related characters, incidents, and dialogue are entirely fictional, and any resemblance to actual people is purely coincidental and unintended.

For Debbie

ACKNOWLEDGEMENTS

I am grateful, firstly, to my wife, Debbie, for the countless ways in which she makes everything possible; my children, Max and Jessica, who never cease to challenge and inspire me; my good friend, Ira Wolff, for his wise counsel, and for providing me with a boost of confidence to see this through. Others include: Nat Lenchner, of blessed memory, for his editorial touches; Sally Kane, my mother and biggest fan; Nancy Schroeder, my research assistant from the early days of this project; Downstate Medical Center/ Kings County Hospital Center, and The New Hope Guild Center/Tikva, for affording me the opportunity during the 1980's to work with and learn about African American and Hasidic populations in the Crown Heights area and throughout Brooklyn; the many African American and Hasidic patients and families I have treated over the years, for teaching me about their respective cultures and lifestyles; the folks at Abbott Press for their support and guidance. Lastly, I am deeply indebted to Denise Lenchner, the world's greatest book doctor.

Sources that were helpful in my research include *Brooklyn, The Way It Was*, by Brian Merlis; *A Report To The Governor On The Disturbances In Crown Heights (Volume I): An Assessment of the City's Preparedness and Response to Civil Disorder*, by Richard H. Girgenti; *A Report To The Governor On The Disturbances In Crown Heights (Volume II); A Review of the Investigation into the Death of Yankel Rosenbaum and the Resulting Prosecution*, by Richard H. Girgenti; Archives of the *New York Times*, *New York Post*, *Daily News*, *New York Magazine*, and *The New Yorker*.

With thee have I pushed into all the forbidden,
all the worst and the furthest:
and if there be anything of virtue in me,
it is that I have had no fear . . .

Nietzsche, *Thus Spake Zarathustra*

PROLOGUE

A slight breeze drifted through the open window, offering little relief from the sweltering August night. Joshua sat in a chair beside Rachel's bed, his eyes fixed on her, his ears on the words of rage from the street below.

Kill the Jews!

No Justice, no peace!

The chanting, the clamor of bottles smashing, windows breaking, cars overturned—it had been going on for two days with no reprieve. Stores had been looted and set afire, pedestrians violently attacked, and still no help from the police. Or anyone.

Rachel was shivering. The months of chemotherapy had left her frail. "Joshua, would it be all right if we closed the window? I'm so cold." As always, her words came softly.

"Of course," he replied, though for him the room was stifling.

On the street, madness reigned. The mob wouldn't stop till it got what it wanted, what it believed it "rightfully" deserved. Already, one innocent scholar had been bludgeoned to death. And instead of contrition, there was only more violence. But here, four stories above the battleground, Rachel was struggling simply to exist, to survive but another day, even a week.

Reluctantly, Joshua approached the window, afraid to be seen by some "hero" with a brick in hand. True, Joshua was a black man—a fact some had accused him of forgetting—but in the dark night, high above the street, he realized his figure would appear but a colorless, indistinguishable shadow, as ripe a target as any.

Keeping himself from view, he reached out and closed the window. The screams were muffled as stillness descended upon the room. Crouching, he turned back to the chair.

Suddenly, an earsplitting sound—glass shattering, a brick crashing through the window. Diving out of its way, Joshua instinctively lunged onto the bed to protect Rachel.

"What's happening," she cried. "Why are they doing this?"

He looked at the broken glass around them, and had no answer. Two long days trapped, a *Kristalnacht* in the middle of Brooklyn in 1991, and no assistance from an entire city that had abandoned them.

A moment passed. Another crash. More shattering glass as a large stone flew across the room, smashing against the far wall. The screaming from the street could be heard once again, as he held her tightly, listening to a succession of windows breaking in yet other rooms and apartments. One after another.

"Don't be afraid, everything will be okay," he repeated. "The police will come. I know they'll come."

Then, a sound Joshua knew only too well: gunshots. Now, despite the heat, he too began to shiver, doubting his own assurances as images raced through his mind. What was he—of all people—doing there, lying beside this daughter of a saintly rabbi, willing to protect her with his life? How did he, once a *wanna-be* hoodlum, a nickel and dime runner for drug dealers, wind up loving this woman who was slowly slipping away? But for a twist of fate, he knew he could certainly have been among the agitators below.

A twist of fate.

And, perhaps, the grace of God.

BOOK I

CHAPTER 1

He was a street-kid. Union Street, President Street, Carroll Street, Crown Street, and Montgomery Street, to be exact. Nine years old, and fortunate to be one of the first black kids to move to the south side of Eastern Parkway. A dubious distinction, indeed.

His old neighborhood, north of Atlantic Avenue, had suited him just fine. But not his mother; she wanted "more," and that meant "living with white folk," as she put it. "You're not going to be another one of those bums out there, making trouble and ending up with nothing," she once yelled, after learning he'd been truant from school for several weeks. "You'll become something if it's the last thing I do!"

He was scared when she spoke that way, which was fairly often. And it wasn't the fury in her voice, nor the fire in her eyes that terrified him, it was the fact that she always meant what she said.

And this time was no exception. For it was soon after that when they moved from the Bedford-Stuyvesant section to the tree-lined streets of Crown Heights, from a dinky walk-up above a grocery store on Lewis Avenue to a bona-fide two-bedroom flat in a building on the corner of Rochester Avenue and President Street, directly across from Lincoln Terrace Park.

Crown Heights was a heterogeneous neighborhood in many respects, reflecting a spectrum of social classes. Joshua's new home was on the top floor of a four-story, red and brown brick apartment building with the name *Rochester Court* engraved in the cement arch above the entrance. Beneath the arch, two glass doors stood, framed and protected by swirling black wrought-iron. A four foot high black iron fence also ran the length of the building along Rochester Avenue, and the width down President Street.

President Street had both apartment buildings and private homes. The private homes were attached, two-story red-bricks with driveways and above-ground basements. A few blocks down, past the intersection of Troy Avenue, there were brownstone and limestone row houses interweaving among the apartment buildings, and even further down, past Kingston Avenue, were the large private homes that the locals called "mansions."

Joshua and his mother were privileged to live in this place—at least that's what his mother thought. Loretta Eubanks often reminded Joshua that they were one of two black families in the entire building, and one of thirty within a five-block radius. "Don't you go messing up our lives here," she repeatedly warned him, "I worked real hard to get us here, and you best not forget it!"

She was referring to her job as a housekeeper for a wealthy, Jewish family out in Long Island. She had worked for them eleven years, the first two as a live-in. But as soon as Joshua had arrived on the scene, the lady of the house, Mrs. Sims, told Loretta that she would have to find her own place.

Joshua never believed that his mother was actually angry with him, no matter how harsh her words. He understood that her true antagonism was toward Mrs. Sims, her employer, to whom she could never express such a sentiment. And she was also angry with herself. As he was growing up, Joshua often wondered why Loretta seemed to loathe herself, her life, her position, perhaps even her color.

She was also disgusted with the way men frequently reacted when they saw her on the street. In the old neighborhood, the black men would constantly whistle and jest, while in Crown Heights the white men silently gawked.

She was a tall woman, about five-feet eight, slender but nicely endowed. Her ebony hair was long and wavy, her skin dark chocolate, and her face bore North African features, a sharp nose and full lips. Her voice was raspy, and she spoke with a deep black-southern inflection. And while Joshua may have portrayed her as harsh from time to time, the one thing he never doubted was her love.

They moved into their new home in 1959. Loretta was twenty-eight years old. The other black family consisted of Mr. Williams, the building superintendant, his wife Mary, and their two children, Jerome and Celeste. Luckily for Joshua, Jerome was his age. Celeste was a year younger.

The other tenants were mostly lower middle-class Jews and Italians. The wealthier Jews in the neighborhood lived in the mansions on President Street, between Kingston and New York Avenues. They were large, red-brick palaces set back from the street, each standing on slightly less than a quarter of an acre. The only thing these homes had in common was that they all had lawns and gardens; otherwise, no two were alike. One was three stories, while its neighbor was five. One had old-fashioned, white, plantation pillars in front, another an open terrace. One had a flat roof, another an arched roof.

A few blocks west of the mansions was the Irish section, in the heart of which stood the Church of St. Ignatius Loyola and Brooklyn Preparatory School. What most of the Irish didn't know was that their church and school were located on the plot of land upon which the Kings County Penitentiary had once stood. The prison had been built in 1846, and torn down almost a century later because of the growing community around it.

The Irish lived predominantly among their own. Their confines were the brownstones of Carroll and Crown Streets between Bedford and Nostrand Avenues. But the Irish kids often journeyed to Joshua's side of the neighborhood to hang out in the park, play handball against the Italians, and pick fights with the Jews.

Loretta frequently praised Mr. Alfred Sims, her Jewish employer and illustrious landlord of their new premises, for his generosity in providing this home rent-free. Joshua never wondered about that, for in his nine-year-old mind, it seemed that this was the way things were supposed to be. As for the other tenants, there may have been suspicions about Loretta's rent-free status, but nothing ever surfaced.

Surprisingly, their immediate neighbors, the Eisenmans, were quite gracious. They were an elderly Jewish couple, and Mrs. Eisenman would check on Joshua regularly whenever Loretta was running late from work. The old lady even told Joshua once how lucky she thought Mr. and Mrs. Sims were to have someone as hardworking as his mother. "Giving you poor people this apartment is the least those rich suburbanites can do," she added. It would be years before he realized this wasn't exactly a compliment.

Joshua had never met Mr. and Mrs. Sims, nor their only child, Paul. He was, however, resentful of the fact that Paul was the one his mother took care of while he was left wandering the streets. Of course, that wasn't Loretta's intention. She needed to earn a living, and had always made arrangements for Joshua to be looked after. Even when he was an infant, Loretta had enough unemployed friends to do for Joshua what she was doing for Paul. But as soon as Joshua began to understand anything, he realized he was getting the short end.

Joshua was one year younger than Paul. He believed his mother really loved "that white boy," as he often put it. Loretta didn't mean to make comparisons, but sometimes she just couldn't help herself. It was no secret that she wished Joshua had been more like Paul, occasionally saying things like, "Paul is such a wonderful student; he gets A's in all his subjects."

She somehow imagined that Joshua was interested in her endless accounts about the life of Paul Sims, and that he was grateful for all of Paul's hand-me-down clothing she brought home over the years. A roof over his head in a choice location, his own bedroom, clothes on his back: he had much to be thankful for. At least that's what Loretta thought.

"We got ourselves a good thing," she often remarked. "So you best fit in, go to school, and do what you're supposed to be doing!"

At times like this, Joshua wondered what planet she lived on. Here he was, a poor black kid from Bed-Stuy, in a middle-class white world, and she was telling him to "fit in."

CHAPTER 2

On a sunny mid-June day in Washington Square Park, Anshel Simenovitz waited anxiously for his name to be called. As he sat among the class of 1948, he began to sweat in his black cap and gown. But the twenty-five year-old ignored his discomfort, for soon he was to join the ranks of power and success. Soon he was to officially graduate from New York University Law School.

The law school dean was a tall, robust man with a ruddy face, bulbous nose, and deep set eyes. His raspy voice resounded over the loud-speaker. "Lawrence Manchester," he announced as one of Anshel's classmates approached the podium to receive a diploma. Anshel knew he was next. The dean cleared his throat, as he did every five or so names, and then spoke the two precious words Anshel had been waiting for: "Alfred Sims."

Anshel's classmates and family looked bewildered. Who was Alfred Sims? It was a name that Anshel alone recognized: it belonged to him, part of his master plan to become powerful and successful. For a name like Anshel Simenovitz would only be a liability. So, a few weeks prior to graduation, he finalized the legalities to assume his new identity. He hadn't told his classmates, mother, or any of his relatives, many of whom were present in the audience. The only other person who knew was his fiancée, Yeda Voratitsky, who recently underwent a similar transformation. She became an Evelyn, still Voratitsky, but soon to be Sims.

Growing up on East 53rd Street in Brooklyn, between Foster and Avenue G, Anshel couldn't have known the difficulties of being an Anshel. After all, his friends were Moishes, Shloimes, and Hymies. And although the Italian and Irish kids frequently gave the Jewish kids a hard time, the names themselves didn't seem to matter so much as the fact of just being Jewish. But among the WASPs, whose antipathy toward Jews was more subtle, Anshel believed that a name change could make a difference.

He had learned this from his four years in the Navy during World War II, stationed on a supply ship in the Philippines, the only Jew among one hundred and fifty sailors. Although he was smart and educated, his ethnicity kept him at the three blue stripes of a Seaman, never to advance. His peers were mostly Poles, Irish, and Italians—just the sort of people he'd been accustomed to dealing with. A few fist fights and pranks, and soon he managed to gain respect. He was a tough kid from Brooklyn, not to be messed with.

They nicknamed him "Angel," an obvious takeoff on his real name, and an allusion to the fact that he was quite the ladies' man. Tall and muscular, with thick black, wavy hair and green eyes, he was the desire of all the island girls and many a Navy nurse. The envy of all. A powerful and successful man.

Yet, notwithstanding his social achievements, Anshel Simenovitz realized that there was one circle in which he would never be welcome: that of the WASPs. Most of the officers were WASPs, especially at the higher ranks. A well-educated Catholic or Baptist occasionally got a shot as well. But never a Jew.

Even among those few of his fellow seamen who were WASPs, there existed an odious undercurrent. They, like the officers, shied away from him. They were, of course, always formal and polite, but never quite accepting. It wasn't long before Anshel came to recognize this as the most insidious form of anti-Semitism he had yet encountered. And it wasn't long after that, he swore to himself that he would never fall victim to it again.

Now, four years after his discharge, Anshel Simenovitz and Yeda Voratitsky had officially become Alfred and Evelyn. Now, they could "pass" in the gentile world. Nothing stood in the way of achieving power and success. Nothing—except maybe Anshel's mother.

"Vhat is dis Alfred Sims business, Anshel?" she asked angrily as the family gathered around at the end of the graduation ceremony. "If your father—God rest his soul—vere still alive, this vould surely send him to his grave."

Anshel's sister, Brindle, and his Uncle Izzy and Aunt Rivka pretended to ignore Sheindle Simenovitz's rebuke. They might have harbored similar feelings, but they knew better than to start up with Anshel. Everyone seemed to fear him, save his mother. She, like him, feared nothing. She had been through too much in her life to ever be intimidated by the likes of Anshel. She had seen her first children, two daughters, raped and murdered as teenagers during a pogrom in Russia. She fought with her bare fists as the same butchers nearly beat her husband to death. And in her own struggle, she had lost her left hand and had been stabbed through her stomach. No, she wasn't afraid of Anshel.

"Will you ever stop with that nonsense about how everything I do would cause my father's death? He's gone already, and so—by the way—is *Anshel*," Alfred responded.

Evelyn came over and interrupted. "Congratulations honey," she said as she embraced and kissed him.

He responded, "Thank you," a bit coldly, still affected by his mother's comments.

Evelyn stepped aside, and held Alfred's hand while facing the others. "An *emesse* lawyer, a real lawyer, yes?" she exclaimed heartily. She would have to lose that Yiddish inflection, Alfred thought to himself. Aside from that, she would make a perfect wife.

That was his plan—the perfect wife, the perfect family, the perfect home. Nothing would get in his way. Soon enough, the striking, tall, full-figured brunette with blue eyes, Evelyn Voratitsky, the princess of Bradford Street, would be taking diction lessons.

They were married that August. Three months later, they abandoned the basement apartment of Sheindle Simenovitz' East Flatbush home for a large new home in the exclusive town of Hewlett Harbor, one of the famed "Five Towns" on the south shore of Long Island. Ten years earlier, Alfred had inherited a substantial amount of money from his father, a successful furrier on the Lower East Side.

Since his law school tuition had been courtesy of the GI Bill, and as a student he kept his living expenses to a minimum, he was able to save and invest. In those years, the stock market was his forte. He did quite well. Now, his sights were set higher, properties and buildings in the five boroughs. Real estate would be his future. Buying, selling, managing, and perhaps even developing.

"Vhat is it you vent to law school for, to learn to be a salesman?" his mother asked, standing over a plate of smoked fish at the *bris* of his son Paul, just a year after he and Evelyn were married. Alfred had been talking up his latest venture to some of the guests and was caught off guard by the remark. "No, mom, I went to law school to learn how to argue with you," he responded. Touché. He seemed to enjoy this thing with her.

In truth, law school, as everything else, was simply a vehicle for Alfred. Practicing law was smalltime compared with what he had in mind, but he knew that the prestige of being a member of the Bar would be an asset. As a lawyer, people would be afraid to "screw" him. Alfred always thrived on the fears of others.

Everything was going exactly according to plan. Until, that is, the exotic Loretta Eubanks entered the picture. Alfred had a weakness for black women. He was excited by them because they were taboo for a proper Jewish boy from Brooklyn.

While he had regularly been fooling around on the side, he respected his home and kept his family insulated from his escapades. But when Evelyn hired Loretta as a live-in, things began to change. It wasn't two months before he was sneaking into her room downstairs in the middle of the night. The danger of this made it all the more enticing, for both Alfred and Loretta.

Loretta may have harbored fantasies of stealing Alfred from his family, but deep down she knew that she was no more than a mistress, not very different from many of the slave girls in the South a few generations earlier. She tried not to let that bother her, and the satisfaction of being more desirable than the white woman, in whose house she lived and worked, seemed to help. In the end, however, she knew she had no choice in the matter. It was either play along with Alfred, or find another job.

For a few months, Alfred managed to keep his gallivanting under one roof. It was rather convenient while it lasted. Then, something happened. Loretta learned that she was pregnant with his child. This changed everything. He pleaded for an abortion, but she—a Southern Baptist—would have none of it. "Don't you go worrying yourself about anything," she told him, "I can take care of this child on my own."

Evelyn appeared to be unsuspecting, and assumed that the deed had been done by some boyfriend during one of Loretta's weekends off. In any event, she didn't want Loretta living in the house once the child was born.

As for Alfred, he had a plan. His conscience wasn't so far gone that he could just abandon Loretta, so he would set her up in a place of her own, and she could keep working for the family as long as she desired. He would pay her rent, and take care of whatever the child might need. Even if she refused his help—which, in fact, she did for the first nine years—he was confident he would eventually persuade her to accept it. Everything would be fine. The perfect life.

CHAPTER 3

Joshua was his Christian name. But on the streets of Bed-Stuy he was called "Peanut," a title bestowed upon him by "Big Bob," one of the neighborhood bosses. While "Peanut" was a reference to his having had light brown, peanut butter colored eyes, just being given any street name at all was considered an honor. It was an indication of Big Bob's admiration for him and his ability to deliver packages quickly and discretely. He had been doing this since he was eight-years-old, and had never inquired about the contents of the bags Big Bob gave him, nor the envelopes he was supposed to bring back in return for them, or why Big Bob needed a young kid to do this sort of thing. Joshua never even peeked. He just did what Big Bob wanted, and gladly accepted his compensation.

"Good job, Peanut, my man," Big Bob would say whenever Joshua handed him an envelope. "Good job!" he would repeat, holding his free hand out for Joshua to slap him five. Always the same script.

True to his name, Big Bob was big, at least three hundred pounds. His round head had no hair, and his face was mean: wide bloodshot brown eyes, deep pocked skin, and a sharply trimmed goatee. He wore several thick gold bracelets and necklaces, with flashy bright colored shirts and trousers, and a wide-brimmed white hat—straw in summer, felt in winter. Joshua emulated Big Bob, and was naive enough to believe that Big Bob cared about him. He even fantasized from time-to-time that Big Bob might actually be his father.

"You think that fat ugly hoodlum on the street is your daddy," Loretta reacted when Joshua mentioned the thought. "Your daddy's bad, but he's not that bad," she exclaimed. That was all she ever said on the subject of his father. "And you stay away from that man, Joshua! I best not be hearing you got anything to do with him!"

So Joshua worked for Big Bob just about every day, and hoped his mother wouldn't find out. He began playing hooky from P.S. 44. A quick buck seemed a lot better than wasting his time with the three R's.

"Don't you worry none about school, Peanut, you'll learn all you need to know right here on the streets," Big Bob had once said. "You see all the things I got for myself, my man? Well, I didn't get them studying no science or history. No, I got what I got from the streets."

And "things" he did have. First, there was his fancy green Cadillac. Then, the jewelry. And of course, the women. Yes, Big Bob, as ugly as he was, had quite a harem. They hung around him day and night, constantly massaging him in one way or another. Joshua watched all this, and couldn't wait till he grew up, till the time when he could be just like Big Bob.

❦

One day Loretta received a call from the school about Joshua's truancy. It didn't take long before she learned what he'd been up to. There was lots of gossip in the old neighborhood, and she had her share of informants.

Joshua was walking along the avenue on his way from making a delivery, with one of Big Bob's envelopes in his pocket when she came up behind him. "Joshua Eubanks! What in the Lord's name have you been doing?" she yelled as she grabbed his jacket. She pulled him aside, and held him against the wall of a building.

Perspiration dripped down her face. Saliva appeared in the creases of her mouth. "I hear what's been going on with you, how you ain't been going to school, and how you been hanging around that bad man. What have you been thinking? You wanna be a hoodlum like him? Are you that stupid?"

Joshua stood there, mute and paralyzed, his right hand in his jacket pocket, clenching the envelope. "Now, you're coming straight home with me, and you're gonna stay there till I tell you!"

"But Mama . . ."

"Don't you 'but Mama' me! You do what I tell you!"

She took his arm and led him home. His right hand was sweating in his pocket, still grasping the envelope. Soon, Big Bob would begin to wonder where he was. Big Bob didn't take kindly to anyone being late, especially with business.

They came to the front door of their building, and Loretta dragged him up the stairs to their apartment. When they got inside, she pointed to his bedroom and said, "Now, you go on, and stay there till I tell you."

"But Mama, I have to . . ."

"You do what I tell you!" she shouted. "From now on, you're gonna go to school, do your work, get good grades, and stay outta trouble."

He stopped and looked at her, afraid to speak.

She pointed toward the room again. "Now go on," she said.

He obeyed.

From inside his room he heard her make a phone call. He held his ear to the door but couldn't make out what she was saying. He thought about the envelope in his pocket. There was no window in his room, no escape, no way to get to Big Bob. He thought of telling her about the envelope, but decided it was a bad idea and would only make things worse. *Who knows*, he figured, *she might even go to the police*. Then he'd be in even deeper. He had to find a way out.

After a few minutes, he heard her hang up the phone. A little while later, it rang. She answered it, talked some more, and hung up again. Then, after a half hour, it rang again. A short conversation. He thought for certain she was calling the police, and could feel his heart racing. If he was right, both their days would be numbered.

He heard her footsteps coming towards his room, and stepped back as she opened the door. "Now you listen here," she began, "and you best listen good. I want you to get all your clothes and stuff, whatever you got, and put it all in these bags." She handed him four brown super-market bags—just about enough to fit what he owned. "You do this right now, you hear?"

"Why I gotta do that?" he asked defiantly.

"First, cause I say so. Second, cause I say so."

"You sending me away someplace?"

"I'm taking you away someplace."

"Where?"

"That's none of your concern. You just do what I tell you!"

"Who you been talking to on the phone?" Boldness.

"That is also none of your concern."

"You ain't been talking to the police, have you?" Anxiety.

"There some reason I should be?"

He paused. Silence.

"I'm sure there is," she said confidently. "But I don't wanna hear about it. I don't wanna hear nothing right now. You just start packing, that's all."

"I don't wanna go no place else!"

"What you want don't much matter." With that, she turned and started walking out.

"When we leaving?" he asked.

"First thing in the morning."

Oh shit, he thought. What was he going to do now?

❧

It was the middle of the night. Loretta was asleep on the sofa-bed in the living room. Joshua got dressed, put on his jacket, and quietly opened the door to his room. Slowly, so the hinges wouldn't squeak. But they always squeaked, and this time was no exception.

"Who's there?" Loretta asked from her bed. "Joshua, is that you? What're you up to?"

"Nothing, Mama, I'm just hungry."

"This is no time to eat, it'll be morning soon. Get yourself back to your bed!"

"Yes Ma'am," he uttered, submissively turning back to his room. He closed his door, reached into his jacket pocket, took out the envelope, and stared at it, wondering what to do next. He would wait another hour, then try again. He had to try again. He was sure Big Bob already had some thugs out looking for him. He had to get the envelope to Big Bob before Big Bob got to him. He had to explain things.

❧

The door burst open. The light went on. Loretta's voice. "Joshua, what're you doing sleeping in your clothes like that?"

He looked himself over, barely awake, eyes squinting from the brightness, and suddenly realized he'd fallen asleep. He felt a surge of terror as he frantically started feeling around the bed for the envelope.

"What you looking for, Joshua?"

"Nothing, Mama," he said, continuing to survey the sheets and blanket. "I just thought I saw a bug." He started slapping his hands all over the bed. Quick thinking. There were always bugs in this house.

"Well, never mind that. A cab will be here in about fifteen minutes, so get yourself together."

"Fifteen minutes! We leaving in fifteen minutes?"

"That's what I said. It's about time you start hearing me."

He ran his hand over the outside of his jacket pocket, trying to be inconspicuous, and felt the envelope inside. "Don't I even get a chance to say good-bye to my friends?"

"You mean those hoodlums? They're not your friends, and you'll never be seeing any of them again where you're going."

"Where's that?"

"We're going to live in one of Mr. Sims' buildings over in Crown Heights."

"We're gonna live with white folk, Mama?"

"Yes we are. And if you're smart, maybe you'll learn something from them."

"But Mama, how they gonna let coloreds like us live over there?"

"Don't you worry. Mr. Sims has everything arranged. You just get your stuff together and cut this talking."

"Was that who you were talking to last night, Mr. Sims?"

"If you need to be knowing, yes."

"And he's gonna do all this for us? Why he's gonna do that?"

"Mr. Sims is a good man. And, I keep telling you, this ain't none of your concern. The car'll be here in ten minutes. There's some cereal left on the counter and milk in the ice-box. You best be ready on time."

Loretta went back into the living room to finish her own packing. Joshua was still sitting up and looked around the bedroom in which he had lived for the past nine years. It was about as modest as a room could be. The walls were bare and the only furniture aside from the bed was a rickety old wooden chair and table that Mrs. Sims had given Loretta when Paul's room had been redecorated. Joshua's clothing and belongings were kept in the closet, except for his shoes which were under the bed.

He would miss this place. Perhaps another child might still have harbored hopes of staying. Not him. His mother never wavered.

He removed the envelope from his pocket and stared at it. He had always honored Big Bob's privacy, but it didn't seem to matter much now. He would be a marked man anyway, so why not see what for. He stared at it a few more seconds until he heard Loretta yell, "Joshua, what you doing in there? I don't hear you packing and the cab's due to be here any minute."

His heart began to pound as he tore open the flap, removed the contents, and counted five one hundred dollar bills. The pounding intensified. He had never imagined what so much money would even look like, and here he was, holding it in his hands. He heard Loretta coming towards the room again, shoved the money back into the envelope, and stuffed it in his pocket. At that moment, notwithstanding his fear of his mother and Big Bob, he felt a strange surge of power. He was rich; he had five hundred dollars. Little did he know, just how much that would one day cost him.

❧

So they moved to their new home in Crown Heights, only about a mile away from where they had been living, yet worlds apart. Loretta would finally have her own bedroom with a genuine queen size bed provided by none other than Mr. Alfred Sims. No more sleeping on the convertible in the living room for her. And Joshua's new room was much bigger than the old one, with a window to boot. There was even some furniture: a twin sized bed, a desk, a chair, and even a full mirror attached to the back side of the door. *How convenient*, Joshua thought, as he looked in the mirror and slid the envelope behind it.

❧

Joshua also started at a new school, P.S. 167, on the corner of Eastern Parkway and Schenectedy Avenue, and was one of six black kids in a class of twenty-five. Jerome Williams, the super's son, was one of the others. Within no time, the two boys were the best of friends.

Besides their color, however, they had little in common. Jerome had never known the likes of Lewis Avenue, and had grown up accustomed to being a black kid in a white man's world. His family was from Alabama, and had come north eight years earlier. After staying with relatives in East New York for six months, Mr. Williams found the job as super and the family moved to Crown Heights.

Outwardly, Jerome was soft and refined, always deferential to white people, whether teachers, classmates, or just folks on the streets. Considering Jerome's father's position, Joshua understood why he acted that way toward residents of their building, but with strangers, it was another matter. Joshua was perplexed, and suspected that Jerome was more bitter than met the eye.

Jerome was short, fat, and clumsy. The Italian kids ridiculed and beat on him regularly. And he took it. When he came home with a swollen eye, fat lip, or whatever, his father would blame *him* and finish the job. Jerome took that too.

This was how it was, until one brisk fall afternoon. Joshua and Jerome were walking home from school along the east side of Rochester Avenue, and a group of Irish kids were hanging out at the entrance to Lincoln Terrace Park. Joshua counted five of them, and assumed they were probably looking for trouble. Jerome, obviously thinking the same thing, grabbed Joshua's jacket sleeve to pull him across the street. Joshua resisted.

For almost two months, Joshua had watched Jerome cower time and time again. He hadn't stepped in because he'd hoped Jerome would eventually rise to the occasion, which hadn't yet happened. The kids at school knew better than to mess with Joshua. He was bigger and stronger than most of them, and they also knew that he wasn't afraid. So he wasn't going to act scared now. And neither was Jerome, if Joshua had any say in it.

Joshua pulled Jerome back onto the sidewalk. "Where you think you're going?" he said.

"What you mean, man? Can't you see what's ahead over there?"

"I can see just fine, but what're you so afraid of?"

"That there's the meanest bunch of micks in the neighborhood, and the last time I ran into them I needed fifteen, count 'em, fifteen stitches," Jerome said, flashing his fingers in Joshua's face.

Joshua looked at the group and didn't recognize any of the faces. "They from another school?" he asked.

"Yeah, they're from that Catholic School down the block there. And they don't like no *Protestants* like us. So I say we cross the street and stay out of their way!"

"Jerome, you got to stick up for yourself sometime!"

"It's a bad time right now to start making changes, if you get my meaning. And anyway, you're going to have to do some sticking up for yourself also if we get in a mess here. These ain't like those micks and ginnies in school that'r scared of your size, these are animals, just looking to brag about having beaten up the likes of you."

"So what!" Joshua said, "I ain't afraid, and you ain't gonna be neither!"

"Man, you crazy. I thought you told me they call you Peanut because of your eyes, but I'm starting to think it's got more to do with your brain."

"Listen then, you go ahead, cross the street. I'm walking on this sidewalk, and that's how it's gonna be."

"Have it your way," Jerome responded as he proceeded into the street. Joshua watched him cross and kept walking on the sidewalk. Seconds later, Joshua was ten feet away from the Irish kids.

"Hey guys," a tall red-head with freckled skin said loudly to his friends. "What have we got here? Seems there's a new nigger in town." The others laughed. Joshua kept walking towards them.

"Hello nigger boy," another one said bravely, stepping out and blocking Joshua's way.

"Hello whitey," Joshua responded.

"What'd you say?" the Irish kid asked. He was significantly shorter than the first kid. Jet black hair, very thin. Joshua was confident he could dispose of him with a single blow. Maybe that would scare the rest of them. After all, they were used to beating on the likes of Jerome, totally unprepared for a black kid who fought back. Might make them think twice.

"You hard of hearing?" Joshua asked.

"Oh, we got us a wise one here," the Irish kid retorted, looking at his friends, smirking.

Joshua stepped forward and pushed the kid out of the way with his body. It was easy. The kid lost balance and almost fell over, but caught himself. He hesitated for a moment and looked at his friends again. They appeared shocked by Joshua's boldness. Joshua kept moving, pretending not to notice their reaction, when the kid came back at him with a shove. "What d'ya think, you're some tough nigger or something," the kid said, pushing Joshua again.

Joshua didn't move. Not an inch. He got in the kid's face, stared into his eyes, and waited for the others to do something. But they didn't.

Joshua could have left it at that, could have gone on his way and never had a problem with that group again. But that just wasn't his style. He pushed the kid back. Hard. Hard enough that the kid flew into the others and fell to the ground.

The first punch came from the tall red-head, a perfectly solid shot to Joshua's left eye. The next thing Joshua knew he was tasting blood and holding his eye with both hands. Then the kid he pushed kicked him in the stomach. Joshua keeled over, only to receive another blow to the back of his head.

He was hurt, and for the first time, a little scared. He seemed almost as helpless as Jerome would have been. He took a deep breath, ignored his fear, and focused on his anger. He straightened himself, and went for the tall one first, the one his instincts told him was the leader.

Joshua lunged at the tall one and took him to the ground. Their bodies hit the concrete hard, but neither seemed to feel the pain. The others stood over them and took turns kicking Joshua. But Joshua stayed on top of the tall one, pounding incessantly on his face. One of the others even tried to pull him off, but it was to no avail; Joshua just kept punching. The tall one was hurt, and wasn't even hitting back anymore.

The next thing Joshua knew, the kicking from the others ceased. Something had distracted them. He looked up and saw that Jerome had come to help, and was now fending off the others. Joshua got up, leaving the tall one lying listless on the ground, and watched his friend in action. Jerome wasn't being very successful, but his efforts were impressive. The others hadn't managed to get him down on the ground; they were just surrounding him, landing punches and kicks to his body. Jerome's eyes were closed and his arms were flailing in all directions. He wasn't able to see where his fists landed, but managed to get in a few licks.

Joshua stepped in, pulling two of the Irish kids away from Jerome. The other two saw this and hesitated. They looked over to their leader—still on the ground, his head in a pool of his own blood—and stopped.

"I'm gonna kill you both, you fucking nigger bastards!" the thin black haired kid yelled.

"Oh yeah!" Jerome reacted confidently, "come on, let's do it right now!" he continued as he began to lunge forward.

Joshua held out his arm to block Jerome's way, and said, "Let's go."

The black haired kid cringed, while his friends stood frozen, frightened, eyes fixed upon Joshua and Jerome

"Come on, we're out of here now," Joshua added, pulling Jerome away.

The Irish kids stepped aside to let them pass, murmuring to one another about revenge as their victors walked on. Half a block up, Joshua turned around. The tall red-head was still on the ground, curled up in a fetal position, his friends gathered around him. A voice screamed out, "Fucking niggers," the echo of which could be heard for blocks. Joshua noticed Jerome's triumphant expression and, despite his own wounds, was pleased with his friend's bravado.

CHAPTER 4

The Hewlett-Woodmere public school district was reputed as one of the finest in the country, with unmatched acceptance rates to Ivy League colleges. In the sixties, the student population was mostly upper middle class and Jewish, with a handful of Italian and Irish kids from the lower income areas of Gibson and South Valley Stream. Despite all this, the only child of Alfred Sims was enrolled in the Hewlett Bay Academy, a posh private school for the wealthy and privileged.

"No son of mine is going to have a 'public' education!" Alfred insisted to Evelyn.

"But the public schools here are excellent," she argued.

"Not excellent enough!" And that was the final word. His was always the final word. There was no reasoning with him once he made up his mind. Evelyn knew this, and had grown to hate it. Over the years, she had grown to hate many things.

They fought often, about almost everything. Sometimes it was just words, sometimes things were thrown, and sometimes Alfred disappeared for a night or two. All the while, young Paul watched and listened.

Over the years Evelyn grew miserable yet, among her litany of resentments was never even a suspicion of Alfred's infidelity. She was far too vain to allow for that, so she convinced herself that his problem was impotence rather than disinterest. The outlet for her frustration found expression through compulsivity, incessantly cleaning, wiping, and straightening things. She did this early every morning before Loretta came to clean, and again late at night, after Loretta had gone. The house was never tidy enough.

When she wasn't cleaning, Evelyn Sims was spending money. Clothes, jewelry, shoes, handbags, cosmetics. There was always plenty of money and it seemed to ease her pain.

Paul was also angry with his father, mostly for not being around. As for his mother, who was *always* around, there was plenty of antipathy left for her as well. In as much as Evelyn failed to control her husband, she would more than make up for it with her son.

"I've told you a thousand times to put your colored socks on the left side of the drawer and your white ones on the right!"

"Is this the way to make your bed? Don't you ever listen? The sheet is too loose and there are lumps in the blanket. Now you won't watch any TV for a week, and then we'll see how well you'll listen."

"What's the matter with you? You do things just to annoy me! You're just like your father, always trying to find a way to upset me. I'm telling you for the last time, you better wipe the shower door dry when you're done in there. If I see any soap scum, you'll stay in the house for a month."

Paul grew up understanding that he could never please his mother, no matter how he tried. With his father, however, things were different. Paul knew exactly what Alfred wanted of him—Alfred, who never took him to ball games, fishing, bowling, and never did any of the things that fathers usually do. All Alfred cared about was Paul's school-work, so that became all Paul cared about.

"There will be plenty of time for other things," Alfred often told him. "For now, you must concentrate on your studies."

So that was it: school, making his bed perfectly, putting his socks on the proper side of the drawer, and washing the soap scum off the shower door. The life of Paul Sims.

Burying himself in books became his escape, his only hope for his father's love and attention. And when it didn't work, he tried harder, until he became ensnarled in a vicious cycle, growing more introverted and isolated with time.

For Alfred, everything seemed perfect. But Evelyn, as caught up as she was in her own misery, seemed to know better. As did Paul's teachers, who eventually began calling and requesting conferences.

"Paul is a highly intelligent young man, but has difficulty getting along with other children," the school psychologist told Alfred and Evelyn when Paul was in the sixth grade. "Is there something going on at home that's bothering him?"

At home? What could possibly be going on in the perfect home? Alfred was distressed. A glitch in the master plan.

"This has been going on for years. As you know, his grades have been perfect, but otherwise he has a lot of difficulties. He has no friends here, and I would guess that he has no friends outside of school either." The psychologist was being kind in using the term "difficulties." Neither Alfred nor Evelyn argued, for they knew it was true. "I think some counseling is in order," the psychologist suggested, "individual to begin with, and maybe the entire family at some point."

Alfred responded with a bewildered look. *My boy, seeing some shrink about problems at home? Never!* "I'm sorry doctor . . . what did you say your name was?"

"Goldman," the man replied calmly.

"Frankly, Doctor Goldman, I don't see what the problem is. My son is a brilliant young man who chooses not to waste his time flipping baseball cards or playing knock-hockey with other kids. He enjoys his school work, he's good at it, and that's what he wants to do. In fact, I personally think it's a good thing. I've always encouraged him to concentrate on his school-work. That's why he does it. He's not going to get into law or medical school by winning popularity contests."

Though Evelyn sat silently, Goldman wasn't convinced that she agreed wholeheartedly with her husband. A heavy-set, balding man in his late forties, Goldman was a seasoned professional and had been on staff at Hewlett Bay for almost twenty years. Dealing with parents like Alfred Sims was second nature to him. He wasn't going to push. He knew he wouldn't win. And above all, he knew that sooner or later, one way or another, Paul would wind up in his office.

❦

Weeks passed and nothing changed. Mrs. Robinson, Paul's teacher, reported to Doctor Goldman that Paul was still keeping to himself, and still carrying a distressed expression that seemed to mar his otherwise pleasant features. Paul was often told he was a handsome young man, tall, dark, with masculine features much like his father's, but with his mother's blue eyes. He never saw himself as resembling his father in any way, but possessing his mother's eyes was another matter. He could easily accept that, for her eyes were the saddest he'd ever seen unless, of course, he was looking in the mirror, which he didn't often do.

Doctor Goldman looked at Mrs. Robinson with a knowing grin, and said, "Yes, it seems Paul Sims' problems are far from solved."

Mrs. Robinson called home and appealed to Evelyn to allow Paul to see Dr. Goldman. "I know he has a problem," Evelyn admitted, feeling her guilt as the words escaped her mouth. True, she was unhappy; true, she frequently took it out on Paul. But she was also his mother, and she hated herself for the way she treated him. She struggled to be better, but she was so desperate, so out of control. "I'll see what I can do," she said, realizing that she had to do something.

∽

The following week, Evelyn enrolled Paul in the Cub Scouts. She bought him one of those blue and yellow uniforms, and he began attending meetings. When Alfred heard about this, his response was surprisingly positive. He even praised Evelyn for her ingenuity—something he'd never done before. "What a clever idea," he said. "It will definitely do the trick. They'll teach him how to be a man, and when he gets older he can become a Boy Scout, maybe even a full fledged Eagle Scout." The only problem was Paul. He didn't enjoy being with the other kids, and didn't care much for pledges and tying knots. After three meetings, he refused to return.

But Evelyn was still determined. Her next idea was to sign him up for Little League. This time, Alfred was less enthusiastic, not because he objected to baseball, but because he knew Paul wouldn't take to it.

It wasn't that Paul was a bad athlete; on the contrary, he was fairly well coordinated. He simply had no fervor for sports, or anything that entailed being with other kids. In his first game, he was put in right field, dropped a fly ball that practically landed in his mitt, struck out twice, and was tagged out at first on what should have easily been a double. Luckily, Alfred wasn't present to watch his only son, and his name, be humiliated. On the other hand, had he been there, things might have turned out differently. That first game was Paul's last.

A few months later, Evelyn convinced Alfred to send Paul to sleep-away camp. Paul went, and phoned home every night for two weeks straight, begging them to come and take him home, until his wish was granted. The camp director recommended counseling.

By this time, Alfred became convinced that his son did indeed have problems, but counseling was still out of the question. Evelyn didn't argue. She, too, couldn't bear the thought of the neighborhood gossips getting wind of her child seeing a shrink. As a last ditched effort, they decided to get Paul piano lessons, figuring that a musical instrument might give him an outlet for his feelings, raise his self esteem, and perhaps expand his interests.

Paul's piano teacher was a large German woman with flat grey hair and chronic halitosis. After a few lessons, it seemed that the only thing Paul could do correctly was to look straight ahead at the music sheet, and the only reason he did that was to avoid the *fraulein's* breath. His fingers, however, seldom managed to land on the proper keys. Exasperated, the teacher began slapping his hands, for which she was summarily dismissed by the lady of the house.

Alfred and Evelyn blamed one another, and nothing changed. Alfred remained aloof and absent; Evelyn, compulsive and overbearing. And Paul? There were yet some surprises to come from him.

CHAPTER 5

Joshua was barely twelve when he first noticed Celeste as something more than his best friend's younger sister. She was eleven. Among the five black girls in her class at school, there were two with whom she was close friends. For years the three of them were inseparable, but recently she had taken to hanging out with Jerome and Joshua. Joshua didn't object.

Jerome felt otherwise. He sensed her attraction to Joshua and didn't know how to handle it. He didn't want her hanging around boys, especially his best friend.

"What's that you got there on your lips?" Jerome exclaimed one day as Celeste came out of her bedroom. It was the first time she'd worn lipstick. "If Mama saw you look like that, she'd make your lips so fat, you'd need a ton of that stuff to cover 'em."

"Well, she don't see me, and you ain't gonna tell her!" Celeste responded, while throwing a devilish smile Joshua's way.

Joshua responded with a nod and a wink. She looked good, he thought, she *always* looked good. And the lipstick was just the touch needed for her high cheek bones and large chestnut eyes. It made her perfect.

It was the middle of July. The three of them had been spending most summer days together, watching TV, playing handball in the park, and doing nothing. Just a few months earlier she was in pigtails. Now, her full wavy hair fell down below her nicely developing breasts, and skimpy shorts revealed her shapely long legs. Joshua was stricken.

He'd known Celeste and Jerome for three years now. In that time, he'd managed to stay out of trouble. Jerome had also come into his own. Since that fight with the Irish kids, no one messed with him.

Another change that had taken place was the influx of more black families into the neighborhood. Three more had moved into their building alone. Even Dubrow's Cafeteria, formerly an exclusively white establishment on the corner of Utica and Eastern Parkway, was showing more color at its tables. And black teenagers were now regularly seen strutting their stuff on the basketball courts in Lincoln Terrace Park.

"You boys wanna go out to the park now?" Celeste asked, again throwing Joshua a cutesy grin.

"We ain't gonna go nowhere till you take that there shit off your face!" Jerome said. His heavy body shook when he was angry.

"Well I guess I'm gonna go alone," she replied.

"I said . . . you ain't going nowhere!"

"Yea, well what you gonna do, beat me?"

He was wordless and stunned. She had mentioned the one thing he would never, could never, do. Not to her.

"Well, are *you* coming?" she asked Joshua as she walked out the door.

"She shouldn't go alone," Joshua said defensively, holding his palms up as he followed after her.

Jerome didn't move.

❧

Celeste and Joshua left the building and were about to cross the street toward the park. It was the end of July, a hot and sticky Brooklyn summer day. Joshua stepped off the sidewalk and Celeste grabbed his hand to hold him back. He looked at her, bewildered.

"I don't really feel like another boring day in that stupid park," she said.

Joshua didn't reply; he suspected something was up.

"How 'bout we go someplace else?"

"Like where?" There was an underpinning of sarcasm in his tone. He was not in an adventurous mood.

"I say we go take a look at your old neighborhood. I ain't never been there."

"And you ain't never gonna be, neither!"

"You know you sound like my big fat brother and mean old father when you talk that way. I know you're not like them, but you sure are tryin' to be. So why don't you be the nice boy I know you can be, and take me where I wanna go."

"Why *there?*"

"See where you came from. I hear you talking all the time, how different it is from around these parts, and I wanna see what all your fussing's about."

"And you just gotta do *something* you know you ain't supposed to be doing."

"And what if I do?" she asked.

"First the lipstick, then this. What's next?"

"I don't know. I'll just have to think of something, won't I, now?" She took his hand and led him in the direction of Eastern Parkway.

"Now, wait just a minute!" he said, resisting her tug. "It's dangerous over there. I ain't going!"

They stopped and stared at each other for a moment.

"I'm surprised to see you're chicken," she said. "I thought you were more man than that," she said as she released his hand and started walking away.

"Wait!" He caught up to her. "This ain't right, but if you're going, I'm going," he said, his reluctance still apparent.

She took his hand again. He would have gone anywhere so long as she did that. "It just ain't right," he repeated as they went.

"That's why it's so much fun."

※

They walked to Eastern Parkway, then west one block to Utica Avenue. When they came to Utica, they crossed the Parkway and continued north. The north side of Eastern Parkway was much blacker than where they lived. Most of the shops along Utica Avenue, between St. Marks Place and Pacific Street, had black proprietors, and most of the people on the street spoke with island accents. At one point, Celeste started mimicking some of them under her breath. Joshua hit her lightly on the arm, and said, "You better stop that before someone hears you!"

"And what're they gonna do if they hear me?"

He looked at her the same way Jerome had in the house.

It was a few more blocks to Atlantic Avenue. "You still wanna do this?" he asked, hoping for a change of heart. He pointed to the other side of the Avenue. "You see, over there's a whole different breed of people. Not like these here polite island types. The folks over there are *bad*, through and through, mean and crazy."

"But you ain't mean and crazy, and you're from there," she pointed out.

"Just tell me one thing," he asked as they were about to cross. "Why you have to do this? You know if your daddy finds out, he's gonna beat me worse than he beats you."

"I ain't afraid of him. He don't scare me! He's gonna beat me no matter what I do, so what difference does it make? Now I wanna do this, and I wanna to do it with *you*." She knew that last part was all she needed to say to turn him into putty, and strangely enough, he knew it too.

They crossed the avenue, continued one block to Fulton Street, and another block west to Stuyvesant Avenue. Then they walked up Stuyvesant, deeper into his old neighborhood. The buildings began to look like tenements: broken windows, dilapidated fire escapes, and graffiti filled walls. Celeste seemed astonished.

"I think people are looking at us," she observed.

Joshua had noticed the same thing a few blocks earlier. It was obvious that they didn't belong. He was confident that no one had recognized him yet, but it was only a matter of time. Something bad was bound to happen; he just knew it. He had to take care of her and protect her, and he was starting to realize that this was probably something he would always have to do.

❧

They had approached the intersection of Stuyvesant and Monroe Street when Joshua recognized someone standing on the corner. It was Bones, one of Big Bob's henchmen. He had earned his name from being so thin, his skeleton practically protruded through his flesh. But he wasn't brittle; on the contrary, he was a mean, tall creature, easily more than six feet, with a square face and long sideburns covering most of an old scar from a childhood knife-fight. He stood there alone, as if waiting for someone, dressed in one of his usual outfits—white linen suit, straw hat, and alligator boots.

Joshua quickly turned his face to the window of a grocery store, thinking that if Bones was here, Big Bob wouldn't be far. He tried to hide his fear from Celeste.

"What're you looking at?" she asked.

"Nothing really, just this store here."

From the corner of his eye he noticed a woman in a tight black dress and dirty blond wig approach Bones. The woman moved clumsily. Her dress was scanty, revealing plenty of cleavage and leg, and hung from one shoulder.

Joshua signaled Celeste to be quiet. She sensed something was wrong and stood still. He took her hand, and held it tight as he watched the woman hand something to Bones. Bones, in turn, placed something in the woman's hand, and looked around to make sure no one was watching.

Joshua understood that the woman was one of Big Bob's working girls, a drug addicted hooker delivering money to her pimp and supplier. It was hard for him to imagine that he had once, not so long ago, been a part of all this. He stood frozen, afraid to move, grasping Celeste's hand. He needed to think quickly, and the only idea he could come up with seemed a bad one.

The woman walked off, but it wasn't a few seconds before another woman approached. A similar transaction. Bones was having a profitable day.

"I'm real thirsty," Joshua said softly. It was the truth. He and Celeste had walked over a mile, and the heat was unbearable. He was also trying to get her into the store, figuring that once inside, they would have some time to come up with a plan. The only problem was that the store had its own dangers.

The man behind the counter was attending to another customer and didn't notice them. It was a small store with only three aisles of goods and a cooler in the back. Joshua led Celeste down the last aisle to the cooler.

"You been in here before?" she asked.

"I've been lots of places."

"I bet you have. I bet you been places and done things I ain't never dreamed of."

"Here," he said, handing her a Pepsi. He took another for himself. "Come on, lets go," he continued, gesturing towards the counter in the front of the store. He was desperately trying to devise a plan to get them home.

Celeste followed him to the counter as the front door to the store opened and Bones walked in. Joshua could have kicked himself a thousand times. He knew it was a bad idea to have entered the store to begin with; at least on the street there were places to run. And how could he have been so stupid, choosing one of Big Bob's fronts as a place to hide? He grabbed Celeste, turned around, and hid his face as Bones sauntered in their direction. Celeste stood stiffly by his side. Bones came closer, and passed by, ignoring them, continuing on toward a metal door in the rear of the store. He pressed a buzzer, and a slot opened in the top of the door. A pair of eyes appeared, and a voice asked, "That you Bones?"

"No, it's the fucking tooth fairy," Bones replied, his voice deep and raspy. The door opened just enough to let him slip in, then closed behind him.

"What was that all about?" Celeste whispered.

"Nothing you wanna know," Joshua said. They needed to get outside and make a run for it, but there was still one more obstacle: the old man behind the counter. Joshua's only hope was that the old man, who had a famously feeble mind, wouldn't remember him.

The old man was alone. He looked at Joshua and Celeste as they approached. A smile came to his face.

"Well, well, well," the old man roared, "look what we have here." His eyes fixed on Joshua. "It's been a long time, Peanut. A lo—ng time."

"Yes, Mr. Powell, it has," Joshua responded, his voice trembling. He knew about the buzzer under the counter, but the old man's hands were still in sight.

Powell was tall, well built, and had a full head of frizzy gray hair. Bloodshot eyes. Slurred speech. And a twitch on the left side of his face. The way Joshua had heard it, he was in a drunken brawl over some woman back in the forties and had gotten hit in the head one time too many. Now, he managed this store, and served as a look-out for the boys in the back.

"Where you been hiding?" Powell asked as Joshua handed him a quarter for the sodas.

"Here and there," Joshua answered, trying to appear undaunted. Powell was always a little slow, and Joshua was banking on that.

"Big Bob know you back?"

"Big Bob knows everything that goes on, don't he?"

"He know what folks tell him." Doubting.

"Well then, I guess someone best tell him. I suppose maybe that someone's gonna be you." Powell's hands were still visible. "If you give me a pen and paper, I'll write down where Big Bob can find me, in case he's gotta job for me." Joshua was hoping to distract Powell into looking for something to write with, so Celeste and he could dash out. It worked. The instant Powell turned around to find a pad, Joshua grabbed Celeste and bolted out the door.

They ran just about all the way home. Celeste, surprisingly, followed without uttering a word, until they crossed Eastern Parkway and finally stopped to rest.

"What was that about?" she asked, catching her breath between words.

"It's a long story."

"I like long stories."

He looked at her, and decided to tell her. She listened attentively, mesmerized, her eyes aglow with interest as he shared it all, the sordid details of his past, the five hundred dollars now hidden behind the mirror in his room, everything. He went on for more than a half hour, and she was wordless the entire time. It became apparent to her how much he'd risked by taking her there, and that the only reason he'd done it was because she had wanted it. She took his hand, pulled him closer to her, and embraced him. She kissed him softly on the cheek. He felt a bit embarrassed, standing there, on an open street corner, that way. But he didn't mind.

CHAPTER 6

Paul Sims lay in bed, tossing and turning, trying desperately to fall asleep. Thoughts raced through his mind as they did every night, about home, school, and life in general. Always unhappy thoughts. He could hear some late movie blaring on the TV in the bedroom down the hall where his mother was fast asleep, alone as usual.

That damned, fucking television!

He always blamed her television for his insomnia. Once, he actually dared to walk into her room and turn it off, only to catch hell the next morning. He never tried that again. Now, he just lay there, night after night, wondering how he could just make everything go away.

⟤⟁⟣

About twenty miles away, Alfred Sims was walking through one of his properties, a building across the street from Lincoln Terrace Park in Crown Heights. Every month he personally appeared at the doors of his tenants' homes to collect the rent. Some of the other landlords still did the same, but most had recently delegated the task to their supers. It wasn't safe anymore; the neighborhood was changing.

But Alfred wasn't changing, not as far as this particular building was concerned. He wasn't ready to give up his only excuse to drop in on the exotic Loretta Eubanks, his wife's "loyal" housekeeper.

Since moving to Crown Heights, Loretta had finally accepted his offer to take care of their son, Joshua. It was the least he could do, she reasoned, after she'd spent nine years struggling.

He always made her his last stop, thereby insuring that little Joshua was asleep. He hadn't seen Joshua since the boy was an infant, another thing he didn't want to change. Luckily, Joshua was a sound sleeper, once he hit the pillow, nothing—save an explosion of his mother's wrath—could awaken him.

Lately, however, Loretta had been snubbing Alfred. She loathed his disregard for Joshua, and frowned upon his visits to her home. She was unafraid of losing her job. In that, she knew she was secure.

Her resistance only made Alfred want her more. He continued to visit, but usually ended up leaving frustrated. Tonight, he knew, would be no different. But he still had to see her. He just couldn't help himself.

⌘

The next morning, as usual, Loretta Eubanks arrived at seven-thirty, in time to prepare breakfast for Alfred and Paul. Evelyn slept late; she never got up before ten.

Alfred typically ate alone and was out of the house by eight, before Paul came down. But today things were different. Alfred had overslept—those late nights were taking their toll—and wound up breakfasting with his son. It was quiet at the table. Loretta was accustomed to handling Alfred in one way, and Paul in another. Her discomfort was evident from her silence.

"How are those Bar Mitzvah lessons coming along?" Alfred asked, as he lifted an eye over the daily newspaper.

"Okay, I guess."

"What does 'okay' mean?"

"Everything is fine," Paul said. "Rabbi Weissman thinks I'm doing well." He found his father's sudden interest in his Bar Mitzvah perplexing, especially over a plate of bacon and eggs.

"Well, I hope he's right," Alfred responded. "Those private lessons of yours are costing me a fortune."

Paul felt ashamed of what he was eating as the image of Rabbi Isaac Weissman, his Sunday-school teacher and private Bar Mitzvah tutor, came to mind. He pictured the rabbi's gentle face, soft and deeply set blue eyes, small—almost emaciated—body, and long scraggly beard. But most of all, he pictured the dark rings under the rabbi's eyes, the reminder that Rabbi Weissman was a kindred spirit in the struggle for sleep. In fact, when Paul had confided in the rabbi about his own sleep problems, the rabbi had responded with a wide smile, suggesting, "Vhy not spend that time studying? It's quiet late at night, good for your concentration."

Paul found Rabbi Weissman easy to talk with, and always sympathetic; beyond that, he had a sense that the rabbi understood anguish in a way that few men could. During the summer, the rabbi frequently rolled up his sleeves, and Paul would glimpse the number on his left arm. Paul had learned about the concentration camps in school, and had chosen not to ask the rabbi for specifics. It was a wise choice, for this was a subject the rabbi never discussed.

The private lessons were actually the rabbi's idea. He had been Paul's teacher in Sunday School for two years, had noticed the boy's interest in Judaism, and had brought it to the attention of Alfred and Evelyn, who were both bewildered as to how their son came to care about such things. Alfred had minimal interest in Judaism and, in fact, had worked hard at putting that part of his life behind him. True, he wanted Paul to do well at his Bar Mitzvah, and had therefore agreed to the private lessons, but that had nothing to do with religion. If he and Evelyn were ever in agreement on anything, it was that they didn't want some Hasidic rabbi from Brooklyn, who comes out to the suburbs once a week for extra money, converting their son to the "old ways." After the Bar Mitzvah, the rabbi would be gone.

Paul was silent. The Bar Mitzvah was just three weeks away, and he was suspicious of his parents' plans for the rabbi once it was all done.

Alfred returned to his paper. He had spoken his piece. Loretta observed them from the corner of her eye as she busied herself with the pots and pans. She wouldn't have to fix breakfast for the lady of the house; all Evelyn ever had in the morning was a cup of coffee.

A few moments later Alfred left for work, while Paul sat there, playing with the food on his plate. Loretta watched him for a moment, then said, "He's real hard on you sometimes."

"How can you tell?" Sarcasm.

She walked over to the table and sat herself across from him. She often sat with Paul when it was just the two of them. He didn't mind; she was his friend.

"Your father always wants what he wants, and there's no stopping him once he makes up his mind. I think you can be stubborn too, you know," she said.

"I suppose."

"He just wants you to be the best, and he knows you can be."

Paul nodded, but—in truth—he couldn't see why Loretta had such a flattering perception of him.

"Seems silly, though, his worrying about your Bar Mitzvah, don't it? You're a smart boy, and you're always working hard and studying. There's no need for him to be worrying."

Paul was pensive for a moment. "I suppose I should get going," he said, eyeing the clock on the wall.

"Yes, you should."

They both stood up, and Loretta walked over to him. She put her hands on his shoulders, looked him in the eye, and added, "You know, you can always talk to me if you need."

"I know."

She wanted to hug him, but stopped herself. She used to caress him all the time when he was younger, but hadn't in many years. The same for Joshua. She missed those days, but she understood that boys do eventually have to become men, a thought that left her sad and empty.

❦

It was just a few minutes before noon and Dr. Harold Goldman sat in his Hewlett Bay Academy office reviewing the file on his next client, Paul Sims. *Remarkable*, thought Goldman, assessing the boy's progress. Paul had first come to him over a year ago as a withdrawn, angry kid, refusing to talk about anything. The school had insisted on the treatment, if Paul was to remain enrolled. An embarrassment for Alfred and Evelyn, but by that time they had no choice.

Paul had no choice either, and he never stopped reminding Goldman of his resentment at having been forced to see the school-shrink every week. He even resisted small talk. Goldman would say, for example, "Did you do anything interesting this weekend?" And Paul would respond, "What business is it of yours what I did this weekend?" Goldman would respond, "Just trying to make conversation," and Paul would retort, "Well, why don't you make it with someone else?" Goldman knew that Paul's anger was really meant for his father. "Transference" was the technical term.

Sometimes, Paul was mute for an entire session. Goldman would attempt a few openers, but usually ended up staring at the walls or twiddling his thumbs. But he never gave up on Paul and never became exasperated. And in the end, his tenacity paid off.

At about the same time that Paul started his Bar Mitzvah lessons with Rabbi Weissman. his hostility began to wane, but he still took every opportunity to cancel, come late, or simply forget appointments. Then, gradually, his attendance improved and he began talking. Soon, they were exploring substantive issues, like how Paul felt about the way his parents treated him, or the way they treated one another. Goldman had felt uneasy with the summer break, but was glad that Paul would still be studying regularly with the rabbi. Not therapy, he thought, but somehow therapeutic. Now, with the start of the new school year, Paul had resumed his weekly visits to the psychologist's office, and was embarking on the most painful course of all—how he felt about himself. Their first session went overtime, and Paul had requested an additional visit for that week.

Goldman closed the file, somewhat amazed but mostly humbled. He had originally seen this young man as destined for a difficult, sad life. Now, who could tell what the cards held for Paul Sims? Such transformations were rare in Harold Goldman's business.

❧

Paul knocked on the door at exactly noon. Goldman opened the door as Paul entered and took his usual seat.

Although the Hewlett Bay Academy was a wealthy school, counseling services were not a budgetary priority. Goldman's office was a simple, unadorned room, institutional in character. Pale green linoleum, off-white walls, a few pictures of nature scenes, a gun-metal desk, and a single bookcase filled with psychology texts. Goldman sat in a swivel chair, and behind him were a pair of windows covered by dusty venetian blinds turned open to expose a view of the parking lot. Protruding from the bottom of one of those windows was the office's sole luxury: a rickety old air conditioner with a broken thermostat that was permanently set at high. On hot days such as this, it was either bake or freeze. Goldman chose the latter.

There was a brief silence in the room. Goldman looked at Paul curiously; he always waited for his patients to initiate.

"It's a pretty hot day out there," Paul said.

"You asked for an extra session to discuss the weather?" Goldman wasn't one to waste time on niceties.

"Well, actually . . . yes, in a way."

Goldman waited for more.

"It's the heat, you see. It's been bothering me a lot lately," Paul explained.

"How do you mean?"

"I'm always hot, no matter where I am. I seem to sweat all the time."

Goldman saw that Paul was indeed sweating, despite the frigid office. "Sounds to me like it's not the weather that's bothering you," he observed.

"Then what is it?"

"I would guess, from knowing you, that you're experiencing a great deal of anxiety."

"Anxiety?" There was a short silence, while Paul considered this. "Why do you think I'm having anxiety?"

"*You* tell me!"

"My Bar Mitzvah?"

"Possibly." Goldman pondered for a moment, and said, "Do you have any other thoughts on what you might be anxious about?"

"Well . . ." Paul stopped himself, without revealing what he was thinking. "No, that's not it."

"Why don't you say what just came to mind, and we'll see how irrelevant it is," Goldman suggested.

"I was just thinking about a conversation I had with my father this morning. It was nothing, really. He was complaining, as usual, about how much money he's been spending on my lessons with the rabbi, that's all."

"That's all?"

"Do you think there's something to that?"

"What do you think? The thought came into *your* mind, didn't it?"

Paul considered Goldman's point. He wasn't worried about the Bar Mitzvah per se, he was more than amply prepared for that. Not only had he had the advantage of private tutoring, but he'd also had extra time to prepare. His thirteenth birthday had actually been in the beginning of August and, as with many summer birthdays, his Bar Mitzvah was postponed until September so friends and family who were away for the summer wouldn't miss it. For him, it really made no difference. He had no friends and couldn't care less about his family. For his father, who was planning the most lavish bash ever seen this side of Canarsie, it made all the difference in the world.

"So it has something to do with the rabbi?" Paul asked.

"Possibly." Goldman was noncommittal, not because he didn't know what was bothering Paul, but because he wanted Paul to uncover these things himself.

"Well, I am afraid that once the Bar Mitzvah's over, my private study sessions with Rabbi Weissman will also be over."

"You enjoy studying with him."

"Yes," Paul said, then hesitated. "Very much."

"You stopped yourself for a second, were you thinking of something?"

"I was just thinking about the rabbi."

"What about him?"

"I don't know!" Defensive.

"I'm sure you *do* know."

"It's just that . . . I . . . like him. Not only the studying, but *him*."

Goldman smiled and waited for more.

"The thing that bothers me most," Paul said, "is that he has invited me to his home for the Sabbath this week."

"Why should that bother you?"

"You can't guess?"

Goldman wasn't stupid. He understood that Alfred and Evelyn wouldn't take kindly to the idea of their son spending a weekend with a Hasidic family in Crown Heights. "You mean that your parents would object?"

"Exactly," Paul said. "I don't even see why they sent me to Hebrew School, or even wanted me to have a Bar Mitzvah in the first place."

"There are some things that people can't abandon regardless of how hard they try," Goldman said.

Paul looked at Goldman, surprised, realizing there was something personal in that last remark. He knew that Goldman was a non-practicing Jew like his parents, for Goldman had revealed as much in previous discussions. Beyond that, he knew nothing about the man. It often made him feel strange discussing his feelings about religion, causing him to wonder what his inquisitor thought of it all. He had actually raised the issue once, but Goldman had retreated to "shrink-talk," claiming that Paul's real worry was about how Alfred felt. It had sounded to Paul like a copout then, yet he was certain he would get a similar response now if he pressed. He chose to let it slide.

"I do want to go to the rabbi's house," he said.

"Perhaps you can ask the rabbi to speak with your father. He does seem to have a little influence."

"That's a good idea, but it doesn't solve the other problem about what happens with the rabbi once my Bar Mitzvah's over."

"Why don't we tackle one thing at a time."

⌇

The next morning, at exactly seven, the phone rang in the Sims' home. Evelyn was startled when she picked up the receiver in the bedroom. Still half asleep, she called to Alfred, who was shaving.

He could barely hear her above the noise of the electric razor. "Who?" he called out.

"It's Rabbi Weissman, on the phone, for you," she yelled back. Now she was completely awake.

He thought he heard her say, "Robert Waxman," but he didn't know any such person. He shut the shaver, stuck his head out the bathroom door, and asked again. She held the phone out, gesturing for him to come and take it, and said in a lower but more severe manner, "Rabbi Weissman."

He walked to the phone mumbling, "What does *he* want this early in the morning?"

"Why don't you take the damn phone and find out," she muttered as she handed him the receiver, turned away and stuck a pillow over her head. The rabbi heard this little exchange.

Alfred greeted the rabbi in a friendly, respectful manner. He still remembered that, at least in person, rabbis were to be treated with reverence.

"Good morning, Mr. Sims," the rabbi said in his thick Eastern European accent. The rabbi knew that Alfred cringed at his accent. It reminded Alfred of his parents and grandparents, of the heritage he had so readily discarded. It embarrassed him that there were still Jews who spoke that way, as if they were too stupid to learn proper English. But Rabbi Weissman's problem wasn't stupidity, not in the least, for English was only one of eleven languages in which he was fortunate to have an accent.

"I'm sorry to call this early, but I understand from your son that you are an early riser, and the morning is such a vonderful time to have a meaningful conversation. People think vith such clarity this time of day, yes?" The rabbi knew an evening call would probably not have found Alfred at home.

Alfred listened, wondering what the man wanted.

The rabbi was calling from his home in Crown Heights. "I have to be getting to *shul* for the morning prayers soon, so I von't take up too much of your time." He knew that Alfred was a bottom line sort. "I vas hoping to be able to have Paul visit vith my family for the Sabbath."

Alfred immediately grabbed the pillow off Evelyn's head. He wanted her to hear this. "This weekend?" he asked the rabbi, as he mouthed to Evelyn what they were discussing. She definitely wouldn't be able to go back to sleep now.

"Vell, I vas thinking that Paul needs more vork during the two veeks ve have left before the Bar Mitzvah, and it vould be difficult for me to spend *Shabbos* in your home, yes?"

"But he tells me he's doing well, not to worry," Alfred said nervously.

"Indeed he is, Mr. Sims," the rabbi asserted. In fact, Paul had been fully prepared months ago with the essentials for the ceremony. What he and Rabbi Weissman were presently studying was well beyond that.

The rabbi didn't feel deceptive, for he believed that he was still teaching Paul things that were very much related to entering Jewish manhood. They were toiling through the pages of the *Tanya*, the great book of mystical lore written in 1796 by the first Lubavitcher *Rebbe*, Schneur Zalman of Liady, a disciple of the *Baal Shem Tov*, the original founder of Hasidism. Paul had learned that Lubavitch was only one of many Hasidic sects that had emanated from the *Baal Shem Tov's* teachings, and that the *Tanya* held the path to spiritual enlightenment through the doctrines of *Chabad,* a Hebrew acronym for *wisdom, understanding, and knowledge.* Lubavitchers believed that the true Hasid, or pious one, strives for these three ideals, and therefore refer to themselves as *Chabad* Hasidim.

Another thing that the rabbi was teaching Paul was the history of the *Chabad* Hasidim, and how the name Lubavitch came from the Belorussian village in which *Rebbe* Zalman lived during the last years of his life. Although the *Rebbe* died in 1812, most of the Hasidim remained in the town until 1915 when they were forced to flee because of Russian persecution. They relocated to other parts of Europe, and in 1940, the sixth *Rebbe,* Yosef Yitzchak Schneerson, brought many of them to Crown Heights. Of those who remained in Europe, most eventually perished at the hands of the Nazis.

Ten years after their arrival in Crown Heights, the sixth *Rebbe* died, and his post was assumed by his distant cousin and son-in-law, Menachem Schneerson, a renowned genius who commanded many languages and had been educated at both the University of Berlin and the Sorbonne, in addition to his Torah scholarship. Rabbi Weissman had told Paul that many Lubavitchers believe that this *Rebbe* was to be the last before the coming of the Messiah, and Paul had found it intriguing that a man as intelligent as Rabbi Weissman could accept this. In fact, Paul found most of what the rabbi had to say intriguing.

"But as you know, vone can never know too much of anything," the rabbi added, "there is alvays room for improvement. I vant Paul to be perfect. After all, it is as much a reflection on me as it is on you, yes?"

Alfred had known from the moment they'd met that Rabbi Weissman was a hard man to bargain with. Initially, the rabbi's unassuming presence had Alfred thinking he was a push-over. Just tell him that I'm not interested in my son having a private tutor, Alfred had said to himself, and that will be that. But by the time their first meeting in the Hebrew School classroom had ended, Paul had a tutor for three hours each week, and at twenty dollars for each of those hours.

"I'll have to discuss it with my wife. I'm not sure if she has plans for the weekend." Alfred felt a bit embarrassed at having flaunted his non-observance of the Sabbath in the rabbi's face. The rabbi didn't think twice about it; he was a true Lubavitcher, believing that every Jew has a hidden desire to return to "God's way." That's why he schlepped, each Sunday, from Brooklyn to the Five Towns to teach children like Paul.

Not solely for the money—as Alfred had thought—but to bring the children closer to *Yidishkeit*, to Judaism, and thereby hasten the coming of the Messiah. True, the modest salary of a Talmud teacher in the Lubavitcher Rabbinical Seminary was not enough to support his wife and daughter, and give the required ten percent to charity. But Rabbi Isaac Weissman, a survivor of the Nazi death camps, in which he'd lost his first wife and son, was motivated by more than money. And his interest in young Paul was deeper than Alfred could fathom.

"Of course you vill," the rabbi responded, knowing full well that Alfred usually couldn't care less about his wife's opinions. "And please apologize to her for me, I'm so sorry to have avakened her. I vill hold on for a few minutes vhile you talk to her, yes?"

Not exactly what Alfred had planned. "To tell you the truth, she's only half awake right now. It would be best if I discuss it with her later when she's more coherent." The rabbi knew Alfred was lying, that most men lie when they begin a sentence with "to tell you the truth."

"That vill be fine. Better yet, I vill call her myself, later. There's no reason vhy you should apologize for me. The Talmud teaches us that each person must seek his own forgiveness, there are no intermediaries, yes?"

Alfred was speechless. The rabbi was outsmarting him once again.

"Anyvay, I vill call you back again tomorrow morning, a little later of course. Maybe after the morning prayers, around five minutes to eight, yes?" The rabbi knew that Alfred left at eight. He also figured that stating an exact time would prevent Alfred from avoiding the call. It was an appointment, and missing it would be an insult.

The two men ended their conversation as cordially as it had begun. Alfred hung up and stared into space for a few seconds. Evelyn tried to get him to tell her what was going on, but he was lost in thought, wondering what the rabbi was after.

CHAPTER 7

"Hey, Peanut, wait up!" Celeste called. Joshua was surprised to see her. He was already twenty minutes late for school, and she was always in school on time.

School had started less than a month ago. Loretta usually left around six, and had entrusted the Eisenmans, the elderly Jewish couple next door, to get Joshua out of the house. They were doing their best.

He stopped and waited for Celeste to catch up. "What are you doing here?" he asked.

"Same as you."

"But you're supposed to be in school by now."

"So are you," she said, leaning her body into his.

Close enough to be slow dancing, or other things, Joshua thought as he felt an erection. She pushed her hip into his; it seemed she knew exactly what she was doing. He grabbed her and pulled her into an alleyway. He wedged her between himself and the wall, and kissed her hard, and long. She wrapped her arms around him and held him tightly.

"Let's not go to school today," she suggested as soon as they broke for air.

"So that's why you're here. You wanna play hooky."

"Not just play hooky, but play it with *you*."

"You planned this?"

She smiled.

"And I bet you got some other games in mind, too," he said as she brought her lips back to his.

This time, a short kiss. It was too dangerous for them to stand there for long, even in the alley. Joshua's apartment was empty, but they couldn't go back to the building because her father might catch them. She grabbed his hand and pulled him across the street, toward the park.

They found a grassy spot, hidden within the trees. Joshua was about to sit when he noticed her reach into her bag for a sheet she just happened to have with her. "You sure *did* plan this," he said, as she spread the sheet on the ground.

"We're gonna have a picnic, a lo—ng picnic," she said as she sat down and pulled him close to her.

A few passionate kisses eventually lead to her easing his hand up her shirt, and letting him play with her breasts. The next thing he realized, her hand was in his pants.

"Wow," she said, "they sure ain't calling you Peanut because of this."

They both chuckled as he started returning the favor, and suddenly, Celeste became gun shy.

She froze up and looked at him. "I think we should just kiss."

"Yeah, sure. Fine," he said, concealing his disappointment. In truth, he was really okay with it. He knew that sooner or later things would happen. Many things, in fact, each with its own novelty and excitement, until eventually he would become a full-fledged man. He took it for granted that all this was destined to happen with Celeste. Hell, he believed that everything of importance for the rest of his life was going to happen with Celeste.

⁓

Jerome, for the most part, pretended not to notice what was going on. It was hard for him, because his sister and Joshua were spending a lot of time together. Joshua felt bad that Jerome and he were drifting apart, but couldn't help himself. Luckily, this year there were three new black kids in their class with whom Jerome had become friendly. One in particular, Roy Sharp, was replacing Joshua as Jerome's best friend. Roy, a well behaved and extremely bright fellow, was clean cut, short and thin, bespectacled, and always dressed like a black

"Poindexter." His father was the Reverend Jameson Sharp, pastor of the local Baptist Church which had recently opened in a store-front on Empire Boulevard. Jerome had begun frequenting the church, and also the Sharps' home. The more time Jerome spent with Roy and the reverend, the more he disapproved of Celeste and Joshua.

⏤⏤

That night, at three a.m., in the small bedroom they shared in the back of the their basement apartment, Celeste and Jerome were soundly asleep. All was quiet, except for Jerome's snoring.

Awake in another room, just a few feet away, lay a beast, a creature with inhuman lusts and cravings, sweating, obsessing, hating himself for what he was about to do. He looked at the woman fast asleep beside him. He despised her too, blaming her for not stopping him, for turning a blind eye all these years. For no matter how hard he tried to stop himself, he couldn't.

The door to the children's bedroom opened slowly, creaking hinges breaking the cadence of the snoring. Celeste's eyes opened, but she lay still. The snoring suddenly stopped, but Jerome's eyes remained closed. The children were both awake now, each pretending not to be, each knowing exactly what was going to happen.

The beast slipped into the room like a burglar, leaving the door slightly ajar. The faint light from the hall was just enough to help him navigate. Slowly, he moved toward Celeste's bed.

He crawled in next to her, knowing she was awake, but all too willing to play along with her ruse. This way they could both pretend it never happened.

In the other bed, Jerome lay helpless, tears in his eyes, silently praying that God would make this stop. But it never stopped. And Jerome, like his mother, was afraid to do anything. He had come far with the white kids in the neighborhood, but this was something else.

In the morning, he too would hate himself, would turn away from his sister in shame for not having protected her. He dreamed of a time when he would be stronger, when he would be able to put an end to it. He dreamed and prayed, and that was all he did.

When the beast was done and gone, neither of the children spoke to one another. Jerome lay in the dark, while Celeste used her sheets to wipe the beast's sweat from her body. She felt contaminated, defiled, wishing she could stop breathing. Anything to get rid of the nauseating, lingering smell.

Her mind took her to thoughts of Joshua and this terrible secret she kept from him. He believed her to be pure, and that was what she needed. She swore to herself that he would never discover the truth of how tainted she was.

What she had no way of knowing, however, was that fate had another plan.

CHAPTER 8

Paul Sims heard his Hebrew name, Pinchas ben Anshel, chanted as the Cantor called him to the Torah. The exalted moment had arrived as he rose from his seat next to the rabbi, walked to a large rostrum on which the Torah sat, and looked out at his audience.

It was a gothic chapel, with a cathedral ceiling, mahogany pews, crimson carpet, pipe-organ, and bright stained glass windows along the eastern and northern walls depicting scenes from the Bible. The ark, constructed of marble and brass, stood ten feet high and eight feet wide between two of the stained glass windows, and a massive silver menorah was affixed to the southern wall. And then there were the people, spruced and adorned to perfection, impeccably observant of the decorum.

In the front row were his parents, sharing a rare moment of joy. They appeared nervous, but Paul was poised. Rabbi Weissman had prepared him well, and he knew it.

Next to Alfred and Evelyn sat Paul's grandparents, Sheindle Simenovitz and Gladys and Sol Voratitsky. In the same row also sat his Aunt Brindle with her husband Martin, and his Great Aunt Rivka and Uncle Izzy. The other pews were filled with family and friends of his parents. There were some kids as well, a few cousins, and a handful from school whose parents were friendly with Alfred and Evelyn.

The only one in the room who Paul actually considered his friend was Loretta Eubanks—also the only black person—beaming in her long, flowing mauve dress and matching hat. The two other friends that Paul had in the world, Rabbi Isaac Weissman and Doctor Harold Goldman, were not in attendance.

The cantor opened the scroll, and pointed to the spot where Paul was to begin. Normally, in Reform temples, Bar Mitzvah candidates didn't read directly from the Torah scroll itself. Instead, they read a portion from the *Haftorah*, supplementary readings usually recited after the reading of the Torah, and gave a short speech. But Paul wanted to do it all, just as he had been trained.

Among the lessons Rabbi Weissman had taught him, the most precious was a sense of being "special." Though such a feeling was indeed alien to him, he had come to believe, as the rabbi insisted, that God's hand was at work in his life. The rabbi saw God's hand in everything.

Paul began the blessings, his voice resonating throughout the large sanctuary. The words came forth mechanically, but his mind was elsewhere, contrasting his surroundings with the modest, unadorned sanctuary in which he had found himself two weeks earlier. He recalled the hordes of Hasidic men, all in dark suits and fedoras, crowded into a single room with wooden folding chairs and linoleum floors, and the women in their long dresses, hats, and kerchiefs, crammed upstairs in the balcony. Those who had arrived early enough had gotten seats, but most stood. And the praying was noisy, spirited, everyone swaying back and forth, pouring out their souls.

The entire weekend at Rabbi Weissman's home had been a surprise. First, the shock that Rabbi Weissman had managed to convince his parents to let him go; second, the rabbi's daughter, Rachel, a year younger than he, and the most exquisite creature he'd ever seen.

Rabbi Weissman had often spoken of Rachel, but never of her physical beauty.

"My brilliant Rucheleh never ceases to remind me that in the book of Genesis it is the vomen who are in charge, from Eve all the vay through to her own name-sake, Rachel,"

"My Rucheleh prepared these jelly donuts for Hanukah, for me to give to my favorite students. Here are some, they are almost as sveet as she."

Such adjectives had led Paul to expect a homely, bookish sort.

He had felt uneasy when he first arrived at the Weissmans' small two bedroom apartment. Alfred had dropped him off outside the building, without accompanying him up, using the excuse of having to get to a business meeting.

Rebbetzin Weissman, the rabbi's wife, had met Paul with a welcoming smile. She was younger than he'd imagined—a small woman, thin with a light complexion and dark brunette bangs protruding from under a kerchief, or *tichel*. She took his bag, and led him to Rachel's room. Rachel had given up her bed for the weekend to sleep on the fold-out couch in the living room. He was told that this was routine in the Weissman home whenever there was a guest.

"I hope you're not uncomfortable about staying in a girl's room, it's the best we can do," the *Rebbetzin* said. He noticed immediately that she—unlike her husband—had no accent.

"Oh, not at all!" Polite, though not completely truthful.

"Isaac, I mean the rabbi, will be back in a few minutes. He and Rachel just went out to do some last minute shopping. Can I offer you anything, a cold drink, maybe?"

"No thank you," he responded shyly.

"Okay. Well, I'll leave you to unpack. There's an empty drawer in the dresser, top left, and some room in the closet. The shower is in the hall bathroom, there's soap and shampoo already there. Candle-lighting isn't for another hour and a half so you have plenty of time. Just make yourself at home. And, by the way, my name is Hannah."

Paul unpacked, showered, and dressed for his first *Shabbos*. He wore a light blue suit, white short sleeved shirt with a starched collar, and a Navy tie. Blue, in any shade, was his mother's favorite color, not his.

After he dressed, he didn't know what to do. He heard voices in the kitchen—the rabbi's, Hannah's, and another he assumed belonged to Rachel. His anxiety grew. Hannah had been much prettier than he'd imagined, so now he was curious to see Rachel. He breathed deeply, and went to join them.

"Ah, Pinchas," the rabbi exclaimed as Paul appeared at the kitchen entrance. "Come, join us, ve vere just about to get you." The rabbi put his arm around Paul. "You haven't met my precious Rucheleh, whom I have told you so much about," the rabbi said. "Rucheleh, this is Paul, rather Pinchas, whom I have told *you* so much about."

Rachel was an emerald eyed, strawberry blond goddess – elegant facial features, flawless skin, and a figure that seemed slightly more mature than her years from what Paul could tell beneath her modest

Orthodox attire. She smiled and said, "Hello." Paul did the same, trying to still the tremor in his voice. The rabbi's hand appeared in front of him, holding a yarmulke for him to place on his head.

They all went into the dining room, where the table was adorned with fine china, and two silver candlesticks in the middle. Hannah Weissman drew her husband and daughter near as she struck the match. The wicks came aglow, and Hannah waved her hands over the flames in three circular motions with her eyes closed, while reciting the blessing under her breath. Rachel and the rabbi stared at the burning candles until Hannah completed the blessing and opened her eyes to behold the light. The Weissmans wished each other *gut Shabbos* with kisses all around. Paul wondered what it must feel like to be loved like that.

Paul and the rabbi left for the synagogue, and the women remained at home. They walked down Montgomery Street to Kingston Avenue, and north on Kingston toward Eastern Parkway. Paul was amazed at what he saw on Kingston: a grocery store, a hat store, a drug store, a pizza place, a clothing store, all with Jewish signs, all closed for the Sabbath. He also saw droves of Hasidim heading to the synagogue, some seeming to take notice of him as well. He felt out of place being hatless and in a light colored suit. Most of the Hasidim walked briskly, passing him and the rabbi on their way.

"Why are they in such a hurry?" Paul asked.

"It is a *mitzvah* to pray. It is also a *mitzvah* to hurry oneself to do a mitzvah," the rabbi responded.

"So why aren't we walking fast too?"

"It is also a *mitzvah* to take it easy on the Sabbath," the rabbi answered with a smile.

"I don't understand?"

"Vell, there are sometimes disagreements about which *mitzvahs* are more important than others. I, and my tired legs, believe it is more important to take it easy."

"I see."

Paul wondered why some of the men scooting by seemed to look at him disapprovingly. He was certain the rabbi noticed too.

The synagogue was on the south side of Eastern Parkway, off Kingston Avenue, in the basement of a well maintained, red brick Tudor with a three pointed white cement crown rising above the roof of the facade. It was set back about fifty feet from the sidewalk, and its grounds were enclosed by a waist high wrought-iron fence. The entrance was marked by a white stone arch surrounding an immense mahogany door with two small windows and a large brass handle. Above the arch, a sign read *World Lubavitcher Headquarters*. A line gathered outside as the men shuffled through the aperture and down the stairs into the basement.

Once they were in the synagogue, Paul followed the rabbi through the mob to two empty seats along the eastern wall. It was strange, Paul thought, that these two seats should remain empty with such a crowd. He hadn't known at the time that this was the most coveted section of the synagogue, specially reserved for the scholars of the community, one of whom was Rabbi Weissman. The rabbi took his usual seat, and gestured for Paul to take the one next to it. Paul looked around, still sensing eyes upon him.

The room was large, but still too small for the crowd. It was also noisy, people greeting one another, catching up, chatting about the latest political gossip, or deliberating minutiae of Jewish law. Paul looked around and found it curious the way the Hasidim talked to each other, the volume, the hand motions and dramatic body language that accompanied their words. Everything was imbued with intensity, whether the latest baseball scores—which he was surprised to hear being discussed a few rows behind—or the recent fluctuations of gold prices that two men were commiserating over just a few feet away.

Suddenly, silence fell upon the room as all heads turned toward a door in the northeastern corner. The door opened. A tall, heavy-set, red bearded man donning a black fedora and caftan appeared, then stepped to the side, holding the door, as he looked out at the audience and waited. Paul turned to Rabbi Weissman with a curious expression. "That's Rabbi Shoenfeld, the *Rebbe's* special assistant," Rabbi Weissman whispered. The *Rebbe*, Paul had known, was The Grand Rabbi of all the Lubavitchers. He was regarded as a king, and as with all royalty, the position was usually maintained within one family, passed down from generation to generation.

A moment later a second man entered, and the entire congregation stood up. The man was short, no taller than five six, with a slightly hunched back, but he walked with great deliberateness. His marks of distinction included a hat that was taller and wider brimmed than the fedoras of his followers, and a pure silk caftan. Most outstanding were his eyes—soft, glimmering blue, almost childlike—and his long, full, radiant white beard. Beneath the beard, a pale, wrinkled face with an austere expression.

The *Rebbe* sauntered toward his seat beside the ark as everyone remained standing in silence. The heavy-set man with the red beard closed the door through which they had entered and followed his leader. The *Rebbe* seemed to be ignoring the honored reception, his eyes focused instead on the ark. Just before taking his seat, he stopped for an instant, turned and stared into the crowd. Then, as he sat, his assistant—still standing—pounded his hand on a lectern. A loud thump resounded through the room and the congregation broke into prayer.

Paul was amazed by the aura of the *Rebbe's* presence. He saw Rabbi Weissman was already lost in prayer, so he opened his own book, and started struggling through the Hebrew. He was better in Hebrew than most of his peers back in Hewlett Harbor, but still not good enough to follow at this pace.

After the service, everybody offered one another salutations for the Sabbath. Rabbi Weissman shook Paul's hand and patted him on the shoulder. Paul smiled and uttered his first, "Good *Shabbos*."

Walking home, they were joined by two other men, close friends and neighbors of Rabbi Weissman. The three men spoke in Yiddish, and while Paul couldn't understand a word, he could tell from the tone that whatever they were discussing was a serious matter. He knew it wasn't about him, for Rabbi Weissman wasn't capable of such rudeness.

One of the rabbi's friends suddenly broke into English. "I don't care what they think, let them go to hell," he burst out angrily.

"Reb Moishe," the rabbi stated calmly—*Reb* being a euphemism of respect. "Please, my friend, there is no need to be so angry on the Sabbath. The *Rebbe* has assured us that he will soon speak out against this fanaticism."

"It cannot be soon enough," the second man asserted with slightly less ire than his cohort. "These zealots have invaded our community, they are teaching our children in the yeshivas, and they are spying on us like the *Gestapo*."

"Enough!" exclaimed Rabbi Weissman.

Paul was stunned, for he had never imagined the rabbi could speak so harshly.

"I'm sorry, Reb Itzhik," the second man said to Rabbi Weissman. "I should not have said that," referring to the term *Gestapo*. "I'm very sorry."

Paul wondered what these men were talking about in the first place? Who were the fanatics? Why were they such a threat?

"It is okay," Rabbi Weissman said to his friend as he regained his composure and affectionately took the man by the arm. "As for those fanatics, the *Rebbe* vill deal vith them; he vill teach them the true way of God and the Torah, I am certain."

"I hope you are right, Reb Itzhik," the man named Moishe said.

"Yes, from the mouth of Reb Itzhik to the ears of The Creator," the second man affirmed.

By this time they were standing outside Rabbi Weissman's building. The three men smiled at each other and said good night. The man named Moishe turned to Paul, extended his hand, and said, "*Gut Shabbos*." The other man did the same, and then the two of them continued down the block.

As they walked away, Paul heard them mumbling, and wondered if Rabbi Weissman's words had made any impact. He looked at the rabbi's face, and saw that the rabbi also had his own doubts.

Paul and the rabbi entered the building and walked up the six flights of stairs, elevators being forbidden on the Sabbath according to Orthodox law. The rabbi needed to stop once to catch his breath, but it didn't seem to bother him. He was content with any and all sacrifices for his beliefs.

The rabbi was still panting when they entered the apartment, but it seemed to subside the instant Rachel greeted him with a hug, kiss, and a hearty "good *Shabbos*." Afterward, she turned to Paul and politely added, "Good *Shabbos* Pinchas."

Hearing her speak his name did something to Paul. He looked at her with a nervous smile and replied, "Good *Shabbos*, Rachel."

The rabbi disappeared into the kitchen where Hannah was preparing to serve the meal. Rachel turned away from Paul and sashayed into the kitchen herself. Paul followed.

As they entered they caught the rabbi and Hannah embracing. Rachel smiled, but seemed a bit embarrassed. A similar look came upon the rabbi's face; he had momentarily forgotten that his student was in his house.

"Come Papa, I believe it's time to say *Kiddush*," Rachel interjected, referring to the traditional prayer over the wine.

"Yes, it is getting late, ve should get started," the rabbi responded.

They gathered around the table, the rabbi at one head, Hannah at the other, and Paul across from Rachel.

The rabbi took the overflowing cup in his hand, rose to his feet, and began reciting the blessing. Paul recognized the words from his Bar Mitzvah lessons. In two weeks he would recite the same prayer in Temple, on Friday night before the entire congregation. He felt less nervous about that than he did from the young lady sitting across the table.

The rabbi's eyes were closed as he sang. His body swayed back and forth. Paul had listened to the rabbi's recitation of this prayer many times—he even had a recording of it to help him learn it—but he had never heard it said with such fervor as now. He watched Rachel and Hannah as they hummed softly to the rabbi's melody. On the table, the candles stood aglow and two large *challas* lay beneath a colorful embroidered cloth that depicted a design of the city of Jerusalem.

This was the traditional *Shabbos* table Paul had learned about, had seen in pictures, but had never actually experienced. He wanted to absorb everything; the warmth, the love, the flickering flames, and Rachel's resplendent eyes.

During the meal, conversation was interspersed with the singing of Sabbath melodies. Paul was unaccustomed to singing at the dinner table, unfamiliar with the songs, and his voice wasn't very good. Not wanting to appear inept in front of Rachel, he hummed along, softly at first, until the spirit seemed to grab him, and he found himself singing as loud as the rabbi.

The menu consisted of gefilte fish, salad, chicken soup, roasted veal, kugel, and rice mixed with peas and carrots. It was a job getting it all down. The rabbi and Hannah talked some about family matters; Rachel discussed her studies at school and confessed that one of the rabbis had caught her best friend, Esther Mandlebaum, passing her a note. Paul was surprised that she wasn't afraid to tell this to her parents, and was even more astonished at their laughter about it. It seemed they were confident that the passing of a note wouldn't turn their daughter into a delinquent.

The rabbi turned to Paul and said, "I informed the *Rebbe* that ve vere having you here for *Shabbos*, and that your Bar Mitzvah is in two veeks. He says that he vould like that you be called to the Torah in the synagogue tomorrow morning, yes?"

"But I can't really be called to the Torah until I am actually Bar Mitzvah'd, isn't that what you taught me?"

"Yes, you are correct. But, the truth is that your Bar Mitzvah passed some time ago, it vas the day you turned thirteen. Remember vhen ve calculated your Hebrew birthday as being the eleventh of the month of Av. Vell, that vas your Bar Mitzvah. It is a strange thing, a Bar Mitzvah, vone does not really have to do anything, it just happens automatically. Vhether you celebrate or not, you are still Bar Mitzvah'd on that day."

Paul's anxiety was apparent.

"Nothing to vorry, Pinchas," the rabbi continued. "All you have to do is say the same blessings over the Torah reading that you already know. It is, how they say here in America, a piece of cake, yes?"

Rachel and Hannah chuckled.

Paul was concerned, but knew he had to do it. He couldn't cower in front of Rachel.

The matter was settled without further discussion. A few more melodies, a delicious mocha layer cake for dessert, the concluding benedictions, and the meal was over. Before Paul knew it, he was lying in bed, tossing and turning, dreading the day that awaited.

❧

The next morning, Paul and the rabbi arrived at the synagogue an hour before the services began. It was the rabbi's custom to come early on Sabbath morning in order to study a while before beginning his prayers. There were several men gathered around a large table headed by an elderly rabbi ruminating over a page of Talmud. The elder played with his long silver beard and rocked back and forth as he spoke. Some of the men had their own books, some shared, and some simply listened. Paul and Rabbi Weissman sat close to the teacher.

On route to the synagogue, Rabbi Weissman had explained to Paul that the Lubavitcher community had many different tiers of leadership. Beneath the *Rebbe* were other rabbis, the "elders" of the community, each with their own students and devotees, some with slightly varying interpretations of the *Rebbe's* teachings.

Paul recalled the conversation between the rabbi and his neighbors the night before, as well as the disdainful looks some of the Hasidim had given him. It occurred to him that among these people, slight differences in interpretation could be rather serious.

At the conclusion of the study session, Rabbi Weissman introduced Paul to the teacher. The man, Rav Yehudah Feldblum, spoke only Yiddish, but his smile communicated enough. *Rav* was a special term of respect, reserved for rabbis of the highest order. "He said he is privileged to meet the honored Bar Mitzvah boy," Rabbi Weissman translated.

"But how does he know?" Paul asked.

"Ah, just about everyone in the community knows; news travels very quickly around these parts," the rabbi responded.

Paul was bewildered.

Rabbi Weissman pointed out that the other men around the table were also students of Rav Feldblum, and that Rav Feldblum was an elder of the community, and a special advisor to the *Rebbe*. Paul noticed that this group of men seemed quite accepting of his presence.

The synagogue filled quickly. Similar chattering as the night before and, again, the ceremonious entrance of the *Rebbe*. About an hour into the service, the Torah scroll was taken from the ark. The man who led the prayers marched it around the synagogue and then placed it on a large *bima*, table, in the center of the room. Another man undressed the scroll and sang out the *Rebbe's* name, bestowing on the Grand Rabbi the honor of the first blessing for the reading of the Torah. Everyone in the room rose to their feet the moment the *Rebbe's* name resounded.

A path was cleared for the *Rebbe* to walk through, as he made his way from the front of the room. He moved slowly among his followers, who were awed by his mere proximity. He approached the podium, climbed the two steps, draped his *tallis* over his head, and stood before the Torah scroll. Silence permeated the room.

The *Rebbe* began to recite the words of the blessing in a low, measured tone. The congregation responded loudly with their traditional refrains. The *Rebbe* completed the blessing, and the reader proceeded to chant the initial section from the Sabbath Torah portion. Everyone in the room followed along in their own texts. Paul knew that his turn at the podium was not far off. Rabbi Weissman had told him that he was to be the third person called. "A very high honor," the rabbi had said.

Upstairs, in the women's section, the main attraction was neither the *Rebbe's* blessing nor the reading from the scroll, but the large shopping bag that Hannah and Rachel Weissman had smuggled into the synagogue. Quickly, Rachel and her mother reached into the bag, pulled out several smaller bags filled with candy, and doled them out among the women. The plan was set into motion. As soon as the Bar Mitzvah boy, now known to them as Pinchas, finished his blessing, the bags of candy would descend upon him from the balcony. Such was the traditional way to celebrate a Bar Mitzvah, the throwing of the candy symbolizing the wish for a life of sweetness.

Most of the women were excited, but not all. The dissenters were the wives and daughters of those men who had shunned Paul the night before. These were members of a right wing faction opposed to Rav Feldblum and his students, objecting to any Lubavitcher scholar teaching in a Reform temple, and to Rav Feldblum's belief in reaching out to other Jews. They wanted their community to remain pure, free from outside, "poisonous" influences.

Their leader was another elder, Rav Nachum Schachter, a man reputed to be a great legal scholar, perhaps the keenest Talmudic mind in the community. He was the head of the *Bet Din*, the Rabbinical Court where all communal and personal conflicts were adjudicated. Hasidim never took one another to secular court, but the calendar in the Rabbinical Court was backlogged at least two years. This position made Rav Schachter a force among the Lubavitchers. His judgments were often harsh, his hand was far reaching, and many of his followers were more loyal to him than even to the *Rebbe*.

Rabbi Weissman's hand came around Paul's shoulder as the man on the podium sang out his Hebrew name, along with the title "*Habachur HaBar Mitzvah*," the Bar Mitzvah boy. Perplexed, Paul turned to Rabbi Weissman, who smiled and whispered, "Today is the day of your Bar Mitzvah, Pinchas. Go! Make me proud!"

Paul moved hesitantly toward the podium. He wanted to back out, say forget it, pack his bags and catch the next train back to Hewlett Harbor, but he wouldn't. He wouldn't disappoint the rabbi, and he wasn't going to recoil in front of Rachel. It was his first taste of what "love" can make men do, a fitting lesson on the day he was to become "a man."

He ascended the steps of the podium and approached the Torah scroll. The man who had called his name reached into a blue velvet bag and removed a large white prayer shawl with black stripes and white fringes. Rabbi Weissman had taught Paul about the significance of the *tallis*, prayer shawl, though in his temple they weren't worn. The man helped him drape the shawl over his shoulders. It was large and engulfed his entire body, the fringes reaching the floor.

The man reading from the scroll took the silver pointer, pointed to a word in the scroll, and instructed Paul to take one of the corners of the prayer shawl, touch it to the word, and then kiss it. After doing this, Paul began reciting the short blessing before the Torah reading. Despite his nervousness, the Hebrew was familiar and flowed easily. He was even able to concentrate on the meaning of the words, *Blessed be God . . . Who has chosen us from among the other nations, and has given us His Torah.* Thanks to the rabbi, it was one of the prayers he understood.

Paul concluded his blessing, and the reader began. He tried to follow the pointer as it passed from word to word upon the ancient Torah scroll. He had studied Torah script with Rabbi Weissman, and recognized all the letters. Figuring out the correct pronunciation of words, and their accompanying melody, however, was another matter. That task required vowels and notes, neither of which appeared in the scroll itself. He knew he was going to read from the scroll in his own temple in two weeks. He had spent months memorizing the pronunciation and melody for each word. None of his peers had bothered learning this; instead, they recited only the *Haftorah*, which could be read directly from a book containing notes and vowels. But Rabbi Weissman insisted that Paul do it the hard way. "A true scholar breaks his teeth and suffers to gain knowledge," the rabbi had remarked.

The reader finished, and again instructed Paul to take a corner of the prayer shawl, touch it to the last word read, and kiss it. Paul recited the concluding blessing, "*Blessed be God . . . who has given us His Torah of truth, and implanted within us eternal life.*" As he completed the blessing, he noticed the other men on the podium lifting their prayer shawls above their heads and holding them up like canopies. He had no idea what they were doing, and wondered if he was supposed to do the same. He looked to the man who had been instructing him, but the man offered only a smile. Suddenly, a shower of candy began to fall from the balcony. as the congregation broke into joyous singing and clapping.

Siman Tov Umazel Tov, a traditional song wishing luck and prosperity.

The young children raced to the podium to collect the candy as Paul felt his hand grabbed by the man next to him, pulling him into a circular dance around the Torah scroll. He followed, and began singing along.

Another circle quickly formed at the foot of the podium, then another around that, and still another around the last. Most of the men's section had broken into dance, save for the followers of Rav Schachter, while the women above leaned over the railing, watched and sang along. All, except the wives and children of the followers of Rav Schachter.

Gradually the gaiety subsided, decorum was restored, and the next honoree was called to the Torah. Paul removed the prayer shawl and returned it to the man who had given it to him. The man placed it back in the blue velvet bag, and as Paul descended the podium to return to his seat, the man reached out, stopped him, and handed him the velvet bag with the prayer shawl inside. Paul hesitated, not understanding the gesture. "It is a gift for you from your revered teacher," the man said as he placed the bag in Paul's hand.

Paul took the bag, and returned to his seat, where Rabbi Weissman tearfully embraced him and kissed him on the forehead. Paul stiffened, as he was unaccustomed to such displays of affection. The rabbi looked him in the eye, and said, "*Mazel tov*, my son, *mazel tov!*"

My son, Paul thought, *if only*.

❧

Here he was, two weeks later, reciting the same blessing over the Torah, feeling almost naked without his *tallis* and yarmulke. He had hidden the *tallis* in the bottom of his junk drawer, the only drawer he knew his mother didn't regularly inspect. How kind she was, he often mused, to allow him this morsel of privacy.

He noticed his father looking around, observing the reactions of the others in the room. He knew that Alfred would only be impressed if the guests were impressed.

His Torah reading was flawless, and his conclusion of the final blessing was met with silence. No candy flew through the air, no singing or dancing. He returned to his seat between the rabbi and the president

63

of the congregation, each of whom extended their hands and politely wished him *Mazel Tov.*

He sat, waiting for the service to end, thinking only of one thing: *Rachel.* He imagined her being there, sitting in the pews, watching him breeze through the Torah reading. He knew that in her world men were measured by their scholarship and piety. He lamented not having been prepared to read the Torah in her synagogue, and craved another opportunity to prove himself. *If only she could be here,* he thought, *if only she could see what I can really do.*

If only.

❦

After the service, the congregation gathered in the catering hall for a collation of bagels and spreads. Guests and relatives lauded Paul's performance and wished him well, a mere prelude of what was to come that same evening during the lavish affair that would take place at the Seawane Country Club in Hewlett Harbor. "It will be the bash of all bashes," Alfred had told Evelyn earlier that morning while they were dressing for synagogue. "Wait till they see the parakeets," he exclaimed, referring to the hundreds of little caged birds that would be adorning the dining room, party favors for the guests.

"Just make sure that we don't end up with one of those creatures flying around this house," she responded. "I have enough problems keeping things tidy between you and your son."

"Please," he implored, "don't get yourself all riled up. They live in cages, you know."

So do I, she thought.

It was to be the quintessential suburban Bar Mitzvah affair, replete with glutinous food, a nine-piece band, and enough flowers to fill a rain forest. Parakeets would surely be a new one, Alfred mused, something people would talk about for a long time; something that would go down in the annals of Long Island Jewish History; something an author might even write about one day, only to find his readers reacting, *No way!*

❦

Alfred stood with some of his buddies in the back of the room, next to a small table upon which sat a few bottles of rye, bourbon, and scotch. One of the men, a husky business associate who had a loud and obstreperous voice, called Paul over to join them for a drink. "Come here my boy," the man said as he handed Paul a shot. "Have one in honor of being a man," he continued, slapping Paul on the back while demonstrating how to down the whisky.

Paul followed the man's wrist motion only to end up almost having a seizure. The others laughed, including Alfred. Paul was embarrassed. It was going to be a long day.

Alfred mingled with his guests, practically ignoring Paul. There were no displays of warmth or affection between father and son, but Paul didn't seem to mind. His thoughts were elsewhere. In the past two weeks, not a minute had passed when his mind was free of Rachel.

His imagination was running wild. For in actuality, he knew that Rachel had been rather indifferent to him. He blamed it on his background, and he was determined, in time, to fix that. He also figured she was too devout to even think about boys at this point in her life. He just couldn't fathom any other reason for the way she reacted to him.

What he didn't know was that there was more to Rachel Weissman than he, or anyone who knew her, had realized at the time.

CHAPTER 9

It wasn't that Rachel Weissman didn't like boys; in fact, quite the opposite was true. And while she lived the life of a reverent Hasidic maiden, her fantasies often told another story.

As if being the daughter of a revered scholar in the community wasn't enough, she was also the child of a man who had a son taken from him in one of God's crueler moments. She had never been told the details, but she knew she bore a heavy burden. She would always have to lead two lives—her dead half brother's and her own.

Rachel's mother knew this too. Hannah was almost twenty years younger than Isaac, yet the gap between them was filled by more than time. She never doubted his devotion, but always felt the presence of his past. It wasn't his fault, for he tried to keep it inside, but there was only so much he could conceal.

Hannah had understood this when she'd accepted Isaac's marriage proposal. Having been one of the more desirable young women in the community, strikingly attractive and from a fine family, she could have had her pick of the lot. Almost every *shodchin*, matchmaker, in the neighborhood had been knocking at her father's door. Until, one day, her father came home from a Talmud lecture and announced that he had found her the perfect husband.

"Who needs those ridiculous matchmakers?" Aaron Twersky exclaimed as he came through the door on that cold January night in 1950. "I have just listened to one of the great scholars of our time recite from the holy books. He is new here, from Europe, somewhere in Poland I think. And he is single, so they say."

"So they say?" Hannah's mother, Rivka, asked her husband as he removed his hat and coat. She was a cautious woman.

"Well, I didn't go up to him and ask, but I walked home from the class with Reb Lazar, and he said that he heard from Reb Mordechai, who heard from his wife, Raizel, that the man is single. So how can this be wrong?"

Rivka sighed and Hannah laughed. Hannah trusted her father, and disliked the matchmakers as much as he did. She'd already had some frightful experiences at their hands, and had become skeptical of ever finding a husband. She would gladly do as her father wished.

What Aaron Twersky hadn't told his wife and his seventeen year old daughter was that this brilliant scholar was thirty-six and widowed. He would worry about that in time, but first he would consult the *Rebbe*, for the *Rebbe* always knew what was best. If the *Rebbe* gave his blessing, then the *shiddoch* was meant to be.

The following week, the *Rebbe* weighed in. Isaac Weissman was a great scholar and Hannah Twersky was a dutiful young lady from an esteemed family. Together, they would produce extraordinary children. Nothing else mattered.

Rivka Twersky's anger at her husband was intense at first, as was Hannah's surprise. But in time, as they came to know Isaac, they couldn't help but love and respect him. For he was a "special" man.

After only three months of courting, Hannah fell deeply in love. The wedding took place two months later, and on her wedding night, Hannah learned yet another thing about Isaac that would make her smile each time the thought of him entered her mind: he was a wonderful lover, soft and passionate, far beyond anything she'd ever dreamed. During the time of month when sex was permitted, she spent her days longing for him, craving his touch. And when he came to her at night, she experienced such pleasure, it often brought tears to her eyes. "How could anyone have the right to feel so good?" she once whispered to him as she was catching her breath, lying back on her pillow.

"It is not a right," Isaac responded softly, "it is an obligation."

Hannah knew that Isaac was referring to the rabbinic commandment to enjoy sex. She had learned about this in her bridal class at the women's seminary. *A man who sexually pleases his wife will merit sons*, was the dictum she recalled each time they made love. Yes, they would create extraordinary children. Yes, she would give him what he had lost, many more than he had lost. She would help him forget.

But eight months after their wedding, Hannah's hopes faded into illusions. She had been seven and a half months pregnant, and one evening—in the middle of the night—she began to bleed profusely. By the time she'd finally made it to the hospital, both she and the baby were almost gone. The doctors managed to save both of them, but she would never again bear children.

Rachel was *it*. Hannah knew it, Isaac knew it, and—above all—Rachel knew it. Nothing ever needed to be said; all was understood. Isaac, especially, doted over Rachel and attended to her in ways that were uncommon. When she was an infant, for example, and wouldn't sleep through the night, he convinced Hannah to let him take her into their bed to comfort her, instead of listening to the pediatrician's instructions to let her cry herself to sleep. "Vhen she is ready, she vill sleep alone," he'd said. Hannah had her doubts, but not enough to argue. She saw how much Isaac loved Rachel, and wanted to believe that he knew better than the doctors.

One Friday night when Rachel was six months old, she began crying hysterically in her high-chair while Isaac was trying to recite the blessing over the wine. Isaac took her from the chair and sat her on his lap while he concluded the *Kiddush*. He rocked her on his knee as he sang the blessing, and even let her taste the sweet red wine. When he tried to return her to the high-chair, she protested with more crying and kicking, so he took her back to his seat and fed her from his plate. Rachel never returned to the high-chair, and remained on her father's lap until she was old enough to take her own seat at the table. Isaac couldn't handle hearing his daughter cry; the memories were just too powerful.

Throughout Rachel's childhood, every morning after Isaac finished teaching his Talmud class in the yeshiva, he would come home for a few hours to spend time playing with her. And every evening, after dinner, he would spend yet a few more hours with her. On *Shabbos* afternoons also—a time when he should have been napping to catch up on sleep—he would sit and read to her or take her for walks around the neighborhood. He never seemed to tire or lose patience.

Hannah felt that Isaac should devote more of his time preparing for his classes or resting, but she would not argue. She even began to feel jealous. Still, she wouldn't allow herself to interfere with her husband's joy. She was proud of him, and confident in his love. She wanted nothing more than to make him happy.

For her first two years, Rachel's parents never went out without her. This was despite numerous offers from Rivka and Aaron Twersky to baby-sit for their granddaughter. After that, Hannah and Isaac went out only rarely, for special occasions such as their anniversary or a friend's wedding. Once in a blue moon, Isaac would agree to let Rachel sleep at her grandparents' home so that he and Hannah could be alone. Those nights Hannah was reminded of how wonderful things could be, dampened only by her frustration and longing for the next time which she knew would be far off.

Soon after Rachel mastered walking, Isaac began taking her with him to the synagogue on *Shabbos*. It wasn't unusual for a father to take a child to *shul* early so that the mother could have some time to dress, and maybe tidy up the house a bit for any afternoon guests. When Hannah finally arrived at the synagogue, she would look down into the men's section and find Isaac and Rachel (young girls were permitted to accompany their fathers in the men's section). Isaac would usually be praying and Rachel would be running around with the other children. Hannah waited patiently for the time when Rachel would, at last, be at her side.

Rachel Weissman was plagued by the depth of love she received, and the overwhelming responsibility that came with it. For Isaac, she represented everything he had once lost. For Hannah, she was simply everything. Rachel understood this, and accepted her role as an obedient, noble daughter.

There was no television in the Weissman home, and the radio was permanently tuned to the news station. For entertainment, Rachel learned Hasidic tunes and stories of great Jewish heroes. The protagonist was inevitably a great scholar or *Rebbe*, and by his side was always the righteous wife that every Hasidic woman should ultimately aspire to be.

In school, Rachel was exemplary. By the third grade, she knew the Bible cold, far more thoroughly than most of the other girls in her class. She was also a prodigy with numbers, able to calculate instantaneously in her mind, and easily achieved a perfect score on every arithmetic test. The teachers were amazed, even intimidated.

Her best friend was Esther Mandlebaum, a slightly overweight young lady with brown eyes, curly hair, and a long, narrow nose. No match for Rachel in the looks department, but definitely an intellectual equal. Esther lived in a private house around the block from Rachel, in one of those President Street mansions: four stories, lofty white pillars, sparkling windows, and a huge front lawn with a limestone walkway. Her father, a diamond dealer, was one of the wealthiest men in the neighborhood, and—like Isaac Weissman—a regular attendee at Rabbi Feldblum's Talmud lectures. The girls' mothers were very close friends. From infancy, Rachel and Esther had played together; they were like sisters.

Rachel seemed to be the only one who knew how smart Esther was, for Esther was less concerned with school, and spent most of her time daydreaming about other things. That was how it all began: Esther started sharing her dreams with Rachel, and Rachel started having dreams of her own.

Esther had it easier than Rachel. She was the oldest of four, with two sisters and one brother. Her father traveled a lot, and even when he was around, he gave most of his attention to little Moishie. Rachel often wondered what life would be like with a sibling, how it would feel if everything didn't rest on her shoulders.

Esther fantasized about becoming an actress. Her parents had a television set in their bedroom and would, on rare occasions, allow her to watch. She would play-act scenes from movies with Rachel as her audience. Rachel was a great spectator; she admired Esther's zeal. Esther made her laugh, made her want something more.

Exactly what that "something more" was, Rachel didn't know—an indefinable, yet constant longing. At times, she wanted to be like Esther, to live in a big house, have nice clothes, lots of siblings, and a television. But Esther wasn't so happy either, and Rachel was the first to notice.

Then, one freezing January day when Rachel was nine years old, it came to her. She was on her way to pick up Esther so they could walk to school together, as they did each morning. In her snow boots, she walked up the icy path to the Mandlebaums' front door. Carrying her book bag draped over her shoulder, she lost her balance, slipped on a patch of ice, and hit the ground hard.

Esther and her mother came running out as soon as they heard Rachel screaming. Rachel was lying on the ground at the foot of the stairs, crying, unable to move her left leg. They helped her up and took her inside. As soon as her boots were off, Mrs. Mandlebaum looked at her ankle, realized she needed medical attention, and called Hannah Weissman, who immediately rushed over. Rachel tried to be brave, but was still crying from pain; her ankle was swollen to the size of a grapefruit and badly discolored. Hannah phoned the pediatrician who advised them to go to the hospital emergency room.

They helped Rachel into Hannah's car and drove to the Kingsbrook Jewish Medical Center. Although the Kings County Hospital was closer, Kingsbrook was more modern and upscale, and the Hasidim always preferred a "Jewish" hospital.

They entered the crowded emergency room. Apparently, Rachel wasn't the only casualty of the icy streets. It would have been a long wait had the nurse on duty not felt sorry for the tearful young girl. She discretely shuffled Rachel and Hannah into a treatment room where they waited for a doctor while Esther and her mother remained outside.

About twenty minutes passed before an attractive, tall, vibrant redhead in a white coat entered the room. She smiled at Rachel and Hannah and, without saying anything, picked up the medical chart and began reading. "Excuse me, nurse," Hannah interrupted, "do you know how long it is going to be before we see a doctor. My daughter is in a lot of pain."

The woman glanced up from the chart. "Oh, I'm sorry, I neglected to introduce myself." She smiled at them both again and said, "I'm Doctor Schiffman."

Hannah was taken aback and immediately responded, "Oh, I'm sorry. It's just that . . ."

"It's okay," Doctor Schiffman interrupted, "it happens all the time. I'm quite used to it."

Though Hannah tried to be mannerly, Schiffman read the discomfort in her face. True, it was the late fifties and female doctors weren't such a rarity, but among the insulated Hasidic communities, the notion was completely blasphemous. It was one thing if a woman had to work in a bakery or dress shop, which was the case if her husband's income was insufficient, or if he were a scholar and studied the holy books all day. But to actually pursue a career and spend endless years studying in college and graduate school? That was absurd. A Hasidic woman made a career out of getting married and having as many children as God would provide.

Rachel was having other thoughts, however. As the doctor examined her ankle, Rachel took notice of the woman's wavy hair and the gold wedding band on her left hand. A Jewish woman, married, with no head covering, she thought. And a doctor too. Rachel was intrigued.

Doctor Schiffman also had an air of confidence about her, in the way she moved, the way she examined Rachel's leg. Her touch was both soft and strong at once. And so pretty, Rachel thought, such delicate hazel eyes, and slight freckles beneath the makeup on her nose and cheeks.

"I'm afraid this ankle might be broken," the doctor said, looking at Hannah. Rachel had been so lost in her thoughts, she'd hardly felt the doctor manipulating her leg. "We need to take her down the hall to Radiology for an X-ray to be sure. Who is your pediatrician?" she asked Rachel.

"Doctor Bronstein," Hannah interjected.

Schiffman nodded.

"You know him?" Rachel asked.

"I most certainly do," Schiffman replied with a smile. "He's famous around here. He takes care of lots of the children in the neighborhood."

"He's on staff at this hospital," Hannah said in a tone that indicated she wished he were there in the room with them at that moment.

"I know," Schiffman replied, not taking Hannah's discomfort personally. Most Hasidic patients preferred to be treated by their own, and Bronstein was a Lubavitcher. "If you like, I'll see if he's in the hospital."

"No, its okay, that won't be necessary," Hannah responded, feeling somewhat embarrassed.

"Good," said Schiffman, "but if you change your mind, let me know." She turned to Rachel and added, "And you, young lady, let's get you to X-ray."

"It really hurts," Rachel said as Schiffman slid open the curtain to summon an orderly.

"Don't worry, we're going to give you something for the pain right away," Schiffman responded. She smiled again at Rachel and Hannah. "I'll see you two as soon as the X-rays are developed," she added as she slipped away to attend to another patient.

A moment later, two orderlies came in and transferred Rachel onto a gurney. "We'll have her back in a few minutes," one of the orderlies said to Hannah.

As they wheeled Rachel out, Hannah was reminded that with all the tumult she'd forgotten to call Isaac. Rachel was already halfway down the hall when Hannah waved to her and rushed out to a phone in the waiting room where Esther and her mother were still sitting.

Rachel watched the ceiling move as the orderlies pushed the gurney toward the X-ray room. She was no longer afraid, and despite her pain, even managed a slight smile. Doctor Marcia Schiffman had entered her life, and in that, she had finally found her answer, her way out: Rachel Weissman was going to become a doctor.

⌘

But that wasn't all.

The trouble really began a few years later, one balmy June afternoon in 1963. Rachel had just turned twelve; Esther's birthday was a month away. They were on their way home together, as usual, from the Beth Sarah School for Girls where they were inculcated, day after day, with the do's and don'ts of maidenly Hasidic life.

"Let's not go straight home, today," Esther suggested. "I have something I want to show you."

Rachel looked at her. She knew Esther well enough to guess when the girl was up to no good. "And what might that be?"

"Why tell you and spoil the surprise? Trust me, my dearest, and all will meet with your complete satisfaction. I guarantee it." Esther always tried to make herself sound dramatic.

Rachel figured it had something to do with boys; these days, that was the only thing Esther ever thought or talked about. "I just know you're taking me someplace we ought not be going, Esther Mandlebaum, down the path of temptation I would bet."

Esther twirled herself around as if she were dancing. "How clever, my dear, how clever indeed. But 'clever' is thy middle name, is it not?"

"Indeed."

"Then, let us not waste another moment, *the day is short, and there is much work to do,*" Esther said, citing a well known Talmudic dictum.

Rachel chuckled at the blasphemy. "So it is," she said. She loved to banter with Esther; she loved Esther's *joie de vivre*. And though she was more reserved than Esther, she always loved the adventure.

They walked up Carroll Street to the corner of Rochester Avenue, and then across Rochester to the entrance to Lincoln Terrace Park. "So what do you think?" Esther asked as they stopped in front of the park.

"About what?"

"This," Esther exclaimed, pointing to the basketball courts about a hundred feet away. Rachel could see the courts, and could hear the tumult of the games, but didn't understand what Esther was so excited about. "Those are basketball courts, Esther," she observed.

"Ah, yes, but not just any basketball courts. Come, my dearest, let me show you."

They walked toward the courts, and Esther inhaled deeply through her nose. "Such fresh air."

Rachel smiled.

They approached the tall wired fence surrounding the basketball courts when Rachel finally realized what the hullabaloo was about. Before her was a group of young men, mostly white, all in shorts, and some shirtless. They were running, jumping, pushing, and shoving. Strutting their masculinity.

"Take a look at that one," Esther said, pointing to a well-built, dark haired young man of unquestionably Italian stock.

"Quite appealing," Rachel confirmed. She stood and observed the young man for a moment, and found that she enjoyed what she saw. She enjoyed watching him sweat, watching him bump up against his opponents, watching his muscles tighten and his hair fly as he jumped through the air. She felt a tinge of guilt over her feelings, but that didn't stop her from looking, or from liking it. She was forced to admit that Esther Mandlebaum had most definitely discovered something worthwhile.

For her and Esther, it was most unusual to find boys like this. The boys they knew were scholarly and, even on the hottest days of the year, wore several layers of clothing. It was forbidden for a Hasidic young man to be out on the street without his black hat and jacket. Beneath the jacket, a shirt was always buttoned fully except for maybe the very top; beneath the shirt were the *tzitzis*, a garment with fringes on the corners to remind one of the Torah's commandments; and beneath the *tzitzis* was always an undershirt to keep the sacred garment from touching the body. Hasidic boys were well shielded, too well, Rachel now thought.

She became mesmerized by the sight. This one young man was surely outstanding, but several of his friends weren't bad either. She was taken, also, by another shirtless young man on the opposite team, a tall, freckled red-head, with green eyes and a sweet face. Glistening from perspiration, his legs and arms looked powerful and muscular, so much so that she couldn't help wondering what it would feel like to be next to him, to touch him. Her mind was out of control.

She assured herself that this was merely innocent fun, fantasy. It wasn't real; it could never be real. Not with a Gentile, not even with a non-religious Jew. She loved her parents and her religion, and though she was to become a doctor—something she hadn't yet shared with her parents—she was still planning to marry a scholar and lead as much of a Hasidic life as a female doctor could. She imagined her husband as having all the outward appearances to satisfy her parents, and all the inner passions to satisfy her. She believed that such a man existed, constantly telling herself, *If I exist, so does he.* Of course, none of the Hasidic boys she'd met ever seemed to measure up. They were robots, espousing the usual thoughts and perceptions, not daring to deviate an inch. But somewhere, she knew, she would find her *basherte*, her intended. As for now, that Adonis on the basketball court would do just fine.

Rachel and Esther were quiet, lost within themselves. The boys on the court were too engrossed in the game to even notice the ogling lasses in their ankle length skirts and long-sleeved blouses. It was apparently an Italian versus Irish wrangle, the sort of contest that was taken most seriously in these parts.

"How did you find this?" Rachel asked, disturbing the silence.

"By accident, really. It was about a month ago. I had a fight with my sister, Shira, because she refused to let me borrow one of her dresses for *Shabbos*. You know how she can be about those things."

Rachel nodded in agreement. Esther had often complained to her about Shira's stinginess.

"Anyway, I stormed out of the house, and it was good that I did. I swear, I was ready to hit the *fabissina*."

Rachel chuckled at Esther's reference to her sister as a "bitch." Strangely, she regarded her friend's penchant for vulgarity as yet another sign of emancipation.

"It was a beautiful day," Esther continued, "not as hot as today, but just as sunny. So I decided to walk off my anger and, somehow, God brought me to this spot. The rest, as they say, is history."

"And how many times have you been here since?"

"Ah, the third degree. Okay, I'm sorry. I suppose you have a right to be pissed that I waited so long to tell you, but . . ."

"It's all right," Rachel responded, knowing quite well why Esther delayed sharing her secret. They both knew that Rachel was more attractive—by far—and it was understandable that Esther had felt threatened.

"It's too bad we can't stay here all afternoon," Esther said, changing the subject.

"I'll second that!"

"It is getting late. We have to be home soon, or explanations will be required."

"My thoughts exactly," Rachel responded, wondering what she could possibly dream up to explain her tardiness. But that was just her guilt talking, for if she got home soon, it wouldn't be necessary to explain anything. Rachel often came home a little late, and Hannah never inquired, for she usually assumed that her daughter was at Esther's house. At this moment, Rachel appreciated her mother's assumptions. It was one thing to keep secrets, another to lie.

As they turned to leave, Rachel noticed a group of young black men playing in their own game on a far court. She stopped for a second to watch, and then turned away. "I wonder why they don't play together," she asked.

"Don't be ridiculous! Just thank God they're not killing each other. My father says that there are a lot more *shvartzes* in the neighborhood these days, but not to worry, the Italians and the Irish are going to force them out."

"You think that's the right thing to do?"

"I don't know. I guess so. I mean, they don't belong here."

"I'm sure some people say that about us, too."

"Maybe. But I don't really care all that much what happens here. I'm not going to live here forever, you know. Hollywood awaits me."

"Indeed it does," Rachel replied as she took her best friend by the hand.

CHAPTER 10

One crisp, sunny Saturday afternoon in the second week of November, 1963, Alfred and Evelyn Sims were riding in their Lincoln on the Van Wyck Expressway, traveling to Manhattan to purchase a mink coat for Evelyn from one of Alfred's father's old business associates. Alfred occasionally gave his wife extravagant gifts, hoping they might pacify her. It rarely worked.

The traffic in their direction was light and, strangely, the other side of the Expressway was barren, not a car for miles.

"Why do you think that is?" Evelyn asked as she pointed to the empty road.

"I don't know," Alfred answered. "Could be a major accident up ahead."

They continued driving, still curious, for another minute or so, until they saw a long motorcade led by police cars and motorcycles. Sirens, flashing lights, and limousines passed by on the opposite side of the highway, and in the middle of the entourage was an open car carrying President John F. Kennedy, his wife Jacquelyn, Attorney General Robert Kennedy, and another lady Evelyn recognized from her society magazines as Mrs. Peter Lawford.

Evelyn was awestruck to have witnessed such a thing out of the blue. Alfred then recalled that he'd heard on the news that the President had been in town overnight for some special dinner, and surmised that the group was now on its way to Idlewild Airport for their return to

Washington. He mentioned this to Evelyn as he tried to contain his own excitement at seeing the President, for Alfred was no longer a Democrat from Brooklyn. Now that he was a true Republican from Nassau County, it would be unbecoming to be thrilled by the sight of a few Kennedys and a Lawford.

"I can't believe they let him ride around in an open car like that," Alfred said, astonished. "Somebody could shoot him."

"Don't be ridiculous!" she reacted. "Everyone loves Kennedy."

"Yea, you think so, huh." Arrogance. "A lot of people hate him!"

She looked at him with disdain. She couldn't stand it when he was cocky, which was just about all the time. But she tried to focus on the mink coat, and the fact that she'd just seen one of the most handsome, dashing men she'd ever laid eyes on, in person: John F. Kennedy.

Less than two weeks later, on November 22, Kennedy was assassinated while riding down a Dallas street in an open car. Evelyn was devastated. She wept for several days. Not only for the President, his family and the country, but for herself, her dreams and her hopes, for all the things that were obliterated by the life she led and the man with whom she led it. It was as if she blamed Alfred for the assassination; after all, hadn't he predicted it?

Yes, she could blame Alfred for this, and all the other ills of her existence. And in doing so, she would never really have to examine herself, or any of the things she'd done to contribute to the very circumstances she so despised.

CHAPTER 11

The winter of 1963 brought numerous snow storms, and few days with temperatures above freezing. Schools were frequently closing, sometimes for several days, though that made little difference for Celeste and Joshua. They were somehow managing to miss a lot more school than that.

They usually played hooky at least once a week. A day here, a day there, forged notes about illnesses and family tragedies, doctoring of report cards before their parents signed them, and re-doctoring again before handing them in. They even had Celeste's father's work routine memorized, what he did and when he did it, thus allowing them to sneak into Joshua's empty apartment undetected.

Their physical relationship approached new frontiers. They experimented in all sorts of ways, but always stopped just short of intercourse. Joshua was hoping that his thirteenth birthday—just four months away—would give him more to say for himself.

Jerome, referred to by Celeste and Joshua these days as Saint Jerome, was aware of all this, but turned a blind eye. He knew the consequences could be quite severe for Celeste. Their father didn't need much of an excuse to beat either one of them.

Joshua's neighbor's, the Eisenmans, had become too old and deaf to detect anything, and their television usually blasted through the walls throughout the day. Mrs. Eisenman typically checked on Joshua around four o'clock each afternoon, and every hour or so after that. By then, Celeste was home.

Everything was working out, until one Wednesday afternoon in the third week of February. It was about 3:15, the time Celeste and Joshua were expected home from school. They had spent the day in Joshua's room, and their usual routine was to look out the window at 2:30 to watch Mr. Williams leave the building for the hardware store to pick up supplies. He did this twice a week, Mondays and Wednesdays, always at the same time, and was always gone for an hour. Celeste often joked about his having a girlfriend or something; she had just turned twelve and had a fertile imagination.

On this particular day, Joshua and Celeste had gotten so carried away with each other, they neglected the 2:30 lookout by a few crucial minutes. When they realized this, they convinced themselves not to worry. Mr. Williams was indeed a creature of habit.

Celeste was about to leave, and stopped to give Joshua a last kiss. She had her coat on, books in hand, and as she slipped into the stairwell she turned around and threw him a wicked smile.

After she disappeared, Joshua stepped back inside, closed the door, and sighed. Another perfect day with the girl of his dreams, he mused, picturing the spirited look on her face as she departed. It would be the last time he would ever see that.

❧

The next morning he waited for her at their usual meeting place, the alleyway across the street from the park. After fifteen minutes, at about a quarter to nine, he realized something was wrong. She had never stood him up, had never been more than five minutes late.

He grew impatient, looking down the street towards their building to see if she was coming. He thought that she might have gone to school, might have misunderstood their plans. Yet, even so, she would still have had to pass this way. Something *was* wrong.

He paced, thinking what to do next. Then, he stopped thinking— always a bad idea—and walked back to the building. He looked around to see if anyone was watching. When he came to the front door, he peered through the glass into the lobby. The coast seemed clear.

The Williams' apartment was in the basement. Celeste and Jerome's shared bedroom had a small window facing the back of the building where the trash was collected. Joshua figured he would knock on her window to see if she was there, hoping she was just sick.

The back of the building was accessible by going through the lobby and out the back door, or by walking around the block into an alley that was shared with several neighboring buildings. Joshua chose the quickest way.

As he entered the lobby, someone came at him from behind. At first, he thought he was being mugged, until he saw the face of his assailant. It was a raging face, eyes steaming and lips trembling. Mr. Williams.

Williams threw him to the floor and stood over him. Joshua was certain he was about to get the beating of his life, but then something happened. Williams froze.

Joshua waited, prepared for his punishment, but Williams remained paralyzed. Suddenly, Joshua realized that Williams was probably afraid to hurt him. After all, Williams worked for Alfred Sims, as did Joshua's mother, and beating Joshua might have complications. Joshua felt a trace of relief, but only a trace.

"I know what you've been up to," Williams said.

Joshua didn't respond. He tried getting up, only to be pushed back down. He didn't try again.

"You got anything to say for yourself?"

"I don't know what you're talking about."

"You don't, do you?"

Joshua didn't know what to say next. The last thing he wanted was to provoke Williams. He also didn't know exactly what Williams knew.

"Well, what you got to say?"

"About what?"

"*About* what you and my little girl have been up to!" Williams deep voice echoed through the lobby, making him sound ominous.

"I still don't know what you're talking about."

"No need to go into details. I know what the two of you have been doing! I've already taken care of her, and have the mind to do the same to you, but I'll leave that to your Mama. I understand she's got a temper of her own."

Joshua didn't respond, thinking Williams was waiting for a reason to explode. He wasn't in an accommodating mood.

He wondered what Williams meant by "taking care" of Celeste. There wasn't a long list of choices, not with someone like this. He vowed to get even if Williams had hurt Celeste. He promised himself that much, even as he lay quivering at the man's feet.

Williams stood, staring down at Joshua for a few more seconds until old lady Eisenman appeared in the lobby with a shopping cart full of packages. She almost didn't see them as she pushed the cart toward the elevator, but Joshua started moaning to attract her attention.

"Vhat's going on?" she exclaimed at the sight of Joshua on the floor. "Is dat you, Joshua?" she continued, adjusting her bifocals.

"Yes, Mrs. Eisenman, it is."

Instinctively, Williams took Joshua's hand and helped him up. "It seems that Joshua fell. Right Joshua?" he said.

"Yes, I suppose I did." Tentative.

Mrs. Eisenman watched curiously. "Shouldn't you be at school now, Joshua?" she asked.

"Yes ma'am," he said. "I was on my way there, running because I was late. That's how I fell." A bit more conviction this time.

"Are you okay? Do you need to come up for anything?" she asked.

"No, thanks to Mr. Williams here, I'm just fi-ne." Joshua turned to Williams with a smirk.

"Vell, then I suggest you go off to school right now. Ve vouldn't vant you to be any more late than you are already, vould ve?"

"No ma'am."

Joshua walked to the front door, feigning a slight limp to impress the old lady. But as soon as he came out onto the sidewalk, he lost the limp, dashed up the block to the corner, and down the alleyway toward the back of the building.

He approached Celeste's bedroom window out of breath. It was a dangerous and stupid move, he knew, being alone in the back of the building after his confrontation with Williams. Williams might have expected this, and could be waiting to finish what Mrs. Eisenman had interrupted. But Joshua didn't care, his only thought was of Celeste. He needed to know if she was okay.

He tapped on the window, looking over his shoulder all the while. Her hand appeared and lifted the curtain. The window, though dirty, was clear enough for him to see dark swollen welts on her face and tears in her eyes. She looked as if she'd been beaten with a lead pipe.

She tried to open the window from inside, but it was stuck from not having been open in years. There was nothing Joshua could do to help. Her pushing quickly turned into pounding. It didn't seem to faze her that the window might break or that her pounding could be heard throughout the building. The window didn't budge.

The door to her bedroom burst open. She screamed with fear as she was pulled away. Through the grimy glass pane Joshua could see her father attack her, swinging at her head and body. Joshua slammed his fist through the glass, and barely noticed the blood on his hand as he started kicking the frame. Celeste's screaming grew louder as he dislodged the frame and tried to squeeze through to get into the room. What he would do when he got in, he didn't know.

Williams turned from his daughter, and seeing Joshua stuck, violently pulled Joshua's legs, trying to drag Joshua into the room. Joshua kicked frantically to break free, pulled himself back out from the frame, and got to his feet. He ran back around to the front entrance of the building, raced up the stairwell to his apartment, went straight to the kitchen, and pulled open the knife drawer. He grabbed the largest knife he could find, hid it in his coat, and rushed back down the stairs.

He wasn't sure what he was thinking, only that he needed to protect Celeste.

He made it to the basement, and at the front door to the Williams' apartment he heard the mayhem from Celeste's bedroom. Mrs. Williams was trying, unsuccessfully, to break it up, while Celeste was screaming, and Williams was yelling at his wife to get out of the way.

Joshua tried the door. It was open. He went into the living room, took a deep breath, and stepped into the bedroom. His hand was behind his back, clutching the knife.

Williams saw Joshua and charged, saliva drooling. Instinctively, Joshua took the knife from behind him, but Williams, too frenzied to notice, kept coming. He lunged, fell upon the knife, then backed away, standing erect, horrified, staring down at the blade handle protruding from his abdomen. He stumbled, looked bewilderingly at his wife and daughter, then fell over backwards to the floor.

Joshua saw that Mrs. Williams and Celeste were both in shock. He held his hand out for Celeste, but she was frozen, her face wet, her body shivering. He wanted her to grab him, to run away with him and never come back. But she just stood there, gaping at her father on the floor, a pool of blood forming around his body.

He was still breathing when Mrs. Williams came to her senses, ran to the phone, and called for help. Joshua tried again to get Celeste's attention, but to no avail. The next thing he knew, he was running away. Alone.

⌘

The police picked him up a few hours later, wandering in the vicinity of Troy Avenue and Empire Boulevard. He wasn't really trying to hide, just roaming the streets, thinking about what to do next. When they found him, he was actually relieved.

They took him to the precinct in the back seat of a patrol car. When he arrived there, he was processed by two plain-clothed officers. He figured they were detectives; they looked like the kind he had watched many times on TV. He loved police shows like *Dragnet* and *Adam-12*, but *The Naked City* was his favorite. It never bothered him that there weren't any black heroes in any of those shows; that's just the way things were.

The taller cop's name was McQuade. He had thin, dirty blond hair, and a filterless Camel between his lips. He tried badgering Joshua about what had happened, but Joshua offered nothing other than where his mother could be contacted. Growing up on the streets had taught him when to keep his mouth shut.

The other cop had jet-black, greasy hair, a neatly trimmed mustache, muscular build, and olive skin. He didn't bother telling Joshua his name, but did try the "buddy-buddy" routine. Joshua figured these guys took him for a fool, but he wasn't going to fall for it. "I don't know. When's my Mama coming?" was his answer to each and every question.

He was, surprisingly, worried about Mr. Williams, but more so about Celeste. He also wondered about Jerome and Mrs. Williams. He was smart enough not to ask the cops anything, not to let on that he knew why he was there. Thank God for television.

The cops eventually became exasperated and placed him in a holding cell, where he sat for another twenty minutes, as they talked among themselves. Finally, his mother entered the squad room with a tall, dark-haired, middle-aged white man in a sharp, expensive looking suit. Joshua had never seen this man before, but assumed him to be Mr. Alfred Sims.

The detectives walked over to greet Loretta and Mr. Sims. Joshua moved closer to the bars to get a better look, and tried to listen to what was going on. His mother was crying, and it seemed Mr. Sims was consoling her while talking with the cops. Loretta turned toward Joshua with a look reflecting more sadness than anger. Joshua was taken aback; he had never seen such an expression on her.

It appeared that Sims was in control of the interchange, which lasted but a few moments. Detective McQuade then walked over to the holding cell, unlocked the door, and let Joshua out. "You're a lucky kid," he said.

Joshua kept silent.

McQuade escorted Joshua to Loretta and Sims, turned to Sims and said, "Here he is Al. Better keep a close watch on him if you don't want him to end up here again."

Sims nodded with a smile. "Thanks, John, I owe you one."

Joshua was surprised that Sims and McQuade were so acquainted.

Sims shook hands with each of the detectives, the three of them smiling. Loretta barely acknowledged Joshua's presence. He knew he was in deep trouble.

◈

Joshua sat in the back seat quietly, as Alfred Sims drove him and his mother home. The first and only thing Sims said to him was something about not needing to worry about the cops. He was finding it hard to focus, and hadn't heard the exact words. In any event, it seemed that Sims had somehow managed to convince the detectives to forget the whole thing and lose the paper work. From this, Joshua figured that Williams must be doing okay, and probably wouldn't being pressing charges, all things considered. It seemed to Joshua that his mother's employer wielded much influence, though he wondered just how much all this had cost.

Loretta remained silent in the car, but Joshua believed she would eventually make him wish he'd stayed in the holding cell. Sims dropped them in front of the building, said good-night to Loretta, and gave Joshua a stern warning about straightening up. Joshua thought it odd for this stranger to be so authoritative with him, but realized that the guy had saved his hide. He owed Sims, so the least he could do was pretend to listen.

When they got upstairs, Loretta sent him to his room and added, "I'm gonna make some supper. I'll call you when it's ready." That was all she said.

Joshua sat on his bed, thinking about Celeste. He could take whatever punishment his mother would dish out, but Celeste—he just couldn't bear to think what her father was capable of. He tried taking comfort in the hope that Williams might change now that Mr. Sims and others were aware of the beating. But Joshua knew better. He had instincts about such things, a peculiar familiarity with evil for someone his age. Big Bob had been right about the lessons you learn on the street.

Several hours passed before Loretta called him into the kitchen for dinner. They sat across from one another at the small table, and Joshua helped himself to a hefty portion of macaroni and cheese from the serving bowl.

Loretta didn't eat, and didn't speak. She just sat there and looked at her son with that same expression she'd worn in the police station. Joshua tried ignoring her, stuffing his mouth with food, but the tension got to him. He wished she would say something, chew him out and pronounce his sentence. The silence was unlike her; she'd found a new weapon.

Without realizing it, he'd polished off the macaroni. He looked at the empty serving bowl, and said, "I'm sorry Mama, guess I was hungry."

"Guess you were," she replied. "You should be, after not eating for a whole day." She got up and took the dishes to the sink.

He waited for her to say more, but she didn't. "I'm also sorry about today," he said, a quiver in his voice.

No reply.

"I know you're angry, Mama, but . . ."

"Now listen here, Joshua," she jumped in, "before you go offering excuses, let me tell you a thing or two." She turned from the sink and looked at him. "First, it ain't none of your business if Mr. Williams got what was coming to him, or not. That there's The Lord's concern. Your place is in school, and if you'd been there as you're supposed to be, none of this would've happened."

"But that's not true Mama, he beats her always, he don't even need a reason!"

She stopped, pondered his statement, and asked, "If he beats her for no reason, then why go and give him a reason?"

Joshua didn't answer.

"That's my point, Joshua—you had no business missing school with this girl, no business being in this house with her. And I don't wanna know what the two of you been up to when you were here."

So that was her lecture. Surprisingly, nothing about his having stabbed Williams, only for having gotten himself into that situation in the first place. It was as if she believed that Williams had gotten what he deserved, but wished it hadn't come from her son.

Joshua knew that it was his lying and deceit that had hurt her. It was also that she blamed herself, the long days away at work, leaving him alone to fend for himself. All these years she had tried to protect him, to teach him the right way. And now, she believed she had failed.

For Joshua, realizing all this was punishment enough. Well, not quite enough. His mother added something extra: he was grounded for the remainder of the school year, four months to be exact, confined to the house after school and on weekends, without television, and no friends over either. Mrs. Eisenman would be checking up more frequently to insure compliance, though to Joshua's thinking that wouldn't be necessary. He was certain he would do as he was told.

CHAPTER 12

"Look young man, this is my home and *I* decide what we eat. You are not going to take over our lives with your religious fanaticism!" Such were Evelyn Sims' words when Paul finally refused to eat the pork chops she had served for dinner. It was about a year after Paul's Bar Mitzvah. "If you don't want what I give you, then don't eat. Or move in with that rabbi and eat what his wife makes."

"I don't understand what you're so upset about, I just don't want to eat that kind of meat anymore, that's all," he said.

"What I'm so upset about," she yelled. "*What I'm so upset about* is the way you've tried to take over our lives. We've given you everything, and now you behave as if that's not good enough!"

"Please, Evelyn, stop screaming," Alfred interjected, seeming more engrossed in his food than in the problem. "It's just a phase he's going through, don't worry about it."

"A phase," she parroted angrily. "With you, everything is a phase. After all, he's not criticizing what *you* made for dinner . . ."

"I'm not criticizing anything," Paul asserted.

"Don't interrupt me when I'm speaking young man," she said. "Or didn't your rabbi teach you about honoring your parents?"

Paul was seething. At this point in an argument with her, he would always seethe. He knew there was never any winning, or reasoning. She believed what she wanted.

In past years, he had occasionally resorted to temper tantrums, banging on walls and throwing things. Once he had gotten so enraged, he actually spit at her. He wasn't proud of these things; there were simply times when he just didn't know what else to do. He bore the brunt of her misery, he was her scapegoat, and he was trapped. Doctor Goldman had helped him with his temper, but at moments like this he felt tested.

He sat there, trying to control himself, recalling his last session with Goldman, in which he had revealed an incident that had occurred when he was seven years old. Evelyn was going to visit her sick father in a hospital somewhere in New York City, and took him along because she couldn't find a sitter. The details were scanty, but Paul had remembered that they were stopped at a red light and it appeared as if smoke was rising from the hood of the car.

"Look Mommy, there's smoke coming out!"

"Oh my God!" She opened the car door and jumped out to see what was happening. Paul followed. They examined the car and looked underneath, and discovered that what Paul had seen was not smoke from the engine, but steam rising from a man-hole. Of course, young Paul's intentions had been completely innocent, but that didn't stop his mother from grabbing him by the jacket and dragging him back into the car, yelling, "I'm going to punish you for this. You knew there was nothing wrong with the car. You were just trying to aggravate me! You're just like your father, always trying to upset me!"

Then too, Paul had tried to explain to her; then too, it was pointless.

It might have been easier for him if she was purely evil. He could simply hate her and that would be that. But she was a contradiction, a cross between an overprotective Jewish mother and a wretched neurotic. He never knew which to expect.

Whenever he was sick, she was at his side, sometimes through the night. Once when he was ten years old, he had come home from school shaking and nauseated, on the verge of vomiting. Evelyn hadn't been there, so Loretta rushed him to the bathroom, and tried to help him vomit.

"I can't!" he protested, sitting on the floor by the toilet, afraid of gagging.

"If you let yourself throw up, you'll feel better," Loretta said, her hand on his shoulders to comfort him.

"Where's my mother?"

"She's out shopping. What does that matter?"

"If she were here, maybe I could."

"You need her here to throw up?"

"I don't know, I just can't do it till she gets here."

"Well, that may be a while yet, and you look like you best throw up soon."

Lucky for him, he heard his mother come through the front door at that very moment. "Maaaa," he called from the bathroom.

"What's the matter?" Evelyn yelled.

He hadn't had the strength to answer.

"He's up here, in the bathroom, Missus Sims. He's pretty sick by the looks of him."

Evelyn hurried up the stairs. "What's wrong?" she said as she came into the bathroom.

"He needs to throw up, but he won't do so without you," Loretta explained.

Evelyn knelt on the floor beside him. "It's okay, Paul," she said calmly as she began gently rubbing his back.

Within seconds, he vomited.

Because of incidents like this, Paul Sims knew he loved and needed his mother. And he believed that, however strange her way of showing it, she loved him as well. The problem was her inconsistency, and that was why he had become so fearful of people in general. He never knew just what to expect, never felt quite secure or safe from somehow being hurt.

Thus, the appeal of Rabbi Isaac Weissman's world—a life centered around books and learning, structured and consistent, everything according to the dictates of the law. The axioms were simple: study, and you will know how to be a righteous Jew; be a righteous Jew, and you will find fulfillment.

And there was also Rabbi Weissman himself, the first person with whom Paul had ever felt completely at ease. The rabbi had never pushed Paul to become Orthodox, for that would have created more problems for the boy than solutions. He was also careful not to provoke Alfred and Evelyn into terminating his services or depriving Paul of the occasional Sabbath visits to his home. Moreover, Rabbi Isaac Weissman was a patient man, certain that God would decide the right time for Paul to join the fold.

And Paul, in his desire to gain favor with the rabbi's daughter, was giving God's plan a little push.

∝∾

A few weeks later, Paul found himself once again at the rabbi's Sabbath table, this time donning a dark suit and fedora. He had coaxed his mother into buying the navy blue suit, dark enough for him and blue enough for her—a rare compromise.

As for the hat, he had purchased that on his own, with his allowance savings, and kept it in the rabbi's house for Sabbath visits. He didn't ask the rabbi outright not to tell his parents about it, but he had confidence in the rabbi's discretion.

Paul was proud of his new outfit. In it, he felt he belonged. The followers of Rav Schachter, however, still seemed weary of his presence. He sensed continuing hostility in their eyes, and wondered about it. He had become more aware of the divisions in the community, of Rabbi Weissman's prominent position among Rav Feldblum's flock. Even earlier that very evening on the way home from the synagogue, Rabbi Weissman's neighbors had once again been complaining about Rav Schachter's followers, referring to them as "fanatics" and the like. Again, Rabbi Weissman had insisted that the *Rebbe* would soon address the problem. It had been over a year since Paul had first heard those words from Rabbi Weissman, yet still there had been no reaction from the *Rebbe*, causing Paul to wonder who the *Rebbe* really favored.

Rachel helped her mother serve while Paul and the rabbi discussed the weekly Torah portion and sang Sabbath melodies. As usual, the meal was sumptuous; everything homemade. Challah, chicken soup, gefilte fish, roast veal, potato kugel, a cooked carrot and prune mixture called *tsimmes*, and three different types of cake for dessert.

By now, Paul was acquainted with the words and melodies of the songs. He sang loudly, often looking to Rachel for approval. Usually, she acknowledged him with a slight, yet perfunctory smile. He knew he had yet more work to do to make that smile shine.

∝∾

That night, after the rabbi and Hannah had retired for the evening, Paul sat in the living room brushing up on his studies. It was a small, oak floored room with a red velour couch, matching recliner, mahogany coffee table, and three large overloaded bookcases. One wall was dedicated solely to a picture of the *Rebbe*, and the other walls bore family pictures and a few old portraits of rabbinical looking men that Paul took to be Rabbi Weissman's ancestors.

Paul was stretched out on the recliner, trying to keep his eyes from closing as he struggled with the Hebrew book in his hands. Rachel sat patiently on the couch reading a chemistry textbook, waiting for the stroke of eleven when the automatic timer would turn the light out so she could open the fold-out bed and go to sleep. She was used to Paul remaining in the living room until the last minute and she knew why. It didn't amuse her.

He looked over his book at her. She ignored him. "You know, the *Rebbe* said that *Moshiach*, the messiah, will be coming any day now," he commented out of the blue.

"Yes, the *Rebbe* has been saying that for many years," she responded.

"You sound as if you don't believe it."

"Do I?" she asked, nonchalantly, her eyes still in her book.

He wasn't taking the hint. "Your father taught me that every Jew is supposed to believe that The Messiah is coming tomorrow."

"I'm sure he did."

He hesitated for a moment, realizing that it might be a good idea to change the subject. "You know, I've learned that it's forbidden to study secular things on the Sabbath."

"Is it?" she asked.

"Oh yes, it certainly is. *Shabbos* should be devoted only to holy matters and religious studies."

"Even if one has a chemistry exam on Monday?"

"One must trust in God. If you follow His commandments, he will see to it that you pass *all* the tests of life." He was proud of how wise his words rang, of how much he sounded like her father.

"Have you ever studied The *Rambam*?" she asked.

"The who?"

"The *Rambam*, Maimonides, the twelfth century rabbinical scholar who was also a physician."

"Oh yes, I've heard of him, but . . ."

"Well," she interrupted, "if you had studied him, you'd know that he believed that science *is* a religious and 'holy' subject!" She realized she wasn't being kind, but she couldn't help herself.

Paul didn't respond. He sensed her impatience.

She continued, "He believed, in fact, that studying science is one of the necessary paths to knowing and appreciating God. In order to truly have a relationship with God, one has to understand the mysteries of nature and the universe."

"But you said you were studying for a test, not to have a relationship with God."

"It doesn't much matter why I am studying science, just like it doesn't matter why you are sitting there with a book you can hardly read. We each have our own reasons, and *none* of them, I suspect, are religious in nature." She was surprised by her own candor, even felt bad about it, but only a little.

Before either of them could say anything else, the lights went out. Just as well, Paul thought, considering the tenor of their exchange. He sheepishly excused himself and bid her good-night.

On his way to the bedroom, Paul moved slowly, somewhat unsteadily, as if stumbling over his embarrassment. Growing up with his mother, he had never known that a woman could have such clarity of mind. This intimidated him, and he wasn't sure how to handle it. On the other hand, it also challenged him and strengthened his resolve to make her his. And therein was his problem, for Rachel Weissman would never belong to anyone.

CHAPTER 13

"Joshua," Loretta said, knocking on his bedroom door. It was six-thirty in the evening and she had just come from work.

As opposed to all those times she'd burst in, admonishing him for one thing or another, tonight was different. He'd actually done something that would please her, and he knew it. "Yes, Mama," he said.

She opened the door and entered smiling. She hadn't removed her coat yet, and in her hand was the report card he'd left for her on the kitchen table. He was sitting in his chair, facing her. She glanced at the desk behind him. The lamp was on, a textbook and notebook lay open, and his pencil was still in his hand. She was wordless.

"Yes, Mama."

"Joshua, I just don't know what to say," she remarked, alluding to his having received straight A's in every subject, and a personal comment from his teacher about his "astonishing turn-around." She waved the card. "You didn't even give yourself such good grades when you were fixing your report cards."

He laughed. It felt strange, and good, to bring her pleasure.

"I knew you were gonna make something of yourself, I just knew it!" she said as she walked over and kissed him on his forehead. "I always knew you were smart enough to be anything you want. I prayed hard to God that you would one day know it too." A tear fell down her cheek. "There ain't no reason you gotta end up like those bums with nothing to show for yourself. You're smart, Joshua, smarter than most folks, and if you use that, you'll be all right in life."

He nodded, though he wasn't completely convinced. He hadn't seen much of the world, but he'd seen enough to know that it was unlikely a black kid could become "anything." But he would try, try at last to make her happy, for now he knew he could.

It had been three months since the stabbing incident; coincidentally, the day before his thirteenth birthday. Loretta hadn't mentioned any plans for celebrating. She hadn't been talking to him much at all over the past few months. He was expecting his usual gift—some articles of clothing he needed anyway—and not much else, though in the back of his mind, he hoped the report card might change things.

"Well, I best start preparing supper," she said, turning to leave. "By the way, tomorrow night I'm gonna make you something special." She stopped and pondered. "Yes, I think I'm gonna bake you a cake."

"Strawberry shortcake!"

"Yes, that one," she said, smiling. "Strawberry shortcake, your favorite, I believe."

"You believe right, Mama."

"Yeah, I suppose I *do* know you pretty well, Joshua." She turned to him one last time. "Now you get back to your studies. I'll call you when supper's on the table."

"Yes, ma'am."

He returned to his books, but couldn't concentrate on anything other than the look on her face as she held that report card. He'd worked hard these past months, he'd done it for her, to prove that he was as good as anybody. She had always known he was, had always told him as much, but he never believed her. Until now.

It hadn't been easy for him to turn things around, though he had some help from not being allowed out of the house after school. She had locked the TV in her closet, so he had nothing to do except read his comics, listen to the radio, and stare at the walls. Within a week, he had become bored, so he decided *what-the-hell*. He started opening his school-books, and soon found that he was getting decent grades. Then came the praise from his teacher. He realized he could actually do this, he could succeed. And whatever that might mean in the end, for now it meant pleasing his mother and proving that Paul Sims wasn't the only smart one in the world. For now, that was enough.

The next day, during recess, Joshua told Celeste what had happened with his mother the night before.

"How come you didn't tell me you've been doing so good in school?" Celeste asked, sounding betrayed.

"I don't know; it didn't come up."

The two of them talked regularly in school, though they weren't allowed to have any contact at home. Today, Joshua thought, was a perfect day to change that, to chance some time together after school in the park. He figured he could get away with coming home a "little" late, and even if his mother found out, she might overlook it, things being what they were.

He shared the idea with Celeste. "What am I gonna tell my mama about coming home late?" she replied.

"It'll only be for an hour or so. You could think of an excuse, if you really wanted to."

"I guess I can tell her I stayed after school for extra help or something," she said, her voice lacking enthusiasm. He figured she was still angry that he hadn't told her about his school-work, and hoped that by the end of the day she'd forget it.

They rendezvoused at their usual place in the park. It was a pleasant, mild afternoon; a clear sky and soft breeze bore the scent of grass and trees. Much had changed since the stabbing: Celeste, like Joshua, was attending school regularly, and Mr. Williams was supposedly behaving himself. Joshua figured Mr. Sims had really put the screws to him.

One thing that hadn't changed was that Joshua was still a virgin. He was planning to change that. A fitting birthday present.

They talked about missing the time they used to spend with one another, and fantasized about having a future together. They believed that there was too much between them to allow anything to tear them apart, and they vowed eternal fidelity.

After about fifteen minutes of this, they lost control. Joshua reached for her hand, leaned over to kiss her, and she wrapped her arms around him. They began to moan and pull at one another. Joshua maneuvered himself on top, rubbed his body against hers, and found his way beneath her blouse. She pressed her thigh into his crotch, and put her hands under his shirt.

They were shielded by the shrubbery, but not enough to go any further. Joshua suggested they sneak back to his apartment. Like old times.

"I don't think we should," she said, hoping he wouldn't get upset.

He looked askance at her; she was acting unusual. He started to get up, when she grabbed his hand and said, "Wait, don't be getting mad!"

"I'm not," he said, his tone belying his words.

She thought for a moment. "I changed my mind; I wanna go."

"You sure?"

She nodded.

"You don't have to."

"I know."

⟨≈⟩

They managed to sneak into his apartment, and when they got to his room she became uneasy. She put her books on his desk, stood, and looked around. He walked over, took her hands, and kissed her lips.

She felt tense. He knew she was afraid. "It's okay," he whispered.

Suddenly, the nervousness left her. She pulled him tightly against her and began kissing him hard as they clumsily fell on the bed. Her hand made its way to his crotch, she caressed him and thrust her tongue into his mouth.

It was wild, and he felt like he was going to ejaculate in his pants. He pulled her hand away, and began removing her blouse and skirt. She lay there, moaning. He tore his clothes off and got on top of her.

They kissed and rolled around some more. Her brassiere and panties found their way to the floor with his underpants. They had come close before, but had never been completely naked. This was turning out to be the best birthday Joshua ever had.

Until, that is, he tried to put himself inside her.

Suddenly, she stiffened, pulled away from him, curled up, and began to cry. He reached out to touch her, but she pushed his hand away, jumped out of the bed, grabbed her clothes, ran to the bathroom and locked herself in.

He ran after her, knocked on the door and called her name. The only thing he heard was crying. He asked her to open the door; she ignored him. Minutes passed before she spoke.

"Please leave me alone," she said.

"Celeste, what's the matter?"

"Just leave me alone. I wanna go home."

"Okay."

"Will you go back in your room so I can go?"

"Why don't you just come out. I won't stop you from leaving."

"No, I don't want you to see me. I just wanna go. Please!"

He went back to his room and began putting his clothes on. In a short while, he heard the bathroom door open, faint footsteps, and then the front door. He ran through the living room and opened the front door, but she was gone. He heard her running down the stairwell, and wanted to go after her, but he knew it wasn't wise. He stared down the empty hallway until Mrs. Eisenman opened her door.

"Is that you, Joshua?" she asked.

"Yes, ma'am."

"I thought I heard something."

"No, just me. Stayed late at school for a science project."

"Oh." Skeptical.

"I don't mean to be rude, but I have to go inside and do my homework."

"That's a good idea. Just this morning your mother told me that you are doing very vell vith your studies. She's very proud, yes?"

"Yeah, she is."

"That's gut. It's very important to do vell in school. Go! Do your vork. I'll stop by later to check on you. Your mother told me that she didn't think it vas necessary anymore, but I told her it vas no bother; I enjoy it. I hope you don't mind."

"Oh no, I don't mind."

"Gut then, I'll see you later."

"Yeah, see you later." He closed the door, went back to his room, sat down on his bed, and thought about what had happened with Celeste. He was at a loss to understand any of it.

That night, as Loretta served the strawberry shortcake, she said, "I hear you got home late from school today."

"Mrs. Eisenman?"

"Well, she wasn't ratting on you. I told her how good you been doing in school and how proud I am, and that she doesn't really have to check on you so much anymore. She couldn't wait to tell me that you stayed after school for a science project."

"That wasn't it," he said under his breath.

"Well maybe she got it wrong. She don't hear so good, you know."

"She heard just fine."

"What do you mean?" The smile left her face.

"I'm saying that Mrs. Eisenman told you exactly what I said, only it wasn't true."

"You lied to her?" Her eyes began to moisten. "Sounds like you're back to being your old self."

"If I'm back to my old self, why am I telling the truth now?"

She didn't answer.

"I was with Celeste today." He was glad he said it. No pretense, no lies, and no explanation. He started to eat his cake.

Loretta was silent for a while, then said, "I hope that whatever you do, you don't let nothing get in the way of school. You got a gift, Joshua. Be a shame to forget that."

"I know Mama. I won't forget."

CHAPTER 14

"I'm sorry to bother you, Mr. Sims, but we can't have this sort of thing going on at our school," said the principal of the Hewlett Bay Academy, speaking sternly into the phone receiver. Paul sat quietly, observing, as the man reclined in his burgundy executive chair and listened to Alfred's reply. Doctor Goldman sat beside Paul, both of them listening to faint sounds of Alfred's voice oozing from the receiver, neither able to make out what Alfred was saying.

The principal, Mr. Harvey, was a thin, fit looking gentleman in his mid-fifties. His full head of salt and pepper hair and stark black eyebrows lent an air of distinction, as did the large mahogany desk and the countless diplomas and awards gracing the walls.

"Well, I'm glad you agree, and thank you for your understanding, but it appears that Paul is being less than cooperative. Frankly, he is forcing our hand. We will have to suspend him until he complies with regulations," Mr. Harvey said.

Paul tried to appear undaunted; Goldman seemed concerned.

The issue at hand was Paul's having arrived at school that morning wearing a baseball cap, and having refused to remove it when asked to by his homeroom teacher. The teacher had immediately sent him to the principal's office, and the principal had asked Doctor Goldman to join them in the hope that maybe the psychologist would talk some sense into the boy. No such luck. Paul refused again, claiming it was his religious obligation to cover his head.

"Yes, I know that is why he is doing it," Mr. Harvey continued, "but it's a baseball cap he's wearing, not a yarmulke. And in any case, I must admit that we would not allow him to wear a yarmulke either; it's simply against school regulations to have any head-covering in the building."

There was more inaudible mumbling from the receiver, then Mr. Harvey added, "Yes, I'm glad that you understand, and I'm sorry it has come to this. I just want to reiterate that Paul is absolutely welcome in our school so long as he removes the hat. It has nothing to do with religion; it is purely a matter of standards. We cannot make exceptions, I'm sorry. I have Dr. Goldman here with us, and we will both try to speak with Paul one more time, but if he doesn't comply . . ."

Alfred said something else into the receiver, and Mr. Harvey's expression indicated that the two of them were in agreement. Paul wasn't surprised at this, considering his father's antipathy towards his Orthodoxy. He knew he would get an earful when he got home, but he was used to that. Above all, he certainly wasn't going to remove his hat.

Mr. Harvey hung up, looked across the desk at Paul, and asked, "Well, what's it going to be?"

Goldman was in an unenviable position. Mr. Harvey was his boss, and Paul was his client. He remained silent.

Paul wondered if he would be allowed to cover his head if he'd had an injury, or had lost his hair from some illness. He chose not to ask. There was no point in arguing. "I'm sorry, Mr. Harvey, but nothing that you, Dr. Goldman, or my father can say will convince me to take off my hat."

Goldman, aware that Harvey was waiting for his input, was also aware that there was nothing he could say that would make a difference. He had gotten through to Paul on many things, but when it came to religion, the boy was inflexible. Goldman also suspected that this entire situation was coming off exactly as Paul had hoped. Paul had confided in Goldman about his desire to leave this school and attend yeshiva, and about his frustration over his parents' disapproval. *What better way*, Goldman reasoned, *than getting suspended like this, to change their minds?*

"I suppose you understand the consequences of your refusal to follow the rules," Goldman said, only because he had to say something.

Paul seemed to understand perfectly well.

By the time Paul got home, his mother had been alerted to what had happened. "You see, I warned you that your fanaticism would get you into trouble. You just don't listen, do you!" she harangued as he came through the door.

Trying to ignore her, he started up the stairs to his bedroom.

"Don't you dare walk away when I'm talking to you!"

"You're not talking to me, you're screaming." He continued on his way.

"This is my house, and if I want to scream, I'll scream," she shouted, following after him.

He turned to her, pointed to his ears, and said, "And these are my ears. If I don't want to listen, I won't." With that, he slammed his bedroom door.

He waited for her to open the door and really give it to him, but the phone rang. He figured it was probably his father, checking on the situation.

A few minutes passed before his mother burst in, saying, "Your father wants you to stay right here in this room until he comes home." Paul was sitting at his desk, wearing his yarmulke, and hovering over one of the books of the Talmud. "While you're at it," she added, "take a look in there for what it says about slamming doors in your mother's face and talking back to her. Or did you skip that chapter?"

She left before he could reply, though he really had no response. Unable to concentrate, he closed the book. He felt antsy, and didn't care that his father had grounded him. He wanted to go out.

It wouldn't be the first time that he'd left through his bedroom window. When he was younger he had done it often, for no other reason than to prove he could. His parents had never suspected.

There were two windows, one that looked out to the front of the house, and another that bordered part of the roof. He opened the latter one, hoisted himself up on the ledge, and climbed out onto the roof.

As soon as he was on the roof, he made his way to the side of the house, where the branches of a tall sycamore were in reach. He looked down, smiled at how easy it was, and grabbed onto one of the tree's solid branches.

He walked across the front lawn to the road, reached into his pocket and felt a dollar and some change, more than enough for a candy bar and a coke. His house was on Everit Avenue, near the entrance to Hewlett Harbor. "The Harbor," as it was called, was considered by *The New York Times* as one of the five wealthiest communities in the country, inhabited by mostly Jews, with a smattering of WASPs and white Catholics. It was rumored that Sammy Davis Jr. had once attempted to purchase a home there, but had somehow been dissuaded.

Everit Avenue was close to the shopping district of the town of Hewlett, and less than a mile from the bay, where the most expensive homes were. But even on Everit, there were homes that qualified as "estates," some of which were surrounded by more than an acre of land. While Paul's house wasn't quite that large, it was still impressive by most standards. Sitting on about half an acre of fastidious landscaping, it was a three story edifice with four bedrooms and two baths on the top floor; dining room, living room, den, study, maid's room, eat-in kitchen, and two baths on the ground floor; playroom, four walk-in closets, laundry room, guest bedroom with bathroom, and finished sitting room with a fully stocked bar in the basement. Outside, in the back, was an in-ground pool, which was seldom used. Alfred was never around, and Evelyn didn't like Paul "traipsing" through the house in a wet bathing suit. It was there because, like everything else, it looked good.

The neighborhood was quiet. The kids on the block were still in school, not that Harbor children were ever found playing in the streets anyway. Paul could smell the pollen from blooming trees and fresh cut grass as he sauntered past the houses. Hewlett Harbor was definitely a nice place, he had to admit, but he preferred Brooklyn. At least there he could wear his yarmulke in peace.

Suddenly, he realized he still had his yarmulke on, and that he had forgotten his baseball cap. He was halfway down the block, and couldn't go back, so he kept walking. The end of Everit Avenue intersected with Broadway, the main street for the town of Hewlett. Just before the intersection sat the local public high school. Kids from "The Harbor" generally didn't attend public school.

As he neared the high school, he heard a bell ring from inside. He looked at his wristwatch and realized it was the end of the school day. A few seconds later, the doors to the building opened and hordes of teenagers burst out.

He felt uneasy wearing the yarmulke. In the past, he'd had a few scuffles with public school kids, especially some of the Italian and Irish kids from the middle-class neighborhood of Gibson, who liked to bother him and other Academy students. Sometimes things got physical; mostly it was just heckling.

Paul realized that, under the circumstances, it would be wise for him to remove the yarmulke. But he didn't. *A Jew must cover his head! I cannot be a hypocrite! I will not be afraid!* He told himself these things as he recalled Rabbi Weissman's stories of Jews who refused to shave their beards or remove their head coverings in Nazi Europe. "You must be proud to be a Jew," the rabbi had said, "and sometimes you must suffer because of it!" Paul pictured the rabbi's soft eyes turn ablaze with those words, and became ashamed of his fear.

He was walking fast, and came to the corner of Everit and Broadway. The candy store was just on the other side of Broadway, half a block down. The traffic light was against him, he had to wait. He heard rowdy voices behind him, and the beating of his own heart.

It was a group of five kids, and they were less than ten feet from him when the light finally turned. He started to cross the street and thought he heard the word "Jew-cap" followed by laughter. He wasn't sure if he was being paranoid or not, so he continued crossing, trying not to appear frightened. The kids were right behind him. He quickened his pace; they quickened theirs. Now, he was certain he wasn't paranoid.

"Hey Vinny," one of his pursuers said, addressing a tall, dark, good looking kid who seemed to be the leader, "the sissy is a *yid*."

They all laughed.

"What you gotta say, sissy? Maybe you gotta a bald spot youze covering or somethin'?" another added.

Paul ignored them. By the time he reached the curb he decided to make a dash for it, but as soon as he started to run, two of them grabbed him, and two others blocked his way.

Vinny, the leader, stood proudly, watching his henchmen at work. Paul tried to wrestle free, but couldn't. Vinny began to laugh again. He had a sadistic look; he was enjoying this. "Is it true, sissy, that your people killed Christ?" he asked, peering directly into Paul's eyes.

Paul didn't respond, and stopped struggling.

"Vinny asked you a question," one of the others said, "or are you deaf along with being dumb?"

"Why don't you do what you want and get it over with," Paul said.

"Okay guys, lets grant the Jew-boy his wish," Vinny said as he pointed toward the back of the shopping center. Paul was scared, but did a good job of hiding it. He would let them get their kicks, then it would be over.

⁓

"My God, what the hell happened?" Evelyn exclaimed as Paul came through the door, his face bloodied and swollen. She was so beside herself at the sight, she forgot he'd gone AWOL.

Paul groaned, indicating that talking was painful, and went directly to the freezer for some ice. She noticed the yarmulke and had the answer to her question.

She followed him to the kitchen. "Let me help you," she said, taking the ice tray from his hands. She started preparing an ice pack.

She handed him the ice-pack, helped him sit, and asked, "Who did this?"

He shrugged, pretending he didn't know, then grunted again, reminding her that he couldn't speak. She left him sitting at the table, and went to the bathroom for some iodine and bandages.

"Did some kids do this because you were wearing the yarmulke?" she asked as she came back into the kitchen.

Paul winced at the sight of the iodine. He dreaded what was coming next, the real punishment. He looked at her and nodded, "Yes." *Why not tell the truth*, he figured, hoping she might appreciate the strength of his convictions. *Maybe she'll respect me*, he thought, though he knew she wouldn't.

"Well, I hope you learned a lesson. It is just plain stupid for you to wear that thing all over the place, especially in school and on the street." She reached over and began to clean his face with soap and warm water. Unlike her words, her touch was soft.

He flinched from the sting of the iodine, as he wondered why she hadn't yet mentioned his sneaking out of the house. Then, it occurred to him: she was probably leaving that for his father. *I'm sure she is*, he mused, wondering how he was going to deal with that.

⁓

Alfred entered the house and was removing his coat when the private phone in his study rang. He had a special line installed about three months earlier, after years of Evelyn's complaints about his tying up the house phone in the evenings. What she had wanted was for him to stop conducting business at home and spend more time with her. She should have known better.

Thinking it was an important call—what else could it be at this time—he hurried and grabbed the receiver by the third ring. The man on the other end identified himself.

"Yes, good evening Rabbi Weissman," Alfred said with exasperation, wondering about the rabbi's perfect timing, and also how the rabbi had gotten his private number.

"I hope I'm not disturbing you," the rabbi said.

"Well, I just got home and . . ."

"Then I'll only be a minute. You see, I've spoken vith Paul today and I understand there's been some problems in school, and some trouble vith kids in the neighborhood."

Alfred hated the way the rabbi replaced W's with V's, pronouncing *vith* instead of with. *Why can't he speak like an American*, Alfred wondered. *And why can't he stay out of my fucking life.*

"I would say so," Alfred said. Evelyn had called him earlier to tell him about the shopping center incident.

"Vell, I'm calling to tell you that I have a solution to all this."

What the hell is "vell," Alfred thought. *Maybe I should ask him. Yea, that's a good idea. Hey, rabbi, what's "vell"? And he'll probably answer, "Vell, Mr. Sims, is a vord."* Alfred said nothing.

"I've been thinking about how Paul maybe vould be better off in a yeshiva, yes?"

"In a *what?*"

"A yeshiva," the rabbi repeated, acting as if Alfred hadn't actually heard him.

"Look rabbi, with all due respect, my wife and I will handle this our way, and that doesn't include putting Paul in a yeshiva."

At this point Alfred's voice grew loud enough for Evelyn to hear from the den where she'd been watching TV. She got up and came into the study to listen to Alfred's end of the conversation.

"Please, Mr. Sims, before you make any judgments, it seems you should consider how committed Paul is to being a Torah Jew. You can ignore this if you vant, you can even try to change it, but in the end he vill still be what he vants to be. I suppose you could say that he's maybe like you in that respect?"

Alfred listened to the rabbi's point. He knew he had long ago lost control over his son, and also realized that Paul was now sixteen, not quite a "boy" anymore. But yeshiva? That was something else. How could he, Alfred Sims—neé Simenovitz—send *his* son to a yeshiva, after having spent most of his life shunning his ethnicity. It was too much to digest. *What's next*, he asked himself. *Who knows, maybe the kid will want to become a rabbi?*

"There is vone more thing I should tell you, Mr. Sims, though you probably already know."

Alfred waited.

"The boys in our yeshiva don't get drafted into the army. Ve claim they are all rabbinical students, and the government doesn't bother them."

Being a vet himself, Alfred was aware of 4-D deferments. He often thought about the Vietnam war, and what would happen if Paul were drafted. A kid who could barely make it in Hewlett Harbor wouldn't fare very well in Southeast Asia. The rabbi had struck a chord.

Evelyn noticed the defeat in Alfred's eyes, something she'd never seen before. She also knew what it meant. She and Alfred had been far from ideal parents, and now it was time to pay.

The rest of Alfred's conversation with the rabbi was short. Within himself, he couldn't deny that Paul's tenacity was indeed inherited. He recalled a Biblical passage from his childhood, the one about the sins of the fathers being visited upon the sons, and realized that his own proclivities had come back to haunt him.

When he hung up, he was silent for a moment, then looked at Evelyn and said, "Well, I guess that's that." His tone wasn't flippant, just resigned.

She shared a final glance with him, and left the room.

Alone in his study, Alfred looked around, reflecting over what his life had become. He pictured his mother, how she would have been proud of Paul in a way she had never been of him. He also reminisced about his father, a simple man from the old country who, though forced to work on the Sabbath, never lit a cigarette from sundown Friday through Saturday evening. Avrum Simenovitz, a devoted Jew, would have been appalled at the life his son had chosen, yet would have found great satisfaction in his grandson. *Yes Mama*, Alfred thought, *now Papa is really turning over in his grave. Turning over and laughing.*

A week later, Paul Sims was enrolled in the Yeshiva O'havei Torah on Eastern Parkway in Crown Heights, a high school yeshiva for boys under the auspices of the Lubavitcher Hasidim. That Sunday, his father accompanied him, and most of his worldly possessions, to the dormitory. As the car pulled up, Rabbi Weissman was waiting outside on the sidewalk, holding the black fedora which Paul had kept at his home. Alfred and Paul emerged from the car, shook hands with the rabbi, and the rabbi handed Paul the hat.

Alfred watched, wincing as his son put the fedora on, relieved that Evelyn had chosen not to accompany them. He looked at Paul, and realized for the first time that his son was truly a stranger. And deep in his heart, sadly enough, he understood that this was exactly what he had forced the boy to become.

CHAPTER 15

"If I ran away, would you come with me?" Celeste asked.

"What are you talking about?" Joshua replied.

"One day I'm gonna go," she said. "I just wanna know if you're coming." Her eyes were pensive, her voice soft and serious. She looked past him, at the trees behind the park bench on which they sat.

"Where do you think you're going?"

"Don't know," she answered hesitantly, her eyes still looking elsewhere. "Don't matter."

"I thought things were okay now."

"What's okay?"

"You know, your father don't hit you and Jerome any more. And you and I are okay, too."

"Oh." Impassive.

"Oh *what*?"

"I guess you're right," she said without conviction.

He let it drop, but was still worried. He wanted to tell her he would go anywhere with her, only he couldn't. A year ago there wouldn't have been a question, he would have packed his bags on the spot. But now things were different. He'd been off the streets, getting straight A's in school, and his mother had been treating him like a man. Moreover, Loretta was growing tired and needed him around. He wanted to be with Celeste, but he had responsibilities. He hoped she would understand that he couldn't choose between her and his mother, and prayed he wouldn't have to.

❧

The next day, Celeste didn't show up in school. Joshua wanted to ask Jerome if everything was okay, but they hadn't spoken since the stabbing incident. It would have been a poor ice breaker for him to remind Jerome of his continued involvement with Celeste.

Joshua couldn't figure Jerome out. He believed Jerome hated his father, and might one day even kill the man himself. In any event, Jerome had become quite the "holy roller." He attended church several times a week, and spent most afternoons and weekends at Roy Sharp's home, studying religion with Roy's father, the preacher. Joshua wondered if it helped.

After lunch, Joshua noticed that Jerome didn't return to class, and wondered if Jerome had also been concerned about Celeste's absence. He reassured himself that she wouldn't have run away without him.

Or would she?

Just as the class was about to begin, he got up and hurried home.

❧

He tapped on her bedroom window, but she didn't appear. Harder, and still nothing. Something was wrong. He tried the back door to the building, but it was locked, so he decided to go around to the front.

He ran up the alley and down the block. As he approached the building, he saw a large crowd gathered out front. In the street sat two police cars and one unmarked car with a flashing red light. On the sidewalk, he saw Mr. and Mrs. Williams and Jerome talking with two plain clothed policemen whom he recognized: good ol' Detectives McQuade and What's-His-Name.

He came a little closer, and was about to ask a bystander what was happening, but before he could, Mr. Williams spotted him, pointed angrily, and yelled. The next thing he knew, the police were running toward him.

Now, there were many things Joshua had learned on the streets, and paramount among them was that when the cops run, so do you. It didn't matter why, or what they suspected he may or may not have done; he could ponder all that later. For now, fleeing was the only option.

He ran up Rochester, onto Eastern Parkway, and by the time he passed Dubrows Cafeteria, it seemed the police had stopped giving chase. He slowed down, caught his breath, and started walking. He assumed Celeste had probably run away, and that the police were betting he had something to do with it. Now that he had run, they would be certain.

He had to find her. He wandered the neighborhood, searching alleys all afternoon, and once it was dark, he ventured back out to the street. He figured the night would camouflage him, for these days there were lots of "brothers" roaming around the neighborhood, and to the cops they all looked alike.

It was past midnight. He'd been searching for almost twelve hours, was tired, hungry, and worried about his mother. Celeste had either disappeared or had already returned; in either case, he was convinced he was wasting his time. He decided to go home and face the music.

As he sauntered down Rochester, he noticed some hookers across the street, outside the park. He knew there was prostitution in the neighborhood, but had never been out late enough to actually see it. He stopped, stood still, and watched for a while as several cars cruised by.

Suddenly, he was grabbed from behind and lost his balance. Someone was pulling him backwards into an alley. He couldn't tell who it was, and tried to resist. His sneakers scraped the concrete as he struggled to free himself, but his assailant was too strong.

Once in the alley, he was thrown to the ground, and noticed a third person watching. He got up slowly, looked at his foes, and swallowed hard. Faces from the past.

Big Bob wore a cool expression. "Well, well, look what we got here," he said.

Bones grinned, but said nothing.

Joshua was also silent.

"Long time no see, Peanut, my man," Big Bob continued. He smiled widely, revealing a large mouth of browned teeth and gold caps.

Joshua nodded. It was a good time to be agreeable.

"You got nothing to say for yourself?" Big Bob asked.

Joshua looked at them; he had to figure a way out. "You know, the police are looking for me all over. So is my Mama and her friends. They're probably not far."

"Poss-ib-ly," Big Bob responded, "but seems they ain't found you yet, don't it?"

"But they will, probably soon."

"I suppose we should be scared," Big Bob said as he and Bones chuckled.

Joshua realized he was stuck there. His fear was showing.

"I heard about you and that girlfriend of yours," Big Bob said. "Seems you bought yourself some trouble."

"You know about that?"

"I know everything, don't you realize that by now? Ain't nothing happens on these streets I don't know."

Joshua didn't respond.

"Another thing I know is what that young girl's daddy been doing to her, and I don't mean those little beatings."

"Huh?"

"I'm saying her daddy been doing her." He and Bones chuckled again.

"Bullshit!" Joshua barked.

"Now, you ain't that stupid, are you?" Big Bob asked, looking directly into his eyes. Bones was still laughing.

"You were always a liar!" Joshua said, shedding his fear. He didn't care what they did to him at this point.

"Suit yourself," Big Bob said.

"Where'd you hear that?"

"What difference does it make? You don't believe it noways."

"That's right, I don't!"

"Good! So let's get down to business. First, you owe me, and I intend to collect on that debt."

"I still got the money. I can go get it."

"I'm sure you can, but I ain't that dumb. I let you go now, I'm gonna have to come looking for you all over again, and I don't got time for that. Now, I also believe there's some interest due. And last, there's a little matter of loyalty—it don't look good for business if I let someone get away with what you did, understand?"

Only too well, Joshua thought. "So, what are you gonna do?"

"What am I gonna do?" he mimicked. "I ain't *gonna* do nothing. Fact is, I already done it." More laughing. "You see, Peanut, my man, I know where your little girlfriend is. Like I said, I know everything. Get my meaning?"

Joshua knew Big Bob wanted more than to simply kick the shit out of him. "Where is she?" he asked.

"She's safe, for now," Big Bob answered, as he looked out the alley, across the street toward the hookers. He turned back to Joshua with another wicked smile.

One day I'm going to kill you, Joshua thought; "What do you want?" he said.

"You sure you wanna do business? You know, that girl is a lot safer with me than with her daddy. At least with us, she makes good money for doing that sort of thing."

Bones laughed hard.

"What do you want?" Joshua repeated. He tried to stay calm, despite what he'd heard about Celeste's father.

"Looks like the boy wants to do business," Big Bob said to Bones.

"Seem so," Bones replied.

Big Bob was pensive for a moment. "This here's what I want from you. Listen now, so there ain't no misunderstanding!" He looked at Bones who nodded and echoed, "No misunderstanding!"

"First," Big Bob began, "I want my five hundred dollars. Second, I want an additional five hundred dollars interest . . ."

"But I ain't got . . ."

"*Don't* interrupt me, boy!" He looked at Bones. "I think we might have to teach the boy some manners."

Bones nodded again.

"Now, where was I?" Big Bob mused. "Ah yes, the third thing—your disloyalty. There are many ways to make you pay for that." He stuck his face in Joshua's, and pressed his forefinger into Joshua's chest. "Many ways," he repeated. "But I'm in a generous mood tonight, so I think I'll just tack on another five hundred dollars."

Joshua's face burned.

"Yes, another five," Big Bob said again. "What's that come to?" he asked, looking at Bones.

"One Thou-sand Five Hun-dred Dollars," Bones proclaimed.

"That sounds about right," Big Bob confirmed.

"Where do you expect me to get that kind of money?" Joshua asked.

"I hear your Mama has a rich boss, the same boss your girlfriend's daddy has. I also heard this man once paid a lot of money to get you out of trouble with the police. He'll pay again to get you out of this."

"What if he won't?" Joshua asked.

"If he don't," Big Bob said, leaning in to Joshua's face, "then your little girlfriend's gonna have to work it off in trade! Get my meaning?"

Loud and clear, Joshua thought.

"Now, you get going and round up the money. You got twenty-four hours, not a minute more. Tomorrow night, at this time, I want you to walk up and down the sidewalk. I'll find you. Any cops or surprises, deal's off, and the girl stays with me." He looked at Bones, adding, "That wouldn't be so bad, she's a nice looking thing."

❧

It was close to one in the morning when Joshua entered the front door of his building. He had been dwelling on Big Bob's assertions about Celeste and her father, which made some sense in light of Celeste's recent behavior. He walked through the lobby, and took the stairs to the basement. He came to the Williams' door, rang the bell, and waited.

Through the space under the door he could see that the lights were on, and figured they were still awake, waiting for news about Celeste. The door opened and Mr. Williams' face appeared.

Williams, who had probably been expecting the police or even Celeste herself, appeared shocked. He instinctively grabbed Joshua by the shirt, pulled him inside, and threw him across the room. Joshua knocked over a lamp and some other ornaments, landing hard on the wooden floor. The lamp came down on his head and fell to his side.

"What's going on?" Mrs. Williams yelled, running from the kitchen. She saw Joshua on the floor, and was about to help him.

"Stay where you are!" Williams demanded. "I'm gonna teach this boy a lesson."

Joshua was lying face-down; the room was spinning; he felt nauseous. He vaguely heard a woman yelling, "*No, No!*" but it was hard to hear anything above the ringing in his ears. Through blurred vision, he was barely able to see Williams come at him a second time. He tried to get up, but couldn't.

Williams lunged through the air. Joshua managed to turn on his side to avoid getting crushed, causing Williams to also land on the floor.

Joshua saw that the impact had weakened Williams, and tried once more to hoist himself up. But Williams' arm reached out and held him down, though the man's face was also on the floor.

Joshua saw the solid brass base of the broken lamp about two feet from his eyes. He reached and grabbed hold of it, feeling it was heavy enough to be useful. Without hesitation, he swung it with all his strength and smashed it into the back of Williams' head. Williams' hold loosened, then went limp.

Joshua pulled away.

Williams wasn't moving.

Joshua figured Williams was unconscious, and was about to drop the lamp. But he couldn't, he had to make sure that Williams would never again bother Celeste. He had to finish the job. All he knew was madness as he raised the lamp and delivered the final blow.

CHAPTER 16

Rachel Weissman and Esther Mandlebaum tried to be inconspicuous as they stood across the street from the main entrance of the Kingsbrook Jewish Hospital. They'd been waiting several hours, and Esther was growing impatient. "Just a few more minutes," Rachel pleaded, "I'm sure she'll be coming out soon."

Rachel was referring to Doctor Marcia Schiffman, the wondrous young resident Rachel saw as possessing all the things she wanted for herself. Over the past few months, Rachel had replayed her encounter with Doctor Schiffman for Esther *ad nauseam* until, finally, Esther had agreed to see for herself what the big deal was. Of course, Esther thought Rachel was crazy, these plans of becoming a doctor and all, but figured that she should at least humor her friend. After all, Esther had crazy dreams of her own.

"Look! There she is," Rachel exclaimed as Doctor Schiffman emerged from the hospital. "Wait! Stand over here, or she'll see us!" It was too late; the girls had done a poor job at hiding, and Doctor Schiffman happened to be looking their way. Rachel was nervous, but figured the doctor wouldn't recognize her; it was so long ago.

But Marcia Schiffman's face lit up when she saw Rachel. It was hard for her to forget the young Hasidic girl who showed so much interest. Rachel saw Schiffman's smile from across the street, and felt embarrassed.

"Oh, *Gut'n himmel*, God in heaven, she's coming this way," Rachel said. "What if she suspects we've been spying on her?"

"Don't worry so much, dear," Esther said. "We haven't been spying on anyone. We've just been out for a stroll."

Rachel knew that the excuse was lame; this side of the neighborhood had changed much over the past few years; it was no place for Hasidic girls to be "strolling." But Rachel also knew that Esther could pull off almost anything.

"Hi," Doctor Schiffman said, approaching the girls.

Rachel said a faint hello, looking to Esther for help. Doctor Schiffman saw that Rachel was anxious. "I remember you," Schiffman said, pointing a friendly finger at Rachel, "but I must apologize; I don't remember your name."

"Rachel Weissman," Rachel answered, trying to conceal her nervousness.

"Yes, Rachel with the broken ankle," the doctor remarked, smiling.

Rachel prayed for Esther to jump in. "This is my friend, Esther Mandlebaum, the one whose steps I fell on," Rachel said. She turned to Esther: "This is Doctor Schiffman, the doctor who took care of me."

"Ah yes," mused Schiffman, recalling the details of Rachel's accident. "Nice to meet you," she said.

"Nice to meet *you*," Esther responded.

"What brings you girls around here?" the doctor asked.

"Oh, we were just out walking," Esther answered. "We come by this way all the time."

Rachel nodded in agreement. Marcia Schiffman nodded too.

"And we should be getting home," Esther added, glancing at her wristwatch. "It's almost dinner time."

Rachel looked at her watch and concurred.

"Well, if you do this much walking, your ankle must have healed nicely," Schiffman observed.

"Oh, it has," Rachel said, feeling foolish.

"I'm glad," the doctor said, "but I think you girls should let me drive you home. It's getting late and you probably shouldn't be out walking these streets at this hour."

Rachel looked at Esther.

Esther shrugged her shoulders, but Rachel knew she was disappointed. The original plan had been to stop by the park on the way home. But it was late, and Doctor Schiffman was right about walking the streets.

The three of them huddled into a two-door Datsun. The ride was short. Rachel and Esther were quiet, but Marcia Schiffman struck up small talk about what the girls were learning in school. When they pulled up in front of Esther's house, Marcia Schiffman said, "It was nice meeting you, Esther."

"It was nice meeting you, too, Doctor Schiffman," Esther replied.

Rachel followed Esther, and also exchanged good-byes with Schiffman. The girls walked toward the house, when Rachel suddenly stopped, turned around, and called out to Schiffman as the car was about to pull away.

"What are you doing?" asked Esther.

"Wait here a minute!" Rachel said, running back to the car.

Rachel leaned through the passenger window. "I was just wondering," Rachel began nervously, stopping to catch her breath. "I was . . . wondering if I could come by the hospital to visit some time?"

"You mean to volunteer?" Schiffman asked.

"Something like that."

"Well, that's an excellent idea. The hospital is always looking for young volunteers. Let me give you the phone number of the director of volunteers. I'll talk to him and tell him to expect your call. I'll even try to get you assigned to me in the emergency room. You'll like it, there's always a lot going on, a lot to learn."

Rachel didn't know what to say. She was beside herself. The thought of working closely with Doctor Schiffman was overwhelming, a dream come true, and a step closer to her ultimate aspiration of becoming a doctor. The only problem would be convincing her parents. But she couldn't think about that just yet, she would deal with it later. For now, all she wanted to think about was this wonderful day.

⌘

Paul Sims sat in the study hall, breaking his teeth over a page of Talmud. The schedule in the yeshiva was grueling: up at five, breakfast at five-thirty, religious studies at six, prayer at nine, Talmud classes at ten, lunch at twelve. Afternoons were for secular subjects, and evenings were for reviewing the morning's Talmud lecture.

He was finding it difficult to stay awake. His mind raced with thoughts of Rachel Weissman. The last time he saw her was a week earlier, when the Rabbi had invited him for *Shabbos* dinner.

Suddenly, his parents came to mind. Strangely, he missed them. He had to admit that absence did do something to the heart after all.

He also missed the creature comforts of his Hewlett Harbor home. It was difficult adjusting to the tiny dorm room with the linoleum floor and squeaky beds. The worst thing was sharing with a roommate, especially one as saintly as Meir Rosenzweig, the upper classman he'd been paired with. It was policy in the yeshiva to team up freshmen with veterans, thereby assuring proper influences at all times.

Meir was two years ahead of Paul and, like all students at Yeshiva O'havei Torah, from a non-Orthodox home. He was tall, with a scraggly beard covering much of his face, and tortoiseshell glasses. He was also soft-spoken and likeable, two characteristics Paul appreciated. What Paul didn't appreciate was not being able to lie in bed at night, think about Rachel, and indulge in a little harmless masturbation. For such was not so harmless in the sanctified world of the yeshiva.

There were a few occasions on which he'd managed to steal some time alone in a bathroom stall, but he always had to be quick about it, for there was the constant danger of someone barging in. He knew he would have been better off not thinking about her. All it brought him was frustration. But he couldn't help it.

All in all, yeshiva life took some getting used to. He was determined, however, to do what he had to do, anything to make him more acceptable to Rachel Weissman. In that, he was single minded.

CHAPTER 17

Elija Williams was buried on Thursday, May 20, 1965. Present at his funeral were his son Jerome, his wife Mary, Alfred Sims, Loretta Eubanks, and several other tenants from his building. Reverend Jameson Sharp officiated, and the reverend's family was also in attendance. Celeste Williams was nowhere to be found, and Joshua Eubanks was being held in the juvenile division of the Brooklyn House of Detention.

The magnanimous Mr. Alfred Sims secured an attorney for Joshua—a specialist in criminal law—at his own expense. Joshua felt uneasy about Mr. Sims' occasional involvement in his life. He also didn't want a lawyer. He was planning to plead guilty and accept his punishment.

❧

Mr. Arthur Rothman, the lawyer, had introduced himself to Joshua in the prison conference room the morning after the killing. Rothman was short and stocky, sharply dressed, with thick salt and pepper hair, deep brown eyes, and a cleft in his chin. "You're mother's employer, Alfred Sims, has asked me to look into this case and see if I can represent you," was the first thing he said.

Rothman placed his briefcase on the table, removed a legal pad and some other papers, and took a fancy black fountain pen from the breast pocket of his three piece, charcoal-gray suit jacket.

"I don't need any lawyer," Joshua stated, "and I don't need favors from some white guy just because my mama works for him!"

"I suppose you're planning on defending yourself," Rothman responded.

"No I ain't. I did what I did, and that's that. No two ways about it. I don't need a trial or a lawyer. I'm ready to go to jail."

Rothman leaned over the table and brought his face closer to Joshua's. He lowered his tone to a whisper and responded, "Oh yes, I understand, you want to be a martyr. You killed your girlfriend's daddy, and now you feel bad about it, so you want your just desserts. You want to take what's coming to you, so you'll feel like a man, and your girlfriend—wherever she is—will think you're a man. And when you get out—if you ever do—the two of you can march into the sunset, and everything will be okay because you'll have paid your debt.

"Well, let me tell you a few things so you understand. First, *nobody* is going to send you away for nearly the amount of time you'll need to purge your conscience. And you know why?" He hesitated, observing Joshua's dumbstruck expression, then continued, "*Because nobody gives a shit!* See, in this world, when one black guy kills another black guy, everybody's happy because there's one less black guy. What they really want to do is give you a medal or something, but instead they'll send you away for a few years so it looks right.

"Now, I'm here only because my friend, Alfred Sims, asked me to be. It isn't exactly my hobby defending kids like you. If you really want me to go, I will, but just realize that whether you want a lawyer or not, the court's going to appoint one, probably some idiot public defender with an overgrown caseload. He'll likely get you two years in some juvie pisspot like Spofford and you'll be out by your eighteenth birthday, not exactly a lifetime if you get my drift. So if you're planning on being a martyr, you better find another way."

Rothman saw that he had Joshua's attention. "See, I think probation is a definite possibility here. First, the guy you killed was a first class dirt-bag, and everybody knows it. Second, according to the facts I have, it's pretty clear you killed him in self defense."

"That ain't true!" Joshua responded. "I went there to kill him. I could have left him on the floor. He was still breathing, but he was out cold. I didn't have to do it." He felt his body tremble as he spoke. Tears welled up in his eyes. "I murdered him," he muttered.

Rothman looked into Joshua's eyes, placed his hands on Joshua's shoulders, and said, "Listen kid! He attacked you *first*, and that's what matters. As for these thoughts you had in your mind, I suggest you keep them to yourself! Like I said, nobody gives a shit. That is, nobody, except your poor mother. And I'm sure it would destroy her to see you go to jail.

"I don't know about your girlfriend. No one's seen or heard from her, and I wonder if anyone ever will. But your mother, I'm sure she would like *you* to let *me* do my job. So why not keep a lid on all this talk about being guilty, and I'll keep you posted."

Without even waiting for a reply, Rothman quickly gathered his papers, stood up, and walked towards the door. The guard opened the door for him.

Joshua contemplated Rothman's point. *Nobody gives a shit!* He couldn't argue with that.

Rothman stepped out into the hallway, and as the door was about to close, Joshua called his name. The guard held the door as Rothman peered back into the room. Joshua stared at the lawyer for a second, hesitating. Rothman looked at him impatiently.

"Do what you have to," Joshua said.

CHAPTER 18

Rachel Weissman sat pensively at the dinner table.

"Rucheleh, is something bothering you?" her father asked.

Her mother also looked concerned.

Rachel knew she couldn't hide her feelings from them much longer. She would have to say something, *but what?*

"No Papa, everything is fine. I'm just worried about my finals in school."

"Well, no need to worry. You'll do just fine," her mother reassured her.

They resumed eating.

"Well, there is *something*," Rachel said.

Hannah and Isaac looked at her. They had been suspecting for a while that there might be an issue concerning boys. Hasidic girls usually started dating at sixteen in order to marry young and have lots of children. Soon it would be time to contact the matchmaker. They wondered if Rachel was anxious about that.

"I mean, it's no big deal," Rachel continued, "it's just something I would like to do and I'm not sure how you will feel about it."

Isaac looked at Hannah, then back at Rachel. "Vell, ve von't know how ve'll feel until you tell us vhat it is." He always spoke gently, and at moments like this, it only made things harder.

"Well," Rachel began hesitantly, "I saw Doctor Schiffman from the hospital. You remember her Mama?"

Hannah nodded.

"Esther and I were just taking a walk and we happened to pass the hospital," Rachel continued, figuring that a small "white" lie was harmless.

"What were you doing in that part of the neighborhood?" Hannah asked, her tone more acerbic than the rabbi would ever have been.

"We didn't even realize where we were. We were just walking, and got so involved in conversation, next thing we knew we were in front of the hospital."

Isaac and Hannah didn't completely buy it, though they did know that when Rachel and Esther were together, the two girls often seemed as if they *were* in another world. They kept silent, awaiting the rest of the story.

"Then, you wouldn't believe it," Rachel continued. "Doctor Schiffman just happened to be coming out as we were passing. She remembered me and said hello. She offered us a ride home because it was getting late."

Rachel saw that her parents were growing impatient. She went on, "Well, in the car, Doctor Schiffman asked us about school and all. I told her that science was my best subject. One thing led to another, and she ended up inviting me to visit her at the hospital. You know, watch her work, help out, stuff like that. She said I could officially become a volunteer."

"Did she make the same offer to Esther?" Hannah interjected.

"No, I suppose not." Tentative. "I mean, she probably would have, but I guess she saw that Esther wasn't interested."

"I suppose she did," Hannah responded.

Rachel was hoping her father would offer something, but he was still digesting it all. That was his way.

"Well, there isn't anything wrong with volunteering at the hospital; it's a mitzvah to visit the sick, isn't it Papa?"

"Yes, Rucheleh, *bikur cholim* is a great mitzvah," the rabbi answered. "But volunteering in a hospital is something else, no? It vould take time avay from your studies, yes?"

"Oh, Papa, I promise it wouldn't. You know how good I am about my studies. I wouldn't let anything interfere with them. And soon it will be summer . . ."

"But you have plans for the summer," Hannah interrupted. "You're going to be a counselor in the Beis Rivka day camp."

"But I've been going there since I was five. Can't I do something else, something new?"

Regardless of how reasonable it sounded, Rachel knew she was asking for something that was unusual for a Hasidic girl. There was no way it would sit well with Isaac and Hannah. All her life, they'd shielded her from Gentiles and Jews who weren't Orthodox. That was their job, as dutiful Hasidic parents, to protect her from the "poisonous" influences of the outside world. And now she wanted a piece of that world, however small. There was no telling what she would see.

Isaac and Hannah looked at one another, neither appearing enthusiastic.

"Okay," the rabbi said, "but under vone condition!"

"Yes Papa, anything." Excitement.

"Before you start, I vant to speak with this Doctor Schiffman."

Rachel had expected as much. Her father needed to make sure that Doctor Schiffman was aware that there were certain things that a Hasidic girl shouldn't be exposed to, medicine or not. "I'm sure Doctor Schiffman would love to meet you, Papa," Rachel responded, avoiding eye contact with her mother.

Rachel had won this little battle. The rabbi had no idea that this was only the beginning, but Hannah suspected otherwise. She knew Rachel differently than Isaac did, the way that only a mother could know a child. She had sensed Rachel's discontentment in the past—whether from Rachel's fascination with science and other secular subjects, or her relationship with Esther Mandlebaum—and it had often given her cause for concern. She had overheard the girls making fun of the Hasidic boys. Until now, she'd dismissed it all as the playful musings of adolescents, and had believed that her daughter would one day come to value the piety of the young Hasidic scholars, many of whom would be lining up to take her hand in marriage. But now Hannah wasn't so certain. Now, she was frightened.

Hannah could hide her feelings from Isaac, but not from Rachel, who was as perceptive about her mother as her mother was about her. The two women looked at one another, each understanding exactly what the other was thinking. And even Isaac's naiveté wouldn't last very long.

❧

It was three-thirty, a half hour after school had let out at the Hewlett Bay Academy. Doctor Harold Goldman sat at his desk, finishing up paper work, eager to enjoy the beautiful spring afternoon with his five mile run. Goldman ran three times a week, religiously, even in the dead of winter. He only relished it, however, on days like this.

The other two afternoons, Mondays and Wednesdays, he spent seeing private patients in an office he sublet from another psychologist in the nearby town of Hewlett. He looked outside his window, and thanked God it was Tuesday. This was no day to be cooped up with patients and problems.

He was just about finished, ready to go, already in his shorts and T-shirt, when someone knocked on his door. He answered, "Yes," wondering who was still in school at this hour. He thought it was probably one of the teachers working late, coming to discuss a student. This occasionally happened when he stuck around too long, but he knew how to deal with it. A few words, maybe a joke or two, and "We'll talk it over tomorrow, at lunch or something." He could be quite smooth when necessary.

The door opened, and so did Harold Goldman's mouth when he saw his visitor. "Oh, Mrs. Sims," he reacted, unable to contain his surprise. "Please, come in, take a seat." Harold Goldman had met Evelyn Sims only once, at a family conference about Paul. He sensed then, as he did now, that she was a deeply troubled woman.

Evelyn anxiously sat herself down. By the look on her face, Harold Goldman knew that his run was cancelled.

There was a brief moment of silence before Evelyn said, "I'm sorry to have barged in on you like this."

"Oh no, it's quite all right. What can I do for you?"

"I'm not sure, really. I just . . . I've been feeling like I need to talk about things."

Goldman looked at her curiously. She seemed different from when he had last seen her, and very much unlike the person Paul had described. But it was always this way in Harold Goldman's business, people ended up being other than expected. He wasn't surprised.

"It sounds like you're not certain why you're here, but you feel you should be," Goldman observed.

"I suppose that's it." Tentative.

"Well, what are these 'things' you want to talk about."

"I don't really know. I'm sorry, maybe I shouldn't have come," she said more definitively, rising from her chair.

"Wait, please sit." He indicated the chair.

She complied.

"I know this is hard for you, but if there's any way I can be of help, I'd like to."

She looked directly into his eyes. "You know, I'm not as terrible as you probably think I am," she said sadly, her hands trembling.

"I don't think . . ."

"Please, don't lie to me, Doctor Goldman. I'm not a stupid woman. I won't be placated."

Goldman kept silent.

"I just want to explain things; I *need* to explain things."

"Do you feel it's your fault that Paul left?" Goldman asked.

"Of course it's my fault! *Everything* is my fault! I'm the boy's mother after all, whose fault could it be?"

Goldman was taken aback. "I guess you could say that, but there are other ways to look at it."

"I'm a very unhappy woman; I suppose you already know that." Tears were forming in her eyes.

Goldman nodded.

"I know that's a poor excuse, but it's the only one I have."

"Maybe it's not as 'poor' as you think."

Evelyn thought about that. "My husband," she began, then hesitated. She wasn't sure how far she should go with this man, this stranger who knew so much, yet so little, about her life. "My husband cheats on me," she said, not completely aware if the words had really come out. She'd suspected for years, but had never voiced it.

"You're certain?" he asked sympathetically.

"Certain," Evelyn reflected, "that's a funny word. I suppose I'm not exactly 'certain,' but I'm pretty damn close. Call it—intuition."

"Based on?"

"Based on years of knowing the man I live with." She became pensive again. "It started in the beginning of our marriage, maybe even earlier. He was in the war and all, and I guess it did something to his head. Or maybe it was his mother; she's something else. I'm no expert like you, but I've heard that war and crazy mothers can screw up a man's head."

"They most certainly can," Goldman said with a faint smile. He didn't want to interject too much; he wanted her to tell her story.

"Well, we had what I suppose was a normal sex life, at least in the beginning, but after a while, it happened less often. It wasn't long before he lost interest. I thought he was impotent; at least that's what I wanted to believe. I guess I just couldn't accept that he didn't want me anymore. He started coming home late in the evenings, working on weekends, and things like that. A typical scenario, I know, but I was too stupid—or stubborn—to see it." Evelyn removed a tissue from her bag and dried her eyes. "You're the first person I've ever told this to."

"It's a difficult thing to admit, even to yourself."

"Yes, I suppose it is."

"Tell me, Mrs. Sims . . ."

"Please, call me Evelyn. After what I've told you, I think it should be okay to call me Evelyn."

"Yes, of course. Well, what I was going to ask—and I don't intend to be callous—but what I wanted to know is why you've come to see *me?* Why am *I* the one you chose to reveal this to?"

"That's a good question. I guess it's because I needed for you to know that there was another side to the story, that I wasn't simply a monstrous mother who tortured her son. I've had a horrible marriage, I've felt worthless, dejected, and things that I cannot even find words to describe. I was desperate, I was—I am—miserable, and I took all of it out on Paul. I know that. I was unfair to him," she said, sobbing, "and now I'm paying for it."

"Paying?"

"I've lost him, haven't I?"

"Again, you might say that, but there *are* other ways to look at that too."

"Like how?"

"Like, perhaps you weren't as 'monstrous' as you think, and perhaps you haven't lost Paul at all. You can still build a relationship with him." Goldman waited for a response, but there was none. "Look Evelyn," he said, leaning toward her, "Paul has his problems, but he also has some things going for him. First, he's smart, smarter than most kids his age, and when he's interested in something, like Judaism, he really gets focused. He's basically a good kid; he's not into drugs, crazy music, or breaking the law. I'd say, on the balance, you didn't do too badly."

She considered his words. "Yes, you do have a point, Doctor Goldman, but it's hard for a mother to look at things that way—'on the balance,' as you say."

"It is hard, I concede, but it's the truth. Just as it's important for you to give me a complete picture of yourself, it is helpful to have a complete picture of Paul. You only see your disappointments, and because of that, you blame yourself. You're making the same mistake with Paul that he makes with you."

"Perhaps."

Goldman would have preferred a more affirmative response, but this was a start.

"I guess I've taken up enough of your time, Doctor."

Goldman smiled. "I hope I was helpful."

"You were," she responded. "I think I needed to hear myself say a few things."

"To get them off your chest?"

"Yes, you could put it that way."

"Listen," he said as he opened his desk drawer, "if you ever feel that you want to do this again, here's my card." He handed her the card with the address and phone number of his private office.

Evelyn took the card, appearing appreciative of the gesture. In a more cynical moment she might have suspected him of drumming up business, but no such thought crossed her mind. She trusted him, though she would probably never avail herself of his offer. She had said what she'd come to say, and that was the end of it. She'd harbored no illusions that her confession would ease her remorse, and left Harold Goldman's office feeling much the same as she had upon entering it. Nothing was different, and in her mind nothing ever would be. She simply lacked the strength to change; otherwise, she would have done so years ago.

CHAPTER 19

Joshua received five years probation from a deal worked out with the DA. A charge of involuntary manslaughter, an explanation to the judge as to what had happened—absent his editorializing—and that was that. His sole lesson from all this was that Rothman was right: nobody gave a shit.

It was odd that Jerome and his mother, both of whom were present at the hearing, didn't protest. Odd, but not surprising. Joshua figured Alfred Sims was probably going to take good care of them.

He was home within two days, and had the weekend before returning to school. He wasn't worried what the kids in school might say or think, all he cared about was finding Celeste. Nothing else mattered.

His mother insisted he stay at home until Monday. It was becoming harder for him to defy her, without feeling guilty. He promised himself this would be the last time.

"Joshua, where do you think you're going?" Loretta asked as he walked toward the front door. He didn't answer, for she knew exactly where he was headed, and the determination in his step made it clear that he wasn't going to be stopped. She didn't go after him, didn't yell or say anything else. The only sound that followed her question was the door as it closed.

He got off the elevator, and looked at the stairway leading to the basement. He paused for a second, feeling a surge of anguish. Loretta had told him that Jerome and his mother had moved out just after the funeral, yet he could still hear screams coming from downstairs. He wondered when the screams would stop.

He walked out into the street, knowing precisely where he would begin his search. As he headed towards the old neighborhood, he swore he would find Celeste, bring her home, and personally deliver her to her mother and Jerome, wherever they were. Perhaps that would make amends. He also swore to himself that he would avoid trouble at all costs. He couldn't break his mother's heart again. How he would do all this, however, he hadn't a clue. He would leave it in God's hands. His first religious moment.

⁓

Joshua approached the corner where Big Bob conducted most of his business. Instead of Bones, another thug was standing around, negotiating with the ladies. Joshua didn't recognize him. *New blood on the streets.* He figured Bones was inside with Big Bob, counting the day's profits.

He walked into the store and over to the cash register. Mr. Powell was listening to the horse races on a small transistor radio.

"Well, well. Looky what we got here," Powell commented.

"Go right ahead and press that buzzer," Joshua said, trying to appear undaunted.

Almost immediately, the back door opened and Bones stepped out. He saw Joshua right away. "I'll be, see here what the cat dragged in," Bones muttered.

Joshua was silent.

"I hear you been having some problems with the law," Bones said, giving Powell a laugh. He walked toward Joshua. "Word is, you killed the girlfriend's old man and got away with it because of that rich Jew your mama works for."

Joshua was still silent.

Bones stood in Joshua's face. "I suppose you ain't got that money you owe us, right?"

Joshua backed away.

"So then, I ask myself, 'What the fuck you doing' here?' I know you ain't looking for work, so you must be looking for your girl."

"That's right," Joshua replied.

"Maybe I don't know where she's at anymore."

"And that depends on . . ."

"On what you're willing to pay for the information."

As Joshua had expected, it all came down to money. He also knew that what he already owed Big Bob wouldn't cut it at this point. "Guess I should be talking to Big Bob," he said, needling Bones, who wasn't empowered to negotiate.

"Yeah, well, maybe you got that right," Bones said, his anger showing. "I'll see if he's available." He turned and walked toward the back room.

Joshua stood, waiting, staring into space. Much of his youth had been spent hanging around this store, running errands, doing this and that for Big Bob. He wondered if he would ever truly get away from it. He glanced over at Mr. Powell, who was sitting on a stool behind the counter, still listening to the horses. The old man's expression was impassive; just another ordinary day in the neighborhood.

Joshua heard the door in the back open as Big Bob emerged.

"So I hear you wanna see me, talk some business?" Big Bob said.

Joshua nodded.

"I hear you ain't found that poor girl yet. Also heard her daddy met with a terrible accident." Big Bob brandished his sneer.

Joshua wondered why anybody would constantly show off such disgusting teeth, but figured Big Bob relished displaying all his gold, wherever he had it.

"Then you know why I'm here," Joshua answered.

"Then *you* know its gonna cost you."

Joshua looked into Big Bob's eyes, waiting for the terms. The look was to let Big Bob know that he wasn't intimidated any more. And he wasn't. True, Big Bob could hurt him, even kill him, a convenient way to send a message to others about the consequences of disloyalty. But Joshua wasn't scared. He saw Big Bob for the low-down, dirty, slime-ball, pimping, drug dealer he was, a man who probably wouldn't last much longer, before one of his aspiring underlings got too ambitious. It was a liberating realization, one that helped him see himself more clearly. Perhaps there was hope for him yet. But first, there was the matter of Celeste.

"Here's what I'm gonna do for you," Big Bob said. "First, I'm not saying I know where the girl is. Let's make that clear from the start."

Joshua nodded. It wasn't time to argue, it was time for business. Big Bob couldn't be trusted, but that wasn't important. All that mattered was the money, and Joshua knew that if he had it, Big Bob would come up with the girl.

"What I *am* saying is that I—as you know—have a way of finding things out. But as you also know, these things come at a price."

Joshua nodded again.

"Now, If I'm correct, you're already into me for . . ." He stopped to calculate in his mind; this too, Joshua knew, was part of the ritual.

"Fifteen hundred," Joshua interjected.

"Yes, I believe that's it. But that was a few days ago; now, I guess a fair price would be, about, let's see . . ." He hesitated again. "How about, twenty five hundred?"

The question was rhetorical. Twenty five hundred would be the amount, and if Joshua didn't produce it soon, it would increase. His problem was, where was he going to get it?

Big Bob, guessing Joshua's thoughts, said, "Why don't you ask that Jewish lawyer your mama works for? Seems he's got some interest in you. I wonder why that is?"

"Oh, I suppose you got a story about him, too." Sarcasm.

"No story. I ain't got no *stories*, only facts. And the fact, Peanut, my man, is that your mama seems to be a little more than a maid for that man. Who knows, maybe that's how you got those eyes of yours?"

Joshua held his temper, and tried to stay focused. He knew Big Bob wanted to unravel him, if only for the pure pleasure of it. He'd long suspected something about his mother and Alfred Sims anyway, though suspecting was one thing, while *knowing* was another. Now, he knew.

⌘

The next morning, Loretta took off from work to escort Joshua to his first meeting with his probation officer. She wanted to make sure he didn't somehow get "lost" along the way, and also wanted to meet the officer. She didn't mention to Joshua about his having walked out the night before. He wasn't surprised; she never wasted words.

They entered a small, windowless cubicle. There were three chairs, one behind a dark gray aluminum desk, and two in front of it. The dull green walls were lined with aluminum file cabinets, the same color as the desk, and both the cabinets and the desk were covered with piles of papers.

In the chair behind the desk sat a bespectacled, balding man in a dark suit. The baldness was the first thing Joshua and Loretta noticed, for when they walked in, the man was looking down at a file: Joshua's file. The other thing they noticed was that atop the man's head sat a black skullcap.

Without looking up, the man gestured for them to sit. Joshua couldn't help but stare at the yarmulke. Loretta noticed, and nudged him with her elbow. He got the message and stopped.

Suddenly, the man looked up from his papers. "I'm Mr. Kimmel, your probation officer," he said softly. Beneath the man's long scraggly black beard, Joshua discerned a welcoming smile.

"Good day sir," Loretta said, her polite southern manner shining through. She knew exactly how to address white folks, especially Jewish ones. "I'm Loretta Eubanks. This is my son Joshua."

"Yes, I know," Kimmel answered as he glanced back at his papers. "I can see that Joshua has been having a hard time lately," he observed, flipping through the file. He looked again at Loretta and Joshua.

"That would be putting it lightly," Loretta replied.

Kimmel smiled again, obviously appreciating her frankness. "Well," he said, turning to Joshua, "it's my philosophy that the past is the past, especially with someone your age." He stopped himself, as if to give his words a chance to sink in. "I'm here to help you in whatever way I can, and I hope you take advantage of that help."

"Yes sir," Joshua said. Loretta had forewarned him that these were to be the only two words to come from his mouth.

"Now, I see from your school records that you made quite a turnaround before this unfortunate incident. It says here that, in the past year, you became a straight A student." Kimmel looked curious.

"Yes sir."

"Well, it's clear you're very bright and that you have a lot of potential. If you can keep that up . . ."

"Don't worry," Loretta interjected. "Joshua's gonna take care of his school work. I'll see that he does."

Kimmel looked for a reaction from Joshua, who nodded in agreement.

This was turning out quite differently than Joshua had anticipated. Instead of being an apathetic bureaucrat, Kimmel seemed sincere, even friendly. And then there was the beard and the yarmulke. Joshua guessed that Kimmel was Hasidic, for the only Jews he had known who looked like that were the Hasidim of Crown Heights. Joshua had often heard Hasidic Jews talking on the streets, but he'd never heard any speak English. He also never imagined one working as a probation officer. He had always thought them to be rabbis or business owners. And he'd also imagined them as harsh and unfriendly, though he had never been given reason to. In all, Kimmel perplexed him.

"I think it would also be helpful if we could find Joshua a summer job," Kimmel said. "School will be over in less than a month; it would be good to earn some money."

I need a lot more than 'some' money, Joshua thought, though the job wasn't a bad idea. It would keep him off the streets and give him some responsibility. He knew that this was exactly what Kimmel had in mind, and appreciated the man's not having framed it in that way. He was liking Kimmel more by the minute.

"And what kind of job do you suggest?" Loretta asked.

"Well, I see you live in Crown Heights, which, coincidentally, is where I live. I know a lot of people in the neighborhood, and I might be able to find something close to home. Let me make some calls; I'll get back to you in a couple of days, okay?"

Loretta nodded.

"Okay with you, Joshua?" he asked.

"Yes sir."

⁂

It wasn't a few days. In fact, it was that very same afternoon that Mr. Kimmel called to tell Loretta he'd found something. Joshua would be helping the custodian of the Lubavitcher synagogue on Eastern Parkway and Kingston Avenue, just a few blocks from home. He could start as soon as school was over. Kimmel gave Loretta the phone number of a Rabbi Weissman, who would be setting everything up.

"Would that be Rabbi *Isaac* Weissman?" Loretta asked.

"Yes, it is," Kimmel responded. "Do you know him?"

"Yes, I do."

Loretta explained the connection, how Rabbi Weissman used to come to the Sims' home to tutor Paul, and how the Rabbi was always polite and respectful to her even though she was the housekeeper. She also mentioned that Paul was now studying and living in a yeshiva on Eastern Parkway. Joshua, overhearing his mother's end of the conversation, was surprised, for he had never been told any of this. Just then, he realized that it had been quite some time since she'd mentioned Paul altogether.

Loretta was almost speaking with Kimmel as though he were an old friend. When she hung up, she turned to Joshua, and said, "He's a fine man, that Mr. Kimmel, a mighty fine man, I'd say."

She picked up the phone again, and dialed the number Kimmel had given her. "Hello, is this Rabbi Weissman?" she asked.

"Yes, who is this?"

"Good afternoon, Rabbi, I don't know if you remember me, but I'm Loretta Eubanks . . ."

"Of course I remember you!"

They chatted for a while; some about Paul, but mostly about Joshua. Loretta expressed her gratitude for the rabbi's help, and assured him that Joshua would be exemplary in his new job. She repeated what a "fine man" Mr. Kimmel was, and how coincidental it was that all this ended up in the rabbi's lap.

When she hung up, she turned to Joshua. "This is a small world, Joshua. It strengthens my faith in the Lord when things like this happen. Rabbi Weissman has done a lot for Paul Sims, and if you let him, he'll do some good for you."

Joshua thought to ask what it was that this rabbi fellow had actually done for Paul Sims, but didn't bother. He wasn't in the mood to hear about Paul Sims.

Loretta got busy in the kitchen, while Joshua went to his room. He knew he should open his school books, for tomorrow would be his first day back in over a week, and he had some catching up to do. Instead, he stared out his window, wondering how he was going to come up with Big Bob's money.

Outside, while it was getting dark, kids were still playing ball in the park, and other folks were just standing around. He thought about Celeste, and the times they used to sneak into that very same park. He knew those days were over and would never return, that things would never be the same. But he also knew that he had to find her and bring her home, no matter what it took.

At dinner, Joshua drank a gallon of milk. He wasn't a milk lover, but it was the only way he could devise to get his mother out of the house. It worked; after clearing the table, she decided to run down to the market to pick up milk for the morning.

As soon as she left, he went through her bag, searching for the small red phone book she kept there. He found it, turned to the names and numbers listed under "S," and saw two numbers for the Simses. One of them, marked *Alfred—private*, was the one he needed. He knew he was taking a chance, but he had no other choice. He lifted the receiver and dialed the number.

The phone rang three times on the other end, before a man's voice came on the line, saying, "Hello."

"Hello, this is Joshua Eubanks." Trembling.

"Oh, yes, Joshua." There was a long hesitation. "Yes, how are you?" Nervousness.

"Well, not so good." Joshua stopped himself, thinking, *this is a bad idea, I should hang up now!* He took a deep breath, and said, "I was wondering if you could meet me tomorrow. There are some things I need to talk to you about." He couldn't believe he was actually doing this.

Another hesitation at the other end, and then, "Okay, what time would you like to meet?"

Joshua, even more shaken by Alfred's willingness, answered, "How about three o'clock, after school?"

"That sounds okay. I'll come to your apartment at three."

"One more thing."

"Yes?"

"This is just between you and me, okay?"

"Yes, that's fine."

When he hung up, Joshua couldn't make heads nor tails of what had just happened. He was glad this part was over, but knew the worst was yet to come. He wasn't sure what to expect of Alfred Sims, the man he now believed to be his father. But he was convinced that if there was any hope of finding Celeste, Alfred was it.

⤸

The doorbell rang a few minutes after three. Joshua opened the door, and Alfred entered the apartment, acting as if it were his first time there.

Joshua showed Alfred to the living room, and they sat down.

Alfred looked at his watch, then at Joshua. "Well, what can I do for you?"

"You want a drink or something?" Awkward.

"That's okay," Alfred answered, glancing at his watch again, "I don't have too much time."

"So I guess I'll just get to the point."

Alfred waited.

"I don't know if Mama told you yet, but I have a job."

"Yes, she mentioned it just this morning. Congratulations."

Joshua wanted to just come out with it, and ask for the money, but he couldn't. "Yeah, guess it's a good thing, keeps me out of trouble."

"I think it's a great thing."

Gee, thanks, Pop, you can't imagine how much your approval means to me.

"The reason I wanted to talk to you is because I need some money, and I didn't know where else to go."

Alfred appeared curious.

"I'll pay you back, every cent plus interest, with the money from my job." *Please, say something!*

"How much do you need?"

"A lot."

"And exactly how much is that?"

Joshua hesitated. "Maybe this isn't a good idea." He rose from the couch and began pacing.

"Look Joshua, I can't give you an answer until I know how much money you're talking about."

Joshua stopped pacing, looked at Alfred, and asked, "Why are you here, anyway?"

"What do you mean?"

"I mean, why did you come here today? Why did you help me with the police? Why did you get me that lawyer? Why do you do these things?"

"Because your mother works for me and my wife, and I like her very much." Defensive. "We think of her as family, you too."

There were many things running through Joshua's mind, but he needed to stay focused on Celeste. "I need twenty-five hundred dollars," he said, matter-of-factly, figuring he could still save his own five hundred for a "rainy day."

"Yes, that is a lot of money." Pensive. "What do you need it for?"

Having anticipated the question, Joshua had also decided to answer truthfully, hoping to appeal to Alfred's sense of decency. He told the story about Celeste and Big Bob, as Alfred stared in disbelief. Joshua thought he even saw concern in Alfred's eyes.

Alfred thought for a moment, then said, "It seems this young lady has been the source of all the trouble you've been getting yourself into."

"I guess you could put it that way."

"And what do you think your mother would do if she ever found out that I helped you to continue your relationship with this girl?"

"This ain't about me and Celeste; it's about Celeste only, and helping *her*. We aren't together anymore."

"Are you sure of that?"

Joshua waited a beat. "Yeah."

"How can you be sure this Big Bob character will keep his word and tell you where she is? And even if he does, how do you know she'll come home with you once you find her? It doesn't sound like she's exactly been kidnapped."

Alfred was a businessman to the end, covering all bases, making sure his investment would be prudent. Joshua assured him that Big Bob, also a businessman, always delivered for the right price. "That's what Big Bob wants folks to think. If he went back on his word, people would hear and nobody would trust him no more."

Joshua spoke in the language Alfred understood. As for the question about Celeste's cooperation, he had no response, for he too wasn't convinced.

"Okay, Joshua, I'll give you the money. But on two conditions." He looked at Joshua closely, scrutinizing the boy's reaction.

Joshua was impassive, waiting to hear the conditions.

"First," Alfred continued, "you have to promise me that after you find this girl, whether you get her home or not, you'll forget about her. She's brought you nothing but trouble, and you can't spend the rest of your life making good for what happened to her father. Second, this money will be regarded by you as a gift, not a loan. I want you to save the money you earn. One day you'll use it for school or something. I don't need it."

Joshua smiled, he didn't have a problem with either condition. He knew there could never be a future with Celeste anyway, and the idea of not having to pay back the money suited him just fine. He also knew that the only reason Alfred was helping was guilt, a motive with which he himself was well acquainted.

Like father, like son.

⟨⟩

To Joshua's surprise, it was one of the better apartment buildings in Bed-Stuy; red-brick, five stories, graffiti-free, windows intact, front door-lock and buzzer system operational. As he stood in the entrance, about to press the buzzer for apartment 5-K, it occurred to him that he should have expected no less. Big Bob lured his girls with promises of comfort and riches. It made sense that he would treat them well, at least at the start. Then, once they became dependent upon him and his "free" drugs, he would put them on the streets to earn their keep.

Joshua's only hope was that Celeste had not yet fallen too deeply into the trap. Big Bob was a fast mover, and Celeste was vulnerable. He didn't know what to expect.

Big Bob had gladly taken the money, seeming nonchalant about losing one of his girls, almost as if he was certain that Celeste would stay put. Joshua wondered about this, and understood that there were no "money-back guarantees." He had one shot, and if he couldn't convince Celeste to come with him, it would be good-bye to both her and the money.

The voice on the intercom asked who it was.

"Sunshine," Joshua responded, using the password Big Bob had given him, knowing that in a few hours it would change.

The door buzzed, Joshua pushed and entered. He took the elevator to the top floor, found apartment 5-K, and pressed another buzzer. Next thing he knew, he was face to face with Celeste.

Her expression lacked surprise, making him wonder if Big Bob had told her he would be coming. She held the door, stepped aside, and let him in without an utterance. He looked at her and realized she was on something.

He surveyed the apartment with his eyes, turned to her, and said, "I've come to take you home."

She was unresponsive.

He wondered if she'd heard him. "Where are your things?" he asked.

Still no reply.

He grabbed her arms, looked in her eyes, and said, "I *am* taking you home. *Now!*"

Tears suddenly formed in her eyes. She broke free and sobbed, "*No, you can't! You Can't!*"

He reached for her again. She held her hand up to ward him off, and continued crying.

"I'm sorry," he said softly.

"You did nothing to be sorry for," she replied, looking away.

"But I did. I killed your . . ."

"You didn't kill no one! At least no one that didn't deserve killing. You did me a favor."

"Look, we gotta go. *Now!*"

"Where do you think we're gonna go?"

"Home."

"I don't have a home."

"Yes you do." He moved closer to her, and wiped her tears with his hand.

They embraced.

"Come," he said, "we got to get moving."

"I can't."

He stepped back and looked at her. "What do you mean, you *can't?*"

"Just what I'm saying. I can't go! Don't you see, I can't go back to my Mama and Jerome. There's nothing for me there. My Mama never did anything to help me. She just let *him* do what he wanted. She never said nothing! Acted like she didn't know what was going on. But she knew all right. She knew everything. And Jerome, he ain't no better. *Hell,* he was in the room, in the next bed, always pretending he was asleep. He never did nothing either."

"But they *do* love you, and I know they're worried sick over you. They probably were afraid and didn't know what to do. You know your Daddy was *real* big, and *real* angry. What could they do?" He hoped she would see his point, even though he wasn't convinced himself.

"That's bull. *You* did something; you're the only one who ever did anything. Don't go making excuses for them!"

"What I did wasn't right."

"It sure was right. You stopped him, and now I never have to worry about him again."

"I could have done other things to stop him, but now's not the time to talk about any of that."

"And Jerome and Mama could have done something, but they didn't. It don't bother me if I never see them again. I ain't going!"

"So what are you gonna do, stay here with Big Bob and become one of his girls? You know what they do for him?"

"He don't treat me like that. He treats me good, takes care of me mighty fine, not like my daddy."

"How? By giving you drugs!"

"He's giving me a nice place to live, and he don't make me take drugs, he just offers me a little something now and then, makes me feel good. What's wrong with that?"

"And you think he's doing all this for free? Don't you see, it starts off as 'a nice place to live,' and 'a little something now and then,' and soon it becomes a *lot* of something, *all the time*, and you're gonna have to work to pay for it."

"That's what you say!"

"What I know! What I've seen!"

"Well you're *wrong*, and I wouldn't go back to Mama and Jerome even if you were right."

"Then just come with me, we'll go somewhere else."

"And where's that?"

"You'll stay with me and Mama for a few days, we'll figure something out." Not very convincing, he had to admit.

"You think your mama's gonna let me stay with you?"

"Don't you worry about it; I'll take care of it."

"Yeah, say you do; then what? I'm gonna stay with you forever?"

There had been a time when he would have said yes to that, but "forever" was no longer in the cards for them. "I don't know," he said, "but there's got to be some place better than here."

"It's not so bad here; you just think it is. Big Bob's been good to me, he says I'm special, he's gonna take care of me."

The next thing Joshua knew, tears were flowing from his eyes. He couldn't recall the last time he'd actually cried.

She reached out, touched his face, and moved closer to hold him.

"Look, Peanuts," she said, "you know where I am, and you can come visit anytime. That's better than it used to be."

"You think so? Listen, Big Bob's never going to let me get near you again. He's gonna watch you like a hawk. And you're not staying in this nice place forever, trust me on that."

She didn't respond; she wasn't listening. He knew he had lost her.

He looked in her eyes. "Wherever you are, if you need me, you call. Even if Mama answers, you just tell her where you're at, and I'll get to you."

She began crying again. "But you can come see me anytime you want," she said, as she fell into his arms. They stood there, holding one another for what seemed an eternity. Only, it wasn't.

❧

He came out of the building, and began his trek back to Crown Heights. Daylight was dwindling, he had to move quickly. He raced against the sun, which was slowly descending somewhere beyond the tenements. Not much of a sunset, but the best these streets had to offer.

His thoughts were muddled, and his spirit was defeated. He had lost the money and Celeste, and had made a mess of everything. He tried contemplating his next move, but was too demoralized to consider the future. Yet, despite this, he knew there would be a next move. *Somehow. Sometime.*

BOOK II

CHAPTER 20

The first time Joshua saw Rachel Weissman, he was sweeping the stairwell of the synagogue. It was his third day on the job, a few minutes past seven in the evening. Quitting time was seven; he was running late.

He was between the first and second floors, and she was ascending the stairs. He moved aside to let her pass. Their eyes met for a split second. She smiled politely and said hello.

He watched her continue up the stairs. Something about her; no, *everything* about her struck him. She exited the stairwell, the door closing loudly behind her. He ran up, taking three steps at a time, eased the door open, and stuck his head out to see where she was going. She stopped outside one of the classrooms in which a group of men gathered every evening to study. She leaned against the wall and waited.

She didn't notice him watching. He came out of the stairwell and started sweeping the hallway. He had already swept it ten minutes earlier; *what the hell.*

She looked at him and smiled once again. The cordial, obligatory sort of smile that one usually offers a stranger. He tried to smile back, but his face froze. He guessed her to be around his own age, and figured she was probably waiting for one of the men in the class.

In the three days working in the synagogue, he had encountered some rather strange things. The first was the notion of grown men still attending school. They were all at least in their thirties, and every night they came to study for hours and to listen to an older rabbi give a lecture.

Outside the classroom, Joshua was able to hear what went on, though he didn't understand a word of it. The men spoke mostly Hebrew, or Yiddish, with a little English here and there. And they spoke loudly, as if they were always yelling at each other, flailing their arms all over.

He'd asked Calvin about it, but Calvin had told him to mind his own business. Calvin was his boss, the custodian, and seemed an okay sort. But Joshua could tell that Calvin was ticked off about having him around. From the moment Rabbi Weissman had introduced them, Calvin seemed less than welcoming.

Joshua understood that Calvin had been working in the synagogue for over five years, was older, and had a family to support. He figured that Calvin had probably been doing a fine job, didn't need any help, and felt a little threatened about having an assistant. Joshua knew he would have felt the same way if the roles had been reversed.

He tried to explain to Calvin that Rabbi Weissman was doing someone a favor. He even told Calvin about his parole and all. It helped some, but not entirely.

Calvin reminded him of his mother, a hard working, serious sort. She would also have told him to mind his own business about the goings on in the synagogue. They both would probably be clobbering him right now if they knew what he was up to.

Calvin was big, muscular, well defined, and looked as if he spent a lot of time lifting weights. He had a crew cut, and a bushy mustache, both of which were starting to show some gray. And he was always sweating.

Joshua had told his mother about Calvin after his first day. He had pointed out that she would probably think Calvin was good looking, despite the fact that he was married. She'd told him to shut his mouth and mind his own business.

So here he was, sweeping a clean floor, watching this girl, when suddenly the classroom door opened and the men came out. Rabbi Weissman, who was among them, greeted the girl with a warm embrace and a tender kiss on her forehead. They shared smiles and a few words, and then started towards the stairwell, holding hands. As they walked past Joshua, the rabbi stopped to ask him how things were going.

"Good," he answered, trying to hide his anxiety. "Calvin's been showing me the ropes."

"Oh, by the vay, this is my daughter, Ruchel," the rabbi said, pronouncing her name in Hebrew.

Rachel, realizing Joshua's unfamiliarity with Hebrew names, politely interjected, "Rachel."

The sound of her voice was pleasing. Joshua managed a stiff smile, and said, "Hi."

She smiled back, this time with a bit more warmth. One could fall deeply into her emerald eyes, with no hope of returning to his former life.

"Vell," the rabbi said, "I'm glad everything is vorking out. Have a good evening and regards to your mother."

As they walked away, Joshua watched her from behind. He wondered if she knew he was watching, and figured that she probably didn't even care enough to think about it.

It wasn't just her beauty that struck him; there was something more, though he couldn't quite put his finger on it. Perhaps it was the ease with which she held herself, or the tenderness of her smile. Whatever, he had found it quite affecting.

And she didn't do anything to encourage this; on the contrary, he was certain she had no interest in him whatsoever. But that didn't matter, nor did the fact that she was the daughter of a Hasidic rabbi and he was a black kid working as a janitor. *Nothing* mattered, not even his sordid past. All he could think of was that he wanted to know more about her.

He promised himself he'd work late every evening.

CHAPTER 21

The first few days in the emergency room were exciting, though there wasn't much for Rachel to do. Doctor Schiffman had explained that they didn't usually have volunteers in the ER, for most of the work that was done there had to be performed by doctors and nurses. "Unlike the regular floors, patients are here only temporarily, so there's really no time to get to know them," she said as she scrambled from one treatment room to another with Rachel by her side. "That's what volunteers usually do: talk to patients, bring them books and stuff. But here there's no time for that. We'll just have to make up a job for you as we go."

Rachel followed the doctor around, taking in every word and gesture. At the start, she had trouble just keeping up with Schiffman's pace, but after a couple of days, she was well in stride.

"So what do we have here?" Schiffman asked as she opened the curtain to one of the small cubicles. Inside, a young Hasidic boy, not more than five, was crying in pain, sweating profusely, his mother standing next to him. Schiffman picked up the chart, turned to the boy and his mother, and said, "I'm Doctor Schiffman." She walked over to the boy, placed her hand gently on his forehead, and said, "Don't worry, everything is going to be okay."

Rachel saw the boy's mother eye Schiffman in much the same way her mother had when Rachel had broken her ankle. She recognized the woman from the community, but didn't know her name. It was another of the many faces she usually passed in the synagogue or walking the avenue. The woman seemed too preoccupied to recognize Rachel.

"He was feverish last night," the mother answered, reluctantly. "We called the doctor, Doctor Bronstein, and he said to give him aspirin. It helped a little, but this morning he woke up screaming in pain and the fever was worse."

The mother's mention of Doctor Bronstein prompted Schiffman to smile at Rachel, recalling the almost identical situation that had occurred when they had first met. Rachel returned the smile, realizing that this probably happened to Schiffman fairly often.

"Yes, the nurse who just took his temperature recorded it as 104.3. That's pretty high," Schiffman stated. "Did you call Doctor Bronstein this morning?"

"Yes, and he said to bring Shloimie here right away. He said he would meet us here," the mother added, impatiently looking at her wristwatch.

"That was good advice to bring him here. I'm sure Doctor Bronstein will join us shortly. Tell me, where is the pain?"

"I think it's his stomach, that's what he says."

It was difficult to hold a conversation with a screaming child and a skeptical mother, but Schiffman managed. Rachel observed how the doctor took control, and imagined herself in Schiffman's place. She liked the feeling that it gave her.

Schiffman turned to the boy. "Shloimie, could you point to exactly where the pain is?"

The boy complied.

"Rachel," she said, her eyes still on the boy, "where is he pointing?"

"His stomach." Rachel wasn't certain of her answer, and figured that if Schiffman was asking, it was probably a trick question. She was becoming acquainted with the doctor's style.

"Close, but not quite," Schiffman said.

The boy's mother was growing more anxious. She kept looking at her watch. Again, she asked, "Where could Doctor Bronstein be?"

Rachel wondered if Schiffman was ignoring the boy's mother, or if she was so engrossed in what she was doing, she just didn't hear what was said. Schiffman moved closer to the boy. "Shloimie, I'm going to have to remove your pants to examine you. Rachel, please help me."

The mother appeared stunned. She looked at Rachel, about to assist the doctor, and suddenly recognized her. "Aren't you Rabbi Weissman's daughter?" the woman asked.

"Yes, I'm working here for the summer, helping Doctor Schiffman. She's a friend of my father's." It was a small lie, but Rachel thought it might help set the woman at ease. If the doctor was a "friend" of Rabbi Weissman's, she must be "okay."

"Rachel," Schiffman said, ignoring the interchange between Rachel and the boy's mother. "I need you to help hold Shloimie still while I remove his pants. This is going to hurt a little," she said to the boy.

The boy started jumping around and Rachel tried to hold him down. As his pants came down, the boy shouted, "No! No! No!" He was embarrassed about his genitalia being displayed in front of women. His mother looked embarrassed as well. So did Rachel.

Schiffman kept her mind on business, palpating around the boy's abdomen. Cries of pain resounded. Then, she stepped away and recorded something in the chart. "Rachel, please help Shloimie get his pants back on." Despite his agony, the boy angrily pushed Rachel aside and did the pants himself. She turned away, allowing him his dignity.

At that moment, Doctor Bronstein entered. Schiffman turned to him and the boy's mother, and said, "Acute appendicitis."

Bronstein nodded as if that was what he'd suspected when he'd first heard from the mother earlier in the day.

"Oh my God," the mother exclaimed, "does that mean he needs an operation?" She looked at Bronstein for an answer. He turned to Schiffman.

"I would say so," Schiffman said.

Again, the mother looked to Bronstein, who gave his nod of approval.

At that moment, seeing the respect Doctor Bronstein had for Doctor Schiffman solidified Rachel's dream of becoming a physician. True, she already had what most Hasidic girls would pray for. Being the daughter of Rabbi Isaac Weissman had afforded her much homage in her community, and heaven knew the hordes of matchmakers lining up for her because of her father's prominence, offering the most pious of scholars from the wealthiest families for her to choose from. And her physical beauty—something of which she was becoming more aware—didn't hurt either. But, it all just wasn't enough. She wanted to be regarded for her intellect, not for lineage, appearance, or ability to be a wife and mother. She wanted to know that she, too, could use her mind to study and achieve all her God-given potential. Of course she wanted to marry a scholar and bring up her children as she'd been raised, but she also wanted more, and now she knew that with greater certainty than ever before.

The doctors conferred for a few minutes, then Doctor Schiffman requested an orderly to move the boy to pre-op. "We should operate as soon as possible," Doctor Bronstein said to the mother, who appeared unnerved, but nodded.

Rachel approached Bronstein and the mother. "Ah, Rachel," Doctor Bronstein acknowledged, "it seems you're doing well here with Doctor Schiffman." He wasn't surprised to see Rachel, for Rabbi Weissman had consulted with him about her working in the hospital.

"Yes, I'm learning many things," Rachel answered.

"Mrs. Glustoff," the doctor said, addressing the mother, "this is Rachel Weissman . . ."

"Yes, I know who she is," the mother reacted with a disapproving tone. Doctor Bronstein looked at Rachel, as if to say, *forget it.*

"Well, anyway," Bronstein continued, "I think you should go and call your husband. He should be here with you."

"Yes, I should," the woman repeated. She appeared stupefied, unable to accept any of this—her son with appendicitis, a female doctor, the rabbi's daughter—it was all too much to handle.

Bronstein showed the mother to a phone, and left Rachel standing alone. Rachel looked around, a statue amid the commotion. She liked the ER, and felt she could learn more here than she could ever learn in the women's seminary. And she *would.* She would go to college and medical school, no matter what it took. As for the condemnation from others, she would deal with that, for she knew there would be more of it to come.

Later that afternoon, Rachel met Esther at the hospital entrance, wearing her excitement.

"What's up, darling?" asked Esther.

Rachel proceeded to relate the day's events, but she could see that Esther's mind was on other things.

"So what's new at camp?" Rachel asked after finishing her spiel. Esther was spending the summer as a drama counselor in the Lubavitch day camp in which Rachel had spent previous summers.

"Oh, not much, really. The kids are putting on a play about Joseph, the coat, the brothers, and all that. I really wanted to do something with David and Bathsheba, but you know how it is." She held her hands up, gesturing quotation marks, "*It's not for the children!*"

Rachel worried about Esther's derisiveness. It seemed her friend was becoming more scornful of Hasidic life with each passing day.

"Don't be so harsh. Maybe it isn't a good idea for children to learn about David and Bathsheba, at least until they're old enough to understand the story."

"And *you* understand the story?"

Perhaps not, thought Rachel. "You know what I mean," she said.

"Yes, I suppose I do. But it just bothers me, all these rules and restrictions. And it bothers you too, *Miss-lady-doctor!*"

Esther had a point. Rachel kept quiet, not knowing what to say.

The girls continued on their way to the park. It was another dog day, perfect for their purposes. None of the boys would be wearing shirts.

They stayed in the park for a while, watching the boys, laughing, chatting, and eventually went home. On the way they passed four Irish boys, hanging out in the street. Unseemly types, obvious trouble makers. The boys noticed them, whistled, and offered a few lewd comments. Rachel became frightened, but Esther lifted her skirt, just a drop, to tease them.

Rachel hit Esther on the hand to knock down the skirt. "What are you doing? Are you crazy?"

"Just having some fun, darling. No harm done."

Rachel grabbed Esther's arm and dragged her along more quickly. At that, one of the boys ran up behind them and said, "Looking good today! Hey babe, maybe you wanna pick that up a little more, or maybe ya want me t' do it for ya?"

Esther turned around and blurted out, "Sorry honey, you're not man enough."

Rachel was shocked. She held Esther tighter and started running. The boy didn't bother after them, but yelled out, "You come back 'round here, and I'll show you how much man I am!"

Rachel promised herself that this was the last of their jaunts to that part of the neighborhood. From now on, she was going to have Doctor Schiffman drive her home from the hospital.

But Esther had other ideas, for she had actually enjoyed the confrontation. And while she knew what Rachel was thinking, she was confident she could convince her friend to reconsider. In any event, she was certainly going to try.

CHAPTER 22

Joshua managed to see Rachel almost every night. He even changed his routine, making sure he was working in the hall outside the classroom when she arrived. Her presence still made him nervous, even shy. He didn't know what to say or do to catch her attention. Usually, he simply nodded as she passed, and was rewarded with that same polite smile.

He sensed that Calvin was becoming suspicious. Calvin always left on time, just about when Joshua was taking the broom and dustpan up to the second floor. Earlier that evening, as Calvin was leaving, he turned to Joshua with a curious expression. *Yes*, Joshua thought, *he must know*.

Joshua predicted that Calvin's lecture would come the next day. He would deny everything, of course, and would have to be less obvious in the future. He wondered just how obvious he had actually been, if either Rachel or her father suspected anything as well. That could mean real trouble. *Heck*, he was used to trouble.

In any event, he wasn't sure how much longer he could keep up the charade with the broom and dustpan, and figured this was as good a night as any to break the ice. Lucky for him, she happened to be carrying a biology textbook. It made things easier.

"I see you're studying biology," he said, trying to hide his uneasiness.

She was taken aback, faltered, looked down at the book, then at him. "Yes, I am. I'm working at the hospital this summer and I was reading up on things."

"Me too. I mean, I took biology this past year." *Good*, he thought, now they were equal. *But not exactly*, he still had the broom and dustpan.

"Really!"

He guessed her surprise was because she probably didn't figure a black kid who was a janitor's assistant for biology. "Really," he said, "Ontogeny recapitulates phylogeny and all that." *I'll show her.*

She smiled, this time a bit more genuinely. She knew he was trying to impress her. "And what exactly does that mean?" she asked, a touch of cynicism in her voice.

"Is this a test?"

Now *she* appeared embarrassed. "Just kidding," she answered.

For a moment she seemed vulnerable, easing some of his anxiety. "That's okay," he said. "I'll tell you anyway, in case you don't know, or if you're confused about it or something." No harm in a little arrogance.

"You see," he continued, "it's like this. The embryo, that's like the egg that grows into the fetus. Well, it goes through all sorts of changes as it grows, sort of like real people, except it changes fast, and in weird ways too." He knew he was running at the mouth, but she was listening, *and ooh, that smile*. He couldn't help himself. "Anyway, as this embryo grows, and goes through those changes, they're the same changes that the whole species went through as we evolved. That's what "recapitulates" means, repeating the changes of the species. Cool, huh?" He knew all that studying would pay off.

"Yeah, cool," she repeated, a bit awkwardly. It was the first time she'd ever used that particular adjective.

"Bet you thought I didn't really know what I was talking about, huh?" He wondered if he was being too impressed with himself, and coming off like a jerk. She acted amused, so he figured he wasn't.

The classroom door opened and the men piled out. Rabbi Weissman emerged, and Joshua returned to his work. The rabbi glanced down at the book in his daughter's hand, seemed to disapprove, and asked, "Vhat is *this?*"

"It's a biology book," Rachel answered, trying not to be defensive.

"I thought school vas over?"

"It is, I'm brushing up on things for my work at the hospital."

"Vhat does this have to do vith your vork at the hospital?"

"Biology, Papa, is the foundation for medicine."

"Ah, I see." Reserved. Tentative.

Joshua, overhearing the interchange, found it interesting that Rachel's father wasn't pleased about the biology text. He wasn't at all schooled in the Bible, but knew enough to figure that all that evolution stuff in biology books didn't quite cut the kosher mustard. He'd never gone to Sunday School. His mother hadn't talked much about religion, and they seldom attended church. He had, however, learned a lot about the subject from TV, particularly the movie *Inherit the Wind* with Spencer Tracy and Katharine Hepburn. Tracy played a lawyer defending a school teacher for teaching evolution, and Hepburn, as usual, played Tracy's lady. Joshua had enjoyed the movie, and even fantasized about one day being a lawyer himself. When he watched cops, he wanted to be a cop; when he watched lawyers, he wanted to be a lawyer. He never really wanted to be a criminal, but he just never saw any black lawyers or cops on TV.

There seemed to be much unspoken between Rachel and her father. Rachel's face carried a look of determination, and the rabbi's bore one of fear. Joshua suspected that Rachel wasn't typical.

As Rachel and the rabbi walked toward the stairs, Joshua looked down. He concentrated on his work and pretended not to notice them. "Good night, Joshua," Rabbi Weissman said as they passed by.

"Good night, Rabbi," Joshua replied, lifting his head.

Rachel said nothing, but as Joshua watched them leave, she turned and caught his eye. Then she quickly turned again, so her father wouldn't notice. And as they disappeared into the stairwell, Joshua wondered what other little secrets she kept from her father.

CHAPTER 23

Midnight, an early-summer heat wave. A small dormitory room with no air conditioning, windows wide open. Clamor from the traffic outside, the forever bustling Eastern Parkway. Paul Sims lay in bed, restless, staring at the ceiling, sweating, mulling over his latest conundrum.

He had just turned eighteen, the customary age of marriage for men in the Hasidic world, and he knew that it was also time for Rachel's parents to be seeking a *shiddoch* for their daughter. He couldn't bear the thought of losing her to another. So he obsessed, tossed and turned. Nothing unusual, just another thing keeping him awake.

For weeks he'd been unable to concentrate on his studies. Even during the summer, the demands of yeshiva life were endless. Time usually spent on secular studies was now devoted to additional religious studies. There was never a break from learning God's word.

It was a Saturday night. *Shabbos* ended quite late this time of year, a little after nine-thirty, and from ten till twelve there'd been the usual evening study session in the *Beis Midrash*, where Paul and his colleagues reviewed their Talmudic lessons, usually in groups of two or three. The following day, Sunday, was just another ordinary day in the yeshiva, not a day off as it had been in Hewlett Bay Academy. Paul was growing weary.

He considered taking tomorrow off, but was reticent. Not because he would get in trouble, but because his absence would be noted and an explanation required. He pondered that, still staring at the ceiling.

His plan was to disappear for the morning, maybe take a walk, clear his head, just get away from all this for a while. He was feeling stifled. He even thought about visiting Loretta. He'd been in Crown Heights for almost five months and hadn't visited her yet. He missed her, and often considered dropping by, but still hadn't gotten around to it.

It seemed like a good idea now. He figured he could go over there at around ten-thirty a.m., late enough for a Sunday visit. First, morning prayers with the yeshiva's *minyan*, then breakfast in the dining room, then the disappearing act. Maybe a stroll past Rachel's building—*one never knows who might be outside!* Eventually, Loretta's place. He had her address, she'd given it to him when he left home. "Come any time," she'd said, "We live right there, and I'd love for you to finally meet Joshua."

Meeting Joshua. Paul wondered what that would be like. He felt as if he'd known Joshua his entire life, yet they'd never seen one another in person. Notwithstanding the few pictures that Loretta showed him through the years, he was sure he wouldn't recognize Joshua, even if they passed on the street, which—he would soon discover—had actually already happened.

⸙

He rang the buzzer for the Eubanks' apartment, and waited. A faint, muffled voice came through the intercom, asking who it was. He could barely make it out, the intercom was definitely in need of repair. As was the cracked glass on the front door, the chipped tile on the walls, and the busted up mail boxes in the lobby.

He thought he recognized the building from several years ago, when his father had taken him along to collect rent, the only time he'd ever gone to work with Alfred. At first, he wasn't sure. He was thrown by the disrepair and neglect. But after some scrutiny, he became certain. This *was* one of his father's buildings. *Why were Loretta and Joshua living here,* he wondered. No one had ever told him about this.

"It's Pinchas, I mean *Paul* Sims," he shouted, figuring the reception on the other end was probably just as bad.

The door buzzer sounded, and he entered. *At least that works,* he told himself, approaching the elevator.

A few moments later, he was standing in a dim, musty hallway, facing the door to Loretta Eubanks' home. He reached for the buzzer, wondering why he hadn't come sooner. It was strange, considering that she was the woman who'd practically raised him. *Strange indeed*, he mused, being so close to a person in some ways, yet so removed in others.

He pressed the buzzer, and listened to the latches turning, wondering if it was Loretta or Joshua on the other side. He didn't have much time to think about it before the door opened.

It was Joshua.

◦≫◦

Paul froze. He didn't believe his eyes, he immediately recognized Joshua as the "black kid" who worked in the synagogue. Now, looking at him more closely, Paul could see the remarkable resemblance to Loretta: tall, slender, handsome.

Joshua, however, didn't recognize the young man, who appeared to him basically indistinguishable from the myriad of Hasidim he saw every day. He had occasionally wondered if one or another might be Paul, but the face before him was not one of those he had seen before.

They studied each other for a long, awkward moment, until Paul held his hand out and said, "Hi, I'm Pinchas Sims."

Joshua offered a tense hand, responding, "I'm Joshua."

A voice from inside the apartment yelled, "Joshua, if that's Paul, invite him in!"

Joshua stepped aside, gesturing for Paul to enter. Paul walked in, and looked around. Loretta came out of the kitchen, stopped a few feet from Paul, and thundered, "Well, I'll be! Take a look at you!"

Paul was self conscious, realizing that his getup made him look quite different from the last time she'd seen him. He smiled uneasily.

Loretta stepped up and gave him a hug. "It's been a long time!" she said.

"It has," Paul agreed. "I'm sorry I didn't visit sooner."

"I see you met Joshua," she said.

Paul and Joshua simply looked at one another.

"Why don't we all go sit in the living room," Loretta suggested, leading the way. "Would you like a cold drink?"

"I'll have some water," Paul answered.

Loretta smiled, knowing that Paul chose the water because it was kosher. She got up and went into the kitchen.

Paul and Joshua sat in the living room. The silence was unnerving. He wished he hadn't come. The animus in Joshua's eyes didn't help.

"I've heard a lot about you over the years," Paul said, his voice frail, equivocal.

"Me too," Joshua answered. Forced civility.

Paul didn't know what to say next. "I guess you've heard that I'm in school just a few blocks from here?"

Joshua nodded.

"I see you around sometimes in *shul*, I mean synagogue."

"I *know* what a *shul* is."

Paul nodded apologetically. "I'll bet you probably know a lot of Yiddish words by now."

"Some."

"Do you like it?"

"Like what?

"Working in the *shul*."

"It's okay."

Loretta's reentrance seemed a welcome reprieve to both boys. "Here's some water for you, Paul, and some soda for Joshua." She placed a serving tray on a frayed oak coffee table.

Paul leaned forward, took his glass, sat back on the couch, and looked around the dimly lit room. He tried to be subtle, but wasn't doing a very good job. It was obvious that he wanted to see how the "other half" lived.

It was clean, of course; he'd expected no less from the woman who kept his mother's house. The furniture was worn and rickety, and the paint on the walls was peeling. The dull green vinyl couch on which he sat had seen much use, its torn surfaces covered by a large, hand-knit, rust-colored woolen blanket. The decaying wood floor was covered by a threadbare brown rug to prevent splinters. He concealed his dismay.

"So you boys were talking while I was in the kitchen?"

"Yes, we were," Paul answered.

Joshua remained silent.

"I've actually seen Joshua in the synagogue," Paul said.

"And you *didn't* known it was *him*?"

"Exactly."

"That's funny all right, don't you think, Joshua?"

"Guess so." Impassive.

If looks could talk, the one Loretta gave Joshua would have said, *Get conversational!*

"How are my parents doing?" Paul asked.

"You haven't talked to them?"

"Once in a while I call, but you see them every day." He was discomfited by the question; he'd barely spoken with them at all recently. He knew that Loretta had known this, for there was nothing in the Sims' home that escaped her awareness. She was only trying to drop a hint for him to be more mindful about being in touch with them.

"They've been okay," she said, "but your mother's been acting a bit strange lately."

"What do you mean?"

She looked at Joshua, wondering if it was appropriate to discuss this in his presence. She knew he was just waiting for an excuse to leave, and didn't want to give him one. Reluctantly, she responded, "Well, she's been real quiet, keeping to herself all the time. She hasn't been going out much, and she doesn't ask for much either. I think she's got a touch of melancholy."

"I think I will call her later," Paul said, knowing that he wasn't really going to, and suspecting that Loretta knew it too.

"Can I bring you another drink?" Loretta asked.

"Not really, thank you. I have to get going. I have to be back for lunch and afternoon classes."

"Oh," Loretta said, seemingly disappointed that the boys didn't get time to talk.

Paul rose from the couch. "Well, it was good finally meeting you," he told Joshua, as he held out his hand.

"Good meeting you," Joshua replied indifferently.

Loretta led the way to the door, opened it, and embraced Paul. "Now you know where I live," she said. "Come *anytime*, whenever you want!" Her eyes welled up, as if she knew it would be a while before she would see him again.

⟨≈⟩

Joshua stood beside his mother, observing her sadness as Paul walked down the hallway to the elevator. He had always been jealous of Paul Sims, for all Paul had, and for the way his mother felt about Paul. But now, it was no longer jealousy that he felt. It was something much more venomous, albeit equally primitive, a feeling with which he was becoming increasingly more familiar as his life progressed: hatred.

CHAPTER 24

Rachel Weissman thought it was a bad idea, but she went along anyway. Not because Esther Mandlebaum had promised it would be the last time—Esther's promises held little credibility—but for her own adventure. There was no denying it, the boys in the park enticed her.

So there they were, Rachel and Esther, despite their last encounter, en route to the park. It was mid-October, and Indian summer temperatures were well into the seventies: perfect for the occasion. Perhaps this *would* be their final excursion, for the days would soon grow cold.

It was just after school, and Rachel wasn't scheduled for the hospital that afternoon. She worked with Doctor Schiffman only two afternoons a week—a compromise she'd arrived at with her parents. She was glad for even that, considering her father's apprehension. But she had stood her ground, and her mother's silence on the matter had helped as well. Isaac Weissman was becoming weary of losing such battles, but his love for his daughter seemed to soften the blow.

They sat on a bench, pretending—however poorly—not to ogle. They teased one another, trying to enhance the pleasure of this final performance, masking their embarrassment at the thought that the boys might be on to them. And then it was over. The sun had fallen behind the buildings bordering the west end of the park, and the coolness of the night began to settle in. The crowd on the courts was thinning, and for Rachel and Esther it was time to go home. They looked at each other with sadness.

"Well, I guess that's it," Esther said.

Rachel knew how important all this was to Esther—not only because of the boys, but because of their strengthening bond and mutual act of defiance. She knew it because she felt it too. "Yes, I suppose so," she sighed. "I'm glad we did this today."

They stood up. Rachel picked her sweater up from the bench, and draped it over her shoulders. "It's getting chilly," she said.

"Yeah, I know."

They walked slowly to the park's exit, and as they came out, Rachel said, "Do you think we should take a different route this time."

They looked at one another—the sort of look that only the closest of friends understand. They would return home the same way they always had. They weren't going to be intimidated. One last act of defiance.

Determined yet cautious, they started down Crown Street. All was quiet for a short while, till they reached the middle of the block and heard familiar voices up behind them. It was too late to turn back.

"Well, look what we got here," one of the boys said while the others chuckled.

"Hey Tim, ain't these those kike bitches we run into a few weeks ago," another added.

Rachel took Esther's hand as they hastened their pace. But the boys closed in quickly and jumped in front of them.

Rachel scrutinized the four faces, trying to get a good look at each one, hiding her terror. Esther was starting to quiver. One of the boys looked at Esther with a snide grin, and said, "You afraid of something, honey?"

Rachel tugged Esther's hand. "No," she answered, "she's not afraid of anything, so why don't you go on and find someone who is!"

"Ooh, nice voice, sexy," the one named Tim said, stepping forward and moving into Rachel's face. Rachel figured him for the leader of the pack by the way the others stepped aside. She wondered if she should act scared, let them get their laughs, and maybe they would be on their way. She didn't know what was best, she just did what came naturally. She didn't retreat.

The one who was looking at Esther said, "I bet you *are* scared, real scared," as he reached over and put his arm around her. Rachel grabbed her friend and pulled her away from him, as Esther let out the loudest scream Rachel had ever heard.

Joshua kept his summer job after school started, working four afternoons each week. His probation officer liked the fact that he had somewhere to go; his mother liked it that her son was being responsible; he liked seeing Rachel Weissman. Everyone was satisfied.

Calvin had let him off a few hours early this evening to study for a test. Loretta had suggested Joshua skip work altogether, but he had been keeping up nicely with his schoolwork, and he was confident he would ace the test. Loretta reluctantly agreed.

Joshua was strolling down Crown Street, taking his time getting home, thinking about Rachel. Since school had begun, he'd been seeing less of her. Her appearances in the synagogue were rare, and she seemed rather inattentive to him. It was always on him to initiate conversation, and he felt silly, especially knowing she was nothing more than a fantasy. But he just couldn't help himself.

He considered the possibility that this was all nothing more than a distraction from Celeste. Celeste was forever in his thoughts, as was his determination to free her from Big Bob. He needed a plan, but was sidetracked with Rachel. From one impossibility to another.

Suddenly, he heard a loud scream, a girl's voice. He looked down the block, and saw a bunch of boys surrounding two girls. For a second he thought they were playing some sort of game. Until he recognized the girls.

He didn't see anyone else around. He counted four boys. Bad odds. He considered getting help, but heard another shriek, this one coming from Rachel. There was no time.

One of the boys was grabbing at Rachel's breasts, while another held her. Joshua came up behind the one holding her, pulled him off her by his hair, while Rachel broke free from the other one.

Still holding the hair of the first one, Joshua wrapped his free arm around the neck of the second one, and brought them both down with him. They rolled around on the ground, Joshua kicking and punching with all his might. He landed a punch, hard into the nose of one of the boys, who cried out in pain.

The girls were screaming for help. They were free because all the boys were on top of Joshua. He tried squirming out from underneath, without success.

"Dirty little nigger!"

"We're gonna kill your black ass!"

They overpowered him and began beating him. The girls kept yelling as he struggled. Suddenly, he felt a piercing, sharp sensation in his lower back, a harsh burning unlike anything he'd ever known. He screamed, his agony nullifying everything else around him. Then, silence and darkness.

⟎

He awoke in a strange bed, his arms attached to tubes and a beeping sound coming from a machine close by. He looked around and saw his mother in a chair next to the door, asleep. He called to her, but his voice was weak. He called again, this time straining to be heard. She jolted to consciousness.

"Joshua," she said, hurrying to the bed. "Joshua, are you okay?"

"What happened? Where am I?"

She brushed his face with her hand. "Everything's all right, don't worry."

"Where am I?" He could barely get the words out.

"You're in the hospital. You've been hurt, but you're okay." Tears rolled down her cheeks. "You're tired, so rest now. We'll talk later."

He *was* tired. His entire body ached, except for his left leg, which he couldn't feel at all. It was as if the leg wasn't there.

"Mama, I can't feel my leg."

"I know," she said. "Don't worry about that." More tears. "It's the middle of the night, go back to sleep. I'll be right here. We'll talk about everything in the morning."

He was freaking over the leg; it was obvious she knew something and wasn't telling him. He tried to move it, and couldn't, so he reached down to touch it. His arm and shoulder ached, every movement was tormenting. He finally had his hand on his leg, confirming it was still there. He was relieved, somewhat.

Loretta stood over him, coaxing him back to sleep. The drugs were strong, and he was finding it difficult to stay awake. He wanted to know more about the leg. She kept telling him to stop worrying and get some rest. Against his will, he found himself obeying her, drifting off into the darkness from which he'd emerged. It was a safe place, so it seemed.

The next time he came to, the room was bright and crowded. His vision was blurred, his eyes stinging from the light. He was still too groggy to make out the various voices. It took a few minutes, but gradually everything became clearer. He remembered where he was, and saw his mother, beside the bed, standing next to a strange woman in a white coat.

At the foot of the bed was someone else he knew: Rabbi Weissman. Next to the rabbi was Rachel and another girl. He thought for a moment, then recognized the girl as Rachel's friend. He was beginning to remember some aspects of the incident—a good sign. But he still couldn't feel his leg—a bad sign.

"Joshua, you're awake!" Loretta said. Her enthusiasm made him worry even more.

"Mama." He looked only at her, as if no one else was in the room.

"Yes, Joshua."

"I still can't feel my leg."

Loretta was about to say something, when the woman in the white coat interrupted, "Joshua, I'm Doctor Schiffman. I'm the doctor who admitted you."

He turned to her and asked, "Why can't I feel my left leg?"

"That's what I'm here to find out," she answered.

She was about to remove the bed sheet to start her examination, when the Rabbi signaled her to wait. "Joshua," he said, "you have done a great *mitzvah*, a great deed. You have saved my daughter, Rachel, and her friend Esther from harm, and I vant you should know that you are a hero. Ve vill not forget this, never." The rabbi began to weep.

Rachel put her arms around her father. "Don't worry, Papa," she said, "everything's all right, we're okay." She wiped his tears with her hand.

"Yes," the rabbi said, "you *are*, thanks to Joshua."

"Excuse me," the doctor interjected, "but I really must examine Joshua now. I think it would be best if everybody left the room except for Mrs. Eubanks."

"Miss. Eubanks," Loretta corrected. It was just like her to make sure folks got things straight, even at a time like this.

"Yes, ve vill leave," the rabbi said as he stepped closer to Joshua, reached out, and put his hand on Joshua's forehead. "But ve vill be back to visit our hero, and ve vill be here for anything you need. He turned to Loretta, took her hand with both of his, and added, "Anything you need!"

With that, the rabbi walked out, Rachel and Esther following. As she was about to exit, Rachel turned her head to Joshua and mouthed the words, "Thank you."

No one else seemed to notice this private exchange between them. He was pleased by it, but his mind was really on his leg and the doctor's examination.

"Let's see what we have here," she stated, lifting the sheet. "Now, Joshua, I'm going to ask you some questions, and I'm also going to ask you to do some things for me. Just try to do your best."

He nodded. Loretta stood by, watching closely. Her expression made him nervous.

"First," Doctor Schiffman said, "has anyone told you what happened to you?"

"No!"

Schiffman looked at Loretta with surprise. "He just woke up," Loretta said defensively. "You see that for yourself."

"But you told me that he also awoke during the evening," the doctor stated.

"I couldn't tell him then," Loretta answered.

"Tell me *what?*"

"Joshua, when you were fighting with those boys in the street, one of them stabbed you," the doctor said.

"*Stabbed me!* Where?"

"In the back, I'm afraid. That's why you're having that problem with your left leg. You see, there are nerves that run from your back into your legs, and it seems that the knife went into one of these nerves and damaged it."

"What does that mean? I'll get better, won't I?"

"I hope so, but it's too early to tell."

Loretta ran her hand through his hair. "Of course you're gonna get better, Joshua. You're a strong young man, and you'll be just fine."

In the past, he would have found her words soothing, but now he wasn't sure. Doctor Schiffman looked at his legs, and said, "Okay Joshua, I want you to wiggle the toes on your left foot."

His head was propped up and he could see his toes. They weren't moving.

Doctor Schiffman tried reassuring him. "Don't worry," she said, "I'm sure you'll do better tomorrow."

He found her unconvincing.

"Now try to move your foot around by rotating your ankle," she said.

Nothing.

"Try to lift your whole leg up in the air."

This time he struggled, turned, and pushed down from inside his gut. He created some interesting contortions, but produced no movement in the leg. Schiffman took a pin out from her pocket, and touched it to his big toe. "Do you feel a prick or anything?" she asked.

"No."

She proceeded with his other toes.

"No." Each and every time.

She worked her way up his leg, and as she got above his knee, he began to respond. The higher she got, the more he felt. "A good sign," she stated, noting her findings in his chart. Neither he nor Loretta asked just how good.

She performed the same examination on his right leg. He felt everything.

"It seems the only involvement is with the peripheral nerves on the left side," she said.

Joshua and his mother looked curiously at the doctor.

"Oh, I'm sorry," Schiffman said, looking up from her notes. "That means that the damage was only on the left side, and mostly to the nerves that affect the lower leg. That's good, it means that the damage is very localized, small and contained, which also means that your chances of recovering your feeling and movement are good."

"Are you talking about a complete recovery?" Loretta asked.

"It's hard to tell right now just how much of a recovery, but my gut feeling is positive."

Joshua was beginning to like this doctor.

Schiffman gathered her things together, and said, "I have to go now, but I'll be back in a few hours to check on things. I'm also going to have a neurologist come in. That's a doctor who specializes in this kind of thing." She touched Joshua's arm. "Get some rest, and *stop* worrying!" To Loretta she said, "You too!"

She smiled, turned, and left them alone.

❧

Later that day, Joshua awoke again from the darkness. Loretta's chair was empty. Behind the curtain, in the next bed, he heard someone groaning and snoring. The noise was annoying, but he was glad to know he wasn't alone.

It took about a minute for him to notice that there was a third person in the room, standing quietly in the corner. The room was dim, and his vision was slightly marred from the fight. He thought he might be hallucinating, that the medication was doing funny things to his mind.

But then, she spoke: "I told your mother to go home for a few hours, get something to eat, clean up, that sort of stuff." Nervous, jittery. "I told her I would stay." Hesitation. "That is, until she gets back."

It was her all right; he wasn't imagining at all. She seemed ill-at-ease, and he wanted to change that. He attempted a smile. "Thanks."

"You don't have to speak if it's hard," she said, approaching the bed.

The first thing that hit him was her scent, despite his swollen nose. At once, both calming and enticing. It was hard watching her stand there from a hospital bed; definitely not what he would have planned for their first real moment alone.

"It's okay, I can talk. It only hurts a little," he lied.

"Do you need anything?"

"No." He pointed to the chair. "Please sit."

She sat, and suddenly a tear fell from her eye. Embarrassed, she took a tissue from the box on the night-stand. "I'm sorry, I get stupid sometimes."

"You're *not* stupid!"

"Thank you, but I'm afraid I am. I should be thanking you for what you did, rather than sitting here, crying like a baby."

"I didn't do anything really."

"But you did, you *really* did. Those boys were out to hurt us. Who knows what they would have done if you hadn't come along." She hesitated. "You saved us."

"What happened after they beat me?"

"Well, they didn't exactly beat you. I mean, you got a few licks in of your own. One of them had blood all over his face, and another limped away."

"But what happened to *you*?"

"Us? Oh, nothing. Esther—that's my friend—she screamed the whole time, and I jumped in and tried to pull them off of you." Her tears stopped as she became more animated. "I think I actually got one of them square in the eye; at least, my hand hurts and all." She held up her right hand, proudly displaying the discoloration around her knuckles. "Anyway, someone must have finally heard what was happening, because two big men came over and broke it all up."

"And me?"

She hesitated. "You were unconscious."

"What about the Micks?"

"They ran away," she said, tentatively, fearful the news might displease him.

"Nobody caught them?"

"Not yet, but I'm sure they will. Esther and I gave descriptions to the police, and so did the two men. It's only a matter of time."

He became pensive; her story didn't make him feel like much of a hero.

"You really did save us, Joshua. I'm so sorry for what happened to you."

"I've been hurt before, been in lots of fights. I was okay then, and I'll be okay now!"

She got up, came to the side of the bed, leaned over, and touched her hand to his face. Once again, she began to cry. He managed to maneuver his arm enough to take her hand. Suddenly, his pain disappeared. She squeezed his hand slightly, just enough to let him know that there was now something between them, something undefined yet tangible. Something that bound them together.

The police caught the Irish boys the next day and brought them to Joshua's hospital room for identification. He recognized all four, but didn't know which one had actually stabbed him. He knew from TV that the cops had ways of obtaining such information and, in truth, he didn't really care. He wasn't out for revenge or "justice." He'd had more than enough of both for one lifetime.

The neurologist came. A real professorial type—bespectacled, balding, bow-tie, hushpuppies, and all. He repeated the same examination as Doctor Schiffman had performed, wrote his notes, and went about his work rather impassively. "Doctor Schiffman will be in to see you shortly," was all he said before leaving the room. Joshua sensed it wasn't going to be good news.

About ten minutes later, Doctor Schiffman walked in, a solemn expression on her face. She examined Joshua again. No changes. She looked at Joshua and his mother. "Okay, Joshua, Miss. Eubanks, I'm going to speak frankly now, because I don't want to hold out any false hope."

Dread fell upon Joshua and Loretta.

The doctor continued, "There's been significant nerve damage, affecting the left leg." She turned to Loretta. "Doctor Levy, the neurologist, agrees that we really have no way of knowing just how much sensation or movement Joshua will regain." Then, to Joshua: "What we do know, however, is that whatever you get back, Joshua, you have a long road ahead. I'm not saying that you're going to end up in a wheelchair or anything like that, but you are going to have to work very hard to learn to get around with that leg."

Loretta tried not to cry, for his sake, but that didn't stop him. It hurt for him to cry; it hurt to do just about anything.

The doctor waited a moment before continuing, "Now, we're going to keep you here for a little while, until we see how you progress. As soon as your wounds heel, you'll be transferred to the Rehab wing. That's where you'll get physical therapy, and we'll try to rehabilitate that leg. You'll have to work hard, it won't be easy. And there's no way of telling exactly what the result will be. Do either of you have any more questions?"

They didn't.

"Oh, there's one more thing," she said, looking down at the chart. "It seems every cloud does have a silver lining after all," she added softly, as if to herself.

Joshua and his mother looked at one another, not quite understanding.

She realized she'd lost them. "I'm sorry, I was just noticing in your chart that you're almost seventeen years old."

Joshua nodded.

"Well, then, I also have what I suppose you might call 'good news,' though at a time like this it's hard for you to imagine such a thing."

Joshua identified with the bewildered look on his mother's face.

"Under normal circumstances," Schiffman continued, "you would probably be drafted into the army in another year or so, and shipped off to Vietnam like all the other boys around here. Guess what?"

Joshua had no clue. What did Vietnam have to do with anything? Loretta seemed to understand.

"You're not going to be drafted at all," Schiffman said.

Joshua looked at his mother.

"I suppose that's good," Loretta said to him. "Some boys have been coming back from that place in worse shape than you, a lot worse. I suppose it *is* good."

So this was his silver lining, the saving grace of the single worst thing that had happened to him yet. And somehow, he thought, he would much rather have taken his chances in Vietnam.

<hr />

Rachel visited daily, even on the Sabbath. She told him it was a special *mitzvah* to visit the sick on the Sabbath, and the hospital wasn't a bad walk from her home. She was surprised he knew what a *mitzvah* was; in fact, she was surprised by all the Yiddish terms he'd picked up at the synagogue. He enjoyed surprising her.

After a week, he was transferred to the Rehab unit, where he stayed for over a month. He was receiving the best care possible, no expense spared. He was too preoccupied with his condition to wonder where the money came from, though on reflection he would easily have guessed.

Rachel continued to come every day. On the days that she worked with Doctor Schiffman, she would visit late, after her shift, and one of her parents would come to pick her up. Otherwise, she was with him for the entire afternoon.

Loretta was with him constantly, and knew he wanted to be alone with Rachel. Though she didn't exactly approve, she didn't want to make an issue of it, at least not now. So she managed to disappear for a while when Rachel showed up.

Initially, Joshua thought Rachel was visiting out of obligation. But with time, he grew confident that a real friendship was developing between them. He missed a lot of school, and Rachel took it upon herself to be his personal tutor. She was a whiz at math and science, and he was certainly able to hold his own.

She inspired him, and challenged him to do even better. He knew that when he returned to school, he would be far ahead of the other kids in his class, though he wondered when that would be.

His leg was improving. He had regained most of his sensation, but only some movement and control. During the three weeks on Rehab, he had gone from a wheelchair to a walker, and now he was even managing with a four-pronged cane. The therapists and nurses were encouraging; he had progressed far in a relatively short period of time. But he knew he would never walk and run as he had before. No one ever said it, but he knew.

And Rachel knew it too. Sometimes he felt worse for her than himself. He was always feeling bad for someone, and that included his mother as well. He saw the sadness in her eyes, and was certain that she, too, would rather have seen him eligible for the draft, war and all.

During his final week on Rehab, the therapists worked him harder than usual. They knew that time was running out. He was exhausted after the sessions, too tired for school-work. He also became depressed, his progress was slowing, and his reason for being there was ebbing.

On the second day of that week, Rachel showed up at her usual time, books in one arm, and her bright red wool coat draped over the other. The last time he'd been outside, it had been too warm for a coat. Now it was well into autumn; he could hear a harsh wind howling outside the window. Her cheeks were red from the cold.

"Come on! Snap to it, Joshua! We have work to do. We don't want you going back to school in a week being the dumbest kid in the class, do we?"

"I'm not dumb," he reacted, too sullen to even get angry.

"I was just kidding."

"I know. I'm sorry, I'm just not in the mood today."

"That's okay then, we don't have to study. We can sit here and talk, or watch TV, or do whatever you want."

"I want you to go." Not very energetic, but resolute enough.

"Why?"

"I don't know. I just wanna be alone."

A tear fell from her eye. "Joshua, I know you . . ."

"Please," he interrupted, "I just think you should leave."

She stood up, and slowly gathered her coat and books, almost clumsily. She turned to him, gave him a rueful glance, and started to walk out.

"It's probably best if you don't come back."

Saying nothing, she opened the door and slipped out. She broke into tears in the hallway, and ran toward the elevator. She wanted to turn back, go to him and make things better. Only, she knew she couldn't.

He lay in bed, helpless, wishing he could get up, chase after her, grab her, hold her, and tell her he didn't mean what he'd said, that he never wanted her to leave his side, that everything was going to be okay. But it wasn't. He was going to be a cripple for the rest of his life, no good to anyone, always struggling just to get around. His days of chasing after anyone were over.

CHAPTER 25

Several weeks later, Rachel Weissman came home from school to find her parents at the kitchen table with another man. They were drinking tea and noshing on Hannah's homemade honey cake. As soon as Rachel saw who their guest was, she understood why her mother had baked a cake for the occasion, and why her father had come home so early. She wanted to escape to her bedroom, but forced herself to be polite.

The man was Reb Nachum Blesofsky, one of the Lubavitcher community's most prestigious, and most "expensive" matchmakers. All the young girls in the neighborhood revered him, and every parent tried to engage his services, but Reb Blesofsky's talents were reserved strictly for those from the most scholarly or wealthy of families.

"Ah, Rucheleh," Rabbi Weissman said heartily, "Come in, say *sholom* to Reb Blesofsky!"

"*Sholom*," Rachel said, keeping herself from trembling.

"A beautiful young lady," Reb Blesofsky said, as if confirming something that had been discussed earlier.

Rachel could just imagine what their conversation must have been. The thought of it disturbed her. She had conveniently forgotten that it was time for her to start "dating," that many Hasidic girls her age were already betrothed. She wished she was little again, playing hopscotch on the sidewalk outside Esther's house, a fantasy she had been having quite often these days.

What has happened, she asked herself, thinking of the events of the past few months. Her life had become quite complex, far beyond her parents', or even her own wildest dreams.

She looked at Reb Blesofsky, not knowing how to respond. He was a middle aged, tall, dark-bearded, well-tailored man, who projected authority with his every gesture.

He is going to ask me questions, I know it, Rachel mused. *He is going to interview me, to determine if I will make a fitting wife for one of his scholars. And what should I tell him? Should I lie and talk about food recipes and stories from the Talmud, or should I tell him the truth, that I want to go to college and medical school, that I enjoy watching half naked boys playing basketball, and that my heart aches over Joshua, a black boy who once killed a man and used to work cleaning up in the synagogue?*

"So tell me, Ruchel, what are your plans after you finish high school?"

"Well, I hope to attend *Bet Rivka*, the women's seminary, of course." It sickened her to lie, but what choice did she have? She had planned to tell her parents of her true desires, but hadn't gotten around to it yet. She just couldn't break the news now, in front of one of the most influential men in the community, for she could never embarrass them that way.

"Ah, this is what I like to hear: a young woman who desires to continue her Torah study. It must be the influence of your scholarly father!" The two men exchanged smiles.

"Mama, I'm not feeling very well. I think I'm coming down with something. May I be excused to my room?"

Hannah searched Isaac for a response. He turned to his daughter, and said, "Of course, Rucheleh. Go lie down and your mother vill see you in a few minutes to check on you."

Isaac turned to Reb Blesofsky and said, "I'm sorry, maybe another time?"

"It won't be necessary," the *shodchin* stated. "She is a wonderful, God fearing daughter of Israel. It would be an honor to find her a scholar of unmatched intellect."

The rabbi and Hannah smiled at one another, then the two men shook hands as Blesofsky went on his way. The deal was struck, though no specifics had been mentioned. The rabbi wondered about that, but didn't want to push. He figured that Blesofsky knew that the Weissmans lived modestly, and even a small wedding—to say nothing of a matchmaker's fee—would be a hardship.

"So this scholar of unmatched intellect and character vill also have to be from a rich family," the rabbi said to Hannah as they were clearing the table.

She laughed; he was always able to make her laugh.

∞

Lying in her bed, Rachel thought of Joshua. It had been two months since she'd seen him. She had returned to the hospital once, after he'd asked her not to, but Doctor Schiffman had caught her in the hall, outside his room, and had advised against going in. Apparently, Joshua had shared some things with the doctor.

"You must understand, Rachel, that Joshua is going through a rough time right now, it would be best to give him some space," the doctor had said.

Rachel hadn't wanted to listen to Schiffman, even though the doctor made sense. "Do you think I can come back in a few days?"

"I believe that's probably too soon. If you want the truth, I think you should wait for Joshua to contact you. I'm sure he will, when he's ready."

"But what if he doesn't?"

"He will." With that, Schiffman took Rachel by the arm and began leading her down the hall. "Come, we *do* have other patients to attend to."

Rachel complied. She trusted Schiffman's judgment. She knew that the doctor had been observing her and Joshua over the weeks, and wondered what Schiffman thought about them.

Rachel wasn't sure why she needed the doctor's approval. Perhaps because she knew she would never have anyone else's, or maybe because Schiffman's opinion mattered most. Either way, hearing those two simple words—*he will*—had gone a long way toward lifting her spirits.

And now, two months later, still nothing from Joshua. So many times she had thought about contacting him. It wasn't easy to defy Doctor Schiffman's advice, to ignore the woman she idolized. But after seeing her parents with the *shodchin*, she knew she couldn't wait any longer. Despite her confusion and fear, having no idea what she wanted from Joshua or why she craved his presence, she would go to him tomorrow.

❧

News travels quickly in the Hasidic world, so it wasn't long before Paul Sims learned that the Weissmans had enlisted the services of Reb Nachum Blesofsky. Just two hours after the *shodchin* had left the Weissmans' home, the yeshiva was charged with gossip.

"What do you think, Sims, will it be you?" one of his classmates jested, while several others stood around chuckling.

"Well, I can assure you, Novitsky, it *won't* be you," Paul responded.

It bothered him that his feelings for Rachel had become public knowledge, but it was his own fault. In his efforts to make friends, he had confided in one or two of the boys, believing his secret would be safe. He chided himself for not having known better, then quickly turned his attention to the more pressing issue of how to become *the one*.

He considered talking to the rabbi directly, but deemed it a bad idea. He was certain that the rabbi had long known of his feelings for Rachel; thus, the hiring of Reb Blesofsky could only mean that the rabbi had already dismissed him as a prospect. It was a painful realization, but he wasn't going to let it deter him. He would somehow convince Reb Blesofsky, and let the *shodchin* deal with the rabbi.

And that was what he set out to do.

❧

It was a cold afternoon, overcast and gloomy. Paul waited on the corner of President Street and Kingston Avenue, within eyesight of Reb Blesofsky's home. It was unusual for a *shodchin* to live in such an elaborate house, on the most affluent street in the neighborhood, but rumor had it that Blesofsky had married into money, an excellent way to gain credibility in his chosen profession.

Paul didn't have much of a plan, and didn't know whether Blesofsky was already in for the evening, on his way home, or on his way out. He also didn't know if Blesofsky would give him the time of day. None of this mattered, however, for he was on the mission of his life and had to succeed.

He had considered requesting an appointment with the *shodchin*, but was certain he wouldn't have gotten one. He was a nobody in the community. So here he was, standing in the frigid air, hoping to trap Blesofsky into talking to him. What he would ultimately accomplish by this, he had no idea.

Almost an hour passed. Paul began walking in little circles to keep from freezing. A few passersby gave him strange looks, but he didn't care. He would remain there as long as necessary.

His determination eventually paid off, as the *shodchin* emerged from the house. He'd seen Blesofsky a few times in the yeshiva, and recognized him immediately, walking tall, marching down the path from the front door of the house to the sidewalk.

Paul's anxiety heightened as Blesofsky walked toward him. It was now or never. He had rehearsed this moment a thousand times in his mind.

"Uh, excuse me, sir, are you Reb Blesofsky?"

"Pardon me?" The *shodchin* peered into Paul's eyes.

"I'm sorry to bother you, but are you Reb Blesofsky?"

"I think so." He looked himself over to make sure. Humorous.

"I was wondering, sir, if I might just have a brief moment of your time?"

Blesofsky wore a curious expression that said, *Well, get on with it!*

"My name is Pinchus Sims . . ."

"Is this about arranging a match?" Blesofsky interrupted curtly. "I don't deal with yeshiva students, only their parents. If you want something from me, your parents must phone my office for an appointment. *That* is how it is done." He turned on his heel and began to walk away.

"But that's impossible," Paul asserted.

Blesofsky stopped, impatiently glanced at his watch, and decided to grant Paul a few more seconds.

"You see, my parents aren't from around here."

"I know that, otherwise I would have recognized your family name."

"They're not Lubavitchers."

"What else is new?"

"They're not even Hasidic," Paul said, feeling humiliated.

"Are they Jewish?" Sardonic.

Paul hesitated, then answered, "They're Reform."

Blesofsky reacted impassively, as if he wasn't the least bit surprised. "Look, young man, this is not intended as an insult, but I don't arrange matches for *Ba'alei T'shuvah*. If you're interested in finding a wife, the rabbis in the yeshiva can help you meet someone from a background similar to yours. Things always work best that way. I hope you understand."

"I do, but I'm not interested in marrying just any girl."

"No one is, my friend." Blesofsky glanced at his watch again. "I'm sorry, but I must be on my way, I have an appointment."

"The girl I'm interested in is Rachel Weissman!"

The *shodchin's* pearly white flesh reddened; his eyes became fierce, as if Paul had mentioned his own daughter. "*That*, young man, is out of the question! I suggest you rid your mind of such *nahrishkeit* at once!"

"It is not foolishness," Paul replied forcefully. "I have known her for a long time, I have become *frum* and have studied hard to prove myself."

Blesofsky was dumbfounded; his world had no tolerance for such behavior. There were traditions to be respected, channels to go through, boundaries to be honored. For a young man like this to expect to marry the daughter of a man of Isaac Weissman's caliber was unheard of. He was inclined to admonish Paul, but decided on restraint. As one who had been dealing with matters of the heart for over thirty years, he was able to distinguish love from obsession. The way that Paul Sims had waited for him in the cold night, the expression in the young man's eyes—*this* was an obsession. Blesofsky knew he was confronting a delicate situation, one of those headaches that—without careful handling—could turn out tragically.

"Look, young man, what is your name again?"

"Sims, Pinchus Sims."

"Yes, well, excuse me for forgetting." Blesofsky waited a beat. "I can see that you have become one of us, and I think that is truly wonderful. I will even be willing to break my policy, and help you find a proper wife. If you ask around, you will find that this is an unusual offer."

Paul remained silent.

Blesofsky continued, "But surely you have been with us long enough to understand that in our community we do things a certain way. It is not at all that you are not worthy, or anything like that, but a *B'al T'shuvah* simply cannot marry someone from a family such as the Weissmans."

"And why not?"

"Because it is *not* the ways things are done."

"And I am just supposed to accept that?"

"Well," Blesofsky pondered, stroking his beard. "Why don't you look at it this way? In the Torah, marriage isn't always about love. There are many matches that simply cannot be. Like, for example, a *Kohen*, a priest, cannot marry either a convert or a divorcé. Now, this does not mean that a convert is less of a Jew, God forbid, for Rabbi Akiva—as you must know—was a convert, and he was one of the greatest rabbis of all time."

"But Rabbi Akiva would have been allowed to marry anyone he chose, even the daughter of a *Kohen*, for the marital restrictions of the priesthood do not apply to daughters." Paul welcomed the opportunity to display his scholarship.

"I can see that you have learned much while you have been with us.".

"Actually, I learned that before I came to Crown Heights. In fact, I learned it from Rabbi Weissman. He was my private tutor back in Hewlett Harbor, that's where I'm from. And if you're at all familiar with Hewlett Harbor, then you'll know that *my* parents can afford to pay you whatever fee you request."

"So you actually do know the Weissman family?"

"Quite well. I've spent many Sabbaths in their home."

"Then why haven't you spoken to Rabbi Weissman directly about your desire?"

"Because it is obvious he would say no; otherwise, why would he have come to you for assistance?"

"That is correct," the *shodchin* answered, "and that is what you must respect, what we *both* must respect. We should accept it and look for someone else for *her*, and someone else for *you*."

"I was hoping to convince you to persuade Rabbi Weissman."

"And I *am* convinced, convinced that you are a dedicated young scholar and most deserving of a beautiful, brilliant girl, which I—God willing—will help you find. But I cannot convince Rabbi Weissman, for he has already given us his decision by his behavior, no?" Blesofsky reached out, placed his hand on Paul's shoulder, and continued, "I am asking you to understand, and to trust me that I will find someone for you, someone so perfect that you will immediately forget Rachel Weissman."

Paul realized he was getting nowhere. He had no choice but to back down, for now. "Okay, Reb Blesofsky, I will try to understand. And I will accept your offer to help me find someone. But I must ask one more thing."

Blesofsky was pleased with his victory, almost ready to say, *Yes, of course, anything you want!* But, seasoned negotiator that he was, he held his tongue.

"I ask," Paul continued, "that you tell no one of our conversation, and that it remain strictly confidential so as not to embarrass me." Embarrassing someone was a cardinal sin in Jewish law, equivalent to shedding one's blood. Paul knew that a subtle reminder of this to Blesofsky was more than enough to insure secrecy.

"Certainly." Blesofsky was actually relieved by the request. He, too, wanted this entire matter to go away.

"Thank you," Paul said, extending his hand.

"You're welcome." Blesofsky shook hands with him. "And I will contact you shortly. One with a mind such as yours should be devoting all his time to his studies, while an expert like me finds you a suitable wife."

"Yes, I suppose you're right," Paul responded.

Blesofsky finally, and thankfully, went on his way.

Paul started walking back to the yeshiva, pondering the encounter. Blesofsky was smart all right, but not very likeable. Yet, in the end, Paul had to admit, the *shodchin* did have a point: the rabbi *had* spoken by his behavior.

Paul knew Blesofsky would keep his word about finding another girl, and he would try to have an open mind about it. It couldn't hurt. But he also knew that there was one thing about which Blesofsky had been sorely mistaken: no one on this earth would *ever* make him forget about Rachel Weissman.

No one, ever!

CHAPTER 26

Loretta Eubanks didn't recognize the garbled voice on the intercom, but she'd become accustomed to buzzing people in, so long as they simply responded. She figured, if they answered her, they weren't thieves. Thus far, the building hadn't had any trouble. There was no reason to be paranoid.

A few minutes later, the door bell rang. She asked who it was, again, and quickly turned the latch the moment she heard Rachel's voice. An enormous smile came to her as the two women faced one another. "Well, this is a surprise!" she said.

"Hello Miss. Eubanks," Rachel said nervously.

Loretta invited Rachel in, and showed her to the living room. Rachel looked around, wondering where Joshua was.

"He's in his room, where he always is these days," Loretta said mournfully. "I just don't know what to do for that boy. He goes to school, comes home, stays in that room all day, and only comes out for supper. Then he goes right back. Doesn't say much, either. I told him, 'Joshua, you have to talk to someone, you can't be carrying around all that pain by yourself.' But he doesn't say anything; he just goes back to that room."

"I came to see if I can help," Rachel said. "I want to see him."

"Well," Loretta said, contemplating, "if he'll talk to anyone, it's you. He's got a special liking for you all right. I saw it the first time I watched him look at you." She stopped herself; she was saying too much. She pointed to Joshua's door. "He probably already knows you're here. These walls are paper thin."

⌘

Overhearing the conversation in the living room, Joshua felt that he was ready to see Rachel, though he wasn't sure why. Nothing had changed these past few months; if anything, his depression had worsened. He still used a cane to get around, and he knew he would need it for the rest of his life, which—at times—he'd hoped wouldn't be very long.

He hadn't been talking to anyone, in or out of school, and his afternoons had all been spent in his room, studying, sleeping, or listening to the radio. He had even given up on finding Celeste. Yet, he had to admit that there hadn't been a single day in which he hadn't thought about Rachel. When he heard the knock on his bedroom door, his depression quickly turned to fear.

"Come in," he said.

The hinges squeaked as the door opened. He was sitting at his desk, facing the window, not quite ready to look at her.

"Hi," she said.

"Hi." Lifeless.

From the corner of his eye, he watched her walk across the room and sit on his bed.

"How've you been?" she asked softly.

"Okay, I suppose. You didn't have to come."

"I wanted to."

Silence.

He turned to look at her. "Why?"

"Because I missed you."

"I don't need anyone feeling sorry for me."

"I know."

"But you *do*."

"I do. But that's not why I'm here. I'm here because I like you." She faltered a moment. "I want you to be part of my life."

"What does that mean?"

"It means that I want to be able to see you, spend time with you, be friends, that sort of thing."

"That sort of thing?"

"Look, Joshua, I'm not going to sit here like this if all you're going to do is interrogate me. It wasn't easy for me to come here . . ."

"I'm sorry."

"It's okay."

"I guess I've been feeling sorry for myself."

"Sure sounds that way."

Another silence.

He looked at his bad leg. "You know, sometimes I think I deserve this."

"How can you say that?"

He thought for a second. "Cause I killed a man."

"But you were defending yourself; he was a horrible man."

He wasn't surprised that she knew, he'd suspected her father had told her. "Maybe so," he said, "but I didn't have to kill him."

"So you think you're being punished?"

"Sort of."

"Well, maybe God wanted you to kill him. Maybe you were God's messenger."

He looked at her askance.

"Do you know the story of Pinchas in the Bible?" she asked.

He shook his head, "No."

"Well, Pinchas was a righteous, God-fearing man, who killed another man for having forbidden sexual relations with a woman. And the Torah applauds what he did."

"I didn't see anyone applauding what I did."

"If I would have been there, I would have applauded."

She probably would have, he thought. It didn't mollify his guilt, but it was somehow comforting. He managed a smile.

She smiled back. Then, out of the blue, he laughed.

"Why are you laughing?" she asked.

"I can't tell you, it's stupid."

"No, you have to tell me. If we're going to be friends, we must tell each other everything."

God, she killed him. He just couldn't help himself in her presence. "It's the name, Pinchas." He had trouble pronouncing the *ch*, it came out more like a *k*. "I know someone who goes by that name, and he ain't nothing like that guy in the Bible."

"That's so funny," she exclaimed. "I do too."

"That's right," he said, realizing the connection. "You *do* know him."

She appeared bewildered.

"Pinchas, you *do* know him," he repeated.

She thought for a moment, then figured it out. "Of course, it's the same Pinchas. That's how your mother knows my father. They both worked for his parents."

Simultaneous smiles.

Such a small world.

CHAPTER 27

Rabbi Isaac Weissman stood in the doorway, wearing his nervousness. "Please, come in," the rabbi said, beckoning the young man into his home.

"Thank you," Benjamin Frankel responded, appearing equally uncomfortable.

They shared a clammy handshake and forced smiles. The rabbi took the young man's coat, and led the way to the living room where Rachel and Hannah were waiting.

"Hannah, Rucheleh, this is Benjamin Frankel, the young man that Reb Blesofsky has been telling us so much about."

A moment of silence loomed as Rachel's eyes met Benjamin's. *A pleasant looking fellow*, she thought. Tall, thin, dark-haired with soft blue eyes, and sharply dressed in a navy pin-striped suit, starched white shirt and burgundy tie. She took special note of the tie, a sign that he wasn't one of those rigid Hasidic men who refused to wear ties, fearing it made them appear like the gentiles. Seeing that he was more like her father, and some other Lubavitchers who were more liberal about such things, brought a sense of relief.

"My friends call me Binny," the young man said, as he and the rabbi took seats.

A gentle voice, Rachel noted. "My friends call me Rachel," she said.

The young man seemed to ease up a bit. Rachel had been told that this was also his first *shiddoch*, and that he was a shy sort. She had a sense, from the way he looked at her, that he was as pleased with her appearance as she was with his.

"So, your family is from South Africa?" Hannah asked, trying to make conversation. She had already known almost everything there was to know about the young man.

"Yes, there is a small Lubavitcher community there. My father is in diamonds."

Rabbi Weissman: "And they sent you here to study?"

Binny: "Yes, to study, and to be closer to the *Rebbe*."

Rachel had to admit she was impressed, though still apprehensive. She'd been told by her parents that he was one of the brightest rabbinical students in the seminary. *Should bode well for our children*, she thought fleetingly, and then it hit her—*children* would be what a man like him would want, *lots of children, as soon as possible*. And her job would be to take care of them, run after them, and keep the home. That, after all, was the Hasidic way.

She felt a sudden wave of anxiety. How could she possibly marry someone like Benjamin Frankel and fulfill her dreams? How could she tell her parents the truth without breaking their hearts? But she couldn't think about all that right now, it was much too overwhelming.

"It's funny, I've never seen you around the neighborhood," she said.

"Rucheleh, Binny is a rabbinical student," her father said. "He doesn't have time to hang around the neighborhood, or stand outside the *shul* on *Shabbos*, looking at the girls. He studies, eats, and *dovens* in the yeshiva! Yes?" He looked to Binny for a reply.

The young man nodded. The rabbi was quite accurate. In the Lubavitcher community, the rabbinical students were known to be isolationists. They studied, day and night, amongst themselves, and they held their own private services in the yeshiva on the Sabbath so as not to waste time traveling to and from the synagogue. They rarely ventured out for any reason, and the younger students often competed for the honor of doing their chores, for they were not to be bothered with mundane worldly matters.

Binny Frankel was well suited for such an existence. He was from a wealthy family, a large home with many servants, and had been catered to his entire life. There had been no pressure on him to work, so he was able to come to New York and continue studying for as long as he wished. His plan was to complete his rabbinical studies, and eventually join his father's business, setting up a branch in New York. But that would wait until he was ready. First, he would find a proper wife: an obedient, dutiful daughter of Israel. And it seemed to him, as he sat in the Weissman living room gazing at his first such prospect, that Rachel Weissman was perfect for the job.

⬥

Unable to sleep, Rachel found herself besieged with thoughts and feelings about the evening she had spent with Binny. The worst of it was that she had actually enjoyed herself. It would have been simpler if she hadn't.

Pictures of him passed through her mind; detailed images, the clarity of which rendered her powerless to ignore. Haunted by sensations of unwanted delight, what was she going to do?

In truth, it had been a rather short date—about an hour of conversation in the living room after the rabbi and Hannah had excused themselves; a walk to a small dairy restaurant on Kingston for some coffee and Danish; another walk around the neighborhood. Small talk, nothing serious. Tidbits of life in South Africa, happenings in the yeshiva, and the exchange of some extremely sanitized jokes.

At the end of the evening, he asked to see her again. It bothered her that she'd said yes so readily.

"Next week, perhaps?" he added.

"Next week is fine." A slight hesitation.

"Sunday evening?"

"Okay."

"I'll call in a few days, just to confirm."

He accompanied her upstairs to her apartment, and said good-night at the door. It was already late, and a good time to end the evening. She found her parents waiting in the living room, her father engrossed in a religious text, her mother perusing a newspaper. They looked up and asked about the date. Her answers were evasive, unrevealing, telling them only that she thought he was "nice enough," and that she would see him again. They were thrilled.

Despite the hour, she needed to call Esther. There were two phones in the Weissman home, one in the kitchen, the other in the master bedroom. She used the one in the bedroom and closed the door for privacy. This was nothing new for Isaac and Hannah; they had grown used to it, sometimes even *kibbitzing* about their daughter's idle chatter with girlfriends. This time, however, they were curious.

Rachel told Esther everything. She described Binny in vivid detail, and seemed to have lost control over her mouth while doing so. That was, until Esther's father had to make a business call. The girls hung up and promised to talk more tomorrow.

Now, lying in bed, Rachel couldn't get this young man out of her mind. Despite her efforts to find fault with him, she came up empty. *Don't worry,* she told herself, *I'm sure he'll give me a reason to be rid of him soon enough."*

She had to believe that. She desperately needed for it to be true, for she could allow nothing to stand between her and her dreams.

⁓

As consolation prizes go, Paul Sims regarded Chava Feuerstein as perfectly acceptable. The first time he saw her, he was surprised; he'd expected a real *meuskheit,* a homely one, as punishment for his audacity. He had even considered cancelling the *shiddoch,* but when Chava came to the door, he was glad he hadn't.

She was average height, had a pleasant face, curly brown hair, and a seemingly shapely figure, though it was hard for him to tell just how shapely considering the way Hasidic women dressed. She also had an inviting smile.

Their first date had seemed a bit dull, however. She didn't talk much, and he could have sworn she wasn't interested. When Reb Blesofsky had left a note for him to call her again, he was puzzled. But agreeable.

She was the daughter of a poor shoe salesman, and her mother suffered from manic-depression. Both facts placed her very low on the *shiddoch* list. Like Paul, she was eighteen, and she had already dated several boys from Hasidic families, all with situations similar to hers, but nothing had worked out. Now, she was agreeing to date boys from non-Hasidic homes. Paul was the first.

Reb Blesofsky was actually pleased with the match, despite the reasons for which he'd originally gotten involved. He had checked Paul out, and had learned that the boy hadn't lied about coming from a wealthy family. The only snag was that Alfred Sims would probably sooner strangle the *shodchin* than give him a nickel.

Paul's decision to see Chava again was partly because he'd heard that Rachel had gone out with Benjamin Frankel several times. He wasn't acquainted with the young scholar everybody referred to as "Binny," but he'd had more than an earful about the young man's wonderful qualities. The word was that Rachel and Binny would soon be engaged, and Paul was starting to realize that he needed, somehow, to get on with his life.

On their second date, Paul and Chava both seemed more self-assured, for each knew that the other was now there by choice.

"You know," Paul said, "things are much different in Crown Heights than I'd thought they were before I came here."

She looked curious about what he meant.

They were sitting beside one another on a couch in the T.W.A. terminal at Kennedy airport. It was the middle of winter, and there were few indoor places for Hasidic couples to go. Bars and movies were *verboten*, so the airport was a popular spot.

Paul had borrowed a car from one of his teachers for the occasion. The rabbis in the yeshiva would do almost anything to help their students get married. It was a great *mitzvah*.

"I mean," Paul continued, "I never realized how much of an outsider I would always be, no matter how hard I tried to fit in."

"I know the feeling." She almost whispered, as if she were talking to herself.

"You do?"

"Yes. In many ways, I'm also treated like an outsider."

"How's that?"

She hesitated for a moment, then said, "Well, my mother's illness, which I'm sure you've heard about, and the fact that my father doesn't make a lot of money. They discriminate against such things."

Paul had known all this, of course, but it felt good having her share it. "That's okay, my mother's crazy too," he said.

She was silent. At first, he thought he'd offended her, wondering how he could have been so stupid to say such a thing. She looked into his eyes; he couldn't tell what she was thinking. And then she started to laugh. Relieved, he began to laugh too.

He told her the story of how he had become a Lubavitcher, offering frank details about his parents, and even mentioning that he'd seen a psychologist. He talked about his relationship with Rabbi Weissman— which had been dwindling as of late—and he also brought up Rachel.

Of course, he downplayed his interest in Rachel, describing his feelings only in the past-tense.

Chava talked about her family as well. She, too, was an only child, and her father had to work very hard to support her and her mother, especially with the psychiatric bills. "He often has to work so late at the store, he doesn't get home till after ten. That's why you haven't met him yet."

"And why haven't I met your mother?"

"These days she doesn't get out of bed much," she said sadly.

Paul didn't know how to respond. After a few seconds of silence, he noticed an airplane pulling out toward the runway. "Come," he said gently, standing up, "let's go watch the planes."

She looked at him and smiled. It was one of those moments in which ordinary people might have shared a kiss or a tender touch, but such was forbidden for unmarried Hasidic couples. The smile would have to do.

⌘

By her fifth date with Binny Frankel, Rachel Weissman knew she was running out of time. In Hasidic circles it was expected that a man would propose marriage at this point. Prolonged courtship was frowned upon.

Rachel had known from the start that, by all objective standards, Binny was a catch. Fearful of hurting her parents, she'd played her role flawlessly. She would make the perfect wife.

"I want to live in a house, a big house," he had said on their third date. "I want my children to have a lot of room to run around, as *I* had in South Africa."

"Yes, I agree. Growing up in an apartment is less than ideal," she had responded, without letting on that she'd felt slighted by his statement.

"It's nice to have many children, a great *mitzvah*." This he had said on their fourth date, adding, "I don't believe in birth control. I know that there are some who practice it against the *Rebbe's* ruling, but it is wrong to prevent what God intended."

Rachel, too, wanted lots of children, as many as God would allow, for she had felt disadvantaged as an only child. She didn't appreciate, however, the assumption that *she* would be home all day, caring for these children and the home.

It was time to set him straight about her aspirations. Even if it would end their relationship—which she didn't want to happen—she had no choice, she could pretend no longer.

"Binny, there's something I have to tell you."

They were sitting in the same dairy restaurant they'd been to on their first date, at the very same table. He looked at her and realized that what she was about to say was serious. It was a blustery night, and there weren't many people out. They had enough privacy to talk about anything, and he had had some plans of his own regarding a topic. But she had beaten him to it, and by the look on her face, his guess was that his agenda would have to wait.

"I want to go to college." *There, I've said it*, she told herself. *The act is over.*

He was speechless, as if he hadn't heard.

"Binny, I want to go to college, and I also want to go to medical school." There was no way he didn't hear that.

The dumbfounded expression left his face. "Oh," he said, wearing his disappointment. "I see."

"I'm so sorry I didn't tell you sooner, but I . . ." She stopped herself mid-sentence.

"You?"

"I was afraid."

"Afraid? Of what?" His tone was serene, but she could tell he was shaken.

"Of everything, I guess. I know that this changes things, that you probably won't want to see me anymore." She became tearful.

He didn't know how to react. He felt deceived; he felt sad; he didn't want to lose her. He had planned to ask for her hand that night. And now *this*. Suddenly, he began to swell with anger. *How could you do this to me*, he thought. "How could you do this to *us?*" he said.

She was silent.

He stared into space for a moment, then stood up and gathered his things. "Come, I'll take you home," he said, putting on his coat.

Without another word, she complied.

They left the restaurant, and kept silent as they walked the three blocks to her apartment. At the front door to her building, he politely said good-night. She could see that he was trying to control the hurt that she had brought upon him.

She kept back her tears, turned from him, and walked into the building. She stood, waiting for the elevator, flushed with anguish. And terrified of how her parents would react.

⚬

The following morning, the phone rang in the Weissman home at six o'clock. The rabbi was preparing to leave for the morning prayer service at the synagogue; Rachel and Hannah were still in bed. Hannah was awakened by the ringing, but Rachel had already been up, she hadn't slept at all.

From her bed, Rachel was able to hear bits and pieces of her father's end of the conversation. "Vhat do you mean?" "Yes, I see." "Of course, I vill talk to her immediately and find out vhat happened." "No, you didn't disturb me at all." "I vill certainly phone you as soon as I know something myself."

After he hung up, Rachel overheard a conversation between her parents:

"Who was it?" her mother asked.

"Reb Blesofsky," her father answered.

"Well, what did he want?"

"He said that it is *ois shiddoch*, the match is finished, over."

"*Ois shiddoch!* How can that be? They seemed to like each other . . ."

"He said he didn't know vhy, only that Binny had called him last night and told him it vas off. That's all."

Sometime during their conversation, Rachel had gotten out of bed, and had walked to their bedroom. She was now standing in the doorway. They looked at her, waiting for her to say something.

"I told Binny last night that I want to go to college. To medical school. To be a doctor."

Lost in her own thoughts, she ignored their reactions. She held back her tears, and added, "I don't think he wants to marry me anymore." She stood there, almost dazed for a moment, and then began to cry.

Hannah jumped out of bed, went to her, and held her, trying to console her. Isaac remained seated on the bed, visibly shaken.

"Papa," Rachel said, regaining her composure.

The rabbi didn't answer.

"Isaac," Hannah called out.

Still blank.

"Come," Hannah said to Rachel, "we'll go to the kitchen and talk there." She began to escort her daughter to the kitchen when a faint voice said, "Vait!"

They turned and looked at the rabbi. "It vill be okay," he said. "Vhatever you vant, Rucheleh, as long as you are happy. It vill be okay."

He stood up, walked over, and held his arms out. Rachel stepped into his embrace, and wrapped her arms around him. They held each other tightly, wordlessly. Hannah watched, her heart feeling heavy. All that could be heard was their crying.

❦

Standing in prayer, draped in his *tallis* and *tefillin*, Rabbi Isaac Weissman was unable to think of God. He yearned for the serenity that his prayers usually brought, but his mind was distracted, tormented by images from the past. He knew he couldn't erase the images, he had tried to so many times and had failed. They were part of him, now and forever.

A room illuminated by candles; a familiar woman sitting across the table; a two year old boy sitting on his lap, tugging at him as he sang Sabbath melodies.

Flames from outside a window; a door burst open; soldiers storming in. A dark, crammed cattle car; a woman beside him; a boy in his arms.

Echoes of wailing; a line; hundreds standing in the cold; soldiers with guns; a man with a list in his hand.

A boy and a woman at his side; a man pointing to the left.

A woman and a boy being dragged away; a soldier's hand against his chest; a struggle; screaming.

Darkness.

He tried to reach into the darkness, to bring back the boy and the woman, just as he had tried so many times before. But, as always, his mind was empty, blank. They were lost in the darkness.

Suddenly, he felt tightness in his chest. Difficulty breathing. He sat down in a chair, and one of the other men in the synagogue noticed he was sweating and pale. The man walked over to inquire if he was okay. Some other men saw what was happening and gathered around.

"It's nothing," he said, laboring to speak. "I'll be fine, I . . ." He tried to catch his breath, but never finished the sentence.

❦

He regained consciousness in the hospital, lying in a bed beneath a plastic oxygen tent, tubes in his arm and electrical attachments affixed to his chest. Through the tent he could see the distorted images of his daughter and wife standing beside him. He attempted to maneuver his hand outside the tent to touch them.

"Stop! Yitzchak. Just relax, don't move," Hannah said.

He complied, resting his hand by his side. Then he tried to speak, but couldn't.

"Papa."

He looked at Rachel.

"Don't speak, Papa. You need to save your strength. You're going to be okay."

He managed a smile, more for her and Hannah than himself.

"Papa. I want you to know that I've reconsidered. I've thought about things, and I really don't need to go to college or be a doctor."

Her mother looked at her, astonished.

"I'm going to marry Binny, so don't worry. I'm going to marry Binny, and you're going to have plenty of grandchildren to look forward to. You just get well, okay." She struggled to keep her smile.

He wanted to speak. To tell her that she didn't have to do this for him, that he would live no matter what, that she shouldn't blame herself for what happened. He wanted to say all this, and more, but was unable.

A nurse entered the room. "Oh, you're awake, Rabbi Weissman. Good," she said as she came around the other side of the bed. "Everything is going to be fine, you've had a heart attack, but you're doing well and it's going to be okay." The nurse smiled reassuringly, turned to Rachel and Hannah, and added, "I think we need to let him rest now. The doctor will be in soon to check on him."

"Yes," Hannah responded, placing her arm around her daughter. "He needs to rest." She looked at Isaac. "Yitzchak, we're going to be in the waiting room down the hall. We'll be back after you rest." To the nurse, she added, "Would you kindly ask the doctor to find us after he sees him?"

"Of course."

Rachel and Hannah went down the hall to a small visitors' lounge. It was empty, except for a seemingly healthy patient in a hospital gown, sitting in a corner by the window, reading the newspaper. They smiled at the man as they entered, and he smiled back before returning to his paper. They sat next to one another on a couch, as far away from the man as the room would permit. Hannah tried to speak softly so as not to disturb him. "What is this you're saying about changing your mind?"

"I don't have to go to college, it's not that important."

"It seemed like it was important this morning."

"Things have changed."

"Look, Rachel, you can't blame yourself for what has happened to your father . . ."

"I can't?" Rachel interrupted. "Why not?"

"Because it's not your fault."

"Right." Sarcasm.

Hannah realized that her daughter wasn't going to listen to reason. She thought of postponing this talk until later. Rachel began to cry. Hannah reached over, took Rachel in her arms, and held her. The man by the window got up and left.

They sat for a few minutes until another man in a white coat appeared in the lounge. He was a short, thin, bespectacled, and balding fellow, somewhere in his early thirties. Rachel recognized him from around the hospital; she realized he was Doctor Levine, the chief resident in cardiology. "Excuse me, are you Mrs. Weissman?" he asked.

"Yes." Hannah stood up to greet him.

"I'm Doctor Levine. I'm handling your husband's case." He recognized Rachel and greeted her with a smile.

"How is he doing?" Hannah asked, skipping formalities.

"Right now, he's out of the woods. But I'm afraid he's had a rather serious heart attack, and it's hard to tell what will happen."

"What does *that* mean?" Agitation.

"Well, in situations like this, it can be touch and go for several days."

"You mean he may die?"

"I mean," he hesitated, "it's unlikely, but possible. We need to watch him carefully, which—I can assure you—we're going to do. I'm afraid that's all I know. Does he have a family doctor or an internist?"

"No, not really. None of us have ever been ill. We've always used Doctor Bronstein for Rachel, and once, when my husband had a bad cold, Doctor Bronstein gave him some medication, but that was it."

Doctor Levine listened without surprise. He was used to hearing things like this from the Hasidic Jews. They trusted in God a bit too much, he thought.

"Well, that's fine. I'll be following him while he's in the hospital, so there's no need to worry."

No need to worry; that's just great, Hannah thought. *My husband may die and there's no need to worry.*

"Would you tell Doctor Schiffman that we're here?" Rachel asked.

"Oh yes. You're one of her volunteers, I recognize you from the ER. I'll let her know right away. I'm sure she'll be up to see you." He turned to Hannah. "You can go back in and see him in about an hour, but keep your visits short. I want him to rest." With that, he turned and left.

Hannah walked over to the window and looked down at the street below. "I told him he was working too much, running too much," she whispered to herself. "I told him to take it easy, but he wouldn't hear of it. He just wouldn't listen. He's so stubborn, so *damned* stubborn!"

"I'm sorry, Mama. Now, Papa's going to be sick and your life is going to be hard. I'm sorry I did this to you." Weeping.

Hannah turned to Rachel and shook her. "Rachel, there's *nothing* for you to be sorry about. Your father is going to be fine! He's a strong man, and he's survived a lot more than this."

"I'm sorry, Mama, I should never have told him that I wanted to be a doctor. I'm going to marry Binny, I promise. I'm going to make Papa happy. He's had such a hard life; he deserves to be happy."

Hannah realized she was getting nowhere. *Rachel, my little Rucheleh, such a beauty, so smart, so much passion for life. And so stubborn, like her father.* They embraced, and as they turned around, they saw Doctor Schiffman standing there.

"I didn't want to interrupt," the doctor said.

"It's okay," Hannah answered.

Rachel was shocked, and wondered just how long Schiffman had been there.

"I just passed Doctor Levine in the hall and he told me," Schiffman said.

"We asked him to," Hannah replied.

"Is there anything you need, anything I can do?"

Hannah thought for a second. "No, but thank you."

"Doctor Levine is an excellent physician. He's the chief resident in cardiology. The rabbi couldn't be in better hands." She looked at Rachel. "If you need to talk, you know where to find me. I'll stop in on the rabbi often and make sure he's okay."

Rachel nodded, but was still wordless.

"I have to get back to work, but I'll see you both soon," Schiffman said. She placed a hand on each of their shoulders. "Don't worry, the Rabbi is a fighter," she continued, "He'll fight and win. He's going to be fine." She turned to leave, and added, "I promise!"

At that moment, Hannah Weissman finally understood what her daughter had seen in this woman doctor. She understood, and even felt jealous. But, more than that, she was proud. It would be no embarrassment to have a daughter like that.

❦

But Rachel would have none of it. Convinced of her responsibility for her father's illness, she was committed to doing anything to ease his life, no matter the sacrifice. In the scheme of things, marrying Binny Frankel, becoming a *Rebbetzin*, and having lots of children wasn't "all that bad." She could do it. She *would* do it.

Rabbi Weissman grew stronger in the hospital, and came home after five weeks. Hannah and he had frequently discussed Rachel, and they decided to leave things alone. They had mixed feelings about her decision, and wanted only for her to be happy. But they also believed that the true path to happiness was the Hasidic way. "Let us leave things in God's hands," the rabbi suggested. And that was what they did.

Binny was delighted. He, too, wondered about Rachel's sudden change of heart, but he chose not to question God's design. The engagement was finalized, and the wedding date was set for the middle of June. A wedding under the stars. The Hasidic way.

CHAPTER 28

Rachel told Joshua of her decision. During her father's hospitalization, she had stopped by his house often. He was her confidant, and there was nothing she didn't tell him. Including things she knew would hurt.

Deep in his heart, Joshua knew it could be no other way. He had his dreams, and wondered if she had them too. He liked to assume that she did. It was what he needed to believe.

Almost five months had passed since his injury, and he was hobbling around pretty well with the cane. Spring was approaching and with it, his depression was beginning to lift. He was getting out of the house more, and had even accompanied Rachel a few times on visits to her father. He liked it that the rabbi was always pleased to see him.

On the day that Rachel showed him her engagement ring, the reality hit. He became despondent. He had expected this sooner or later, but was still unprepared for it.

They were on a bench in the park. The weather was a little chilly and there weren't many people around.

"I'm sorry," she said, reaching over to touch him.

"Sorry about what?" Trying to appear happy.

"Sorry if this upsets you."

"Upsets me? Of course not! It's great news. It's what you want." It was a cheap shot, for he knew she wasn't doing what she truly wanted.

She was quiet for a few seconds. "I'll always love you, Joshua. You'll always be my best friend, even better than Esther . . ."

"Stop!" He put his hand over her mouth. "You don't have to say that. I know we'll always be friends. Come," he said, holding out his hand, "let's walk."

She took his hand, stood up, and then let go as they began walking. He hated that touching and letting go thing that she always did, but took it for what it was. He knew that she shouldn't be touching him at all, but also knew that she sometimes just couldn't help herself. He understood the last part only too well.

⁓

Spring arrived, and Joshua was feeling stronger. He had never given up on Celeste, nor his quest to bring her home. He was sure Big Bob had been moving her around, and had no idea where to begin. He would have to go back to square one, and knew it would once again take money. He was also a lot less confident about roaming the old neighborhood with his bad leg. It would be difficult if he had to move quickly. *What the hell.*

One day he removed the five one hundred dollar bills from behind his mirror, and stared at the money. He thought about himself, when he had first hidden the money. Had he really changed that much? It was hard for him to think so, standing there with the bills in his hand.

He knew five hundred wouldn't be enough, so he pulled one of his old school books from the shelf in which he had hidden his savings from the job in the synagogue. In all, it came to seven hundred and forty three dollars. He wondered if even that was enough. But it would have to do. And with what he was cooking up, he figured it might just work.

⁓

He waited, out of sight, across the street from the store for about an hour. He watched Bones doing his thing, collecting his money, and walking in and out of the store every twenty minutes or so. As the evening progressed, things got busier. He needed to speak to Bones privately, and was prepared to wait all night for the opportunity.

Just after two in the morning, Bones emerged from the store and started walking in the opposite direction from the corner. Joshua figured the pimp was calling it a day. He quickly took the money from his shoe, searched a garbage can and found a paper bag with rotted fruit in it, dumped the fruit, placed the money in the bag, and hid it under the pail. He didn't think it wise to have the money on him when he met up with

Bones, and figured he wasn't going to be gone long enough for anything to happen to it. Not his best idea, he knew, but neither was anything else he was doing.

He stayed in the shadows, crossed the street, and followed Bones as quickly as his foot allowed. It was a few blocks before he was sure he could approach. There was no one else in sight. His cane made it hard to sneak up on anyone, so he just hobbled along the sidewalk and called out, "Bones!"

Bones turned quickly, as if ready for an attack. When he saw it was Joshua, he loosened up some, and asked, "What you doin' here?"

"I need to talk."

"You know you could get killed, comin' outta nowhere like that. Truth be, you could get killed just hangin' 'round these parts this time of night." He noticed Joshua's cane and smiled his wicked smile.

"I know, I don't care."

"Right, you a brave one. Stupid too."

"Listen, I didn't come to get your opinion of me, I came to find the girl."

"What girl?"

"Look, if you're gonna bullshit me, we don't do business."

"Business? What kinda business you wanna do?"

"I've got seven hundred dollars says you know where the girl is." He needed the rest for cab fare home.

"Seven hundred dollars." Pensive.

"And no one has to know."

"Let's just see this money," he said.

"You think I'm stupid enough to walk these streets with that kind of dough at night?"

Bones didn't answer.

"I got it stashed, not far from here. You tell me where the girl is, and I'll tell you where the money is."

Bones was thinking. Joshua knew he'd sell out, but wasn't sure that seven hundred was enough. "What happened to your leg?"

"It's a long story. Not important right now."

"You already paid a lot for this girl, now you wanna pay more? She ain't even gonna go with you!"

"That's my problem. Look, we have a deal or not?"

"Yeah, okay, deal." Bones took the bait, seeing it as a win-win: seven hundred dollars he wouldn't have to share with Big Bob, plus his confidence that the girl wasn't going anyway. "One thing," he added.

"Yeah, what?"

"Whether the girl goes with you or not ain't my problem. Whatever happens, you don't tell her how you found her. Don't want her goin' and blabbing to the boss, if you get my meaning."

"I got it."

Bones told Joshua where Celeste was, and Joshua told him where the money was.

"Boy, you dumber than I thought." Bones said. "How you go off leavin' seven hundred dollars under a garbage pail in an alley?"

"Look, it'll be there, just where I say it is." He tried to sound reassuring. "I only put it there a few minutes ago."

"It better be."

❧

The instant Joshua saw the place, he wished Bones had lied. It was a drug house, an abandoned, rundown, decrepit building that looked like it had been bombed out during a war. The front entrance had no door, and the windows were either boarded up or barren.

He entered the building, and was immediately hit with the foul stench of decayed food and garbage. There was no light, and all he heard was the squeaking sounds of rats. Then, he heard something else: heavy breathing.

He followed the breathing until he stood over a young black woman, barely clothed, squatting in a corner, staring out into nowhere. He looked at her face, and thanked God it wasn't Celeste. His eyes adjusted to the darkness, and beside the girl he saw a syringe lying on the floor. It took her a while to notice his presence.

"Want somethin'?" she asked.

"Yeah, I do."

"Well, what'll it be?"

"Just some information."

"Information?"

"Yes."

"What kinda *information*?"

"About a girl."

"What's wrong with me that you interested in someone else?"

"Nothing's wrong with you, I'm just looking for a friend."

"Friend? I'll be your friend!"

He knew he wasn't getting anywhere, so he reached into his pocket and took out the last of his money, a five dollar bill and change. He gave her the five. She looked the bill over, and said, "A friend, you say. What's her name?"

"Celeste."

"Don't know no Celeste." She put the bill in her pocket.

He described Celeste, at least what she'd looked like last he'd seen her.

"Oh, you mean Cocoa!"

"Cocoa, I suppose so, if that's what Cocoa looks like."

"Sure sound like it."

"Okay, so where is this Cocoa."

"She's here."

He looked around and didn't see anyone else."

"Upstairs. One of the rooms upstairs."

"Which one?"

"*One of them*! What you think, I'm a hotel clerk or somethin'?"

"Yeah, sure," he said, turning away, looking for the stairs.

He walked up to the second floor, and heard more sounds: breathing, coughing, groaning. He began checking out the rooms, one by one. The first had two girls and one man, each sleeping in separate corners. He approached all of them, examined their faces, but none was Celeste. They were the living dead, so strung out nobody moved or even acknowledged his presence.

The next room had one girl. Again, it wasn't Celeste. The last room had two girls. The first was another stranger, the second wasn't. His heart stopped. It was her, or what was left of her. Disheveled and sickly, but definitely her. He shook her a few times. She didn't respond. He jolted her more severely until she came to.

She looked up at him. "Joshua?"

"It's me, Celeste, I've come to take you home."

"Joshua, is that you?"

"Yes, it's me."

"What are you doing here?"

"I've come to take you home."

"Take me home?" Her words came slowly, slurred.

He put his arms around her, and lifted her up to her feet. She could barely stand on her own. "My God," he said. "What's happened to you?"

"To *me*? What do you mean?" She sounded innocent, as if she really didn't understand.

"We'll talk about it later." He began leading her out of the room.

"Talk about what? Where are we going?" She stopped, resisted him, and suddenly came to life.

"Come, Celeste, I'm taking you home."

"I keep telling you, Joshua, I ain't got no home!" She spoke as if she'd had no sense of time, as if they'd just had this conversation yesterday.

"I'm taking you home with me, to my house."

"Your house. I can't go to your house. I have to stay here." She turned and started back towards her corner.

He grabbed her arm. "Celeste, you can't stay here! I'm taking you with me. You'll stay with Mama and me, and we'll get you some help."

"Help? I don't need no help!"

"Celeste, please! Just come with me. It's late, come home with me, sleep over, and we'll talk about it in the morning."

"Sleep with you," she said, moving in closer and rubbing herself against him. "Sure, I'll sleep with you."

"Not *with* me." He stepped away. "You can sleep in my bed, though. I'll sleep on the couch, or something. We'll figure it out when we get there."

"Get where?" She was losing it again.

"My house. Come on!"

"Sure, I'll sleep with you, Joshua. Anytime, cause you're my man," she said dreamily, ambling alongside him. The resistance had gone out of her. "I'll always sleep with you."

⌘

He had enough change left for both of them to take the bus, and thanked God the buses ran all night. By the time they got home, it was close to five. He tried being quiet, so as not to disturb his mother, but she was awake, and had been all night. Silly of him to have expected anything else.

When Loretta saw Celeste, her face turned crimson. "Lord in heaven," she gasped, bringing her hand over her mouth.

There was no need for explanations; Loretta understood. "I'm gonna let Celeste sleep in my room tonight," Joshua said.

"Yes, of course," Loretta replied, still stunned.

He brought Celeste into his room, and said good-night. "You're really not gonna stay with me?" she asked.

"I'll be right outside, in the living room."

He promised they'd figure everything out tomorrow, and went into the living room. Loretta was making up the couch. She looked at him, and said, "It's okay, Joshua, if you wanna sleep in the bed with me. There's enough room for the both of us." The couch was about three inches shorter than he was.

"Come," she said, as she walked into her bedroom. "It's late. You need to sleep, and you ain't gonna get any sleep on that couch."

He went in and lay down beside her. She turned off the lamp. "What are you planning on doing for that girl?" she asked in the darkness.

"I don't know."

She was silent for a while. "We'll figure something out," she said.

⌘

Joshua drifted off to sleep, only to be awakened by his mother's alarm clock less than an hour later. He opened the door to his bedroom quietly so as not to awaken Celeste. He might as well have been blowing a bugle because she wasn't there.

Loretta stood behind him. "Well, I'll be," she said. "Seems our guest sneaked out while we were sleeping."

"Seems so," he said, still looking at the bed.

"What are you gonna do now?"

He thought for a moment. "I don't know."

"Maybe it's best. That girl don't want help, Joshua, or else she would've stayed. There ain't nothing you can do for someone who don't want help!"

He knew his mother was right. Celeste was gone, and this time she would make sure he wouldn't find her. Suddenly, he felt himself unraveling. He couldn't stop the tears. Loretta took him in her arms.

"It's okay, Joshua. You did all you could. It's in God's hands now."

With all he'd been through, he couldn't remember ever having cried until now. And here he was, in his mother's arms, weeping like a helpless infant. He cried for Celeste, but also for himself, his leg, and his anguish over Rachel. For all the things he would never have.

CHAPTER 29

Rachel Weissman's engagement came as no surprise to Paul Sims. The blow was softened by the fact that things had been progressing well with Chava Feuerstein. He was trying to convince himself, and others, that he was okay, though he sensed that Chava had her own conflicts about him because of his background.

They had recently begun to discuss marriage themselves. In keeping with the custom of consulting the *Rebbe* on all major life decisions, they had sent a letter asking his advice, and had received a prompt reply with his blessing.

The most difficult part would be selling the idea to Alfred and Evelyn. While Paul had long forsaken any hope of gaining their approval, he and Chava would definitely need financial help. There was also the matter of Reb Blesofsky's fee, which in this case would not be able to be paid by the bride's parents.

Paul knew he would need assistance in confronting his father, but he had no idea where to turn. In the past, Rabbi Weissman had proven an effective ally in dealing with Alfred, but Paul's relationship with the rabbi had become strained by the situation with Rachel. He consulted Chava, and she suggested Rav Schachter.

"He is a great leader in the community, and has tremendous influence," she said.

"But I've heard he's a fanatic, that he doesn't accept people from backgrounds like mine. He would *never* approve of our engagement!"

"Those are just rumors from those who fear his influence. He has many followers, you know."

"Are you one of them?" Puzzled.

"Well, my father is."

Paul found this strange, considering her own predicament.

"Rav Schachter didn't make my mother ill," she explained, reading his mind. "He didn't create the prejudices that people have toward me because of that, either. In fact, he was the one who convinced Reb Blesofsky to help me. That's why I'm certain he'll help you."

Paul considered her point. "You think a man as important as Rav Schachter would take the time to speak with my father?"

"I believe that a man like Rav Schachter would seize any and every opportunity to do a mitzvah."

⁂

Rav Nachum Schachter's sanctum was a limestone house on the South side of Eastern Parkway, half a block down from the yeshiva dormitory. It was an impressive, three story building, in which the elder rabbi lived and worked, a shrine and gathering place for his followers, and a site surpassed in eminence only by the *Rebbe's* residence.

Paul arrived on time for his appointment, but still had to wait a good hour. When his turn finally came, one of the rabbi's assistants escorted him up three flights to the rabbi's study on the top floor. Paul traipsed up the stairs behind the assistant, failing to keep pace, and was more than a mite winded when he got to the top. The assistant, obviously accustomed to the stairs, offered a quizzical look, which Paul ignored.

Paul was led into the Rabbi's study, a small but well adorned room with bookcases, a large desk, and several hand carved wooden chairs, all of burnished oak. The assistant instructed him to take a seat.

Rav Schachter sat behind the desk, stroking his beard, scrutinizing his visitor. The rabbi was an imposing man, stout, with grievous brown eyes, bushy reddish-brown hair, and touches of gray at his temples and in his beard. The desk was orderly, except for a few open religious texts which the rabbi was working on. The rabbi closed the books, slowly and deliberately, and signaled for his assistant to shelve them. The disciple did as commanded, then left the room.

It was dark, and Paul felt like he was in one of those interrogation rooms he used to see in spy movies. The only light came from a dim reading lamp on the desk. Another, more substantial lamp, sat behind the rabbi on a small table, but for some reason, it wasn't on. Paul wondered about this as he waited to be addressed, apprehensive of what he might be asked and how to respond. He was tempted to get up and leave, but he froze. *This was a bad idea*, he told himself, though it was too late.

◈

Rabbi Nachum Schachter was a keen observer of human nature, and understood that the less men saw the more they feared. Routinely darkening his study before meetings, even with his closest colleagues, was one of many ways in which he maintained his edge, augmenting the mystique of his already revered presence. It was a necessary, albeit manipulative ruse to inspire fidelity among his followers. And most effective.

"So you are the one who is to marry Chava Feuerstein," the rabbi said.

"Yes, I am." Tremulous.

"Her father tells me you are a fine young man."

"I am honored to be entering his family."

"That is *gut*. The Feuerstein name is a worthy one. A pity it has been marred by such tragedy."

"Yes, it is. I hope to bring joy and honor to the family."

"*Gut*. Then what can *I* do for you?" The rabbi glanced at his watch.

"There is a problem, at least I believe there will be a problem, when I tell my parents of my intentions."

"You mean you have *not* told them?" Feigned consternation, for the rabbi had already been briefed on the purpose of the meeting.

"Yes."

"How does one become engaged without informing his parents?"

"In this situation, the circumstances are such . . ."

"Yes, I am aware of the circumstances. But when a young man leaves his home, for whatever reason, he does not forget to honor his parents, does he?"

"No." Sheepish.

"Then, you must tell them immediately."

"What if they object?"

"So they object. That is not the issue. You are an adult. If you want to marry, you should marry. But you owe your parents the honor of telling them, that is all."

"But I would prefer if they didn't object."

"And how do you think you can control that?"

"With the rabbi's assistance." Paul spoke to the rabbi in the third-person, as he had been taught in the yeshiva, not unlike the way a loyal subject addresses his king.

Rav Schachter reflected for a moment. "And what is it that you would like *me* to do?"

"Talk to my father, if it wouldn't be too much of a burden."

"You think that would help?"

"My father is a difficult man to deal with. He doesn't listen much to what I have to say, but he has always listened to Rabbi Weissman. He frequently disagreed with the rabbi, but he listened."

"So why don't you have Rabbi Weissman talk to him?"

"I don't speak to Rabbi Weissman that often these days." Faltering.

"Oh, I see." Hands stroking his beard. "And why, if I may ask, is that?"

Paul didn't want to go into this. He was surprised by how uninformed Rav Schachter was, surprised *and fooled*. He dismissed the issue, answering, "Rabbi Weissman and I have been having some differences."

"Your father, I am told, owns many buildings in our neighborhood."

"Three or four I think."

"Yes, I've heard his name." The rabbi stopped, and stared into space, calculating something in his mind. *This young man could be useful in the future.* "Yes, perhaps I will speak with him."

CHAPTER 30

Rachel's wedding was in June, and Joshua had the dubious distinction of being the only black guest among several hundred. He attended and held his head high. The ceremony was outdoors, under the stars, and the reception was in a catering hall next to the synagogue. There was a lot of food, music, and religious dancing. He couldn't dance because of his leg, not that he was inclined to dance with a bunch of men. But he drank, more than enough to help him forget his sadness.

During the months prior to the wedding, Rachel and he had continued seeing one another, though not as often as before her engagement. She'd visit him at home, call, or meet him in the park every few weeks. They always had much to talk about, though she never stayed for more than an hour.

Joshua hadn't met Binny until the wedding. Rachel had rarely mentioned him, and Joshua couldn't tell what she truly felt. She had always managed to avoid the topic, leaving Joshua to wonder if she simply didn't want to hurt him, or if she couldn't betray her own disappointment. He had hoped for the latter, had prayed that she would come to her senses and regain her old self, but now his hopes were gone.

Paul Sims also married, just a few months after Rachel. Joshua wasn't invited, but Loretta was. The night that she came home from the affair, she blabbed incessantly about the food, the music, and the way the guests dressed. Joshua wondered if his mother would ever cease to be impressed by white folks.

Loretta continued working for the Simses. She was growing tired, and it showed. But she never complained; she did what she had to do.

And Joshua forged ahead, keeping his mind on school despite all the things eating at him. He had given up on ever finding Celeste again, though she never left his thoughts. In his heart, he believed that things were not yet over for them, that someday, somehow, their paths would cross again.

Rachel phoned every few weeks, but always on the sly, when Binny wasn't around. Once, in the middle of a conversation, she heard Binny coming through the front door, and hung up abruptly, without even saying "good-by." Another time, she called in the middle of night, whispering that she needed to see him. It never came to be.

In December, 1967, Joshua applied and was accepted to Brooklyn College. His guidance counselor claimed his grades were good enough for him to consider better schools, like NYU or Columbia, but he wasn't interested. He didn't mention any of that to his mother, knowing she would have loved the idea and would have gone to Alfred Sims for help.

The following spring, on the fourth of April, the TV, newspapers, and radio were filled with news of the assassination of Reverend Martin Luther King Jr. That night, when Joshua came home, he found his mother sitting in the living room, her eyes misty, glued to the television as the reports came in. "Oh my God, Oh Lord," she chanted over and over again.

"Mama, you okay?" He asked several times.

"I'm fine," she finally answered. Unconvincing. Lost.

"Do you want me to get you anything? Some water or coffee?"

She didn't hear him.

He sat quietly beside her, for what seemed an eternity.

Finally, she turned to him and said, "I *do* want you to do something for me. I want you to promise that you won't leave the house for a few days."

He looked at her curiously.

"There's going to be trouble in the streets, rioting, I just know it. I want you to stay put for a couple of days."

"Rioting?"

She looked at him as if he should have understood this on his own. "There are people out there who've just been waiting for a chance like this to riot." She pointed to the TV. "Now they've got one."

He considered her point, but felt she was overreacting. He remembered having heard about riots in Harlem and Bedford Stuyvesant four years earlier, after a fifteen year old black kid was killed by a cop, and again last year in Harlem and the South Bronx, after an Hispanic man was also killed by a cop. He hadn't paid much attention to such things, for they only seemed to happen in places ridden with crime and poverty. *Nothing like that could happen in Crown Heights*, he thought.

Joshua obeyed his mother's wishes, though in the end he was right. While there were reports of sporadic violence, rock throwing, looting, and arson for a few days in Harlem and Bedford-Stuyvesant, things remained peaceful in Crown Heights.

"See, Mama, I told you there was nothing to worry about," he said, sitting with her in front of the TV, listening to a news report three days after the assassination.

"Don't get too pleased with yourself, Joshua," she answered. "We were just lucky, that's all. *Lucky.*" She stared off into space, contemplating her own words. "Luck don't last forever," she added, seemingly talking to herself. "Sooner or later, it's got to run out."

BOOK III

CHAPTER 31

Chava Sims, neé Feuerstein, lay in her bed, silently wondering what was happening. She was trying to be sympathetic about Paul's sexual naiveté, but couldn't help feeling wounded by his behavior. In the few times they had attempted relations, they had barely kissed or held one another before Paul penetrated her. A few seconds later, it was all over and he would retreat to his own bed in silence. Now it seemed as if he was avoiding her altogether. She tried to tell herself that he was just embarrassed, and she knew that if they didn't talk, it would only get worse.

"Pinchas," she said softly from her bed.

"Hmm," he groaned, acting half asleep, hoping she would leave him be.

"We don't have to sleep apart tonight," she said, reminding him that she had observed her seven days of cleanliness and had just been to the *Mikvah.*

"I know, I know, but I'm very tired. Maybe tomorrow night."

"But, I think . . ."

"Please, Chava, I must go to sleep! I have a long day tomorrow in yeshiva."

And that was that.

⌘

After a few more attempts, seeing that the situation was not improving, Chava Sims consulted Rav Schachter.

"This happens sometimes," the rabbi said. "As he gets more comfortable, things will be better. You must be patient and understanding."

In the weeks that followed, the rabbi's words proved incorrect, but there was one thing that did change. At first she had thought she'd come down with a virus or something, but after days of unrelenting nausea and vomiting, she realized what it was. She had difficulty believing it, but it was undeniable; it didn't take much for her to get pregnant.

When she told Paul, he was ecstatic. "Oh my God, Chava, this is so wonderful!"

Only, instead of embracing or kissing her, as she had hoped, he ran out to the yeshiva to tell his friends.

That night, she began despising him.

⌘

Rachel Weissman stood in the bathroom, looking in the mirror, feeling a surge of disgust. She had prayed that this month would be different, but still the bleeding came. It had been over a year since her wedding, and she would still have to endure yet another month of waiting, hoping, beseeching God.

She tried to convince herself that it wasn't so bad. A week of menstruating, a week of cleanliness, and then back to the *Mikvah. Next time it will be better.*

She thought about Binny, about their times together in bed. It had all began so wonderfully, filled with tenderness and innocence. Their first time had been both strange and exciting, far from the calamity she'd feared. She had bled from the penetration, and had to wait the week of cleanliness before she could go to the *Mikvah* and be with him again. And what a reunion that had been, one that most certainly should have produced a son. But it hadn't.

Rachel went into the bedroom, and looked around. It was an impressive room by all standards: silk wallpaper with blue flowers against a white background; wall-to-wall light blue carpeting; two queen size beds, the extra one for when they had to sleep apart; walnut night-tables with matching armoire and dresser, and an abundance of closet space for her ever-growing wardrobe. There seemed no end to Binny's generosity.

The three story brownstone on Carroll Street had been a wedding gift from Binny's parents. And what a house; so spacious, Rachel thought, so beautifully adorned and comfortable. Yet, so empty.

Rachel's eyes fixed on her bed. They had made love often, whenever it was permissible, not only for the sake of children, but for the mere pleasure. She had been surprised by how much she had enjoyed being with him, by what an attentive lover he had turned out to be. For these things she could only be thankful, especially considering the ghastly stories she'd heard about the husbands of some of her classmates. But she couldn't help but think that her peers had all succeeded where she was failing. It wasn't fair.

"God will choose the time to bless us," Binny had told her the first time she had been upset over her period. "We have to trust in Him."

How many times she had clung to those words. How many times she had reminded herself of the sincerity in Binny's eyes. *If he could have so much faith, so must I.*

But recently things had changed. Binny, too, was now growing impatient. He was coming home from yeshiva much later in the evenings, and disappearing to study on *Shabbos* afternoons during the time when they used to take walks together. The bedroom had turned chilly, clinical, and sex had become a chore. She tried talking to him about it, and he responded with the same exact words: "God will choose the time to bless us." Except he no longer sounded comforting, and his eyes bore only disappointment.

She had complained to Esther a few weeks earlier when they'd gotten together for lunch. "Oh, deary," Esther had remarked, "what do you expect him to say. They *all* say the same thing; they really don't know much about life."

"But what should I do?"

"Gee, I have a novel idea: why don't you see a doctor?" Sarcasm.

Rachel knew Esther was right, but was scared to take such a step. *Let me give it more time*, she had told herself, *just one more month*. And now that month was up, and time was running out.

She looked at the phone on the night-table, and thought about calling Joshua. It was during moments like these when she thought about him most, when she needed to hear his voice. He was still her protector, her savior. Lately, she'd been calling him more often, and had begun to feel bad about it. Not only because it was almost like cheating on her husband, but also because it was hurting Joshua.

She picked up the phone, dialed his number, and hung up as soon as she heard it ring. She picked up the phone again, but this time she dialed a different number. The woman on the other end answered, "Kingsbrook Jewish Medical Center."

"Yes, hello, may I please speak with Doctor Marcia Schiffman?"

"Please hold."

❧

Esther Mandlebaum had had it with men. Hasidic men, that is. After her fourth failed *shiddoch*, she vowed never to be fixed up again. From now on, she would choose her own dates, and none of them would have hats, dark suits, or peach fuzz on their faces.

Though the decision had been long in coming, her last conversation with Rachel had put the proverbial nail in the coffin. It had been frightening to have seen Rachel like that, so devastated over not getting pregnant. *Good God*, thought Esther, *is that all there is to life? And Rachel, of all people, what happened to her dreams?*

Well, it won't happen to me, Esther told herself. And in truth, Esther had already begun to sow the seeds of her aspirations. Secretly, unbeknownst even to Rachel, she'd enrolled in an acting class with a small repertory company in Greenwich Village. She'd been sneaking into Manhattan, two evenings each week for the past three months, and had been getting away with it. She figured she could also get away with dating "regular" men. She even had a specific prospect in mind.

His name was Steven Butler, a fellow would-be thespian she'd met in drama class. She didn't know if that was his real name or stage-name. Many acting students took stage-names prematurely, probably in the hope of one day being able to use them. She wondered why his name even mattered to her. Probably because Butler didn't sound Jewish.

Why did it make a difference if he was Jewish or not? She tried to tell herself that it didn't. The more sinful, the more enticing. She wanted to escape, to live an unencumbered, expressive life; to be a successful, famous actress. How could something like being Jewish be important? Yet she still wondered about his name.

Looks-wise, he was most assuredly a stunner. At least six feet, trim, jet-black wavy hair, Clark Gable mustache, green eyes, and a square, cleft chin. His mere presence made her shiver, and when he spoke, his deep, raspy voice made him "unbearable." To her, this was what God had intended man to be.

Her only problem was attracting his attention. For the past three months, she'd made several attempts, and while he always responded affably, he somehow managed to make her feel invisible. She wondered if she was being paranoid, if his "indifference" was only in her mind. Her limited experiences with men—the Hasidic "boys," as she called them—had left her bitter and insecure. Of the four she had dated, all had eventually rejected her. Not that she was particularly enamored with any of them, but she had been willing to give things more of a chance.

She had even kept her secrets and, ever the consummate actress, had managed to play the obsequious Hasidic lass. Yet, for some reason, they all eventually stopped calling, and the *shodchin* was running low on new candidates.

Perhaps she hadn't been as good an actress as she'd thought, or they hadn't been as dumb as she'd imagined. Perhaps her masquerade had been a bit too obvious, and the boys a mite more perceptive than she'd expected. That was an explanation she could live with.

But there was another possibility, one that pained her because it related to her appearance. She had always seen herself as overweight and unattractive, and had believed that others saw it too. Her parents and Rachel had constantly disputed this, telling her she was crazy, insisting she was beautiful. But how much truth could she expect from them?

She simply believed she was ugly, and nothing anyone could say would change that. In the past, she had attempted dieting, every diet under the sun, even to the brink of starving herself. But regardless of how little food she ate, each time she looked in the mirror, all she saw was "fat."

She hated herself, and that was why she so desperately needed to escape her life. Her dreams of the stage, of Steven Butler—these were her fantasies, her salvation. If she could attain them, she would be okay. She had to succeed; her happiness depended on it.

But what could she do about her weight? There was only one answer left, one that she had avoided because it had always seemed grotesque. She'd heard about it over the years from some of the girls in the community, but had never believed she could actually do it. Not until now.

It was seven o'clock in the evening, and Esther lay in bed with anticipation. The following night she would once again see Steven Butler. She was so entranced in fantasy, she didn't even realize that she was touching herself. She'd just finished dinner with her family downstairs, and had thought about doing some reading before going to sleep. Her class was working on *The Tempest*, and she'd planned to finish it before tomorrow's session. But she couldn't read, and she wasn't able to sleep either. All she could do was lose herself in thought.

Suddenly, she got up from the bed and went to the bathroom. She locked the door, something she'd never done before, and sat down on the floor. She stared at the toilet for a few minutes, until she built up the nerve to bring herself closer to it. Then, she leaned over the bowl, stuck her finger down her throat, and vomited. The purging took five minutes; cleaning it up, much longer. She wanted everything to be spotless. There shouldn't be a trace of what she'd done.

Afterward, she returned to bed and cried. Yet, despite the awful feelings she had for what she'd done, she was somehow relieved. She was no longer anxious about Steven; she finally had control over her appearance. A few minutes passed, and she was able to pick up *The Tempest* and concentrate. She would sleep just fine.

Esther Mandlebaum now had another secret.

CHAPTER 32

Brooklyn College was located on Avenue H in Flatbush, the heart of Kings County. Its impressive campus of trimmed lawns, surrounded by neo-Georgian red-brick buildings, lent an aura of another place and time, while its perpetual social problems made it very much a place of its time. From its inception in 1937, the campus had been regarded as a hotbed of left-wing ideology, earning it the nickname of the "little red schoolhouse" from its critics. By the late sixties, it had become a center for political and racial upheaval, marked by protests against the Vietnam War, and demonstrations by minority students demanding open admissions.

Joshua's first day was devoted to registration and orientation. There was a large meeting in the assembly hall, at which the dean and other officials gave speeches about registration procedures, college rules, activities, etcetera. Afterward, Joshua was confronted with the task of filling out forms and choosing classes. Much of this was simple. There was a list of required courses for freshmen, which took up most of his schedule and left room for only one elective. The instructions were to pick an elective from one's "major." There came the dilemma.

Joshua sat, pondering the list of potential majors, while the room emptied out. When he realized that he was one of the only students remaining, he forced himself to decide. He stared, once more, at the dotted line, and filled in "pre-law." *What the hell.*

The first recommended course for pre-law majors, he noted, was *Introduction to Political Science*. He got up to hand in his forms.

The line, which had been quite long just fifteen minutes earlier, had dwindled to three, including him. He approached the desk with his papers, and a tired looking black woman extended her hand to take them without even looking at him. She examined the forms, and flipped through some other papers as she entered his name for various classes. It seemed to be going smoothly, until she looked up at him, and said, "Sorry, poli-sci is full."

"Full?" he asked, not quite knowing what she meant.

"Full. You'll have to pick something else."

"What else?"

"How do I know?" Chafing.

"But I'm a pre-law major, and that's the first pre-law class."

"But it's full."

He looked at his list of classes again, and chose the one that came after *Introduction to Political Science*. "How about political science-two?"

"No can do, you need the introduction course first."

"But it's closed."

"That's true."

He went to the next course on the list. "How about U.S. Constitution-one?"

"Need the poli-sci courses first."

He was getting the hang of this. He looked down the list one last time, searching for a course without a prerequisite. There had to be one. Finally, a title struck him, *Introduction to Ethnic Studies*. Without speaking, he showed her the list with his finger pointed to it.

Her expression was disdainful, as if she didn't approve. He returned a hearty smile—*who gives a fuck what you think?* She returned to her rosters, found the class, and entered his name.

He walked away, wondering why she'd been so rude. Here he was, finally entering college, an adult, at the gateway to the civilized world, and getting mistreated. By a black person, no less. It had been naive of him to think that blacks supported one another in the white world. Now he knew otherwise. He wondered what other lessons awaited.

His name was Alvin Thompson, and he was a full professor in the department of Ethnic Studies. He was black; in fact, the only black teacher Joshua had. He was about five-ten, of average build, and good looking. To Joshua's eye, he could have passed as a double for Sidney Poitier.

In temperament, however, Professor Thompson couldn't be compared with anyone. He was reputed as a firebrand, extremely acrimonious, with no concern for what others thought of him. A proud son of the ghetto. Self-anointed messenger of truth.

On first impression, Joshua thought he was okay. He appeared to be a gentleman, impeccably groomed—conservative, brown, plaid suit; starched white-collared shirt; carmine bowtie; maroon hush puppies. And he was remarkably eloquent, not a trace of "street-talk."

He had quite a following, standing room only, flowing into the hallway. Joshua was surprised at that, considering the ease with which he was able to register for the class. But then he realized that most of the audience weren't students at the college. They were Thompson's disciples from outside.

The sole subject of the class ended up being the endless subjugation of blacks in America, and the ways—a' la Thompson—to change that. One of the first things Joshua learned was never to argue with Thompson. He had tried once, during a lecture in which Thompson was going on about living conditions in urban America, and the white man's effort to deluge black neighborhoods with drugs.

"But that's not completely true," Joshua heard himself say, not believing that the words had actually left his mouth.

Thompson looked around the room. "Do I hear a voice of dissension?"

All eyes turned to Joshua.

"Well?" Thompson asked, looking directly at the culprit.

Joshua trembled, wishing for a trap door in the floor.

"Did you have something to add?"

"No, not really." Sheepish. "I was just saying that I don't think that all the drugs in black neighborhoods come from white folks. I think things are more complicated than that."

"Ah, I see." The professor scratched his chin. "*You* think things *are* more complicated than that. Well, why don't you tell us what you mean, Mr . . . ."

"Eubanks, sir. Joshua Eubanks."

"Okay, Mr. Eubanks, why don't you share some of these 'complications' with us."

Joshua didn't think it wise to bare his expertise on the subject. "I'd rather not, sir."

"You'd rather not." Thompson looked around the silent room. "Is that because you really don't know what you're talking about, or because you don't want us to know how much you *do* know?" The crowd chuckled.

Joshua kept silent.

"Well?"

Still silent, Joshua was aware he was letting Thompson intimidate him. He was angry with himself for getting into this position.

"It seems you don't know anything." More laughter. "Well, Mr. Eubanks, in this class we have a rule. It's simple. If you don't know, don't say." He looked out at the audience, as if this were a warning to them as well. Then, he turned back to Joshua. "Okay?"

"Yes."

"Good."

Thompson continued on, his followers spellbound, until he'd gone about twenty minutes overtime. Joshua had heard that this was typical, and surmised it was also intentional—the professor must have enjoyed having his students arrive late for their other classes, for it made him feel more important.

As the classroom emptied, Joshua heard his name called. He turned, and saw Thompson looking directly at him, beckoning "come hither" with his forefinger. Joshua swallowed hard, and hobbled over.

As soon as Thompson and Joshua were the only ones remaining in the room, Thompson looked at the cane in Joshua's hand, then into his eyes, and said, "Tell me, Mr. Eubanks, why did you give up so easily?"

"I realized I had made a mistake."

"A *mistake*? And what might that mistake be?"

"I shouldn't have contradicted you."

"Why not?"

"Because it wasn't my place."

"That's good, Mr. Eubanks. Every *Negro* should know his place, right?"

"Excuse me?"

"You heard me, Mr. Eubanks. Every Negro should know his place, shouldn't he?"

"I'm sorry, sir, I don't understand . . ."

"Of course you don't, Mr. Eubanks, but I bet you're good and angry right about now, huh?"

"Yes sir," Joshua answered, knowing he wasn't sounding nearly as peeved as he felt.

"Then good. You should be angry, because you behaved like a scared little Negro, or would you prefer *boy.*"

Joshua was dumb-struck.

"Well, let me tell you something, Mr. Eubanks. Next time, if you want to be a scared little Negro, then keep your mouth shut from the start. That's the way it's done. But, if by any chance, you desire to grow up and become a man, then *never* let *anybody* intimidate you. And *that* includes *me!*" He stood in Joshua's face. "Next time you have something to say in my class, you say it! Otherwise, I'll be sure to fail you."

"Yes sir."

Thompson turned away, waving Joshua out of his presence.

Joshua obeyed, left the room, and walked down the hallway perplexed. He loathed Thompson, no doubt, but also realized that the professor did indeed have a thing or two to teach him.

⨋

Joshua stood on the Brighton Beach boardwalk, leaning over the railing, looking at the ocean, wondering why Rachel had sounded so desperate on the phone, and why she had insisted on meeting him here. She was late, giving him time to ponder the waves breaking on the sand.

It was an early autumn day, a mite too chilly for the beach. Two teenaged lovers strolled along the edge of the water, and a sanitation worker was combing the area for debris; otherwise, the place was empty. The sky was clear, and the view extended to the horizon.

Joshua had a vague recollection of his mother taking him to the beach as a child, but wasn't sure if it had been Coney Island or Manhattan

Beach. He was certain it hadn't been here. This wasn't a place black people frequented.

The boardwalk was quiet. A few pedestrians meandered back and forth. There was a row of food concessions, most of which were closed. He had walked there from the train, and had passed through streets with large apartment buildings, and an impressive commercial district beneath the El. He had seen only white faces, mostly elderly, and—he assumed—Jewish. He remembered that the Eisenmans, the couple that had lived next door to him, had recently moved to this area. Mrs. Eisenman had told him that they wanted to be with people their own age, but he had known the real reason. White people, except for the Lubavitchers, were disappearing from his neighborhood rather quickly these days.

The Eisenmans had even given him and his mother their new address, and had encouraged them to visit. He had always liked the Eisenmans, and had been thinking of perhaps dropping in on them. He reached into his pocket and removed the crumpled paper on which he had written their address earlier that morning, and stared at it. He didn't know why, but he eventually released his grasp and let it fly away.

It was then that she tapped him on the shoulder. He turned around, and his heart fell. Fifteen months, and she hadn't changed a bit.

"Hi," she said. "Sorry I'm late, the train was slow."

"It happens."

"How *are* you?"

Joshua knew that this was one of those rare times in his life when that question was genuine. "Pretty good, and you?"

She shrugged.

"Come," he said, putting his arm around her shoulder, "let's walk."

She walked beside him, allowing him to hold her. This far from Crown Heights, she seemed comfortable no one would recognize her. Joshua realized that was why she had chosen this place.

They sauntered along the boardwalk in silence for a few minutes, then she stopped, turned to him, and began to cry. "Oh Joshua, I don't know what to do."

"About what?"

"About Binny. And me." Hesitant.

"What about Binny and you?"

"We're having a problem, a big problem."

"What kind of problem?"

"Look at me." She stepped back and postured herself.

"Yes?" *God, she's gorgeous.*

"Don't you see?"

"See what?"

"Joshua, *look at me!*" She put both her hands on her stomach.

"You're pregnant?"

She laughed, almost choking on her tears.

"*What?*"

"I'm *not* pregnant!"

"Oh." He felt stupid, realizing he should have known that a Hasidic woman ought to be pregnant after over a year of marriage.

There was a long silence.

"I'm sorry, I shouldn't be bothering you with this," she said.

"No, it's okay."

"I guess I just needed someone to talk to, someone with a man's perspective. I talked to Esther, and she suggested seeing a doctor."

"Good idea."

"I did. I called Doctor Schiffman, and she gave me the name of a gynecologist at the hospital, a Doctor Silver. I went and he examined me."

"And?"

"And, I'm okay, as far as he can tell."

"Has Binny seen a doctor?"

"That's what Doctor Silver asked."

"And?"

"And, Binny would never see a doctor. He believes it's all in God's hands. So does my father, I imagine. That's why you're the only one I could turn to."

Oh, Joshua said to himself.

"What do you think I should do?" she asked.

"I think you need to convince Binny to see a doctor."

"But how?"

None of this was easy for Joshua, for he really wanted to say, *run away with me!* He would gladly have given her plenty of children. "Rachel, I don't think I'm the right person to be talking to about this . . ."

"You're right, Joshua, I shouldn't have . . ."

"It's okay."

"Come, let's walk," she said, and this time *she* held *his* arm.

They strolled a bit farther. A smile came to her face. "I miss you," she said.

"I miss you too."

"I guess I just wanted to see you. I suppose it was selfish of me, but I needed to know that you still care."

He stopped, turned to her, put his hand on her cheek, and said, "I do. I always will."

"I needed to know."

"Don't ever doubt it."

They walked on, his arm around her shoulder, in silence, feeling safe in this place, so far from the world that divided them. They felt good being together, even for a short while, untouched by complication and intrusion. But, in truth, they weren't safe at all. For somewhere, in the shadow of a nearby shop, Paul Sims stood, observing their every move.

CHAPTER 33

Doctor Marcia Schiffman phoned Rachel to find out how the visit with Doctor Silver went. Upon hearing what the gynecologist had said, Schiffman responded, "Well, there's one other possibility as well."

"What's that?" Rachel asked, hoping it might mean Binny wouldn't have to see a doctor.

"I don't know how to say this, Rachel, but it could be that the problem you and Binny are having isn't medical."

"What do you mean?"

"What I mean is—and I don't understand it completely—but sometimes couples have difficulty getting pregnant because of psychological reasons."

"You mean because they don't really want to?"

"No, just the opposite. I mean because they want it *too much.* It creates a lot of tension and anxiety, which somehow affects the reproductive process."

Rachel took a moment to consider the point. "What do you suggest?" she asked.

"To put it simply, Rachel, and at the risk of sounding crass, you need to stop thinking about getting pregnant, and start thinking about having sex for fun!"

"But I used to enjoy being with Binny. I didn't always do it just for children." Defensive.

"Yes, but somewhere along the line that stopped, didn't it?"

"I suppose so."

"Well, that's what you should work on, if you want my advice. Try it this way for a few more months and let's see what happens. There's always time for Binny to see a doctor, but if you do this, it may not be necessary."

⌘

That very night, Rachel waited up for her husband in bed, ready to implement Marcia Schiffman's advice. She had to admit, she felt rather sexy in the red satin nightgown Esther had given her at her bridal shower, the same one she had worn on her wedding night.

Binny arrived home late, as was his recent habit. She heard him come through the front door, and then heard him rummaging through the refrigerator. For all she knew, it would be hours before he'd make an appearance in the bedroom, if at all. There had been more than one occasion on which she had found him in the morning, sleeping at his desk in the study. *Not tonight*, she told herself, getting out of bed.

She turned on the light and scrutinized herself in the mirror, teasing her hair, and adjusting her gown to make sure it hugged her body perfectly. She went down the stairs, into the kitchen, and sneaked up behind him.

"Binny," she said softly.

He turned around and looked at her. Instantly, a glass filled with milk fell from his hand and shattered on the floor. "Oh my," he said nervously, noting the mess he'd made.

"Don't worry about it," she said, walking over to him, pressing her body against him and pushing her thigh into his groin. She moved her hands up his chest and passionately kissed his lips.

It was a long kiss, and when he finally came up for air, he said, "Rachel, what's gotten into you?"

"Come, let me show you," she said, taking his hand and leading him from the kitchen.

It was a torrid evening, surpassing anything either of them had ever imagined. Rachel delayed actual intercourse, trying other tricks she'd read or heard about instead. She explored every crevice of his body, and spoke to him softly of her desires. After an hour, he was begging to have her, and when she finally gave herself, cries of ecstasy echoed through the house.

When it was over, they lay together, kissing and holding one another. She touched him again, enticed him and tortured him again. He began to kiss her all over, and made love to her a second time. Afterwards, they rested for a while, but only for a while.

In the beginning of their marriage, they had often made love twice in an evening. It had always been wonderful, but nothing like this. The third time was novel, and the mixture of pleasure and pain accompanying their final release took them beyond paradise. Rachel could swear she hadn't had a single thought of getting pregnant. But now, lying apart, fading off to sleep, she couldn't help but believe that if this night didn't bring a child, nothing would.

❧

Paul Sims sat beside his baby daughter's crib, watching her sleep, pondering what he had seen a few days earlier. Even now, during his most blissful of moments, he couldn't erase the image from his mind. He felt embarrassed for having followed Rachel, but mostly he was enraged. He was confused about what to do with what he knew.

He had much to be thankful for these days. God had given him a wondrous gift, a soft, precious child with the face of an angel. He was going to be good to her in every way. She would have all the love of which he had felt deprived.

They had named her Sheindy, after his paternal grandmother, Sheindle Simenovitz, who had died just a few months earlier. He had always been fond of his grandmother, the only person who knew how to put Alfred in his place, and the only one who was proud of Paul's decision to attend yeshiva. Now, he had another Sheindle to make proud.

It was late in the evening. Chava was asleep in the bedroom. It had been six weeks since she'd given birth and she was still exhausted. Paul frequently sat up, watching Sheindy, still plagued by an inability to sleep.

He envied the way Chava slept, soundly and undisturbed. He knew she earned it, taking care of the baby all day while he studied in the yeshiva. Thank God, Rav Schachter had convinced his father to help financially, so he could continue studying for at least another year. He was concerned about eventually having to find a job, for he knew he didn't have any skills.

He figured he could always work for his father, a daunting prospect indeed. He would write to the *Rebbe* to seek council when the time came; there was no need to think about it now.

His thoughts returned to Rachel's tryst with Joshua. A few days had passed, yet he hadn't told a soul. *God works in mysterious ways*, he mused; *after all, what were the chances of discovering something like that?*

He had been on his way to the yeshiva the morning he saw Rachel heading toward the train. He was across the street, and hid himself from her view. She was walking rather quickly, turning around frequently, as if looking to see if anybody was following her. He was struck by this, and wondered if she was up to something sneaky. He had always suspected her as a person with secrets, he had just known it, so he decided to follow, to see where fate might lead. A missed day in yeshiva seemed trivial at the time.

He rode in the car behind hers, standing near the door, watching for when she disembarked. He followed her through the streets of Brighton, staying far enough behind to remain unseen. It was an unlikely place for her to be; he was sure his efforts would prove fruitful.

His curiosity peaked as she climbed the ramp to the boardwalk; his heart pounded as he watched her embrace the black man. And then he saw the black man's face.

He had heard about Joshua's rescue of Rachel and Esther a few years earlier, and had known that Joshua had been a guest at Rachel's wedding. But *this* was unfathomable.

His mind turned, once again, to his little Sheindy. She slept soundly, her breathing heavy, as if she were sucking in every ounce of life. It felt strange being a parent, the responsibility, the angst, the joy. He wondered what his baby would grow up to be like, what kind of man she would marry, what sort of life lay ahead for her. And he remembered how Rabbi Weissman used to talk about Rachel. It seemed so long ago. Pleasant memories, painful memories; for him, the past was always confusing.

He realized that what he knew would destroy the rabbi, and that was something he didn't want. Unclear of his religious obligation— whether Jewish law required him to tell the husband or not—he was, however, certain of the danger in asking the question. For he would most definitely be pressured to reveal the reason for his query. So for now his conundrum would have to remain unresolved.

For now.

One Friday afternoon, Binny Frankel arrived home just before candle lighting. He had been delayed in the yeshiva because of an argument with another student concerning the interpretation of a difficult Talmudic passage. He felt bad for his tardiness. Lately, he'd been spending more time around the house with Rachel, and had been making a point to arrive early on Friday to help with the pre-Sabbath chores.

As he entered the house, he was immediately captured by the *Shabbosdik* aromas—home baked challah, chicken soup, potato kugel, gefilte fish, and a marinated brisket, the recipe for which his mother-in-law had generously bequeathed to his wife. It was a typical Friday night menu in the Frankel home, nothing out of the ordinary.

"Rachel," he called as he hung his coat in the foyer closet.

"In here," she answered from the kitchen.

He walked into the kitchen and saw the candles, already placed in the candelabra, waiting to be kindled. He felt even worse, for it was he who customarily set up the Sabbath candles for Rachel to light; it was the husband's job, a sign of his partaking in the preparation for the Sabbath.

"Sorry I'm so late," he offered, looking as disappointed as he sounded.

She turned to greet him with an unexpected smile. "That's okay," she answered, "sometimes being *late* can be a good thing."

He gazed at her curiously, catching the gleam in her eye. She was not one to speak in riddles.

"You mean you're . . ."

"I think."

Neither of them wanted to actually say the word, for fear of casting an *ayin hara*, an evil eye, on such a delicate matter.

"I'm pretty sure," Rachel added. "It's been a few days."

Binny crossed the room with open arms. Rachel broke into tears at his touch. "I didn't want to tell you until I knew," she said, crying and laughing at once.

"I love you," he replied softly, running his hands through her hair.

"I love you too," she answered, believing her own words. *I do love him*, she told herself, as if she needed convincing. *I will love him, and our child, and our family. I will love my life.*

"Oh my," she exclaimed as she jumped away, "it's time to light."

It was actually a few minutes past the time, but neither noticed. Binny ignored the clock and watched her kindle the candles, wave her hands over them, and bestow blessings of peace for their home, observing intently as if for the very first time.

He took a quick shower before heading to *shul*. He rarely took advantage of the legal dictum allowing men an additional eighteen minutes after candle-lighting to prepare for the Sabbath. He was uncomfortable with the dispensation, regarding it as proper for husband and wife to start the Sabbath together. But tonight there had been unforeseen circumstances, wonderful circumstances. He could make exceptions; he could be late for *shul*. Nothing would bother him.

He stood in the shower, warm sprays of water and rising steam easing the day's tensions. *An indulgence*, he thought, while pondering his new fortune. His wife was pregnant, and because of that she would be permitted to him without interruption until the baby was born. He would start tonight, on *Shabbos*, when it was a double *mitzvah*. He would make burning love to her—*just for the fun of it*.

He began to hum one of his favorite melodies. He only knew Hasidic tunes, and it was expressly forbidden to sing them in the shower. Singing was a sacred rite, a form of prayer and supplication. To perform such an act in the bathroom was sacrilege, but he couldn't help himself. He needed to sing.

CHAPTER 34

"The Jews are not our friends. They pretend to be. They marched with Doctor King and started their Anti Defamation League—which they *say* will help *us*—but all this was rooted in self interest. The Jews stood by us in the South only because they themselves are afraid of the Klan; they themselves are scared of persecution and prejudice, *not* because they give a damn about the black man.

"Take a good look at these Jews, my friends. What have they really done for us? Well, to start, they participated in the slave trade, even owned some of the ships and companies that had transported our grandparents from their homes and villages in Africa to the so-called *New* World. These Jews have made a profit from our servitude, that's what *they* have done for us!

"And today, what does the Jew do for us? He is the slum lord, is he not? He owns our tenements; he does not fix the plumbing or replace the lights in the hallways and stairwells where our mothers and sisters are accosted; he does not repair the chipping paint our babies ingest; he does not provide heat in the winter, and does not replace broken locks on the doors to keep criminals out. All he cares about is filling his pockets, and *that's* what the Jew does!"

Joshua sat in the back of the class, listening to Professor Thompson's final lecture of the semester. The professor had apparently saved the "best" for last, and Joshua couldn't argue. The comments about Jewish landlords rang true to his experience, and the statements about Jews having been involved in slave trading were not without some historical evidence. And as for the reason some Jews marched with blacks in the South, there was some truth in that as well.

Yet Joshua was bothered by the insinuation that all whites, and Jews in particular, were bad. *What about Rachel, her father, or even Mr. Kimmel, the probation officer?*

He was about to raise his hand, but lost his nerve. He knew he was copping out, doing exactly what Thompson had admonished him about, but it just wasn't worth it. Not at this time, in this place.

The class concluded with a thunderous ovation. Joshua, too, found himself on his feet, applauding. Not because he was afraid of sticking out, but because there were things he'd learned from Thompson, and an intangible quality about the professor that he admired, despite the demagoguery.

A few minutes passed before the room started emptying. Joshua gathered his belongings and was headed for the door when he heard his name called.

What luck!

He turned around; the notorious forefinger was beckoning.

He ambled over.

Thompson gestured for him to sit.

He obeyed.

Thompson looked at him. "So you never did speak up," he said.

"About what?"

"About anything."

"I guess I didn't have anything to say."

"You *guess*?"

"I mean, I *didn't* have anything to say."

"Or you would have spoken up."

"Yes, exactly."

Thompson waited a beat. "I'm sure you know that you received the best grade in the class on the mid-term."

"No, I didn't."

"Well, you did. It's obvious that you're a smart fellow."

Joshua said nothing.

"Anyway," Thompson continued, "I was wondering what exactly it is that you plan to do with your brains?"

Joshua wasn't sure how to respond. "Well, I'm a pre-law major."

"Does that mean you want to be a lawyer?"

"I don't know. I guess so."

"You *guess* so. Well, you better be more convinced than that if you really want to be a lawyer."

Joshua nodded.

Thompson pondered a moment. "Perhaps you *will* be a lawyer! Perhaps you will do your people proud one day."

Joshua was dumbfounded.

"I could tell that you don't agree with everything I say," Thompson added.

"How is that?"

"Your face, it gives you away. You would be a terrible poker player." A chuckle.

Joshua vowed to work on his poker skills. "There are some things you say that sound too simple," he said, surprised by his own candor.

"And what might those things be?" Feigned curiosity.

Joshua offered some of his thoughts regarding Thompson's generalizations. Thompson sat, listening with extraordinary interest, silent, reflective, rubbing his cheek. Joshua was afraid he'd said too much.

"Tell me, Mr. Eubanks, where do you live?"

"Crown Heights."

"Ah!"

"Is there something wrong with Crown Heights?"

"No, not really. But it isn't exactly your typical black neighborhood, wouldn't you say?"

"If you mean that whites live there too, that's true. But things are changing. The whites are moving out fast. When we first came there, we were the only blacks in our building, and now there aren't any whites left in *our* building at all."

"And why do you suppose that is?"

"I guess they don't want to be around us, with all the crime and drugs and everything. They're scared, and to tell you the truth, so am I. I grew up in Bed-Stuy, and I've seen what can happen to a neighborhood."

"Bed-Stuy," Thompson said, pondering. "So you do know something about black neighborhoods?"

"Some." *More than I'd like to admit.*

"Tell me, Mr. Eubanks, can I ask you a personal question?"

"Yes." Tentative.

"What happened to your leg?"

"A fight with some white guys, one of them had a knife and got me in the back."

"A fight?" He didn't seem surprised. "Over what?"

"I was trying to help two girls."

"Girls?"

Joshua nodded.

"Were they black girls?"

"No, they were Jewish."

"I see." Again, pensive. He stood up and stretched. "Well, Mr. Eubanks, you should think more seriously about becoming a lawyer. You'll probably make an excellent one; you seem to have a gifted mind. You may even contribute to *your* people one day, help them as you did those Jewish girls. Unless, of course, you're afraid of being wounded again."

"I'll think about it," Joshua said. He would have said anything at this point to have gotten out of there.

"Good, you do that," Thompson replied. "You can go now."

Joshua got up, and walked toward the door.

"One more thing, Mr. Eubanks."

"Yes." He turned around.

"Have you ever heard of *Crow Hill?*" Thompson asked.

"No."

"Have you heard of *Crow* Heights?"

"No."

"You might want to look them up in the library. You might find something interesting." Thompson turned away, giving the impression that he wasn't looking for a reply. Joshua left the room, forgot about his next class, and headed directly for the library.

⚬

Joshua didn't know exactly what he was looking for, but was sure it would be some obscure little historical snippet of seeming insignificance.

Crow Hill.

Crow Heights.

What could Thompson have been alluding to?

Figuring it obviously had something to do with Crown Heights, he searched the card catalogue for titles about Brooklyn. He pulled three books, dealing specifically with the history of Brooklyn, and searched their indices. All had entries for Crown Heights, but the first two had nothing under *Crow*. He was just about convinced he was chasing a ghost, when he came upon an entry in the third book.

There it was, in front of his eyes: *Crow Hill*. He turned to the page and began reading about how, during the eighteenth and early nineteenth centuries, Crown Heights had actually been called Crow Hill. It was regarded as a hill because it was the highest point of land stretching from the hills east of Prospect Park to East New York. The term *crow* had two origins. The first was that, according to folklore, the hill had been infested with crows. The second theory was based on the fact that the area had been settled in the 1830's by freed black slaves, who were referred to as "crows" by whites.

In either case, the black settlers lived in shacks they built on the hill. Many of them had been farmers or craftsmen, while others found work in the fish and meat markets in Manhattan. Years later, as the city limits extended, Crow Hill's abundance of land and centralized location attracted many Protestant middle-class immigrants from Western Europe, who in turn developed the area by building churches, hospitals, parks, museums, and architecturally rich homes. By the early 1920's, the opening of a subway line to the area led to an apartment house building boom, and brought a new influx of immigrants, most of whom were Jewish, Irish, and Italian. Over time, the blacks were forced out as Crow Hill became a highly desirable place for the city's growing urban class to live.

An obscure little snippet indeed.

Joshua sat and reread the chapter. It didn't take much to guess what Thompson was trying to tell him. A story about whites taking over a black neighborhood. Vintage Thompson: the repression of historical truth to maintain the white domination of society.

The only remaining question concerned the change of name, something the book, surprisingly, didn't discuss. It wasn't difficult, however, for Joshua to figure that out; after all, the professor had taught him a few things.

He guessed that the new name, Crown Heights, must have been coined by the whites in their effort to upscale the area and rid it of the negative connotation associated with its former residents. As for *Crow Heights*, a term also absent from any of the books, he guessed that it was either an interim name, between Crow Hill and Crown Heights, or a little quip for those in the know, like Thompson, used as a subtle reminder of a neglected past.

Joshua now understood. He had accused Thompson of oversimplifying, and the professor had responded masterfully, using Joshua's own neighborhood as an example of how truly complex things are. *Touché!*

⮂

Months had passed since Joshua had seen Rachel. She called once to tell him she was pregnant. The conversation had been tense. He had felt her fear of Binny walking in and discovering her on the phone with him. He had been growing increasingly uneasy with the whole situation.

He hadn't shared his feelings at the time, for it had been her moment of joy. He had also liked the fact that she still needed to talk with him, to share things with him. Above all, he didn't want to lose her.

But now he was at a turning point. Perhaps it was Professor Thompson's influence, or perhaps he was growing up; whatever, he needed to do something.

The day finally came in the middle of February, during his two-week intercession from college. She had called and asked for another meeting. It was a bone-chilling afternoon, the streets were covered with wet snow and ice from a recent storm. Rachel insisted on the boardwalk, their "safe" hideout.

As usual, his arrival preceded hers. The boardwalk was barren; the gusts off the ocean unbearable. He saw her approaching in a bright red wool coat and matching hat. *Not very inconspicuous,* he thought.

"It's quite cold here," were her first words. Her hands remained in her pocket, shivering along with the rest of her.

"Want to go inside?"

"Where?"

"There's a little luncheonette a few blocks from here. Nice, quiet, and *warm.*"

She considered for a moment. "Okay, let's go."

They left the boardwalk, and walked the two blocks in silence. The freezing air was nothing compared to the chill Joshua felt from her. The luncheonette was on a corner, just below the El, its fogged windows suggesting a toasty interior.

They walked over to an empty table. Rachel removed her coat and hat, as Joshua noticed how four months of pregnancy didn't do much to alter her appearance. In fact, he thought, she looked even better, as if that were possible. She smiled a bit awkwardly, knowing she was being scrutinized.

"I've put on a few pounds," she said.

"You look great."

"Thanks, you're being kind."

The waitress presented herself. Joshua ordered a hot chocolate. Since the place wasn't kosher, Rachel asked only for some cold water.

"I'm sorry, I forgot," Joshua said.

"It's fine," Rachel replied. "Cold water is good for you, especially when you're pregnant."

He looked at her and smiled.

"Enough about me. How have *you* been?" she asked.

"Pretty good."

"I guess you're learning a lot in college." A touch of envy and sadness.

"Yes, I am." He didn't want to rub it in her face.

"I'm really happy for you." She reached over and touched his hand.

"I'm happy for you, too."

The waitress brought their drinks. The hot chocolate felt good in his hands, even better going down. He felt guilty for her water; he still wanted to take care of her.

"It's really good to see you," she said.

"Why?"

"Why what?" Taken aback, she withdrew her hand.

"Why is it good to see me?"

"Because I've missed you, that's why."

"Okay, if you say so," Testy.

"What does that mean?"

"It means, if you say you've missed me, you've missed me."

"You don't look happy about it."

"Maybe I'm not."

She was silent for a moment. "I suppose I knew this was going to happen."

"Look, Rachel, I just . . ."

"I know," she interrupted.

"Know what?"

"It's wrong of me to keep calling you, to keep suggesting meetings like this. It isn't fair to you."

"And what about *you*? Do *you* enjoy meeting this way?"

"No, I don't. But what else can I do? I can't simply forget you, I just can't!" She began to cry.

He handed her a napkin. "Rachel, there's something I need to know." Now he was touching her hand.

She looked him in the eye, waiting for him to continue.

"I need to know if it's because I'm black?"

"If *what's* because you're black?" Defensive.

"If you didn't choose *me* because I'm black."

"*Choose* you? What do you mean?"

"You know what I mean. Didn't you ever think about it—being with me?"

"You mean, marrying you?"

"Whatever."

Another silence, this time long and onerous.

"Oh Joshua, I'm not going to pretend I haven't thought about it, or how stupid I've been, expecting us to go on forever like this without talking about it. We never have talked about it, have we?"

"No, we haven't."

"And we should have."

"Better late than never."

"Yes, I suppose."

He nodded.

"I do love you," she said. "It's a strange thing, but I know in my heart that I love you." She squeezed his hand. "But I haven't been fair to you and," she hesitated, "I haven't been fair to myself." She stopped and considered what she was about to say. "I suppose your being black has something to do with it. I would be lying if I said it didn't. I *don't* want to lie to *you*. But I also know that my being a coward has a lot to do with it as well. I gave you up just like I gave up my dreams of college and medical school. I was afraid of what it would do to my parents; I just couldn't hurt them."

He hesitated a moment, trying to frame his words as tenderly as possible. "I don't think you can completely blame your rejection of me on your parents."

She thought for a moment. "You're right, I can't. There are so many complications, I just don't know where to start. I love being a Hasidic Jew, not because of my parents, but because *I* really love it. Of course, there are things I would change if I could, and there was a time I believed I could have my dreams and they wouldn't affect anything. But I was naive, *everything* affects everything.

"That's where you come in. I couldn't marry a Gentile, not because I'm prejudiced—though I'm sure some people would say I am—but because I wouldn't be able to have a Hasidic life or raise Hasidic children if I did. And even if you had offered to convert, it still would have been impossible. Not because of my parents as much as the community. My parents would eventually have accepted you—after my father had another heart attack or two—but I believe they *would* have. After all my father's been through, there's nothing more abhorrent to my parents than hatred and bigotry. But the community, that's another thing. They would scoff at us, and their children would scoff at our children. It's wrong, I know, especially considering that the Torah commands us to welcome the convert, and the fact that Moses' wife was both black *and* a convert. But that's how the community is, and the most unfortunate thing about being Hasidic—the thing I hate about it—is that the perceptions of the community are sometimes more important than the Torah itself. So what it all comes down to, I guess, is that my so-called rejection of you has a lot more to do with *my* weakness, than *your* color."

"I don't think 'weakness' is the right word," Joshua responded.

"Then what is?"

"Fear."

She offered a faint smile. "But I sure do feel weak," she said, her face turning sullen again.

"It's okay." he said.

"Is it?"

"Yes. Some of it's even my fault. Just as you can't keep blaming your parents, I can't keep blaming *you*. I need to get on with my life. I need to stop imagining us in ways that will never be."

"I know."

"You *do* look great."

"I'm sure you think so."

"I do."

"It's good we talked about it, isn't it?" she asked.

"Yes, I think it is." Unconvincing.

"At least everything's in the open now."

He nodded, as reassuringly as possible.

"I should be going," Rachel said, looking at her watch.

Usually, she would leave first, and he would wait and catch a different train. He had always thought the precaution silly, but today he was only too glad to steal a few extra minutes of warmth. He watched her put on her scarf and coat. She moved slowly, sadly. She held her hat and gloves in her hand, turned to him, and asked, "Can I still call?"

"You still want to?"

"Yes. I want us to always be friends. *Real* friends."

"We are."

"And you're not mad at me?"

"No more than I am at myself. I'll get over it."

She put her hat and gloves on just as she exited the door. He ordered another hot chocolate, and thought about their conversation, wondering if he would ever see her again. In his mind he knew he would be okay if he didn't, for he realized he needed to move on. But in his heart, well, that was another matter altogether.

CHAPTER 35

At a few minutes past 7:00 p.m., Rachel and Binny Frankel finished dinner. Rachel started clearing the table, and Binny went to the closet for his coat. He was heading back to the yeshiva for the evening, and would return in about two hours. He used to love the yeshiva's evening study sessions—a requirement for all rabbinical students—but as of late his preference was being home with his wife.

He came into the kitchen and kissed her good-by. "I'll be home soon," he said.

She smiled. His love for her made her happy, and at moments like this she wished that could be enough. But it wasn't. Having things out with Joshua had cleared the air, so-to-speak, but she wondered if she'd really resolved anything, or if she ever would. She knew she couldn't rid her life of Joshua. She'd given up too much already, too many of her dreams, but the duplicity was killing her.

After finishing the dishes, she felt unusually fatigued. Her pregnancy often made her tired, especially at night, but this was something else. She decided to go upstairs and lie down for a few minutes. She could make her phone calls and tidy up the house later. She walked toward the stairway and began to feel faint. She held the banister as she started up the stairs, but halfway up she felt she couldn't continue. Fearful of passing out, she clutched the banister and leaned against the wall. A strange sensation ran down her leg as she reached unsteadily to lift her skirt. She gasped at the sight of blood trailing down to the bottom of the stairs. Petrified, she struggled up to her bedroom for the phone, but never made it.

❧

She awoke in the hospital. Her father, mother, and Binny were at her side. "What happened?" she managed.

"Nothing. You're okay. Thank God you're okay," she heard her mother say.

"The baby?" she asked.

"Everything is okay, you're going to be fine." Again, her mother's voice.

"But the baby?"

No one answered.

"Oh my God," she screamed. "Oh my God!"

"Don't worry," her father said, grasping her hand. "Don't upset yourself. You need your strength."

She read the anguish on Binny's face. "I'm sorry Binny," she cried, "please forgive me."

He reached out and touched her. "It's okay Rachel," he said, fighting his own tears. "Everything will be fine."

"I'm so sorry, I'm so sorry," she repeated.

Binny and Hannah started to cry.

"There's no reason to be sorry," her father offered.

She was deaf to the world, lost in her anguish. "I'm sorry," she repeated through her tears. "Forgive me!"

They didn't understand, they couldn't understand. Why was she blaming herself? But *she* understood. Only too well. For it was truly her fault; she had killed her baby, and it was no different than if she had used a knife. Her day of judgment had arrived, and with it the wrath of an angry, vengeful God. He'd been watching all along, just as she'd always been taught. Nothing is hidden from Him, a fact that had never been so compelling as it was now.

You shall not chase after your heart and your eyes, after the things for which you lust.

She had ignored everything she'd ever believed in, and had placed earthly desire above the purity of her soul. And now she was paying the price.

"*Forgive me!*"

She loathed herself for her iniquities.
"Forgive me!"
She loathed God for His harshness.
"Forgive me!"
She loathed Binny and her parents for her own inadequacy.
"Forgive me!"
She loathed Joshua for her agony. She would *never* see him again!

⤫

During her first week home, her mood remained unchanged. Her mother stayed with her. Binny and her father were around all the time, and Esther visited daily. Rachel seldom left her room, and didn't say much to anyone. They catered to her and tried to cheer her up, but she was intent on her suffering.

One evening, after about two weeks, she finally came down and joined the others for dinner. She didn't talk much, but it was a good sign. The next day, in the afternoon, she was sitting in the living room with Esther. Her mother had gone marketing.

"You seem to be coming along better," Esther observed.

"I'll be okay."

"I know you will, you've always been the strong one."

Rachel considered the observation. "Compared to whom?"

"Compared to anyone."

"I think you meant something else."

"You're right." Hesitation. "Compared to me, I guess."

"What do you mean by that?"

"Just that you manage to figure things out and rise above unpleasant situations. I've never been quite as good at that as you."

Rachel raised her eyelids, still curious.

"Well," Esther continued, "you're married—and to a pretty good guy, as far as these guys go. You have a beautiful home, you *will* have children, you'll have it all. Because you're strong. You know what's right."

"Funny, I always thought I have all this because I'm weak."

"I suppose it depends on how you look at it." Sadness.

A moment of silence. Rachel took Esther's hand. "Tell me, what's happening with you?"

Esther proceeded to confess. It was the first time she'd told Rachel, or anyone, about Stephen Butler and, at this point, things had gotten rather spicy. She had finally managed to attract his attention; it had been a simple matter of wearing the right outfit. Those long skirts and ample blouses hadn't been doing the trick, so she had purchased some sexier apparel at a boutique in the village. She had also found a place to change clothes en route to class. She would stop in a coffee shop, order a coffee or soda to please the owner, put on her new ensemble in the bathroom, go to class, and change there again on the way home.

These days, however, she was taking an additional detour on the way home: Stephen's studio apartment. It had all begun on the third night of her new image. He had approached her after class, and asked her out for a drink. A quaint little pub a few blocks from school, a couple of drinks, and next thing she knew, his place.

"What can I say, darling? I'm just a harlot, like one of those pitiful vixens in the Bible."

Rachel sat there, eyes fixed, ears glued to every word. "You mean you've been . . ."

"Just as *you've* been, my dear."

"But I'm married."

"Are you passing judgment?"

"I'm sorry, I have no right to . . ."

"It's okay, I know you didn't mean it."

"I really didn't; I shouldn't have said that; I'm sorry."

Rachel was obviously still fragile. Esther took her hand, and reiterated, "It's okay, it's okay."

"It really isn't," Rachel responded. She had never told Esther of her meetings with Joshua, and this seemed to be the opportune moment to change that. Whether for her own sake, Esther's, or both, it was time to tell someone.

⌘

Esther was stunned by the confession, and Rachel had spared not a single detail. The telling had been heart wrenching, and also cathartic. It seemed to ease both of their guilt.

"So it's over?" Esther asked.

"It's over."

The two friends looked at one another intensely. Suddenly, Esther started to laugh. Rachel hesitated at first, but couldn't keep from joining in. They began to laugh harder; it felt good. Much better than crying. Oh, the mess they'd made of their lives.

"What are you going to do?" Rachel asked, trying to calm herself.

"Who knows? Maybe I'll marry him; he's Jewish, you know. I suppose I can't hold that against him, can I?"

"No, I suppose you can't."

"What are *you* going to do?" Esther asked.

"Me?" Rachel contemplated her response, then: "I'm going to keep things simple. I'm going to love my husband, have lots of children, and make chullent and kugel every *Shabbos*."

More laughter.

⌘

Rachel returned to the synagogue the following *Shabbos*. She hadn't fully recuperated, and could have gotten away with staying home, but she wanted to go. She knew that sooner or later she would have to face the sympathetic stares from the women in the balcony. *It might as well be now.*

There was also another reason for her decision. It had been announced throughout the community that the *Rebbe* was going to deliver a major speech, the topic of which was known only to a select few. Rabbi Weissman had been one of those few, and he had shared what he knew with his family during Friday night dinner. Rachel had been shocked: *the Rebbe is going to talk about racial issues in the neighborhood, unheard of.*

The *Rebbe* had always been aloof from such unseemly matters. And now that was going to change. Notwithstanding her vows of ending her relationship with Joshua, and her belief that this was all behind her, she felt compelled to hear what the *Rebbe* had to say.

She and her mother arrived at the synagogue just in time. They climbed the stairs, and found the usually vacant balcony filled to capacity, standing room only. Rachel was glad to be hidden in the crowd, virtually unnoticed, able to avoid spurious consolation and inquiries as to her well-being.

They stood in the back for less than a minute before silence descended upon the hall. The room was never this quiet, not even during the Torah reading. Rachel had always found it disturbing how the *Rebbe* commanded more decorum than the Almighty Himself, but that was the way things were.

She couldn't see beyond the heads in front of her, but she heard the *Rebbe's* voice emanating from the podium below. He spoke softly, barely loud enough to be discerned, and in Yiddish, the preferred tongue of all Hasidic sects. Rachel had no problem with that; her teachers had all taught in Yiddish, and her parents had often used it around the house. She listened intently, her hand cupped behind her ear for better acuity. Around her, the women were *shuckling*, swaying back and forth with their bodies, believing that doing so enhanced their concentration. Rachel stood still, as did Hannah. The *shuckling* thing wasn't in their blood.

"My friends, this small section of Brooklyn has been our home since the early 1940's, and it will remain our home until, God willing, the Messiah comes to gather us." The *Rebbe* paused for a moment, for words of the Messiah usually inspired cheers and singing among his followers. The crowd responded as expected: *We want Moshiach now! We want Moshiach now! We want Moshiach now . . .*

Rachel looked at her mother with humor. Neither of them chanted, and they knew that, down below, Isaac wasn't chanting either. Isaac Weissman had always stressed that prayer and deeds would hasten the coming of the Messiah, not screaming and yelling.

The crowd quieted after a few minutes, and the Rebbe continued. "Our neighborhood has also been the home of many groups other than ourselves, and over the past few years, some have been leaving for one reason or another."

Rachel knew the *Rebbe* was being intentionally vague, it would be unfitting for him to be more specific.

"This is unfortunate, and much has changed. There is more crime, there is more tension on the streets." The *Rebbe* stopped, as heads all around him nodded in fierce agreement. *The Rebbe is going to take us to live somewhere else*, they thought, *the Rebbe is going to save us.*

"I know that many of you have waited for a sign . . ."

Again, chanting: "*We want Moshiach now! We want Moshiach now!*"

"Many of you have waited patiently for me to consider our problems."

Silence.

"And now, it is time for me to speak out."

"Bring Moshiach now! Bring Moshiach now!"

"My friends, it has always been our faith that the Messiah will be arriving any day to deliver us from exile, return us to our holy land, and rebuild the temple in Jerusalem . . ."

"Moshiach is here! Moshiach is here!"

At this point, just about everyone in the hall was perspiring from the frenzy. The heat was unbearable. Hannah turned to Rachel, seeing that her face was peaked, and asked, "Do you want to go home?"

"No, not yet."

The *Rebbe* continued: "I believe that the day is near. I believe that the day is *tomorrow!*"

More chanting.

"And that is why I say that we must remain *here* in our home, that we must not leave like the others. For this is the place where God has delivered us from the hands of the Nazis. *This* is the place where God wants us to wait for *His* final redemption: the coming of the King Messiah, to gather us, and bring us back to Jerusalem."

A song erupted: *L'shana haba'a b'Yerushalayim*, next year in Jerusalem. The *Rebbe* looked out at his followers, and began to clap along as they sang the words of hope. Within seconds, there was dancing throughout the hall. A joyous occasion. *The Rebbe has spoken. We will stay in Crown Heights until the Messiah arrives. We will not run!*

Even the many who had hoped to be leaving Crown Heights danced. For it was the *Rebbe's* desire that they wait for the Messiah, and the *Rebbe* had said that the Messiah was at hand. Soon, they would leave.

Rachel and Hannah made their way through the crowd and down the stairs. As they came out of the synagogue, some men were standing around and talking. Rachel could have sworn she heard one of them say, "The *Rebbe* is the Messiah."

"Of course, there is *no* question," another added.

She turned to her mother. "Did you hear . . . ?"

"Yes. There's been a lot of talk like that lately. Your father doesn't like it; he thinks it's blasphemous. The first time he heard it, he almost had another heart attack."

Rachel suddenly felt awful. She'd been so wrapped up in her own suffering, she had forgotten about her father's condition. "How is he doing?" she asked, embarrassed.

"He's okay. This thing with you has upset him, but he's handling it."

"I'm going to bring him joy," Rachel said tearfully. "I'm going to give him grandchildren."

"I know you will," her mother answered. "He loves you more than anyone in the world."

Rachel read the jealousy in her mother's comment, feeling ashamed that she had never completely appreciated Hannah's predicament. True, she'd had her own albatross, measuring up to a dead half-brother, always fearful of disappointing her saintly father. But Hannah was doubly cursed, having to compete with Isaac's lost wife, and his obsession for his daughter. *That* was more than anyone should have to bear.

Rachel looked at her mother. The once stalwart enchantress was growing delicate and weary. Years of unspoken aching had taken their toll. "I'm going to bring *you* joy, too, Mama," she said, putting an arm around her.

"You already do."

CHAPTER 36

Joshua wasn't surprised at not having heard from Rachel for the past six months. Their last rendezvous had left him doubtful about their future. He knew that staying away from him was a difficult choice for her, but it was one he would honor.

He escaped in his studies and, after his first year, it paid off with an A average and a place on the dean's list. He had also decided to take Professor Thompson's advice to pursue law as a career, not out of fidelity to the black plight in America, but because he started believing he could actually become one of those criminal lawyers he used to watch on TV. Perry Mason Eubanks.

He tried getting past his feelings for Rachel, and was frequenting social functions on campus. Lectures, dances, holiday parties; he forced himself to attend all of them. Loretta had also given him a push: "You can't sit around all the time waiting on something that just isn't going to be!"

It was hard for him to meet new people. He was fearful of rejection because of his cane, always came late, stood alone, and left early. Until a few weeks earlier, one Saturday night, when everything changed.

Her name was Constance Henderson, or Connie as she called herself. She wasn't the greatest looker: a bit chunky, bespectacled, frizzy hair. But that didn't seem to bother him. He thought she was nice, *real* nice, and sharp too. An adept conversationalist, quick sense of humor, and brassy—considering the way she had approached him.

She had recognized him from Thompson's class. He hadn't recalled seeing her, but politely pretended he had. He wasn't proud of being remembered from that class; his notoriety there had been far from his finest moment. But at least something good had come from it. Another one of those silver linings.

He liked that she laughed a lot, and that she wasn't one of Thompson's blind devotees. Their mutual interest in studying law was the proverbial icing on the cake. They had much in common and, while he enjoyed her immensely, he knew in his heart that they weren't destined for a flaming romance.

Since the night they'd met, they had eaten lunch together daily, seen two movies, and she'd been to his house to meet his mother. They'd started holding hands now and then, and had even shared a few tender kisses. Neither of them seemed particularly ecstatic, but it was okay. They liked one another, and that seemed to be enough.

So here he was, Saturday evening, getting dressed for another date with Connie. He glanced in the mirror, then went into the living room to say good-night to his mother. She kissed him, and said, "Good luck, now. You act polite and gentleman-like, and things will be just fine."

She was referring to the fact that he was meeting Connie's parents. He dreaded the occasion, for Connie's family was from Trinidad, and Caribbean blacks usually preferred their children socializing amongst their own. Joshua loathed the ever growing divisiveness in his own community, the deep prejudices regarding shade of color, purity of heritage, place of birth, and rearing. He couldn't understand any of it, as if there weren't enough problems from the whites.

Connie lived in East New York, a predominantly black neighborhood abutting Crown Heights. It was a clear, warm summer night. He walked two blocks to East New York Avenue, and noticed the hookers gathering around the park. A lump formed in his throat as an image of Celeste came to mind. A day seldom passed without the thought of her, wondering where she was and if she was all right. He continued on his way.

He took the East New York Avenue bus, got off at the corner of Snediker Avenue, and walked the rest of the way. She lived on a block of red-brick, two-family row houses. He looked for her address, and arrived at her doorstep ten minutes early for a Seven-thirty date. He climbed the cement stairs to the front door, and pressed the buzzer.

Her father answered the door. A large man, rotund, dark brown complexion, sharp mahogany eyes, coal black hair, gray at the temples, and a well trimmed goatee also with a touch of gray. His most notable feature at the moment, however, was an angry expression.

"Hi. I'm Joshua Eubanks." Joshua offered his hand.

"Mat Henderson." Frigid. No eye contact. Obligatory shake.

Mr. Henderson showed Joshua in. The living room was nicely decorated.

Wall-to-wall, grass-green carpet, gold and mint patterned wall paper, landscape paintings, an impressive burgundy couch with two matching sitting chairs, mahogany coffee table, and a brown leather recliner. Joshua knew that Connie's father was an auto mechanic; now he knew that auto mechanics didn't do too badly. Mr. Henderson offered Joshua a chair, and took the recliner for himself.

Connie's mother emerged from the kitchen. A short but pleasant looking woman: shapely, *café au lait* complexion, stylish hairdo, and a nicely contoured face. Connie looked more like her father.

Mrs. Henderson, who didn't bother to offer a first name, also appeared somewhat inimical. She attempted a smile, obviously transparent. "Can I offer you something to drink?" she asked.

"Sure." Nervous.

"Pepsi?"

"That would be great."

She left the men alone for what seemed to Joshua the longest minute of his life. He was tongue-tied, and Mr. Henderson had nothing to say either. They sat in silence.

Mrs. Henderson returned, handed Joshua his Pepsi, and took a seat on the couch. Nothing for her husband, and nothing for herself. Joshua, wondering what indignity they might have suffered to drink with him, held his poise.

"So, Joshua," Mrs. Henderson opened, "Constance tells us she knows you from college?"

"Yes, we met at a dance." *Where the hell is she, anyway?*

"Are you studying anything particular?" she asked.

"I'm interested in law."

"Oh." A skeptical grimace. "Constance wants to be a lawyer, too."

Just at that moment, Joshua heard someone coming down the stairs. Connie. *Thank God.* He never thought he'd be so happy to see her. They all turned toward her as she entered the room. "Hello everybody," she said cheerfully, as if purposely intending to break the tension. To Joshua: "Sorry I took so long."

"It's okay. No problem," he responded. She could tell he was lying.

Her parents also seemed relieved by her appearance. "Well dear," her mother said, "where are you off to?"

"The movies, I suppose." She looked to Joshua for confirmation.

"Yes, the movies," Joshua said.

"How nice." Patronizing.

They all got up and walked to the front door. Connie kissed her parents good-night, and her father finally spoke. "Be sure to get home early, before twelve," he enjoined, looking at Connie, though Joshua knew it was for him that the comment was intended.

"Daddy!" Connie said cutely, as if they'd been through this before.

"Twelve," he repeated unflinchingly.

"Twelve it is," Joshua interjected.

⁂

They took the bus to the Kingsway on Kings Highway, at Coney Island Avenue. They were quiet, neither knowing quite what to say after that meeting with her parents. Finally, she turned to him and apologized again for having kept him waiting.

"It really wasn't that bad," he said.

"I'm sure it seemed like it was," she replied.

He chuckled.

"There's a lot they don't understand," she said.

"I'll bet there is."

"Okay, so they're prejudiced; show me someone who isn't."

He thought about it. No answer.

"They're just old fashioned," she said. "And scared."

"Does that bother you?" he asked.

"Of course it does. It's just that I'm used to it."

"What if they told you not to see me again?"

"They wouldn't. They know I wouldn't listen." She took his hand and smiled. "Looks like this is our stop," she added, pointing at the theatre.

The movie was *The Great White Hope*, a film about the persecution and humiliation of a black boxing champion, played by James Earl Jones, and his relationship with his white mistress, played by Jane Alexander. The story took place in the early 1900's, and was supposedly based on the real-life story of Jack Johnson, the world's first black heavyweight champion. It had been receiving a lot of media hype, and was certainly a topic of interest to both of them. Despite all that, they sat in the back row and made out through most of it.

She was home by twelve, but it didn't get Joshua any points. Her parents were awake, and greeted her at the front door, precluding any long good-nights. They didn't invite him in, didn't inquire about how he was getting home, didn't say anything to him, in fact. For some reason, their displeasure had augmented over the past few hours, and Joshua had some suspicion as to why.

He sat on the bus, glanced at his leg and cane, and became rife with anger. It was easy for him to despise his life, and at moments like this, that's exactly what he felt.

⟨≈⟩

Joshua continued seeing Connie, but their relationship never took off. He hadn't really been smitten to begin with, and the other complications didn't help. He was thinking he should give the "woman thing" a rest for a while.

The summer flew by. He had a work-study position shelving books in the college library. He spent his days working, thinking about Rachel and Celeste, and lunched with Connie every now and then. Evenings were for TV and books he borrowed from the library—not much of a life, but at least he was staying out of trouble.

CHAPTER 37

Esther Mandlebaum gazed into Stephen Butler's eyes. She couldn't help herself. They'd been dating for over a year, and still, each time she saw him was as if it were the first.

Tonight, Stephen cooked dinner at his place. In addition to his acting talents, he fancied himself a gourmet. Veal piccata, asparagus with hollandaise sauce, roasted garlic potatoes, and a slightly chilled Chardonnay to wash it down. Dessert: a homemade tiramisu.

Esther had forsaken the laws of *Kashruth* almost as quickly as the prohibition of premarital sex. She had found a new existence, and was determined to enjoy it to the fullest.

Stephen watched how heartily she ate. Since they'd started dating, he'd been amazed by how much she could consume, while actually appearing to *lose* weight. He had even once mentioned it to her, to which she had responded by assuring him that, aside from their meals together, she was a stern dieter. "I only indulge when I'm with *you*," had been her exact words.

After dessert, she excused herself to the bathroom while he cleared the table. Several minutes passed, and he was almost done with the dishes when he became concerned. "Esther," he called out, "is everything okay?"

No answer.

"Esther." This time louder.

Still no answer.

He walked to the bathroom door. "Esther, are you all right?"

He heard her moving around in the bathroom. He knocked on the door. "Esther, please, open the door."

Stumbling in the bathroom.

"Esther!" Pounding on the door. "Esther, open the door!"

Nothing.

He pressed his weight against the door and pushed, but not enough. Again, harder, all his strength. The door flew open.

In front of him, on the floor, she lay, half conscious, eyes open but glazed. A retched stench permeated the air. He looked at her face, the corners of her mouth, the floor, the toilet. Vomit all over.

He bent down, helped her to a sitting position, grabbed a towel off the rack, and began to wipe her chin. "Are you sick?"

She struggled to answer. "I think so."

"I'll call a doctor."

"No! Please, no doctor."

"But Esther, you're sick. You need a doctor."

"No doctor, *please*."

He looked at her, concerned. "Come, you'll lie down." He helped her up and walked her to the bedroom, frightened by how unsteadily she moved.

"I'll be okay," she said. "It's probably a virus."

"Maybe it's something you ate?"

"I don't think so, otherwise you'd have it too."

She was making sense, sounding a little stronger. Good signs, he thought. "You sure you don't want a doctor?"

"Positive."

"You should stay here tonight."

"I can't. I have to go home."

"But how can you possibly get home in this condition?"

"I have to."

"Then I'll take you."

"That's not a good idea."

Stephen knew all about Esther's family, and the fact that she was keeping him a secret until the "right" time. He didn't completely understand; after all, he *was* Jewish, he had often reminded her. There was much he didn't grasp about Hasidic life.

"If you won't see a doctor, you won't stay here, and you won't let me take you home, then what?" He was losing patience.

"I can go home myself."

"I don't think so."

"I can," she said, struggling off the bed. She stood up and started walking toward the door. Faltering and wobbly. He grabbed her before she fell, and helped her back to the bed.

"Now what?" he asked.

She couldn't answer right away.

"Esther, we have to do *something*."

She thought about it for a few seconds. Then: "Okay, I have an idea. My friend Rachel, her number is 555-8974. Call her, she'll know what to do; she'll come and take me home."

⁂

Rachel was lying in bed when the phone rang. Binny had helped her clean up after dinner, and had just left for the yeshiva when she decided to steal some well needed rest. It had been over a year since the miscarriage, and two and a half months ago she'd finally gotten pregnant again. She and Binny had reacted soberly and cautiously to the news. He'd begun helping out around the house, enabling her to take it easy.

Rachel answered the phone thinking it was the usual evening call from her mother to check on things. "Everything's fine, Mama," she said as she picked up the receiver.

"Pardon me," an unfamiliar voice said on the other end.

"I'm sorry," Rachel offered, slightly abashed. "Who's calling?" she asked, thinking it was probably for Binny.

"Is this Rachel?"

"Yes, *who is this?*"

"My name is Stephen Butler."

Rachel recognized the name. "Oh yes, you're Esther's . . ."

"Yes, I am." Stephen explained why he was calling. He reassured Rachel that Esther was okay, only that she needed someone to come and get her. A slight contradiction, Rachel noted nervously.

She hung up the phone, called a car service, got dressed, and left a note for Binny in case he came home before her. It said: "Had to go out to get something. Don't worry. Be home soon." She couldn't come up with anything else to write at the moment. She would explain later.

On the way to Manhattan, she thought about what Stephen had said on the phone. Vomiting immediately after dinner, weakness, stumbling, no fever. It didn't take much for her to make the connection. Esther had steadily been losing weight since she'd met Stephen, claiming she'd been dieting, yet Rachel hadn't noticed any changes in her friend's eating habits. On reflection, Esther still ate lots of sweets, junk food, and almost nauseating portions at meals. There had been stories in high school about girls who threw up. It certainly wasn't unheard of, even in their insulated corner of the world. Esther was perfect prey for this sort of thing.

Rachel felt a sudden surge of guilt, accusing herself, once again, of being consumed with her own problems to the point of obliviousness to those she loved.

⟨⟩

Stephen Butler answered the door and instantly understood why Esther had never mentioned Rachel before this evening. Even in theatre circles, he'd rarely seen someone so captivating. For a split second, he'd almost forgotten why she was there.

Rachel, of course, wasn't surprised in the least by Stephen's appearance. Esther had described him to a tee, sparing not a luscious detail. "Hi, I'm Rachel," she said.

"I'm Stephen," he responded. He showed her in, without offering to shake her hand. Esther had forewarned him that Hasidic women didn't shake hands with men.

He escorted Rachel into the bedroom. Esther was lying on the bed, though more alert than earlier. "I just don't know what happened," Stephen said.

Esther looked at Rachel, and knew immediately that her friend had figured out her secret. Her expression said, *don't you dare say a word!* Her voice said, "It's probably a stomach flu or something."

"Probably." Rachel felt Esther's forehead. "I think you might even be a little warm." Good act.

"I feel like I am," Esther confirmed.

"I couldn't tell, I'm hot myself," Stephen added.

"Well, we best get you home. The car service is waiting downstairs," Rachel said.

Esther sat up on the bed, and slowly got to her feet. "I feel a bit better," she said as she started walking. Rachel moved to help, but Esther waved her off.

"Are you sure you don't need me to go with you?" Stephen asked.

"Positive," Esther responded.

"Don't worry," Rachel said to Stephen, "everything's going to be fine."

They left Stephen's building and got into the car. For the first few minutes, neither spoke. The silence was finally broken by Esther. "So I guess you know what's going on."

"I think so."

"No, you *know*."

"Okay, I know." Rachel tried not to seem annoyed, but couldn't help it.

"It's really not that bad. I'm not going to do it anymore."

"Is it that simple?"

"Yes, it is. It's quite simple, so you can stop worrying."

"Okay," Rachel responded, though she didn't believe it. She had heard too much about bulimia over the years, and had even seen a few cases when she had worked in the hospital. It was an awful addiction, and she knew that Esther wasn't just going to stop, not without help.

Rachel searched for something profound to say, something that would make a difference, but her mind was blank. Confounded, she sat in silence. Esther began to cry. Rachel moved over to put her arm around her friend.

"I feel so sick about it," Esther confessed. "Each time I do it, I feel sicker, then I promise myself not to do it again, but I just keep doing it." More tears. "I don't want to do it anymore, *I really don't*."

"I know."

"I've tried so hard to stop."

"Do you *really* think you can?"

"I don't know."

"Maybe we can find you some help?"

"Where?"

"Doctor Schiffman might know."

"I'm not sure if that's what I want. I'm embarrassed about the whole thing."

"I know."

"Maybe I should try by myself. If it doesn't work, I'll call Schiffman."

"Esther, I don't think it's a good idea to go it alone. You're already weak, and who knows what's going on with your body. You really should get checked out right away."

"You mean tonight?"

"I'll settle for tomorrow."

Esther thought for a minute. "Okay, tomorrow."

"Good, I'll come by for you in the morning."

"*You're* coming?"

"Yes, I am, and I don't want to hear any more about it."

"Okay," Esther said, realizing she had no choice.

They rode the rest of the way quietly, both staring out at the passing city streets. The time passed slowly. The Manhattan Bridge, Flatbush Avenue, Eastern Parkway. Familiar territory. The cab finally stopped in front of Esther's house.

"I guess I'll see you tomorrow," Esther said as she opened the door.

"Tomorrow it is."

"By the way, I almost forgot, how's the baby?" She reached over and touched Rachel's stomach as she asked.

"*Baruch Hashem*, Thank God. So far, so good."

Esther kissed Rachel on the cheek. "Thanks."

Rachel watched as Esther got out of the cab, walked to the house, and went in. She fought back her tears. She would figure out what to tell Binny about where she'd been, but—for the life of her—she had no idea what to do about Esther. Between the bulimia and Stephen Butler, she was at a loss as to where to start.

⸻

The next morning Rachel picked Esther up and escorted her to Doctor Schiffman's office in the hospital. Esther had told her mother that she was accompanying Rachel to the obstetrician. Rachel had told Binny that she had gone out the night before because Esther had been alone at home and had gotten sick. As they sat in the waiting room, reflecting on their respective fabrications, it occurred to them that, in some ways, they were still those rebellious little girls in the park.

Doctor Schiffman wore an ominous expression as she examined Esther. She took a cardiogram, drew blood, and used terms like "dehydration" and "electrolyte imbalance." Her first suggestion to Esther was to consult a psychiatrist, though she knew that was unlikely to happen. She also wrote out a specific diet, and recommended supplements to replenish Esther's system. Lastly, she lectured Esther on the dangers of bulimia.

That was it; there wasn't much more the doctor could do. The rest was up to Esther. If Schiffman was trying to scare Esther, it seemed she had achieved some success.

Schiffman turned to Rachel and asked about the pregnancy.

"Thank God. So far, so good," Rachel answered, choosing the same words she'd used with Esther the night before.

For a long while after the miscarriage, Rachel had been angry with God. But finally, with this pregnancy, came a renewal of her spirit. She began to pray again, to thank God for each day that passed with her baby still strong, to appeal for more such days, and to erase the trepidations that accompanied every minor ache and discomfort.

Rachel looked at Esther. She wished for her friend to rediscover the very same faith, but knew it wouldn't be. Esther needed liberation— from her home, her family, and her God. The only thing Rachel could reasonably hope for was that Doctor Schiffman's fear tactic would have some impact. In the end, however, none of it made much of a difference. Rachel suffered yet another miscarriage within two weeks, and Esther was back in the bathroom, purging her guts out in less time than that.

BOOK IV

CHAPTER 38

On March 29, 1973 the United States troops withdrew from Vietnam. Three days later, a young chaplain who had voluntarily served four tours, arrived from Southeast Asia in Fort Hamilton, Brooklyn. He would be stationed there for a month, his final days before returning to civilian life.

The fort, located at the southernmost tip of Brooklyn, stood at the foot of the Verrazano-Narrows bridge. The bridge, which traversed Jamaica Bay connecting Brooklyn to Staten Island, was the world's longest suspension bridge. Standing outside his quarters in full uniform, Captain Jerome Williams stared out at the massive structure, lost in a reverie of memories and thoughts about the war he had left halfway around the world just a few days earlier, and the war he had left, in this very place, so many years before.

It was late in the day, a few minutes before sunset. Just west of the bridge, Jerome watched the burning ball slowly descend into the horizon, radiating hues of violet and crimson. A pretty sight, though not nearly as magnificent as the sunsets of the Pacific, he thought. No, nothing here was equivalent to anything there, not in beauty, nor in ugliness.

He thought about the war, how many had died, how many of his *brothers* had died. The disproportionate number of black soldiers serving on the fronts had disturbed him deeply, but it was nothing new. Growing up on the streets of Brooklyn had taught him that blood was cheap, especially black blood.

He had missed the first draft lottery, and that had given him time to finish high school and enter the seminary. He had then taken advantage of the 4-D deferment for two years until he decided to volunteer as a chaplain. He had needed a break from school, and from New York. Above all, he had needed a good fight, a tangible enemy on whom he could unleash his rage.

But the rage never waned. With all he'd learned in the seminary, all the killing he'd seen, even the killing he'd done—yes, the chaplain had taken up arms against the *enemy*—nothing had changed.

And soon he would be returning to the streets of Crown Heights. He wondered what awaited him. He wondered about his mother, and about his sister. He had a suitcase filled with hundreds of letters from his mother, and not a word in any about Celeste. So many years since Celeste had disappeared, so many confusing and conflicting feelings about her; he still didn't know why he'd never gone searching for her, nor if he would start now. What he did know was that he had a plan. The first thing he was going to do was return to his mother's house, finish the seminary, and open a new church in the neighborhood. That had been his dream since the time he'd studied with Reverend Sharp.

The reverend had always been a great inspiration, until that tragic day when the telegram had arrived reporting his son Roy's death in the war. From that moment, the reverend stopped preaching. He resigned his position in the church, and refused to see anyone. Eventually, the church had closed, and the empty storefront became yet another lair for drug dealers and whatnot.

Roy had been Jerome's closest friend, and had been drafted right out of high school. The news of Roy's death had shaken Jerome, had made him feel guilty about not having been there to save his friend, the same guilt he had always felt about his sister. Two weeks after Roy's death, Jerome had decided to join the army.

And now, Captain Jerome Williams' service to his country was over. But there were still battles to be fought, both in his soul and in the streets. He had learned many lessons of survival, some from Vietnam, some from the army, but most from an old childhood "friend."

Jerome Williams felt a surge of vengeance whenever he thought of Joshua Eubanks. Yes, there were more battles ahead.

In another part of Brooklyn, on the deserted roadways adjacent to the piers and the Navy Yard overlooking Manhattan's seaport, Celeste Williams turned her tricks and filled her veins with kaleidoscopic juices that helped erase her past. It was a wretched existence, walking the streets day and night, catering to empty faces in cars. Doctors, lawyers, plumbers, each with a different story, all with the same desire. They needed her and she needed them; they paid and she delivered. No pretense, no surprises—at least most of the time.

By all odds, she should have been dead by now. Lowlife pimps, perverts in cars, and all that poison in her veins. Lots of the girls disappeared into the night, and the cops usually never even bothered investigating. But not Celeste, she had the instinct. She always seemed to end up on her feet.

Like the time Big Bob had tried to pawn her off on another pimp, because she'd gotten too strung out and the johns had started complaining. No one was going to sell *her*. So she'd upped and run. Away from Big Bob, away from Bed-Stuy and East New York. Around the piers she would be safe; they would never find her. She had gotten away. But the sad truth was, Big Bob hadn't even bothered to look for her.

The years had passed quickly. It was all about survival, moment to moment. Get the money, get your stuff, catch some sleep, steal some food, and back on the street. No time to think about what might have been, or who was left behind. No time to think about anything; thinking was a bad idea.

Boyfriends were also a bad idea. Some of the girls had boyfriends, usually their pimps. But those girls were always exploited, used, and trashed. Not Celeste, anyone who wanted a piece of her had to pay. *Anyone*. No pretense, no surprises.

CHAPTER 39

On August 9, 1974, Richard M. Nixon resigned the Presidency of the United States, an event which ordinarily would have meant little to Joshua. He didn't much care for Nixon, and hadn't voted for him. But it was a date Joshua would never forget, for that was the same day on which he first met Willie Johnson.

Willie Johnson was a nineteen year old black kid, accused of stabbing and raping a thirty-six year old Hasidic woman in Crown Heights. The incident had occurred in the woman's apartment, where she resided alone. The police report accused Mr. Johnson of following her home, late at night, to her building on the corner of Troy Avenue and Montgomery Street, forcing her at gun-point through the front door, up the deserted stairs, and into her second floor dwelling, where he allegedly robbed, raped, and left her for dead. The only witness was a Hasidic male, who claimed to have seen a man fitting Mr. Johnson's height, weight, and dress leaving the building around the reported time of the rape. The police picked up Mr. Johnson about two hours later, hanging out on a street corner in the vicinity. The victim, Emma Lukins, provided an accurate and detailed report of the occurrence from her hospital bed, but was unable to identify her assailant with any certainty, as he had worn a black ski mask during the attack. The police, however, believed that they had their man, since he fit the general description, was in possession of a gun, and had a record of two previous burglaries.

Joshua had been out of law school, working at the public defender's office for two months, and was already well entrenched in the system. His job, basically, was to help "move cases," which was shop talk for making deals and avoiding trials. The Johnson case was supposed to be just another "hand-job," as they called them: white victim, black perp, nothing to it.

In the life of a PD, concepts like "justice" and "equality" were ephemeral, remnants of an idealism that ceased the moment law school ended. For Joshua, the adjustment was easy, for his idealism had died long ago. He was thankful for what he had, the opportunity to have attended Brooklyn Law School, and the job. Now he had to play the game.

In his case, sealed juvenile court records, an impeccable college transcript, solid scores on the L-SAT's, and a nest egg that Loretta had put away over the years had made it all possible. He'd had some doubts about the extent of the nest egg, and had suspected Alfred Sims' involvement once again. But that was fine with him. Sims owed him.

He'd landed the job immediately after graduating in May. He took the July Bar, and was still awaiting the results. Since he wasn't actually an attorney yet, he was delegated to menial tasks: intakes, assignment of cases to trial attorneys, scheduling court dates, etcetera. He didn't mind, for he didn't plan to stay long, maybe a year at the most. Pass the Bar, behave himself for a while, then onward and upward to private practice. Perry Mason Eubanks at your service.

But then he met Willie Johnson and everything changed. There was something about the kid that made this case different, something that told him that this kid was capable of neither rape nor attempted murder. He just didn't have the eyes. Joshua had learned to read people's eyes, growing up on the street.

Joshua knew that Willie was going down for this crime anyway, regardless of the truth. A white woman was raped and the police needed a perp. It didn't matter that Willie had no history of sex crimes. He was black, poor, had a rap sheet, and wore the right clothes in the wrong place at the wrong time. They weren't going to look for anyone else.

Joshua's boss, Tom Fielding, didn't care much either. He was a tall, jet-black haired fellow with a beer belly who always wore shirts that were too tight around the collar. Middle aged, bad marriage, placid demeanor.

A career PD. Make no waves, pick up your check at the end of the week, and spend it at the bar with your pals.

Fielding had asked Joshua to sit in on his interview with Willie, because Willie wasn't talking. He was the type who figured that blacks stick together; he figured lots of things like that. "Just get him to open up and tell you his story. Make him think you're his best friend. We can't go to the DA looking like assholes," he said.

Their initial meeting took place in an interview room at Riker's Island. It was the first time Joshua had met a client in prison, the first time he'd been involved in a case at this level. The room looked like a cage. A barred metal door, puke-green walls, a rectangular wooden table, four wooden chairs, and plenty of stench. The only window, of course, was sealed and barred.

Joshua sat with Fielding, reviewing their notes. Willie was escorted in by two guards, his hands and feet shackled. Fielding didn't ask the guards to remove the shackles, and Joshua sat there, keeping his mouth shut.

Willie was about the same height and weight as Joshua. His cheeks and eyes were bruised, as if he'd been in a brawl, his affect was flat, he made no eye contact, and he said nothing. The three of them sat at the table in silence.

Fielding gave Joshua a look that said, *see what I mean.*

Joshua wondered if Willie was a punk who didn't give a shit, or if he was just scared. Scared in a way that Fielding could never understand.

"Willie, my name is Joshua Eubanks and I work with Mr. Fielding at the public defender's office."

Willie lifted his head and looked at Joshua. He was silent for a few seconds. "So they sent me some lackey just because he's black."

"Willie, I'm a *lawyer,*" Joshua said, realizing that he'd never actually said that to anyone before. It felt good.

Willie eyed him with disbelief.

"Willie," Fielding said, "this here is Mr. Eubanks, and he *is* a lawyer for the public defender's office. He's going to assist in your case."

"Black boy suckin' up to 'the man,' seems right to me."

Fielding: "Why don't you just tell us your side of things."

Willie: "What difference is anything I say gonna make?"

Joshua: "Hard to tell, until we hear exactly what it is that you got to say."

Silence.

Willie: "I didn't do it."

Fielding: "That's it, *you didn't do it?*"

Willie: "What else you want, man. *I didn't do it.* Didn't rob or rape no lady. Never raped no one."

Fielding: "But you have robbed a few folks."

Willie: "Not like that, I ain't."

Fielding: "Like what?"

Willie: "Never beat no one, never even hit no one. Just broke into a couple a stores late at night, nobody's around, that's it!"

Fielding: "Seems your record here says otherwise." He pulled a sheet out of a pile in front of him. "Says here you robbed a grocery store one afternoon, held a gun to the owner."

Willie: "Yeah, well I didn't hurt him none, just scared him."

It struck Joshua that Fielding was sounding more like a prosecutor than a defense attorney, so he jumped in. "Look Willie, we're here to help you."

"Help me. How you gonna help me if you believe I'm guilty?"

"I don't believe you're guilty," Joshua said.

Fielding threw Joshua a look. He was hoping for a confession, quick deal with the DA, and on to the next case. This was complicating matters.

"Yeah, well *he* don't," Willie said, pointing to Fielding.

"Yes he does," Joshua responded, knowing that Fielding was going to fry his ass. *What the hell*, the kid had his rights.

Fielding sat back. Willie looked down at the table again. Joshua continued to speak. "Willie, why don't you tell us your side of it?"

Willie picked up his head, looking only at Joshua. "Ain't much to tell. I was hangin' with some brothers outside this store all night. Along come these cop cars, three of them. Cops jump out and come at me, I don't know why."

Joshua: "Did you try to run?"

Willie: "No, I just stood there. Didn't know they wanted me till they came at me."

Joshua: "Did you resist arrest?"

Willie: "I know better than to do that, especially with six cops on my ass."

Joshua: "Did you say anything?"

Willie: "I said all kinds of things. So did the brothers. Like, 'what you doin' man? What the hell you rousting me for?' That kinda stuff."

Joshua: "Were the police rough?" He looked at the bruises on his face.

Willie: "Oh no, sir, they were po—lite! They always polite with us, don't you know that?"

Joshua: "Did they tell you why they were arresting you?"

Willie: "Not till we got to the station."

Joshua: "And your friends, what did they do?"

Willie: "They got the hell outta there, that's what they did."

Joshua: "You mean the cops were only interested in you?"

Willie: "Guess so."

Joshua: "Why do you think that is?"

Willie: "Cause they think I raped and beat that white lady, *that's why!*" He looked at Fielding and asked, "Hey, is your partner here stupid or what?"

"Willie, why *you?*" Joshua asked, preempting Fielding's reply.

"I don't know, man. They say someone saw me coming from the building, some white guy. Maybe *we* all just look alike to *them.*" His eyes were fixed on Fielding.

Joshua: "Willie, where are your friends, the guys you were hanging out with?"

Willie: "They around."

Joshua: "Willie, I need more than that. I need them as witnesses to testify that you were with them 'all night' as you said."

Fielding stirred in his chair.

Willie: "I said they around. I don't know where. Why I gotta keep repeating myself?"

Joshua decided not to push, and asked instead, "Your mother, where is she?" He had read in the arrest record that Willie lived alone with his mother in a tenement apartment on the north side of Eastern Parkway. For a moment, Joshua was struck by the familiarity of this, and wondered if that was why the kid had gotten to him in the first place.

"I don't know where she at, sometimes she don't come home for days. Probably out of town with some white dude cheating on his wife or something."

An image of Loretta and Alfred Sims flashed into Joshua's mind, but he quickly regained focus. He wanted to know why Willie wouldn't reveal where his friends were, why they weren't by his side, supporting his alibi. Something was fishy.

"Let's get back to your friends, Willie," Joshua said. "Why won't you tell us where they are so we can talk to them and clear things up?"

"Look man, I told you twice, I don't know."

Joshua: "How about their names?"

Willie: "I don't know any names."

Joshua: "You mean to tell me that these guys are your friends, but you don't know who they are?"

Willie: "They not my friends, just some guys I was hanging with, and I ain't gonna talk no more."

Joshua: "Okay, fine then. We'll play it your way." He stood up, looked at Fielding, walked to the door, and called for the guard.

"That's it?" Willie asked.

"That's it," Joshua replied.

Fielding wore an *I told you so* expression on his face as he gathered his papers and placed them in his briefcase. A guard came into the room—this time only one guard—took Willie by the arm, helped him to his feet, and escorted him from the room.

Joshua watched Willie leave, and thought back to when he'd been a prisoner. He remembered his attitude, not much different than Willie's, and his attorney's haunting proclamation: *Nobody gives a shit.* It was true, nobody had given a shit about him or the late Elija Williams, and nobody gave a shit about Willie Johnson. But a whole lot of people cared about Emma Lukins. So much so, they would settle for Willie Johnson's conviction in a heartbeat, regardless of the evidence. These days, with a black defendant and a white victim, it didn't take much to convince the public that they had the right man, just so long as everyone could feel safe on the streets at night.

Call it instinct, or intuition, but Joshua had a feeling. He figured that Willie and his cronies had been involved in some unrelated crime that same evening, which explained why Willie was protecting them, and why they weren't coming forth as witnesses. The only problem was: what to do about it. In order for Willie's "friends" to provide an alibi, they would have to reveal exactly where they were and what they were doing at the time of Emma Lukins' rape, and if Joshua was right, that would land them in a heap of trouble. Joshua understood Willie's world.

The kid would much sooner do time for something he didn't do, than sell out his friends. It was part of the code.

Joshua was frightened by how easy it was for him to get into Willie's head. Big Bob had been right, *you learn a lot from the streets.* But he had also learned a lot getting off of the streets, and that was what separated him from Willie. Strangely enough, it was also what separated him from Fielding. He wanted to do right by Willie, find those alibis, and get to the bottom of things. But he was alone, with no help from Fielding, or Willie. The odds were against him, but there was nothing novel about that.

❦

Connie Henderson, after going to law school with Joshua, had ended up working in the DA's office. They'd maintained a close relationship over the years, which occasionally ventured beyond platonic. They were one of those couples who were able to keep a lasting friendship, while occasionally sharing a bed. The latter usually happened when they were too lonely to fight it, and too disillusioned to look elsewhere.

Joshua phoned her as soon as his lashing from Fielding was over. Fielding had removed him from the Johnson case, and had assured him that his tenure at the PD's office was in serious jeopardy.

Joshua asked her to dinner, and promised to pay if she would look into what the DA had on the Johnson case. He told her about his meeting with Johnson, his suspicions about Johnson's innocence, and Fielding's reaction.

"But you're off the case," she said.

"Don't worry about that, just find out what you can."

"You know you're going to get yourself fired."

"So what."

"Okay, I'll do what I can. Juniors at seven?"

"Juniors at seven."

Juniors was a restaurant on Flatbush Avenue in Downtown Brooklyn that touted the "world's greatest cheesecake." It was a popular lunching spot for professionals, but usually quiet around dinner time. Joshua often met Connie there because of its proximity to their respective offices. Tonight, however, it wasn't so convenient, for he would be taking a rather lengthy detour to the other side of town.

❧

Professor Alvin Thompson was a creature of habit. He kept the same teaching schedule year after year, which included two evening courses during the summer semester. Joshua knew exactly when to find him in his faculty office.

What Joshua was about to do could most definitely ruin his career. He had to be careful that no one found out. He stood in the hallway, not far from Thompson's door, waiting for the right moment. There was only one other person in the hallway, a male student at the other end, reading a bulletin board. Joshua pretended to do the same, until the student disappeared into a classroom. Joshua walked quickly to Thompson's door, listened to confirm if the professor was alone, and knocked.

He heard Thompson say, "Come in," and opened the door. Thompson was surprised. "Mr. Eubanks, oh my! An old student coming to visit? You *must* have been in the neighborhood." Sarcasm.

"Actually, sir, I wasn't." Nervousness.

Thompson appeared curious. "Come! Sit!" He pointed to a chair. "Tell me, how are you?"

Joshua briefly summarized what he was doing, not yet mentioning the Johnson case or his reason for visiting. Thompson seemed genuinely delighted by his accomplishments, especially the part about being a PD.

"I don't know if I had anything to do with it," Thompson said, "but I always knew you would be a lawyer, and now you can really help your people. Many of our brothers are often wrongly accused in the judicial system. A young man such as yourself can do a great deal."

Joshua had anticipated the rhetoric. "That brings me to the purpose of my visit," he said.

Thompson raised his eyebrows.

Joshua told Thompson about the Johnson case, both facts and impressions, and presented his spin on how things went in the PD's office. Thompson, of course, wasn't surprised, but was, however, puzzled that he hadn't heard anything about this case until now.

"I think it was the Nixon resignation," Joshua said. "The media has been so involved with that, everything else was ignored."

Thompson agreed. "Well, now we must rectify that," he said. "We must bring this matter to the attention of the media, and put pressure upon the judicial system to insure Mr. Johnson gets a fair trial."

Exactly what Joshua wanted to hear.

Thompson looked at his watch. "I must be getting to my next class," he said. "You have taken quite a chance coming to me; it could hurt you if anyone were to find out. You needn't be concerned. This discussion will remain between us." He thought for a moment. "You are going to do great things for our people, great things."

Joshua painted on a smile. He had no intention of forming a pact with Thompson, or becoming an activist. He simply wanted to help Willie Johnson, and Thompson was his only recourse. He knew Thompson would bite—it was an irresistible situation. The easy part was done. Now, he needed to get on with the hard part: finding Willie Johnson's friends.

Connie waited a good fifteen minutes, and wasn't happy about it. She was already seated at a table, munching on a pickle, when Joshua appeared and sat down across from her. He looked contrite.

He had debated with himself whether to let her in on his scheme, and hadn't come to a decision. On the one hand, she was his closest friend and sometimes bedfellow; on the other hand, she worked for the DA. He had no doubts about being able to trust her, he just wasn't sure he wanted to put her in a compromising position. When he saw her sitting there, the issue was decided. He needed an excuse for his tardiness, a *good* excuse.

"I'm really sorry I'm late, but it *was* something important."

"Oh," she responded, lifting her head, "and what might that be?"

"It's related to the Johnson case, and I promise to tell you. But first I need to know what you have."

"Is this some sort of *quid pro quo*?"

"Connie!"

"Okay, okay. You know, I could get into a lot of trouble for this."

"No kidding. Trust me, there's going to be plenty of trouble to go around."

"You're right about that. I peeked in the file, and if you ask me— which you obviously are—I think it stinks."

"My sentiments precisely."

"I mean there's no real evidence. *Nothing.* Just a victim and a suspect. No serious investigation, and everyone seems to want to close the book. I'm afraid to imagine why."

"It doesn't take much imagination," he said.

She reflected on his point. "Okay, so what are you going to do? You can't try cases yet, and even if you could, they wouldn't give you one like this. They don't want a circus, they just want this to go away."

"*That's* why I was late tonight."

"Huh?"

"I'm going to give them a circus."

"How?"

"I've been to see Thompson."

"You've been *where?*"

"You heard me. I went to see Thompson, told him the whole story, and if I'm right, Fielding's going to freak tomorrow."

"You could lose your job for this."

"I could."

"And what difference is any of this going to make with Fielding defending him?"

"Who says Fielding's defending him?"

"Well *you're* certainly not, and the kid's got no money, so who else is there."

"Let's just see how things go."

⌘

Connie wanted to stay with him that night; the lone hero stuff had gotten to her. But he had other plans. He shared them with her, and she understood. She also begged him to be careful.

It had been years since he'd been out on the streets at night. He knew he wasn't going to get anywhere in his work clothes, so he went home first to change into something street-wise. Loretta was home when he arrived. He told her he was going out on some business. She didn't ask about it. He was now her lawyer son, completely trustworthy and revered, above all suspicion for any possible wrong-doing.

It was a balmy summer night, with lots of folks out on the sidewalks in front of their buildings. He found a luncheonette on Troy Avenue, just off the corner of Montgomery Street where Willie and his cronies had supposedly been hanging out the night of the rape. He sat at a table, nursing a cup of coffee till around twelve, when the crowds outside had dwindled.

He didn't have much of a plan; in fact, he was basically improvising. He figured he would walk to the corner, hang out a while, see what happened. Smoking had never been his thing, but he thought it wise to buy a pack and puff on a few, hoping it made him fit in.

It didn't take long before someone approached. A black kid, tall, stocky, scar on his chin, beady eyed, in desperate need of dental work. "Hey man, wahs up?" the kid asked.

Joshua looked at him starkly without answering. The first rule is never appear intimidated. Otherwise, you're done. "You want something?" he said.

"No man, I was wonderin' maybe *you* wanted somthin'."

"Like what?"

"You tell me, man. Girls, horse, reefer, whatever you want, I got."

Joshua hesitated, then said, "Information?"

"Infomation! Got plenty o' infomation. What you need to know?"

Joshua reached into his wallet, pulled out a five, and handed it to him. "I'm looking for a group of kids that are on this corner some nights."

"And who might they be?"

"Friends of Willie Johnson."

For an instant, Joshua thought he saw a scared look on the kid's face. Then: "Willie Johnson? I seem to recall a name like that, but I'm not too sure."

"Look, five bucks is all I have. Give it back, or come up with something." Tough, a lot tougher than he was actually feeling.

"Okay man, okay. Cool out! I know the guy."

"So where are his friends?"

"And *who* wants to know?"

"I'm his lawyer."

"*You* Willie's *lawyer?*" The kid looked askance at Joshua. "Come on man, you ain't no one's lawyer."

Joshua was losing patience. He handed the kid his card. "Listen, that's my name, and as it says, I work for the public defender's office. I represent Willie, and if you know anything, you know he's in a shitload of trouble. I'm trying to help him, but I need to talk with his friends and find out where he really was that night."

"Look man," the kid said, fear showing in his eyes, "I ain't never heard of no Willie, and I don't know nothin' about it." He shoved the five dollars back into Joshua's hand, and started to walk away, but Joshua followed after him.

"Listen," Joshua said, grabbing his arm. "I'm not looking to get anyone in trouble."

"Then you best be gone." He pulled away.

"Willie's going to end up in prison for a long time for something he didn't do, unless you help me."

"I told you. I don't know nothin' about it."

"Okay, okay." Joshua calmed himself. "Why don't you just think about it, talk to some guys who might know what I'm talking about. You have my card."

"Yeah sure." Hollow.

"The deal is, if you help me out, I'll help you out."

"You gonna help me?"

"You never need a lawyer?"

The kid considered the offer. "Sure man, whatever you say." With that, he walked off.

⌘

Joshua spent the remainder of the night awake, ruminating over Willie's fate. He didn't even bother getting into bed. He sat at his desk, peering out the window, watching the emergence of daylight.

He showered and changed his clothes. He had two suits, both seersucker; one blue, one gray. Graduation gifts from his mother, who, upon giving them to him, had said, "By the time fall comes, you'll have some money to buy yourself some warm ones." He enjoyed wearing suits, thought he looked kind of lawyerly in them. As for having money, he wasn't even sure he was going to have a job in a few days.

Willie Johnson's arraignment was scheduled for two-thirty. Joshua got to the office early, so he could leave in time to make it to court. Fielding had been abundantly clear about his being off the case, but that wasn't going to stop him from spectating.

The day flew by. He asked Connie to meet him outside the courthouse. "Why not?" she answered, a bit hesitantly. He feared he had involved her more than he should have, but she didn't seem to want to turn back. Not now.

They met on the courthouse steps. It was one of those New York summer days—hazy, hot, and humid. His tie was loosened, his shirt undone, and he looked like someone who hadn't slept in nearly two days. Connie, of course, was put together nicely, hair coifed, lipstick subtle, eye liner matched to a dark blue cotton summer dress. Ever self-conscious about her weight, she always wore dark colors.

"You look good," Joshua said.

"You don't."

Oh well.

They slipped into the back of the courtroom. There were plenty of seats. The room was quiet; the judge was on a break. Fielding was up front, his back to the audience, waiting for Willie's case to be called. A disheveled looking man with gray hair and tortoiseshell glasses sat at the prosecution table, shuffling through some papers.

"That's Strauss," Connie whispered. "He's the ADA on the case. A bona fide asshole, like Fielding. Been on the job fifteen years, only cares about getting through the day."

"I hear the judge isn't much better."

They watched as Strauss approached Fielding and the two began talking. For adversaries, they seemed rather friendly.

"Word is they party together after work at some pub on Montague Street," Connie said.

"Why am I not surprised?"

The door to the judge's chambers opened, and out stepped the honorable Bernard Wilkens, a short, emaciated old man, with thinning white hair, a crooked chin, and a bulbous nose. He ambled up the podium stairs, and sank, slowly, into his chair.

"I wonder if the judge joins them after work," Joshua asked.

Connie giggled, causing eyes to turn their way.

Fielding shot Joshua a disapproving glance, but Strauss didn't seem to recognize either of them.

Joshua kept a straight face. He was no longer afraid. Once he had decided to visit Thompson the night before, he had prepared himself for the worst.

"He doesn't recognize you," Joshua said to Connie, referring to Strauss.

"He will, next time he sees me."

The judge coughed up some phlegm and cleared his throat. "Okay, bailiff, call the next case," he commanded.

The bailiff announced the case and charges. Two guards escorted Willie and his shackles through a door in the front corner of the courtroom, and sat him at the defense table next to Fielding. The judge took the file from the bailiff and began perusing the papers, as a large group of people suddenly paraded into the courtroom. Black people. The judge looked up from his desk. Fielding and Strauss also turned around.

There must have been about fifty of them, all attired in suits and dresses, all observing decorum, quietly entering the room and finding seats. The last to enter was Professor Alvin Thompson. At his side were two white men, also in suits. One of the white men held a large sketch book, the other, a note pad.

Fielding and Strauss looked at one another, then at the judge. Willie turned around and spotted Joshua smiling. He didn't seem to understand what was happening.

"Mr. Fielding," the judge opened, "can you explain what's going on in my court room?"

"No, your honor, I can't."

"Mr. Strauss?"

"Sorry, your honor."

"Okay then, Mr. Thompson," the judge called out, looking directly at the professor, "perhaps *you* can shed some light on the matter."

It wasn't surprising that the judge recognized Thompson. Over the years, the professor had gained quite a reputation. His charisma had turned his small following of classroom zealots into a popular movement, and his face frequented both the tabloids and television.

Thompson rose from his seat. "Your honor, I, and *these* fellow citizens, and *these* members of the press, have come here today with the simple and pure purpose of observing this great court and witnessing how justice is performed."

"He should have been a preacher," Joshua whispered to Connie.

The judge appeared dumbfounded, as did Fielding and Strauss. He called the lawyers up to the bench. The room stilled to overhear what was being said.

"What kind of shit case is this, Mr. Strauss?" the judge asked the DA, pretending to whisper, but knowing the crowd was listening.

"Your honor, the defendant was found . . ."

"I don't give a rat's ass where he was found. There's no evidence connecting him to the crime, is there?"

Fielding remained silent.

"Your honor, he was dressed similarly to the assailant, and has a past record . . ."

"A past record of *what*, Mr. Strauss?"

Strauss stood there, embarrassed. The judge looked at Fielding. "And you, Mr. Fielding, what kind of advocacy is this, offering to plead your client in a case as flimsy as this?"

"Your honor," Fielding began to say as the judge interrupted.

"Step back gentlemen!" the judge commanded.

The lawyers returned to their tables. Fielding conferred with Willie for a few seconds, but the kid still didn't understand anything. He listened to his lawyer and nodded.

The judge cleared his throat again, sipped from a glass of water, and said, "Okay, Mr. Fielding, does your client wish to enter a plea as to the said charges?"

"Yes, your honor," Fielding answered hesitantly. "My client pleads not guilty."

Professor Thompson smiled with approval as the courtroom broke into applause. Judge Wilkins called for order. "Mr. Thompson," he admonished, "you and your entourage will *not* make a mockery of this courtroom. Am I clear on that?"

Thompson rose again. "Abundantly, your honor. I apologize for this slight outburst. It's just that there has been speculation in the community that a young man was going to be railroaded in this court today, plea bargained for a crime of which there is no evidence against him, deprived of his right to a fair trial and an impartial jury of his *peers*. These rumors were concerning, your honor. They frightened the people into believing that there is not equal opportunity under the law for both black and white, and petrified them into imagining that a young man's life might be sacrificed in the name of expediency. And now, your honor, the people have witnessed that justice does indeed prevail, that there is equal access under the law for all. I do apologize if they display their gratitude too intemperately for your honor's liking. I apologize profusely."

Next to Thompson, the white reporter with the notepad seemed to be recording every word of the professor's speech. The sketch artist appeared busy as well.

"Boy, this guy's good," Joshua whispered.

Connie smiled.

"I appreciate your sentiments, Mr. Thompson," the judge said, "but this is a court of law, not a place for grandstanding. In the future you will limit your soliloquies to appropriate forums!"

Thompson smiled.

"And as for the concerns of the community," the judge continued, "this court is *always* occupied with justice. No one, regardless of race, religion, or anything else, gets *railroaded* inside these walls. *No one!*" The judge waited a few seconds for his words to be absorbed. "Now, regarding the matter of the State vs. Willie Johnson, trial will be set for . . ." He stopped to consult his calendar. "February 20th."

A six month delay was not unusual considering the court's schedule, but most of the people in the room didn't know that. They grew restless at the idea that Willie would have to sit in jail awaiting trial for that long. Thompson, however, didn't protest; he knew six months was typical, and he was also confident of his ability to raise money for Willie's bail. He figured that the time would only help Willie's case. Tempers would calm down in the Hasidic community, and maybe he could even pressure the police to do some real investigating.

Strauss rose to his feet. "Your honor, in the matter of bail . . ."

Wilkins: "Save it, Mr. Strauss. This matter has taken up enough of the court's time already. In consideration of the state's case, which is rather weak at this moment, I am setting bail in the matter of five thousand dollars."

Strauss: "Your honor . . ."

Wilkins: "That's it, Mr. Strauss!"

With that, the judge stood up and left the court, the guards escorted Willie out, and Thompson stood around congratulating his followers. Fielding marched out in a huff, not even stopping to look at Joshua. Strauss followed quickly behind him.

Joshua and Connie were still seated, taking in what had just transpired, when Thompson approached them. "You best pass that bar exam, Mr. Eubanks," the professor said. "This boy is going to need a *real* lawyer in six months, not some flunky. The case is yours, you earned it!"

He walked away before Joshua could even discuss the offer. But Joshua knew it wasn't an offer at all. It was a command, and one which he would gladly accept.

CHAPTER 40

Rachel and Binny came out of Doctor Silver's office; she, in tears; his mind elsewhere as if she didn't exist. He offered no words of comfort, no gestures; in fact, he had withdrawn from her weeks earlier, just after her third miscarriage.

"Three successive miscarriages over four years suggests the obvious," the doctor had said. "The chance of miscarrying again is high, and the blood loss could be quite dangerous."

"Dangerous?" Rachel had asked.

"To be honest, Mrs. Frankel, it could kill you."

"You mean, we can't . . ." Rachel had been unable to complete her own sentence.

"I'm sorry," the doctor had said.

Through it all, Binny had sat silently. He was again the person she had thought she would never see again, the Binny of old. And now, this was the Binny she would be stuck with forever.

She knew in her heart she couldn't put all the blame on him. In her despair, she had also retreated. She had stopped taking care of herself and her home, had stopped trying to keep her marriage strong.

And the fighting. So loud, so harsh, so ruinous. Incessant bickering, constant criticism, such had become their only form of communication. She wanted it to stop, and would do anything to make it better. But it was too late. It had taken on a life of its own.

Paul Sims had heard rumors of Rachel's troubles, for there were no secrets among the Hasidim of Crown Heights. The latest chatter predicted an imminent separation. Something about their not being able to have children, and their disenchantment with one another. No one had seen Rachel for months, but Binny was always around. In the yeshiva, on the avenue, taking his weekly meals in restaurants and his Sabbath meals in other people's homes. To all appearances, he was living the life of a *bochur*, a single man.

Paul's own marriage had its own problems, the result of years of tedium and disinterest, but nothing near the calumny of the Frankels. Chava had given him a second daughter, and he had learned to find unexpected pleasure in his children. But aside from that, he was discontented. Financial considerations had forced him to work for his father, managing four apartment buildings in Crown Heights. Basically, he saw himself as nothing more than a glorified "super." The only saving grace was that it kept him busy, away from Chava.

He worked all day, studied in the yeshiva most of the night, and usually saw his daughters after they were asleep, or on *Shabbos*. As for Chava, she had plenty to keep her busy; she seemed to accept the life God had given her.

Paul had never stopped thinking about Rachel. Often, late at night, awake in bed, he imagined her there with him. Sex had stopped with Chava after the birth of their second daughter, and this was his only release. Thankfully, Hasidic couples slept in separate beds.

He always believed Chava to be asleep while he indulged his fantasies, but he'd occasionally been mistaken. Sometimes she was wide awake, pretending to be asleep, listening. His intemperance both humored and humiliated her. Part of her wanted to be next to him, to have a husband who desired and craved her. And part of her was glad; *better he have himself and leave me alone.*

Isaac and Hannah Weissman were worried about their daughter. They had watched with anguish as Rachel's marriage deteriorated. They had tried talking with her, and Isaac had even spoken with Binny on more than one occasion, but their efforts were to no avail.

Hannah visited Rachel daily. It disturbed her that Rachel was always at home, always alone. She tried to suggest going out together, shopping, lunching, whatever. But Rachel was never in the mood.

Isaac would see his daughter some evenings and on *Shabbos*, but his conversations with her were sparse. The Weissmans had been having Sabbath meals together as if Rachel had never married. Except for the fact that the meals were always served in Rachel's home, for she didn't feel up to leaving. The table was usually subdued. Isaac no longer sang his melodies. The knowledge that he would never have grandchildren had opened old wounds, had infuriated him towards his God, had soured him on life and hope. He tried desperately not to show it, not to let his daughter see his disappointment. But there was only so much one could hide.

One afternoon in early October, Esther Mandlebaum came over to deliver the news to Rachel: she had become engaged to Stephen Butler.

"Esther, you're crazy," Rachel responded angrily, no trace of jest or sarcasm.

Esther knew that Rachel wasn't really angry with her. She understood how anger had become Rachel's only way of relating these days. She walked over and shook her friend. "Rachel, you *must* come out of this slump! I've just told you I'm getting married and you're not even happy for me."

"Are you happy for yourself?"

"Sometimes."

"Sounds good to me."

"Ah, we're beginning to feel a mite better, are we?"

Rachel offered a slight smile.

"Now that's more like it," Esther said. "I'll tell you what. Why don't you go pretty yourself up, and we'll go out on the town tonight, just you and me, to celebrate."

"I don't think so."

"Why not? Come on, you could use it."

"I don't go *out on the town*."

"That's part of the problem, deary, all those *do's* and *don'ts* of yours. How about we forget the rules for a bit and just have a good time, *come on!*"

"I'd really rather not."

"Please, for me." Esther wasn't going to give up.

After a little more prodding, Rachel agreed. She showered, put on some make-up, and tried on three dresses before she was finally satisfied. Esther agreed on the choice.

"Okay, let's go," Esther said as she reached for her coat.

"No, wait!" Rachel went back into the closet and removed her *sheitel* from its box.

"Oh no, not the wig," Esther protested. "You can't wear that thing."

"Esther, I'm still married," Rachel said. "For however long that lasts," she added with a touch of acrimony.

"But the wig, you simply can't."

Rachel placed the wig over her hair, fussed with it for a while, then said, "You're right, I can't." She replaced the wig in the box, went back into the closet, and emerged with four hats. "Okay, which shall it be?" she asked.

Esther made a face, but didn't object. She realized there was no way Rachel was leaving the house without a head covering, and a hat was certainly better than a wig. She looked at the four hats; she had to admit they were all stylish and tasteful. Rachel tried one on, looked in the mirror and scoffed at the clashing colors. The second wasn't much better. But the third, a carmine beret, was just right for her ruby lipstick and royal blue dress. Esther had to admit, it worked.

"Where are we going?" Rachel asked.

"How about the Village? I know some places where we can have a splendid time."

"I'm sure you do."

Esther picked up the phone and called a car service. Rachel walked into the kitchen, opened one of the cupboards, and removed a Rosenthal sugar bowl. The gold trimmed set of dishes had been one of many gifts from her in-laws, and the delicate bowl had always seemed a most appropriate place to keep the "petty" cash. "How much do you think we'll need?" she asked Esther.

"Nothing, deary. It's on me."

"Uh, uh! It's *your* engagement celebration, *I'm* doing the treating!" She opened the jar, removed several bills, and looked at them. "I might as well spend his money while I still have it," she reflected. "How much?"

"Oh, I don't know. How much is there?"

Rachel counted. "Seems there's at least a hundred."

"That should do."

They laughed; Rachel hadn't done that in a long time. It felt good. She looked good. The night held promise.

They heard the taxi's horn, gathered their coats, and left. Rachel locked the door behind her, and as she walked toward the cab, she turned around and looked at the grand house. She felt a lump in her throat, and a force drawing her back inside, but she resisted. She was acutely conscious of the symbolism in her actions, a feeling that with each step, she was approaching another chapter of her life.

Rachel and Esther got into the backseat of the cab, and Esther instructed the driver where to take them. "It's a wonderful little bar on Bleecker Street," she said to Rachel. "You'll like it. Nice crowd, not too rowdy."

Rachel wasn't sure if she would ever "like" going to a bar, but she had to admit it felt good to be out. "So, have you told your parents yet?" she asked Esther.

"Heavens *no*."

"And when do you plan to?"

"Sometime."

"Esther!"

"I know, I know. It's just that it's going to cause such a ruckus."

"Do they know anything?"

"About what?"

"Stephen."

"You mean, do they know he exists?"

Rachel nodded.

"No, not really."

"You mean they don't know . . ."

"*Anything*. And I'd just as soon keep it that way, if I could. But I can't, can I?"

"I don't see how."

Esther laughed. "It *is* funny when you think about it," she explained. "My parents have no idea of the life I live; they're in their own little world. I haven't gone out on a *shiddoch* date in years, and they don't wonder. Perhaps they don't want to wonder, or maybe they've just given up on me. Who knows? Either way, it should be interesting to see their reaction."

"*Interesting* isn't exactly the word that comes to mind."

"I suppose not." Esther reflected. "You know, deary, I was wondering if maybe you could sort of help me out with this." Devilish.

Rachel couldn't imagine what was coming next. "Help you? How?"

"Well, to begin with, we will need a rabbi to marry us."

"Esther, Binny isn't a rabbi yet, and even if he was, I'm sure he would have nothing to do with it. Besides, we're practically separated."

"Who was talking about Binny? I was talking about a *real* rabbi."

Rachel suddenly had a familiar sensation, one she hadn't felt in years. It was the same feeling she had had as a girl whenever Esther schemed. "You can't be serious," she said sternly.

Esther turned to look at her. "Rachel *please*, if your father would marry us, if he would talk to my father, it might save us all from Armageddon. At least it would save me."

"Esther, my father's heart is weak enough without all this."

Esther turned away, disappointed, silent.

"Okay, I'll talk to him."

⌘

Rachel awoke the next morning in a mood she hadn't known in years. It had been a delightful evening. Lots of innocent male attention, even some harmless flirting, and probably a bit too much to drink. All in all, she felt like a woman again.

She looked in the mirror, smiled, and ran her hands over her figure. *Still not too bad*, she thought.

An image of Esther came to mind. Esther had looked awfully thin last night, but Rachel hadn't wanted to mention it. There had been enough to contend with without getting into all that. And anyway, what difference would it have made? Esther believed she had to stay thin to keep her man and her sanity, and Rachel was far from an expert on either of those topics.

Rachel jumped into the shower, got dressed, and went downstairs to fix herself some breakfast. No sign of Binny. He had been asleep when she'd gotten home, and was already gone when she awoke. She figured he didn't even care where she'd been, and that brought back some of her sadness. But only for a moment. She was too absorbed with Esther's problems to worry about her own.

And what problems they were. Esther's father, Lazar Mandlebaum, was a simple man. He would never understand any of this, just as Rachel's father hadn't understood when she'd told him about college and medical school. And this was worse. A lot worse.

At least Rachel understood. *Bravo, Esther, for chasing after the things you knew would make you happy, and shame on me for settling, for allowing myself to end up like this.* But enough with feeling sorry for herself; she had work to do. She had to speak with her father.

❦

"Hello Mama," Rachel said.

Hannah Weissman was surprised to find Rachel at her front door. She looked her daughter over. Cherry red fall coat, matching hat, and a sprightly countenance. The old Rachel.

They embraced. Hannah could barely hold back her tears.

"Now, Mama, let's not get melodramatic," Rachel said.

Hannah didn't respond. She was speechless.

Isaac emerged from the living room, and also began to cry.

"You too, Papa?"

Isaac was embarrassed, but couldn't help himself. His daughter, his *beautiful* daughter, had returned to life. "Come, come in!" he said, waving her into the living room.

Rachel removed her coat and followed her father. Hannah excused herself to the kitchen to prepare some coffee. "You look so *vunderful,*" Isaac said, his lips quivering, as he sat down.

"Thank you, Papa."

They chatted for a short while, about nothing, until Hannah came in with some coffee and cake. Rachel stood to help her mother. "It's okay," Hannah said, "just sit, let me do the work."

"So, vhat's new? Vat's *really* new?" Isaac asked.

"Well, as you can both see, I'm feeling better, *Baruch Hashem.*"

Isaac: "Yes, *Baruch Hashem,* thank God."

Hannah: "*Baruch Hashem.*"

Rachel: "And how are *you*?"

Isaac: "Ve're both *gut, Baruch Hashem,* and now that you're okay, ve're better than ever!"

Hannah nodded along.

Rachel: "I saw Esther yesterday, last night." She had to start somewhere.

Hannah: "And how is she doing?"

Rachel: "Good, I suppose." Tentative. "She's getting married."

Isaac: "*Mazel tov*! It's about time!"

Hannah: "*Mazel Tov.*" Subdued. She could tell from Rachel's tone that something wasn't quite right.

Isaac: "And who is the lucky man?"

Rachel looked at her parents and read her mother's reaction. She knew she could never fool her mother. "His name is Stephen Butler," she said.

Isaac: "Butler," he reflected, "I don't think I know the family."

Hannah: "You wouldn't." Disdain.

Rachel: "Mama!"

Hannah: "Rachel, why don't you tell your father *everything*."

Rachel: "Okay, so he's not Lubavitch."

Isaac: "She's marrying a Satmar?"

Hannah: "No, Isaac, I don't think he's a Satmar, or even a Bratslaver." She hesitated a moment, looking at Rachel. "I don't think he's even Jewish."

Isaac's face turned crimson.

"That's not true!" Rachel protested. "He *is* Jewish, just not religious." As if that made much of a difference.

Isaac: "How has her father reacted?"

Rachel: "Well, that's just it. He really doesn't know yet."

Hannah jumped in. "Rachel, you're not suggesting that we, I mean your father, be the messenger of such news, are you?"

Isaac seemed a bit confused. There was an unspoken communication between the two women that he had never been privy to, a type of mind reading.

"Well," Rachel responded, "I was sort of hoping . . . actually, *Esther* was hoping that Papa might intercede and talk to Reb Lazar."

Hannah: "Rachel, it really is Esther's place to deal with her parents."

Rachel: "I know. It's just that she's afraid of their reaction. But if Papa tells them it's okay . . ."

"Okay, what's okay?" Hannah interrupted.

Rachel was dumbfounded.

"Don't worry," Isaac said to the women, "I'll find a way to talk to Reb Lazar." At that moment, he wasn't going to deny his daughter anything.

"But what will you say?" Hannah asked.

Isaac thought about her question. "I'll tell him that this is an opportunity for him to do a great *mitzvah*, to reach out and bring this young man into the fold of *Yiddishkeit*."

"I'm sure that will go over well," Hannah responded sardonically. "While you're at it, tell him what a *mitzvah* it would be to bring his daughter back to Judaism as well."

Rachel: "Mama, maybe they both *will* return."

Hannah: "And maybe the Messiah will come tomorrow."

Rachel didn't want to argue, she had already won. "One more thing, Papa," she said.

Isaac waited.

"Would you marry them?"

Did he really have a choice?

CHAPTER 41

Joshua and Connie passed the Bar exam, became full-fledged lawyers, and celebrated with steak dinners at Luger's under the Williamsburg Bridge. Dessert was at some flea bag motel a few blocks from the restaurant. The next morning, Joshua marched into Fielding's office, tendered his resignation, and informed Fielding that Willie Johnson would henceforth be represented by private council. Fielding didn't seem to care much about either piece of news. "Better you than me," was all he had to say.

Joshua was now a lawyer with a client, soaking behind the ears, and no place to hang his proverbial hat. He invited Connie to join him in private practice, but she wasn't leaving the DA's office so fast. He didn't really try to persuade her. She would be more valuable where she was.

Loretta didn't object when he asked if he could set up shop in the house. There was nothing she wouldn't do to help her lawyer son, even if he was defending a suspected rapist. If he believed in Willie Johnson, so did she. He only hoped the jury would be as kind.

Another thing Loretta did was present him with a check for a thousand dollars. She said it was the last of the money she had saved over the years for his education. Not fully believing her, he took the money. Using Alfred Sims' money to help Willie Johnson didn't present much of a conflict.

Joshua had also saved a little from his job. In all, he had enough for supplies, a private phone line, and to tide himself over for a few months.

He realized he didn't have much of a case, but figured the DA didn't either. He was also banking on Thompson being in court and handling the media. All the ingredients for an acquittal.

He knew he was being used by Thompson, but thanks to the professor there had been a lot of play about the case in the press, and more than a few hotshot attorneys approaching Willie with generous offers. Willie, however, wasn't biting. He was following Thompson's lead. Thompson had even managed to locate Willie's mother and was now the official spokesman for the family. He had finessed Venice Johnson's transformation from drug addict to solicitous mother, had raised the money for Willie's bail, and had gotten the defendant a full-time job in a grocery store. Everything was looking up.

Joshua was well aware of why he'd been chosen. True, he had believed in Willie, and had brought the case to Thompson's attention in the first place, but the professor was less concerned with rewarding loyalty than with promoting his agenda. Having an inexperienced nobody like Joshua as Willie's lawyer insured that the spotlight would be Thompson's, and his alone.

Joshua nevertheless knew that he was no patsy, nor any less driven by ambition than Thompson. The glitz had definitely seduced him, and he was keenly aware that winning the Willie Johnson case would launch his career. It was tough to keep perspective, to remember the real reason he was there.

There wasn't a lot of preparation involved. He didn't have any witnesses. Willie's mother had wanted to testify as to her son's excellent moral character, and had offered to have some of her neighbors do the same. Joshua had thought it an unwise strategy, considering the defense was planning on using Willie's past record to prove otherwise. There was no sense in offering a bogus defense and losing credibility. Thompson had agreed.

Instead, he would simply attack the prosecution's case. A few holes, the casting of some "reasonable doubt," a lot of noise from Thompson about police racism, and voilà. Joshua had no problem with any of this, it was all true.

❦

The night before the trial, Joshua sat at his desk, trying to review his opening statement. He just couldn't help drifting off and thinking about the twists his life had taken. Tomorrow he would be standing before a judge and jury. As a lawyer.

Loretta came in. "Some men are here to see you. I recognize one of them from TV."

He walked out to the living room and found Thompson waiting with two of his cronies and three kids. Joshua recognized one of the kids: scarred chin, beady eyes, rotten teeth. It was the kid he'd run into the night he had searched for Willie's friends.

"Good evening, Mr. Eubanks," Thompson said. "I wouldn't dream of bothering you on the night before a trial, but I believe that these young men have some information which might be of value to your case."

The kids appeared reticent, frightened. Thompson put his hand on the shoulder of the one Joshua recognized, and said, "Come on now, Arthur, tell Mr. Eubanks what you know about Willie Johnson's whereabouts on the night that Jewish woman was raped."

"I keep tellin' you man, my name ain't Arthur. It's A.J., okay, A.J.!"

"Well, your Mama seems bent on calling you Arthur," Thompson responded. "But that's another matter. Why don't you just tell Mr. Eubanks exactly what you told us."

Arthur, aka A.J., looked at Joshua with trepidation, then at his buddies. "We still have a deal?" he asked Joshua.

"Yes," Joshua responded.

Thompson looked bewildered. "You know this kid?"

"We've met," Joshua answered, and then turned to the kid. "Well, A.J., what's it gonna be?"

"So we got a deal?"

Joshua nodded.

"Cause if we gotta say this in court, we gonna be in a lotta trouble. We'll need a *real good* lawyer." His friends, though silent, seemed to be in agreement.

"Well, Mr. Eubanks is certainly one of the best," Thompson interjected.

"Depending on what you've got," Joshua said, "you may not have to say it in court. If it's good enough, there may not have to be a trial."

They looked at him curiously.

He explained. "If you guys have evidence which proves that Willie didn't rape that lady, then the DA's going to want to dismiss the charges before the trial even starts. See, the last thing the DA wants is the public embarrassment of losing a trial like this. Now, I can still insist we go to trial to expose the prejudice of the DA and the police department, and the DA's going to want to do anything to avoid that. So I offer him a deal: no charges against you guys. Everyone goes home. But this all depends on what you've got."

A.J. looked at his friends. They seemed to agree. Joshua wondered just how Thompson had found these guys, but didn't ask. He figured there were some things he was better off not knowing.

A.J. and his friends told their story. They claimed that Willie was with them during the time when Emma Lukins was raped and beaten. They'd hit two liquor stores, one in Canarsie and one in Sheepshead Bay, and had stolen a little over three hundred bucks without hurting anyone. Willie had used his gun in both robberies, consistent with his previous MO.

Joshua called the respective Precincts and verified that both liquor store robberies did, in fact, take place that night. The first coincided exactly with the time of the Lukins incident, and the descriptions of the perpetrators were remarkably consistent with Willie and his friends. Joshua was certain the DA had seen the robbery reports, and had ignored them in favor of charging Willie with the rape.

He told the kids that he could probably get a deal for them, if they were prepared to go to the wall for Willie. They might have to repay the money, do some community service and probation, but that would be about it. They promised to show up in court the next day, but Thompson sent his "associates" home with them, just to be sure.

Thompson stayed behind. There was something more he needed to discuss with Joshua. "No deals with the DA!" he said.

Joshua knew this was coming. "But we promised those kids."

"Listen to me, Joshua. What the DA did in this case is *unconscionable*. It must be exposed. People have to know what happened here, the world has to know!"

"But those kids . . ."

"Those kids are criminals," he said with all the self righteousness he could muster.

"And Willie Johnson is a criminal too!"

"That's correct. Do you want Willie and his friends to go scot-free for the crimes they actually *did* commit?" More self righteousness.

"Willie has already been punished enough with all this. As for his friends, if they got a break, and saw that there were people they could trust, like *us*, who knows what would happen? I've seen kids like that my whole life, they think the odds are always against them, so they rob and steal what they can. Maybe once, just once, if they saw that the system can work for them the same way it works for rich white folks, they'd have a chance to clean up their act. Because I can tell you one thing: prison won't do them, or anyone else, a bit of good."

"My, you have quite a bleeding heart there."

"Just a heart."

"I'm sorry you feel this way, Joshua, and I'm sorry for those kids, but the trial *must* proceed! *You have to see the big picture here!* This isn't about Willie Johnson; it's about the police and the DA. If there's no public hearing, they'll be able to smooth things over, to say that *they* uncovered new evidence, new leads to pursue and investigate. They'll make themselves look like heroes, instead of the racist scum we know them to be, and *you* will have helped them do it!"

"That's where you're wrong, professor. This *is* about Willie Johnson, and *nothing else!*"

Thompson held his tongue, gathered his coat, and opened the door to see himself out. He turned toward Joshua one last time, his face bearing a warning: *Don't defy me!*

Joshua stared into Thompson's eyes, knowing he couldn't obey, and understanding that it would one day come back to haunt him.

⌘

The deal with the DA came off just as Joshua had predicted, and the DA's statement to the media was just as Thompson had predicted. Joshua stood on the courthouse steps with Willie and his mother, watching the DA play to the press. Nobody was interested in the three of them. So much for his fame and glory.

He offered to take the Johnsons to lunch, but they declined. Venice kissed him on the cheek, thanked him, and promised to be a better mother. Willie shook his hand and promised to stay out of trouble. He wasn't sure he believed either of them.

Professor Thompson hadn't even bothered to show up. There was nothing left in this case for him. Also absent were the many Hasidic spectators that had been awaiting the trial. When the DA had stood up, and had announced to the court that "new" evidence had emerged exonerating Willie Johnson, the Hasidim upped and left in disappointment. They would have to await another day for justice for Emma Lukins.

The press was still surrounding the DA. Joshua watched Willie and his mother descend the steps. He started to walk off, and heard his name called. He turned, and saw a man with a microphone running toward him, and a TV camera following behind.

"Mr. Eubanks, is it?" the man with the mike asked.

"Yes." The camera was aimed at his face.

"Well, sir, do you have any comment about this case? There are rumors that the DA really messed up and is giving us a snow job."

"All I can say is that Willie Johnson has been exonerated of all charges, and that I hope the police work quickly and effectively to bring the true perpetrator of this horrible crime to trial."

"No other comment? We understand that Professor Alvin Thompson was involved in this case, that there were charges of police racism, false arrest . . ."

"I'm sorry," Joshua said as he began to walk away, "I have no comment on any of those things."

CHAPTER 42

Rachel Weissman Frankel caught the eye of each and every one of Stephen Butler's male friends. The royal blue bridesmaid's dress was simply exquisite, and perhaps a bit too fitted for a "married" Hasidic woman. But Rachel chose to wear it anyway. She'd moved out of Binny's house a month earlier, and though she hadn't yet received her *get*, or Jewish divorce, it wouldn't be far off.

Her father had disapproved of the dress, but had held his tongue. He and Hannah had been worried about Rachel. Not being able to bear children was the worst curse a woman could endure in their world, and the stigma of divorce was no picnic either. If this dress would bring Rachel even a glimmer of cheer, they could overlook it.

The bridal party gathered under the canopy. Esther, Stephen, their respective parents, Rachel, Stephen's brother, and Rabbi Isaac Weissman. It had been a bumpy road, but somehow they'd all made it.

Lazar Mandlebaum was a wealthy man, so much so because he'd been obsessed with his diamond business and neglectful of his family. Constantly traveling the world, leaving his wife alone with their four daughters, sooner or later he knew it would catch up with him. His wife, Leah, had warned him that she'd sensed rebellious fires in their eldest daughter, that Esther had needed more love and attention than a mother with four children could afford. But Reb Lazar had pretended not to see.

The day that Isaac Weissman had visited the Mandlebaums had been a sad one, yet the news the rabbi bore hadn't been so shocking. The Mandlebaums would have to find thankfulness in their hearts that the boy was at least Jewish, would have to pray to God to help Esther and Stephen find their way back to a Torah life, and would have to give more attention and devotion to their other girls.

After all the tears and anger, this had been the resolution. And Rabbi Isaac Weissman had acted both wisely and gallantly in helping bring it about. Rachel looked into her father's weary eyes as he offered the betrothal blessings. The last time she'd heard him utter those words had been beneath her own canopy, and his eyes had seemed far more spirited then. He was not alone in having lost his zeal, he was not alone in having become tired, worn, and despairing. And he was not alone in forging ahead despite it all.

Blessed art Thou, oh Lord, our God . . .

&

Paul Sims sat in his living room, staring into space. It was past twelve, and as usual he couldn't sleep. His mind had been ablaze since the news of Rachel's divorce. He could think of nothing else. He had to admit that this gave rise to more than a tinge of guilt, but he was well beyond choice or probity. He had to have her.

He tried rationalizing, reminding himself that the actual biblical prohibition against adultery applied only to married women, not married men, and that—in fact—most of the men in the Bible had several wives. Of course he knew that there were clear rabbinic rulings against such practices nowadays, but he wanted what he wanted.

The only problem was Rachel. She hadn't been interested in him before, so why should he imagine that she would feel differently now? He didn't, but he still had to try. As for his being married, he couldn't see her rejecting him on those grounds; after all, she had been married when he had caught her with Joshua.

And what of Joshua, Paul wondered. Were they still seeing one another? Were they truly lovers, or had he exaggerated their association for his own designs? Soon enough, he mused, he would have answers to all his questions.

Paul waited, and watched her parents' home for days. From shadows and alleyways, he tracked her every move, meticulously calculating just the right moment to approach her.

"Here, let me help you with that," he said, jumping out of nowhere, grabbing the door to her building.

She was returning from the market, with overflowing bags in each arm. "Paul! You scared me," she reacted. "Thank you," she added, trying to catch her breath.

"It's Pinchas now."

"Oh yes, I remember. Sorry."

"How have you been?"

"Good, I suppose." Uneasiness. She was still shaken by his appearance, and was uncomfortable with such questions to begin with. It seemed the entire world had been aware of her travails, and she wished everyone would stop reminding her. She hurried through the door.

"Let me help you," he repeated, following her into the lobby.

"Thank you, but it's not necessary."

"It's nothing," he said, reaching for the bags.

She gave him the bags, but wished he would go away.

Stay Calm, she told herself as she pressed the elevator button. They stood there in silence, the elevator moving ever so slowly. He couldn't help staring; she couldn't help noticing.

This was what God had intended a woman to look like, he told himself.

I can't wait to get upstairs and lock the door to my apartment, she told herself.

The elevator arrived. "Thank you very much, Pinchas, but I think I can handle them from here," she said, attempting to recover the packages.

"Really, it's fine," he insisted. "It isn't right for you to schlep when I can do it for you. Besides, I haven't seen your parents in such a long time."

"My father's in the yeshiva."

"He is? I should have realized. But I would like to say hello to your mother."

Rachel thanked God that her mother would be home. They approached the apartment door, and Rachel took out her keys. She opened the door and, as she walked in, she realized they were alone. Her anxiety had caused a momentary lapse of memory: Hannah was at her weekly Bible class. Pinchas, however, had known all this. He had done his homework.

Paul saw himself to the kitchen, laid the packages on the table, and made as though he was leaving. He approached the door, where Rachel was standing, waiting to see him out.

"Well," she said, "thank you again. I'll tell my parents you came by."

He heard a quiver in her voice. "To be honest, I was really hoping that they wouldn't be here," he said.

"Pardon me?"

"I was hoping we could, sort of, be alone."

"Pinchas, this really isn't . . ."

"Right," he interrupted. "I know." He attempted to sound rational, but his mind was possessed.

"I think you should leave."

"Why?"

"Because I'd like you to." *Stay cool!*

"Am I not good enough for you?"

She sensed his rage. *Careful*, she told herself. "You're married!"

"So were *you* when you were with Joshua. Are you still with him?"

"Excuse me?"

"I saw the two of you together. I know all about it."

"About what?"

"About *this*," he answered as he reached out and touched her. He was out of control, desperate just to feel her in his arms at last.

She backed away, frightened.

"I'm sorry," he said. "I didn't mean to . . ."

"I want you to leave. *Now!*" Trembling.

Paul struggled to restrain himself, to keep from doing something really stupid. Suddenly, almost miraculously, a moment of clarity emerged, ordaining him to heed her demand.

He turned away, wondering if he would ever be able to look at her again, and walked out the door in shame.

He wandered for blocks, confused and dejected, worried about the potential consequences of his actions. *Would she tell anyone? Would Chava find out?* What was he to do?

A thought came to mind. He could blow the whistle on her and Joshua. After that, nobody would believe anything she would have to say. It was cruel, but what choice did he have?

He also knew just to whom such information would be most valuable. The one man who would appreciate it and use it wisely. He quickly turned on his heel and headed to see Rav Schachter.

Paul was flattered at the rabbi's willingness to see him with barely a moment's notice, but wasn't sure what to make of it. Last time, he had waited weeks for an appointment. Perhaps it was divine intervention; it certainly made him feel better to think so.

In truth, however, Rav Schachter had a special interest in Paul, and had known from the start of their relationship that Paul would one day prove to be useful. With all the racial problems emerging in the neighborhood, entrée to a man such as Alfred Sims could be quite valuable.

"Good day, Pinchas, I hope things are going well with you and Chava," the rabbi opened, leaning back, seeming unbothered by the intrusion.

"*Baruch Hashem*, all is well."

"*Gut*, then what brings you here this afternoon?" Right down to business.

"I have come with unfortunate news."

The rabbi raised his eyebrows.

Paul continued, "It is a matter requiring the utmost discretion, a matter that I now realize I should have brought to the *Rav's* attention long ago. It concerns the daughter of Rabbi Isaac Weissman."

Schachter appeared nonchalant, but Paul saw through the mask. He knew the rabbi was eager to hear what he had to say. He proceeded to relate his tale, omitting not a single detail of that afternoon on the boardwalk. A few years had passed since the incident, but his recollection was impressively vivid, arousing Schachter's suspicion of the veracity of everything he was hearing. But Schachter was a pragmatist, and believed in the old adage: where there's smoke, there's fire. This was something he could exploit.

"This is an interesting story, Pinchas, but it is about something that happened quite a while ago. Tell me, do you have any direct knowledge that there is *still* something going on between this man and Rachel Weissman?"

"No, I only saw them that one time."

"And why have you brought this information to *me*, and why *now*, after all this time?"

"I have been grappling with what I saw for a long time. At first, I had considered telling someone or asking someone what to do with such information, but then I thought that I would probably have been doing more harm than good. I didn't know how to proceed, so I kept it to myself. I suppose, in hindsight, that was wrong; a woman suspected of adultery is a serious matter and her husband has a right to know."

Rav Schachter nodded.

Paul continued, "Lately, I have been feeling guilty about the way I handled this. I have been wondering how *I* would have felt if it had been my wife, God forbid, and another man had seen her doing something like this, and had concealed it, as I have. It is unthinkable."

"So why do you come now? The marriage between Rachel and Binyamin is over."

"But the sin has still been committed, both hers and mine. I know I can't do anything about hers, and I suspect that the *Bet Din* wouldn't choose to do anything at this point either, but I can do something about what I have done, or *haven't* done, as the case may be."

"So you have come here to confess?"

"And to ask how I can repent."

The rabbi began to realize that this "penitent" was even more clever and cunning than he'd imagined. "You have expressed yourself quite well," he said, "and you are correct that neither I nor the *Bet Din* would act on such information, considering that such action would serve no purpose for the 'husband.' The fact that you did not come forth when you should have, also seems to have had no actual bearing on the unfolding of events in this situation. The *Eibeshter*, our Creator, has obviously resolved the matter on His own."

Paul nodded, showing appreciation for the rabbi's insight.

"As for your *t'shuvah*, repentance," Rav Schachter continued, "there is no specific prescription in a case such as this. All I can say is that you should learn from what you've done, and if ever a similar situation arises, you will behave differently. After all, isn't that what the *Rambam*, Maimonides, says *t'shuva* is all about? A man truly repents when, if confronted with identical circumstances in which he committed his sin, he behaves differently."

"Yes, I remember learning the *Rambam's* thoughts on this," Paul responded.

"*Gut*, then let this matter take up no more of your precious time."

"And what does the *Rav* plan on doing with the information I have disclosed?"

"I am going to do nothing," Schachter said. "As I explained, the marriage is already over, and all things considered, it is unlikely that Rachel Weissman will easily find another *shiddoch*. Perhaps some unfortunate widower or divorcée who has already fulfilled the mitzvah of having children will take interest in her, and that is punishment enough for such a beautiful young woman. I see no purpose in adding to her misery."

"I understand," Paul said, well aware of the rabbi's duplicity.

⸎

As soon as Paul departed, Rav Nachum Schachter arose from his chair, walked to his window, and looked down upon Eastern Parkway. There, below him, the sidewalks were teeming with soldiers of the Lord, armored in their black and white garb, shielded with caftans and fedoras, pacing briskly from place to place. Some would be en route to prayer, others to study, and still even others to their homes and families. And then there were those who were headed to unspeakable places, harboring treacherous secrets. Sexual indulgences, drugs, gambling—Schachter knew that all those things were out there, that the black and white facade concealed many shades of gray.

The amorality of the world had crept into Schachter's ghetto, and he blamed the likes of Isaac Weissman, and Isaac's teacher, Rav Feldblum, for these vile intrusions. Feldblum was his nemesis, a man "disloyal" to the *Rebbe*, a man who dared question the *Rebbe's* messianic destiny. Feldblum's camp was too embracing of modern society, sending vulnerable yeshiva students onto the streets to proselytize among the secular and forsaken, and accepting outsiders into the community, thereby poisoning the purity of the Lubavitcher lineage.

Schachter wondered how many of the *Rebbe's* followers lived like Rachel Weissman; how many had been influenced by the debauchery and perversions of the outside world; how many had been defiled and enticed.

Stirred by his ruminations, Schachter knew he had to act. Feldblum and his circle of "apostates" had to be discredited. And now he had the means with which to do it, the fact that the daughter of Isaac Weissman had fallen into a life of sin. It was the ultimate irony, superb ammunition. But the mere word of Pinchas Sims wasn't sufficient. Real evidence would have to be gathered, perhaps photos, or credible witnesses.

Schachter turned from the window, pressed the buzzer on his desk, and summoned his assistant. A moment later, the underling appeared in the elder's office, waiting anxiously for instructions.

"There is a matter that requires our immediate attention," the rabbi said.

⁂

Rachel Weissman Frankel had chosen to keep silent about the incident with Paul Sims. She believed she was safe from him, and that he wouldn't be back. Moreover, she was concerned about once again becoming the object of gossip. She'd already suffered enough of that.

For days, she'd been unable to sleep, haunted more by what Paul had said than what he had done. Last night, she finally surrendered to the little yellow pills Marcia Schiffman had given her when she'd been depressed. She had avoided resorting to medication, even during the worst of times, but this had pushed her over the edge.

The pill worked like a charm. The sleep had done her good. She awoke a bit hung over, but feeling far better than on previous mornings. She came into the kitchen for breakfast, made herself some coffee, and picked up the newspaper her father had left on the table.

She thumbed through the want-ads, imagining what it would be like to get a job. Of course, she could easily find work in the neighborhood, but she fantasized about breaking out, doing something like designing clothing in Midtown or selling art in SoHo. In truth, she knew she was terribly unskilled; she also knew Manhattan was no place for a Hasidic woman to be.

She turned to the front section of the paper, national and international news, and skimmed the headlines. Unlike her father, who read the paper from cover to cover every morning of his life, she was rather selective. She landed on a piece about a recent terrorist skirmish in Israel. That sort of thing always grabbed her attention. It never ceased to amaze her how such a tiny scrap of land, on the other side of the world, managed to command so much attention.

It had been over a year and a half since the Yom Kippur War, yet the graphic memories returned whenever she read such articles. She had been twenty-three at the time, consumed in the turmoil of her failing marriage, too demoralized to even attend synagogue on that single holiest day of the Jewish calendar. In fact, it hadn't been until that evening, when her parents had come to break the fast with her, that she actually learned the news. "They are like Nazis, those Arab bastards, to attack Jews in their synagogues," her father had exclaimed. Rachel had never heard him use such language before and, forgetting her own troubles, attempted to comfort him.

She hadn't been very successful, but it wasn't her fault. Isaac Weissman had been inconsolable, the images in his mind too powerful to be quieted. "They vill never leave us alone," he had added, banging his fist on the table. "Never!"

Rachel would never forget that scene, the fierce look in her father's eyes, words and resonance of which she'd never imagined him capable. Each time she came upon an article about an attack in Israel, she could picture his reaction to it, and here was yet another one. She worried about him.

She finished the first section of the paper, and went on to the local news. She usually didn't bother with local news, but today she felt compelled. Perhaps because she was restless, or maybe a tad more inquisitive than usual. Or simply, perhaps, it was the hand of God.

Her eye was caught by a headline: *SUSPECT FREED IN LUKINS RAPE CASE*. She was stunned. Everyone in the Lubavitcher community knew about Emma Lukins' frightful attack six months earlier, and the impending trial. Since the incident, women had been warned to be careful when they walked the streets. There had even been talk among the men about setting up citizen patrols.

Rachel read on:

Chief Assistant DA, Leonard Strauss, announced yesterday that the State's case against Willie Johnson in the rape of Emma Lukins was being dismissed because of lack of evidence against Mr. Johnson. New leads concerning another possible suspect will be pursued. Miss Lukins, a member of the Lubavitcher Hasidic Sect, lived alone in an apartment at 127 Empire Blvd. in the Crown Heights section of Brooklyn. The incident had taken place on August 9, 1974. Jewish leaders had been outraged by the brutality of the crime, and had complained to the authorities about the increasing frequency of violent acts perpetrated against members of the Lubavitcher community. Black leaders have maintained that Mr. Johnson had been falsely accused. There is a wall of silence around the actual events that led to the dismissal of the case against Mr. Johnson yesterday. Joshua Eubanks, Mr. Johnson's attorney, said only that his client has been exonerated of all charges and that he hoped the police would work quickly to find the actual perpetrator.

Joshua Eubanks? Rachel couldn't believe her eyes.

Joshua Eubanks! Not a day had gone by in the past few years in which she hadn't thought of him, and now, here he was, in print. *The New York Times*, no less.

Joshua Eubanks!

She reread the article to convince herself she wasn't dreaming. She had always expected great things of Joshua. A lawyer, no surprise. Willie Johnson's lawyer, *that* was hard to take.

It had been several years since she'd last seen him. She tried to imagine what he must look like, but she could only picture him as he was then. She found herself overtaken by curiosity, and perhaps by something more than curiosity. She wanted to see him again.

She downed the coffee, closed the paper, and got up from the table. Her hands were unsteady and she almost dropped the saucer on her way to the sink. She quickly washed the saucer, and hurried to her bedroom to dress. It took three outfits till she found the right one.

She didn't want to think about what she was doing, or even why she was doing it. Obstacles and consequences be damned. Whether he was married, involved, or how he would react after all this time, none of it concerned her. She wanted only to go to him, talk to him, to hold him, and to feel good once again.

She had suffered enough.

CHAPTER 43

It was a storefront office on Nostrand Avenue, small but just right for Joshua's needs. The first three months' rent would be paid by an interest-free loan from the Nostrand Avenue Commerce Association, an organization of local merchants who wanted to reward Joshua for his performance in the Johnson case.

The commerce association was dedicated to promoting black owned businesses, and establishing youth programs throughout the community. The night after the Johnson dismissal, three representatives from the association had visited Joshua at his home. Their proposition was straightforward. All he had to do was join the association, participate in raising charitable funds, attend monthly meetings, operate fairly in business dealings with other association members, and repay the loan in a reasonable amount of time. A ready-made clientele, prestige, and legitimacy, all wrapped up in one neat package. Amazing what a little notoriety can do.

They had informed him of the availability of the storefront office. The landlord was a member of the association. The rent would be more than equitable.

Joshua was thrilled with all the attention. He'd never imagined himself belonging to such a fraternity. He'd made it, a lawyer, keeping company with local bigwigs. The look in his mother's eyes had said it all.

So here he was, the day after the Johnson dismissal, standing with Connie in the back room of the storefront, figuring how to set up shop. The place was barren and dilapidated, but had potential. "I guess I could put my desk over there," he said, pointing to the corner.

"What desk?" Cute.

"They said they would help with some start-up furniture. Nothing exotic, just some used odds and ends."

"So you want this to be your private office, and the front to be the reception area?" She walked around, gesturing in different directions as she spoke.

"I suppose so." Tentative. "This is really a large room. I could also divide it into two private offices. That way, I'd be able to have an associate."

"Associate? You don't even have money for a secretary!"

"Well, that's why I was thinking of an associate. Someone to share clerical stuff and expenses with. Interested?" He gave her a suggestive look.

"If you mean associate, no. If you mean *partner*, maybe."

"Then I mean partner."

"Equal partner?"

"As equal as the sides of a square."

She looked him in the eye, thought for a moment, and said, "Okay."

"Okay?"

"That's what I said."

They started to embrace, and were about to join lips, when they heard what sounded like a woman clearing her throat. They turned toward the intruder standing in the doorway. "Excuse me, the front door was open," Rachel said in an embarrassed tone.

Joshua's mouth fell into his stomach. He stood there, frozen.

"I hope I'm not interrupting," Rachel said. She turned to Joshua. "Your mother said I would find you here."

Silence fell upon the room. Connie looked at Joshua. Rachel looked at Joshua. Connie and Rachel looked at one another as Joshua said, "Connie, this is . . ."

"Rachel, I presume," Connie interjected.

Joshua had told Connie all about Rachel, on more than one occasion. In fact, Connie had believed that Rachel was the reason Joshua would forever have trouble with other women. Now she understood why.

"Rachel, this is Constance Henderson, my law partner." He liked the sound of that.

The two women held out their hands and shook, while Joshua stood, not knowing what to do or say next. Connie looked at her watch and said, "Oh my, I didn't realize what time it was. I'm late for court."

Joshua glanced at her, knowing she didn't have any business in court whatsoever.

Connie picked up her briefcase, and excused herself. "I'll call you," she said to Joshua. Then, to Rachel: "Nice meeting you," as she marched out.

And there they were, alone, after all this time, staring at each other, the space between them feeling like a stone wall. It was a scene Joshua had often dreamed of, though in his dreams he wasn't paralyzed.

He saw that she hadn't changed much in the looks department. She still had that succulent, dangerous smile, and all the other details he had so often played over in his mind.

"Hi," she said, in what seemed as good an opening as any.

"Hi," he responded, wanting to step closer to her, holding himself from doing so. "Long time."

"Too long."

"Can't argue with that."

Awkwardness.

"How have you been?" she asked.

"Actually, pretty okay."

"So I've read."

"You, too?" He pretended more surprise than he actually felt.

"Me, and probably a whole lot of other people."

"Yeah, should be a real career starter," he said, eyeing his shabby surroundings.

"Should be."

More awkwardness.

"So how have you been?" he asked.

She considered the question for a second. "Not as well as you."

He looked at her curiously. She held up her hand to display the absence of rings.

"What happened?" he asked.

"Life, I suppose."

"Divorce?"

"Bingo."

"I'm sorry."

"I'm not."

"Then I'm not either."

She laughed. He smiled.

"Would you," she said, and then hesitated to wipe a tear. "Would you—hold me?"

He moved toward her slowly and took her in his arms. At first, his touch was tentative, halting. She felt soft and frail, and began to cry on his shoulder. Fighting his own tears, he began to hold her tighter. She lifted her head from his shoulder, and looked into his eyes. He thought about that long, passionate kiss that had always appeared in his dreams, but couldn't do it. It just didn't feel right.

She shared his conflict and stepped back. "So this is where you're going to set up shop," she said, deflecting the tension.

"I suppose so. The rent's right, the location's pretty good." He looked around and frowned. "The place does need some work."

"I'll say."

He showed her the layout that Connie and he had discussed. She liked the concept, and even offered to help. He accepted, realizing it might have been a good idea to have consulted his new partner first.

They left the building and walked up Nostrand Avenue. She told him about her miscarriages, the problems with Binny, and even about the incident with Paul Sims.

"You really should tell someone, especially your parents; he could be dangerous," Joshua said.

"I *am* telling someone—you. I think he's more stupid than dangerous, and I'm not worried that he'll try anything again. He knows it's a lost cause."

Joshua wondered about that. "Maybe I'll pay him a little visit, just to let him know that he didn't get away scot-free."

"Please don't!"

"Still worried what people might think about your association with me?"

"Are you going to start with that black and white thing again?"

"Do I need to?"

"If I wanted to keep you a secret, why would I be walking in public with you?"

"Are you really *with* me? Seems to me there's almost two feet between us."

With that, she moved closer and took him by the arm. "How's this, better?"

"Much!"

They both smiled, but he could feel her discomfort. Although Nostrand Avenue was pretty much an exclusively black part of the neighborhood, one never knew when a Hasid might pop up.

"So why don't you want me to talk to him?" Joshua asked.

"First, I don't believe that *talking* is what you have in mind. Second, I'd just prefer letting it be."

He didn't press, but still had the mind to do something. He would respect her wishes, for now.

"I'm glad you're here," he said.

"So am I."

CHAPTER 44

He was a staunch loyalist, a blind devotee to his master's will. As assistant to Rav Schachter, he enjoyed immense prestige and honor, though the things sometimes asked of him portended neither. He rationalized, believing the righteousness of his mandate. Even in moments such as this.

The camera in his hand was an instrument of God, or so he thought, capturing the baneful sinners soon to meet their lawful reckoning. He lurked, and hid, and stalked, until he got what he'd come for: the evidence. And when it was his, a sudden surge of nausea overcame him, as if he despised both his deed and the chieftain who'd ordained it. But only momentarily, until the rationalizations returned, and once again he saw himself doing his part to uproot evil and depravity. For there was nothing else a man of such position could do.

✥

Rabbi Isaac Weissman paced nervously in the hallway, waiting to be summoned to the inner sanctum. He had no idea why his presence had been requested, and had even been inclined to refuse, but for his curiosity.

What could Rav Schachter conceivably want?

He heard footsteps approaching, lifted his head, and saw the assistant coming his way. It was time.

324

He entered a dark room and beheld what seemed like a large shadow behind the desk. As his eyes adjusted, he saw that the elder was actually turned away from him, looking out the window. A moment passed before Schachter acknowledged his presence.

"Ah, Reb Yitzchak, it has been a long time," Schachter exclaimed spiritedly, swiveling the chair around to face his visitor.

"Yes, it has."

Isaac recalled his encounters with Schachter, almost thirty years earlier, when he had first come to America. Isaac had been but a simple Talmud teacher from Poland, and Schachter, who had been trained in the celebrated yeshivas of the holy land, had been touted as one of the great minds of the community. Many had even regarded Schachter as a candidate to one day assume the position of *Rebbe*, considering that Rav Yosef Yitzchak, the *Rebbe* at the time, had no sons. Isaac was one of many who had attended Schachter's lectures, and had enjoyed a peripheral relationship with the scholar. Yet even then, he had sensed something about Schachter that left him uncomfortable.

It had all crystallized after the death of the *Rebbe*. Instead of Schachter, Yosef Yitzchak's son-in-law and distant cousin, Menachem Mendel, had been anointed to the throne. Schachter had reacted badly: irate, resentful, and eventually vindictive. Rav Yehudah Feldblum, who had been Schachter's closest friend and confidant since childhood—also a great scholar in his own right—was forced to break from Schachter because the man's temperament had become insufferable. A core group of students had followed Feldblum, Isaac among them.

Schachter, not yet bereft of disciples, began to rebuild his ranks. In the years that followed, he became more outspoken on issues dividing the community, and emerged as the leader of a reactionary element within the community. He was appointed to a seat on the *Bes Din*, and gained much influence. Some even speculated that the *Rebbe* had granted all this as a consolation.

Feldblum and his followers had remained quiet for the most part. Feldblum was a soft man, more concerned with studying and teaching than politics, and he encouraged his students to behave likewise. But on some issues, as in the case of allowing outsiders into the community, or permitting rabbis to teach the unaffiliated, Feldblum had found himself forced to contradict Schachter publicly.

Over the years, divisiveness gave way to enmity, yet both men managed to maintain their respective positions as close advisors to the *Rebbe*. Perhaps, as Isaac had once mused, the *Rebbe* was able to see what others couldn't, and thus welcomed contention among his followers.

"I'm glad you could come," Schachter said. "Sit!"

Isaac complied, as the two men scrutinized one another. Schachter wore a solemn expression, and Isaac was not very good at hiding his own tension. Despite not knowing the purpose of the meeting, Isaac was certain it was going to be unpleasant. But that was okay; he had managed far more formidable obstacles than Schachter could possibly ever conjure up. Or so he thought.

"I'm sorry to have taken you from your busy schedule," Schachter continued, "but there is a matter that has come to my attention, and I am sure you would want to know about it immediately."

"And vhat might that be?"

"It concerns your daughter, Rachel." Schachter waited a beat for Isaac's reaction. He enjoyed watching his adversaries cringe. "And I want to say, Reb Yitzchak, that this matter came to my attention by sheer accident."

"Vhat matter is that?"

Schachter lifted a manila envelope from his desk, and said, "In here are some photographs that someone brought me. I can't tell you who the messenger is, only that he is a fanatic, a crazy *bal t'shuva* who believes he is doing some sort of *mitzvah*. I can assure you that I have rebuked him sternly for his behavior, that these pictures will never be seen by anyone other than you and me."

With that, Schachter leaned forward and offered the envelope to Isaac. "And what do these pictures show?" Isaac asked, hesitating to take the envelope.

"It embarrasses me even to describe it. Here, see for yourself."

Isaac stared at the envelope for a moment. He was not one given to premonitions, yet was certain that the instant he opened it his life would change forever. He looked askance at Schachter, and opened the envelope.

Schachter watched Isaac remove the pictures and examine them. He allowed the silence for a few minutes, and then said, "I'm sorry, Reb Yizchak, this is truly terrible for you."

"Vhat do you vant?" Isaac asked, his face crimson, his body trembling.

Schachter feigned innocence. "What do you mean, what do *I* want?"

"It is obvious that you are showing me these for a reason. Otherwise, you vould have burnt them and forgotten about them, so *vhat do you vant?*"

"Reb Yitzchak," Schachter said, "I understand you are upset and, therefore, not thinking clearly, but I can assure you that my intentions are only to shield you from harm. You are correct, I could have burnt these and forgotten about them, but then the situation between your daughter and this man would have continued. Who knows, eventually the pictures might have landed in the hands of someone less discrete than I. I thought it my obligation to inform you, that is it."

Isaac wasn't buying, but knew he had no option other than to play along. "I'm sorry," he said, trying to calm himself. "I am upset."

"Please, Reb Yitzchak, there is no reason for you to apologize!"

Isaac looked silently at the elder.

"It is devastating when something like this happens," Schachter said. "*Truly devastating*! I feel your pain, Reb Yitzchak, as I always feel the pain when any of our children are led astray. That is why I fight so hard to keep our community safe, to keep our children protected from the poisons of the world. We have not always agreed, I know, but now I am sure you will see the value and importance of what I have been trying to teach. Now, that you have personally experienced the anguish that comes from leniency with our ways, *you* will understand why it is crucial to be stern, to keep our gates closed and corruption from our midst."

Isaac contained the rage welling within. He wanted to lash out, to grab Schachter, to strike him. But he did nothing, for he knew that if he lost control, he and his family would forever be marked. He sat there, praying for God to help him hold his tongue.

"I'm sorry this had to happen," Schachter added. "But it is at moments like this when *Hashem* gives us the opportunity to examine our ways and see that we can truly grow. I am sure you don't need to hear this now, but when you go home and think about things, I know you will agree with what I am saying."

"And vhere are the negatives?" Isaac asked, ignoring the sermon.

"Excuse me?" Defensive.

"The negatives, vhere are they?"

"Reb Yitzchak, of course I have instructed the fiend who took these pictures to destroy them. And I can guarantee you that he has done just that."

Isaac didn't bother pressing for the identity of the photographer, for he knew who the real devil was. He replaced the pictures in the envelope, and dropped them on Schachter's desk.

"Don't you want to take them?" Schachter asked.

"No, I don't."

"Then *I* will burn them."

"Yes, I'm sure you vill."

⌘

Pictures of his daughter with Joshua flashed through Isaac Weissman's mind as he walked the street. He understood Schachter's agenda clearly enough, even though it had been couched in code: *Change your alliance, join me, or else!* But Rachel with Joshua, he couldn't begin to fathom that. Where had he gone wrong? What horrid sin had he committed to warrant this? And what was he to do about it?

He walked, and he remembered—painful memories, of which he had more than enough. They came vividly, as they always did, as if they were occurring then and there. *A two year old boy on his lap, a Sabbath melody; flames, soldiers; a cattle car, a woman beside him, a boy in his arms; a line, a man with a list, struggle, screaming; darkness.*

He tried once again to reach beyond the darkness, to capture those final images of the boy and woman being dragged away. But there was only darkness. And Rachel with Joshua.

He walked on, heading nowhere, faltering, unaware of the world around him, images battering him with unrelenting force: Rachel as a little child on his lap at the Sabbath table, singing, rocking in his arms. He hears her voice and feels the softness of her hair against his cheek. He kisses her head. How she has blossomed, so beautiful, so brilliant, so filled with love and life. And now this.

The darkness returned. He stumbled, leaned against a wall, and didn't know where he was. All he could see was the darkness; all he could feel was a great hunger, unlike anything he'd ever known. It was a hunger for air, as he gasped and struggled to fill his lungs. But it was not to be.

He felt himself slipping downward, the hunger subsiding as he merged with the darkness. Almost blissful, even comforting, he relinquished the last morsel of suffering connecting him to this world. He was going someplace else, beyond the darkness, where there was light, luminous and redeeming. And the lost faces of a young boy and a woman, waiting.

⤛⤜

Hannah and Rachel raced into the emergency room. The phone call had come just ten minutes earlier, and had provided no information aside from the fact that Isaac had been brought in by ambulance. They hurried to the reception desk, gave their names, and were asked to wait while the clerk called for the doctor.

Marcia Schiffman suddenly appeared, her face revealing what her tongue could not utter. Rachel and Hannah looked at each other and knew. Rachel turned toward Schiffman again, praying to be wrong, hoping for any words that would dispel the dreadful reality. But all the doctor could say was, "I'm sorry."

Rachel's legs gave way as she collapsed. Schiffman dashed to her side, caught her, and eased her into a chair. Hannah helped, almost forgetting her own despair. Rachel regained consciousness quickly, but was still unable to hold herself up. She fell into the chair, limp, deadened.

Hannah sat down, and put her arm around Rachel, bringing Rachel's head into her chest. She held Rachel the way she had when Rachel was a child. And Rachel was still her child, frail, in need of comfort and reassurance. She had to be a mother for now, her own grieving would have to wait.

Schiffman stood silently, helpless.

Rachel let out a blaring shriek, her body began to tremble. Hannah held her tightly, trying to sooth her. Schiffman watched, feeling a tightness in her throat. Her own mother had died when she was four years old, and her life as a doctor had been much too busy for marriage and children. The scene upset her, she needed to escape.

A few seconds later, Schiffman found herself staring into a mirror above a bathroom sink, tears gushing from her eyes. She was certain that Rachel and Hannah hadn't noticed her slip away, certain that none of the other doctors or nurses had seen her running toward the bathroom.

329

She quickly washed and dried her face. She had to be professional. No time for this sort of thing.

She slipped out of the bathroom and back to the treatment rooms where her patients awaited, figuring Rachel and Hannah wouldn't notice her absence. She promised herself she would phone them later, maybe even stop by the house to see how they were faring. But in her heart she knew she wouldn't, she couldn't. Death was something she still had trouble with, even after all her years in medicine. It was life that concerned her, sustaining it, saving it. Death was always a fact. There was never anything she could do about it, not when she was four, and not now. She needed to get back to work.

❦

The funeral was the next morning. An ominous rainstorm bore heaven's testimony to Isaac Weissman's sainthood. Despite the short notice and inclement weather, there was a good turnout. Neighbors and friends of Isaac's and Hannah's, many of Rachel's girlhood friends, students and teachers from the many different yeshivas in the neighborhood, the Elders, and even the *Rebbe*.

Esther and Stephen stood close to Rachel. Paul Sims, driven by an obligation to honor his former teacher, found an inconspicuous place amid the crowd. He was looking around, expecting his father to appear, but Alfred had arrived late and was hidden somewhere in the back. Also in the back, noticeably separated from the other elders found prominently by the *Rebbe's* side, Rav Nachum Schachter stood with his assistant, both men visibly shaken.

Since he'd heard the news of Reb Yitzchak's death, Schachter's feelings had vacillated between guilt and vindication, the former seemingly stronger than the latter. Part of him reasoned that every war has its casualties, that every true soldier has blood on his hands. But in his heart of hearts, he knew there could be no excuse for his horrendous deed. He would have to live with it.

Schachter thanked God that Reb Yitzchak had left the photographs behind. He would destroy the pictures and the negatives, and spare the Weissmans any more anguish. There was nothing to be gained from a scandal; what Rachel Weissman did with her life would be left for God to judge.

330

In truth, however, his motivations were more self-serving. He knew that if the photographs were ever discovered, his former confrere, Rav Feldblum, would most definitely suspect his involvement. And *that* would be more difficult to live with.

In either case, the connection between Isaac's death and the pictures would be obliterated. No one would know about Rachel and the black man, except Schachter and his assistant, and Rachel. Just as she had blamed herself for Isaac's first heart attack, she blamed herself for his death. Reward and punishment, that was the way she had been bred to understand the universe. People get what they deserve, and for her that was the coffin containing her father's body being lowered into the ground.

It was a simple view of life, and one which she would gladly have discarded if she had been able. But she was stuck with it, the remorse it brought, and the contrition it demanded. Her father was gone, and he had never been so influential in life as he would be in death. There was nothing left to argue, and no one left with whom to argue it. She had always understood, but now she would listen. At last, she would abide by his will, in silence, in agony.

She would never fathom how a man as gentle as he, a man who'd survived the crematoria, could harbor even an ounce of prejudice. She wanted to believe that what she yearned for was not so awful, that eventually her father might have come to accept Joshua. But deep down she knew she was deceiving herself. Her father, as all men, had his limitations.

She hadn't informed Joshua of her father's death, and hadn't wanted him at the funeral. As for why, she didn't know. And as for what she was going to do about Joshua, she also didn't know.

Around her, the crowd wept as the men took turns shoveling the earth upon the casket. It was a great *mitzvah* to bury the dead, but one in which only men partook. The *Rebbe* began to pray and others joined in. The Hasidic way: praising God during life's worst calamities, always awaiting a glorious tomorrow. Rachel had given up on that tomorrow long ago.

CHAPTER 45

Joshua had read about Rabbi Weissman's death in the *Times'* obituaries, and tried not to think about why Rachel hadn't called. He felt angry for having been excluded, and knew it hadn't been an oversight.

He considered paying respects during the week of *shiva*, but thought it best not to. Once again, rejected; once again, a victim of his color. He was growing weary of the fight.

A month passed, and still there was no word. During that time he busied himself with getting things in order: office supplies, furniture, advertising, even building a small list of clients from the commerce association's roster. He visited prospective clients at their businesses, and was always greeted favorably. It was gratifying to see how many people had heard of him, and how willing they were to place their trust in his hands. But it didn't lessen the pain.

On Connie's final day with the DA, she and Joshua were scheduled for dinner to celebrate their partnership. He was sitting at his desk, working on a new client's file, already late for his dinner appointment, when he heard the front door open. He hadn't gotten around to hiring a receptionist. There wasn't any money for that just yet. He got up, and walked out to the waiting room to see who was there.

He wasn't sure if he was surprised, happy, or angry. Rachel just stood there, wordless, looking at him, waiting for a reaction. Without thinking, he walked to her and took her in his arms.

"I'm sorry about your father," he said.

At first, she just leaned her head on his shoulder. Then she looked at him, and said, "I'm sorry I didn't tell you. I didn't know what to do."

He told her he understood, though he really didn't. He waited a beat, trying to contain his frustration. "How's your mother doing?" he asked.

"She's handling it, I suppose."

"And you?"

She shrugged. "Some moments are harder than others."

"If you ever need to talk . . ."

"I know."

He glanced at his watch. He was very late for his date with Connie, but didn't want to leave. "I hate to say this, but I need to be someplace about fifteen minutes ago."

"That's okay," she answered, obviously disappointed.

"Can you come by tomorrow?"

"Tomorrow's good."

"How about five?"

"That's fine."

She waited till he locked up. They said good-bye on the sidewalk outside, shared a stilted embrace, and he watched her walk off, wondering if she would really come back. That was the way things were with her, the way they probably always would be.

❦

The following afternoon he sat in his office, anxiously waiting for five o'clock. Unsuccessfully distracting himself with work, he glanced at the clock every ten minutes. At exactly five on the button, he heard the front door.

He got up to go out and greet her, but Connie, sly fox that she was, had beaten him to it. He had told Connie about Rachel's visit the night before at dinner, and figured that Connie had planned this all day, had waited for Rachel's arrival just as he had. It was her opportunity to prove that she could be friendly and hospitable toward Rachel. Joshua stayed in his office, allowing the women their pleasantries, gathering his wits.

He listened for a minute, took a few deep breaths, and stepped out to the reception area. They both turned toward him. "Hi," he said to Rachel.

"Hi," she responded.

Connie stood there, silently observing. She was more worried for Joshua than jealous.

"Why don't you come on into my office," Joshua said to Rachel. "I just have to clear my desk and we can get going."

The two women exchanged smiles. It was genuine, they shared something and both knew it. They would need to get used to one another, to work out their respective roles. A woman's thing.

Rachel followed Joshua into his office and Connie went back into hers. Joshua gathered some papers, put his files away, and straightened up his desk. He hadn't realized how busy he'd been until he started cleaning. It was a good feeling. He was on his way to success, at least as a lawyer.

It was a nippy afternoon, mid-March. Spring was around the corner, teasing from time to time, but it was still too cool for a long walk. "How about dinner?" she asked.

He was surprised, for they'd never actually broken bread together. He couldn't imagine what exactly she had in mind. All the local Kosher establishments were bound to be filled with people who might know her, and he didn't really think she was inviting him to her mother's home.

"What do you think about going into Manhattan?" she asked. "I know a place there, a vegetarian restaurant where I went once with Esther."

"Okay, sure. Sounds great."

He locked up and hailed a cab. He was a big lawyer now, and could afford to splurge. Okay, not so big, but at least smart enough to know that public transportation was too "public." Which also made him suspect that this vegetarian restaurant was probably some tiny, out of the way dive, suited for bohemians like Esther.

⁂

The place was called The Greenery, and was located above a leather shop. There were eight tables in all, only two of which were occupied when they walked in.

"Is this place Kosher?" Joshua asked Rachel, while they waited to be seated.

"It's vegetarian."

"But that doesn't necessarily mean Kosher, does it?"

"It's Kosher enough." Dismissive.

He let it go. It was obvious that she was making compromises, and wasn't completely comfortable about it.

The manager, an overweight woman wearing an earth-toned gypsy dress, showed them to their table, presented their menus, and told them that their waitress would be with them shortly. They sat on uncomfortable straw chairs, and perused their menus in silence. There had been a lull between them since Rachel's last comment.

"I'm sorry, Joshua," she said, looking over her menu. "This is the best I can do right now."

"Do you think things will ever be different?"

"I don't know. All I *do* know is that I love being with you, spending time with you, talking with you. I can't stand the thought of not being able to do any of those things, not for a second."

"And that's enough for you?"

"No, it's not enough," she answered pensively. "But it will have to do."

She watched for his reaction. She was setting the rules, and hoping he would comply.

"Okay," he said, "We'll try it your way."

CHAPTER 46

Israel Turner looked in the mirror, not for vanity, but for the simple satisfaction of seeing himself. He smiled at his stocky, bearded image. Soft eyes, not a fraction taller than five feet four inches, fifty-four years old, and a miracle. He couldn't get over the fact that he was alive, and fortunate to celebrate yet another Succoth holiday, the time of year when the Jews praise God for protecting them through their travail and wandering.

To Israel Turner, this was a momentous occasion, for he had endured more than most, and had personally experienced the beneficent hand of the Lord. Together with his wife, he had survived the crematoria of Auschwitz and had come to America. They raised children, and built new lives among the Lubavitch community in Crown Heights. And still, Israel Turner took nothing for granted. Each holiday, each celebration, each opportunity to rejoice with his family was a gift. A miracle.

And tonight was a double celebration, not only the final night of Succoth, but also the Sabbath. A paradoxical combination, a time when one is commanded to both rest and revel simultaneously. But the Hasidim never truly rested, not when it came to serving God. So now, after the festive dinner had been concluded, the community would once again gather at the great synagogue on Eastern Parkway for song and dance, into the wee hours of the morning. It was a way of life that suited Israel Turner perfectly.

The meal had been delightful, as usual. His five year old foster son, Zvi, had enthusiastically joined him and his sons-in-law in the melodies; his baby granddaughter cried and fussed; and the three women took turns soothing her. Notwithstanding the difficulties he had walking—a limp, courtesy of the camp guards—and a scar ridden body, there was so much to be thankful for, so many reasons to praise God.

In his present life, Israel Turner had become an auto mechanic. It was a hard living for an honest, religious man, but it was enough. For him, it was more than enough. If he could put food on the table on an evening such as this, it was simply another miracle.

It was late and he was tired, but he would not submit. He rinsed his face, hoping the cold water would bring a second wind, straightened his tie, and went out to the living room to say goodbye to his wife. She would be remaining at home, baby-sitting, while the others went off to the celebration. He kissed her and his granddaughter, and promised an early return. She knew not to take such a promise seriously.

After exiting his building on Empire Boulevard, he walked past his ground-floor apartment window and saw his wife standing, holding the baby, waving to him. He waved back and proceeded with the others, all of whom were walking slowly so Israel could keep up. He smiled, and told a few jokes along the way, ignoring the strain of the journey. Ever the wit, his friends and neighbors would say, always good for a laugh.

Kingston Avenue was teeming with Hasidim, all heading to the main synagogue. It was a beautiful sight, Israel thought, all these *frum* Jews living, worshiping, and celebrating together. Reminiscent of his youthful days in Eastern Europe.

He turned the corner onto Eastern Parkway, and was stunned by the crowd outside the synagogue. Each year it grew, devotees migrating from all corners of the earth just to be close to the *Rebbe*, to celebrate on the holy streets of Crown Heights. He arrived too late to actually get into the synagogue, but the song and dance had spread to the street. It was loud and joyous, and Israel Turner was content just to be there, to witness such jubilation. Another miracle.

He mingled for a while, mixing and *kibbitzing* with compatriots. His limp made dancing difficult, but singing was another matter. He clapped his hands mightily, and sang at the top of his lungs. Yes, God had protected him, had saved him, had brought him and his loved ones to this moment. God deserved his adulation.

It took some time, but eventually his energy waned. He looked at his wristwatch. He had left home more than two and a half hours earlier. The festivity was still going strong. He hated to leave, but sleep was beckoning.

He would never have thought of asking anyone to accompany him home. He had walked these streets so many nights alone. God was always watching. He said his good-byes and went on his way.

As he sauntered down the Avenue toward Empire Boulevard, the sounds of the celebration faded in the darkness. The street grew barren and quiet, except for the clicking of his shoes upon the pavement and the soft humming of his own melody. He walked on, in oblivion, as if the night were his friend.

Suddenly, behind him, he noticed the sound of someone else. He turned to see who it was, perhaps a neighbor. There was nothing. Curious, but undaunted, he continued, turned the corner and approached his building. When he came to the window of his apartment, he stopped, tapped on the screen, and called to his wife. He didn't have a key—carrying was expressly forbidden on the Sabbath—and needed her to let him in. She came into the living room and as she approached the window, she saw what would forever alter her existence.

Israel Turner faced his assailant with the same courage he had shown the Nazis so many years before. He was not afraid. God would protect him.

"Please, leave him alone, he has no money," his wife yelled from the window. She ran to the door, hoping to get outside to help her husband.

Israel tried to talk his attacker down, to explain that Jews don't carry money on the Sabbath, but the man with the .25 caliber pistol wouldn't relent. Before his wife had made it to the lobby, she heard what sounded like two gunshots. She told herself it couldn't be, until she came out and saw for herself.

Lying on the holy streets of Crown Heights was the body of Israel Turner. The miracle was over.

⤜∽⤏

The police broadcasts were transmitted within moments of the shooting. Black man, late teens or early twenties, medium height and weight, wearing a cream colored leatherette jacket and brown pants. Believed to be armed and dangerous.

Seconds later, about three blocks from the shooting scene, a fleeing man answering the description was spotted and apprehended by two patrolmen. The suspect was searched and found to be in possession of a .25 caliber handgun. He was taken into custody, and later charged with the crime when the ballistics report came back identifying his gun as the murder weapon. His name was Larry Pilgrim.

※

Israel Turner was buried two days later, on Monday September 29, 1975. The service was held at the Agudath Israel Synagogue on Crown Street, followed by a procession of at least five hundred mourners trailing the hearse. They marched past Israel Turner's home and onward to the Empire Boulevard police station.

The crowd stopped at the station-house for a brief demonstration to express their anger over the lack of adequate police protection. The demonstration was supposed to be solemn and peaceful, in keeping with proper funeral etiquette. It was anything but.

Prominent members of the community took turns speaking from the station-house steps to the mournful crowd. Onlookers, mostly black people from the neighborhood, began to gather. Directly across the street from the station-house, in Junior High School 61, classes were disrupted as children moved from their desks to the windows to see what was happening.

Suddenly, someone shouted, *"Heil Hitler!"*

Not an ear in the crowd missed it. People turned, looking at one another in shock, looking at the spectators in rage. Then, another shout: *"Hitler was right!"*

Some of the mourners, convinced they had identified the agitator, lunged toward a black man and a woman standing beside him. The police observed the commotion, and charged through the crowd to break it up. During the struggle, they managed to rescue the woman and bring her into the school for safety. The man, however, had broken free and fled, but he didn't get far. Two other officers quickly grabbed him and began escorting him to the station-house. The mourners, however, had another idea.

One of the officers was knocked to the ground while his partner, still standing, was pummeled from all directions. The Hasidim broke through to the black man, and began beating him before reinforcements arrived. The children, watching from the school windows, joined in, hurling more cries of *Heil Hitler!*

Several of the mourners turned toward the school, looking with disgust, but there was no inclination to go inside. A line had to be drawn.

It was a while before the police took control and the turmoil was quelled. The crowd eventually dispersed, the procession moved on, and the body of Israel Turner was taken to its final resting place. The man and the woman who were apprehended later denied having uttered any anti-Semitic slogans. They were identified as Nelson Martin, 22, and his common-law wife, Yvonne Gonzalez, 17, who was in her fifth month of pregnancy. They were both taken by police to Kings County Hospital where they were examined and released. Neither they, nor any of the mourners, were arrested.

The entire ordeal had lasted but a few minutes; the fallout would linger for decades.

CHAPTER 47

Joshua's practice quickly grew. Practically every legal problem belonging to any black person within a five mile radius seemed to land on his doorstep, and he took them all. Real estate closings, partnership formations, wills, personal injuries, and occasional penny ante criminal stuff. He wasn't choosy.

Connie was less satisfied. She ached for another Willie Johnson, a high profile case that could bolster their standing as criminal specialists. She understood, however, that the business they got was the business they did, and why Joshua was thankful for any and all of it.

Eventually there was enough money to hire a secretary. Connie's mother had a friend, a bone skinny, frail looking, fifty-five year old English teacher from East New York who had grown weary of yelling at children. Despite her appearance, she was a toughie, a Caribbean like Connie's parents, stiff and punctilious. The perfect secretary. Her name was Emma, but she preferred Mrs. Sawyer.

Between the three of them, things got organized and moving. Joshua even started getting to the office, and other places, on time. Anything to avoid Mrs. Sawyer's admonition.

Rachel Weissman Frankel changed her name back to Rachel Weissman. She had given Binny the house, the car, the china, the silverware, the money—all the things that had come from his family. She didn't want *anything* that was his.

She found a job selling dresses in a shop on Kingston Avenue. Often, after work, she saw Joshua. They frequented the vegetarian place, The Greenery, which had become their hideout. On warmer nights, or when they simply needed a change of pace, they strolled the Brighton boardwalk or caught an out-of-the-way movie. Whatever they did, it was always surreptitious. And always celibate.

Joshua was frustrated, but chose not to force the issue. For now, the fantasy would have to do.

They found themselves in troubled times. Notwithstanding their difference in religion, which could have been resolved through conversion—his, of course—racial tensions around them were exploding. Between the Willie Johnson case, the Israel Turner killing and its aftermath, they knew they were playing with fire.

And then there was Rachel's guilt over her father's death, her belief that God had taken him from her as punishment for her involvement with Joshua. She had never discussed this with Joshua, but he was keenly aware of it anyway. He tried to understand. It wasn't easy.

❧

"There are two men here to see you," Mrs. Sawyer said, standing in the doorway to Joshua's office.

He waved her in. She took exactly one step, indicating that she didn't appreciate being commanded by hand gestures. He beckoned her closer, not wanting anyone in the reception area to overhear them. Reticently, she approached. Without inquiring as to the identity of his visitors—he figured they were prospective clients—he asked, "Do they have an appointment?" He didn't like the idea of seeing a "walk-in." It made him appear too available.

"No, they do not." Formal. Snide.

"Then, perhaps you should give them one."

"You might want to see them now."

"And why is that?"

"Because one of them is that famous professor from Brooklyn College. Thompson, I believe his name is."

"Thompson," he uttered. "And who is with him?"

"That, I can't help you with, but whoever he is, he looks important."

Joshua thought for a moment. He could have sworn he'd seen the last of Thompson. But maybe it was payback time. Then it came to him: The Israel Turner killing; the suspect, Larry Pilgrim. *Payback time, indeed.*

"Show them in," he said.

A few seconds later, she knocked lightly on the open door. Joshua was attending to some papers, feigning indifference, but as soon as he lifted his eyes, his pretense evaporated. For the man accompanying Professor Alvin Thompson was none other than his boyhood friend, Jerome Williams.

"Good afternoon counselor," the professor said, smirking at Joshua's obvious uneasiness. "I understand you already know Reverend Williams."

"Yes," Joshua responded, attempting what subtlety he could muster. He stood to shake hands. Jerome's was clammy, making Joshua feel that he wasn't the only nervous one. "Please, sit," he said, gesturing to two chairs in front of the desk.

"We're here about the matter of Mr. Larry Pilgrim," Thompson said. "Seems Mr. Pilgrim is in need of legal representation, and your name has come up as a possible candidate."

"Why me?"

"Because of the excellent job you did for Mr. Johnson."

"Mr. Johnson was innocent," Joshua reacted.

Joshua thought he saw Thompson squirm in his chair. The professor had obviously expected him to jump at this, offer gratitude, and beg everlasting forgiveness for past iniquities. Not so.

He looked at Jerome, wondering what his role was in all this. He had heard of Jerome's involvement with Thompson. Jerome had become quite an activist since he'd taken over Reverend Sharp's storefront Baptist Church, mixed up with the likes of the professor, preaching about white oppression, black uprising, and other such things. Reportedly, he was quite effective. A budding community force. Joshua had guessed it would be only a matter of time before their paths crossed. And here they were.

"How have you been?" Joshua asked, looking straight into Jerome's eyes.

"Fine," he answered. Expressionless.

"Celeste?"

Jerome flinched slightly, but kept his poise. "Wouldn't know," he said, almost indifferently.

Thompson was growing restless. Joshua turned to him, and asked, "Who else are you considering?"

"The usuals."

Joshua thought about that. He knew who "the usuals" were, the well established criminal lawyers with successful records and sizeable tabs. He also knew that not one of them would let Thompson run the show. It was the same situation as with the Willie Johnson case; Thompson needed him.

He wondered how Thompson could imagine controlling him after what had happened the last time, then realized that Thompson was the quintessential pragmatist. Thompson still had a better shot with him than with anyone else—*let bygones be bygones, onward and upward, anything for the cause.*

Joshua supposed that this was where Jerome came in. A crafty form of intimidation: *Behave, or the whole community learns about your past, how you murdered the good reverend's father.*

Nice touch, Joshua thought, wondering still why Jerome would go for it. *Wouldn't the story embarrass him too? Maybe not, maybe it would actually help him? What better way to bolster the image of savior than to have once been a martyr? Another hero!*

All this aside, the prospect of representing Larry Pilgrim enticed Joshua, though he wasn't ready to share that with them. He was certain Connie would jump at the opportunity, and was thankful she was out of the office. He didn't want to know about this, at least not yet. First, there was someone else he needed to speak with: Rachel.

"Gentlemen, I don't mean to cut this meeting short, but I'm due in court." He was actually due for a real estate closing, but court sounded better. "Your offer sounds interesting, but I'm not really sure how I feel about it."

"Time *is* of the essence," the professor said.

"Yes, I know. Even so, I will have to think about it. I'll talk with my partner and get back to you no later than tomorrow. I'm sure that's reasonable."

The professor didn't hide his ire very well. He was accustomed to having what he wanted, when he wanted it. Joshua enjoyed delaying the man's gratification, thus gaining leverage in setting the ground rules.

"That will be fine," Thompson said. Jerome looked at him with surprise; he hadn't expected Thompson to fold this easily. Neither had Joshua.

Thompson stood, Jerome followed his lead. They each extended their hands and the three men shook. "Tomorrow, then," Joshua said.

"Tomorrow!" Thompson responded.

Jerome was silent, his eyes far away.

Joshua wondered about Jerome, whether his old friend had somehow resolved the tragedy that had come between them. It was difficult sitting there, silent about it. Joshua wanted to say something, perhaps only to ask to meet in the future for lunch, or just a drink, but he couldn't bring himself to do it.

Maybe someday, he thought.

❧

His next scheduled dinner with Rachel wasn't for two days, but he needed to see her that night. He debated whether to stop by the dress shop, or go to her home later. Either way, it would be ticklish. He decided on her home, thinking her mother would probably be less of a problem than some nosey strangers.

He had first met Hannah Weissman years earlier when the rabbi had gotten him the job in the synagogue, again when she had accompanied Rachel to visit him in the hospital after the stabbing, and a third time at Rachel's wedding. Still, he wondered if Hannah would recognize him, and how he was going to explain his visit. And then there was always the chance that she might be out.

No such luck, he mused as Hannah opened the door. She looked at him and smiled. "Joshua Eubanks!" she said.

"Hello Mrs. Weissman."

Her expression was curious, and he still hadn't concocted a good tale. Some lawyer. Suddenly, she turned sad. "I'm sorry, Joshua, but the rabbi isn't here. He died a few months ago."

"Oh," he responded, "I'm terribly sorry." He knew it was low to play along, pretending he had actually come to see the rabbi, but he couldn't come up with anything better at the moment.

He tried convincing himself that he hadn't actually lied to her, technically speaking. Notwithstanding his duplicitous display of surprise, his sorrow was genuine. Perhaps he was a better lawyer than he thought.

There was a moment of silence, and then she said, "Why don't you come in and have a drink?"

He entered, discomfited, keenly aware of his infringement. He wanted to turn and leave.

"Rachel," Hannah called out, "guess who's here to visit?"

Rachel came out of her bedroom and turned pale at the sight of him. "What . . ."

"Joshua came to visit Papa," Hannah interjected.

"Well," he said, "I actually came to see the family."

Rachel was speechless, her face without expression. He knew he was in it up to his chin, and regretted having come. He should have just taken the Pilgrim case, and dealt with Rachel afterward.

"Why don't you two sit in the living room, I'll make some tea," Hannah suggested.

They moved to the living room, and as soon as Hannah was gone, Rachel turned to him, whispering, "What the hell are you doing here?"

"Shh," he said. "I needed to see you. Something's come up, and I have to speak with you about it before tomorrow."

Hannah entered the room. "I put the water up, it'll just be a minute." She sat down. "So, Joshua, what exactly was it you were coming to see my husband about?"

He felt Rachel's disgust as he looked at her. "Well," he began, "like I said, I wanted to talk to both of *you*. It's about a problem I have, and I would like to know what you think." He could hear the nervousness in his own voice. "As you know, I defended the man who was accused of having attacked Emma Lukins."

"I read about that," Hannah said. "I didn't realize it was you, though."

"Yes," he answered. "Anyway," he continued, "I suppose that some of my old friends in this community weren't very happy with me for having done that."

Hannah: "I don't know about other people, but I can assure you that the rabbi never said anything derogatory to me about it. Come to think of it, I don't recall his having mentioned it at all. Do you, Rachel?"

Rachel: "No."

Joshua: "Well, that's good to hear, because my intention was only to help my client. You folks were always kind to me, and I was concerned about how you felt."

Hannah: "There's no need for you to be concerned. I'm sure the rabbi was proud of how you turned out, even if he only played a small role in it.

Joshua: "He actually played a large role. He gave me a break, got me a job when I needed one and no one else would hire me, and he didn't even know me."

Hannah: "Well you paid him back tenfold with what you did for Rachel when those hoodlums attacked her and Esther."

Rachel feigned a smile as her mother looked in her direction.

"The reason I'm here tonight," he said, "is because another case has been offered to me and I would like to know what you think before I decide whether to take it. Your opinions are important to me."

"And what case is that?" Rachel asked, almost as if she were alone with him. Her mother looked at her strangely.

He swallowed hard and uttered the name, "Larry Pilgrim."

Rachel and Hannah looked at one another, both wondering if they'd heard correctly.

Hannah: "The man who killed Rabbi Turner?"

Joshua: "I didn't know he was a rabbi."

Rachel: "Most people didn't. He was a humble man who worked as a mechanic; as far as everyone knew, that's all he was. But when a man dies, you learn the truth, things you never knew before."

Joshua hadn't read anything in the press about Turner having been a rabbi. Strangely, the new information made a difference. He knew it shouldn't have—a human being is a human being and all that—but it did. Isaac Weissman, a rabbi, had been his friend.

He could see Hannah's disappointment, while Rachel's face remained barren. It ate at him; he would have preferred being chided.

"I'm not sure what you want from us, Joshua," Hannah said.

"I'm not, either," he responded.

Hannah: "I understand you have to do your job, but this is so . . ." She couldn't finish her own sentence.

"Ugly," Rachel added, making no eye contact with him.

The word pierced him like a dagger, right into his gut. He stared at her, hoping she would glance back, but nothing. "I suppose I wanted to hear it was okay," he confessed.

"And why is that important?" Hannah asked.

"Because I respected the rabbi, I respect both of you, and your feelings mean a lot to me."

"It sounds to me like you're looking for absolution," Hannah said. "In our religion, absolution comes only from God, and from doing the right thing. I believe my husband would have told you the same thing had he been here."

"I suppose so," Joshua said wearily, realizing this was as far as he was going to get. He rose to his feet. "I'm sorry I bothered you so late at night."

"No bother, it was good to see you," Hannah said, also rising.

Rachel remained seated, lost in some place he couldn't get to.

"Well, thank you both for seeing me."

"You are welcome always," Hannah said, as she escorted him to the door.

Rachel remained in the living room.

He stepped into the hall. "Thank you again, and good-night."

"Good-night, Joshua, and may God help you find the answers you seek."

⁂

It was two o'clock in the morning. Loretta was asleep in her bedroom, and Joshua, unable to sleep, was up watching late night TV in the living room, trying to rest his mind. The doorbell rang, followed by a loud knock. He knew who it was.

He responded quickly, hoping Loretta hadn't been awakened. He barely had the door halfway open, when it came crashing into him. Then, a slap, hard and mighty, threw him off balance, as he heard the words: *"How dare you!"*

She walked past him, straight into the living room. At this point, he was certain his mother was awake, and equally certain she would remain in her room, pretending not to be. He used his hand to sooth the sting on his face, and looked at Rachel. He wasn't angry with her; he knew he had no right to be.

"How could you do that to me?" she exclaimed.

"I was wrong, I shouldn't have . . ."

"*Shouldn't have*! Whatever were you thinking?"

"That's just it, I wasn't thinking."

She looked at him, seething.

"How did you get here this time of night?" he asked.

"I walked, rather *ran*."

"But the streets . . ."

"The streets are perfectly safe, safer than ever. Since Rabbi Turner's murder, they've formed community patrols. They're all over the place."

"Who's *they*?"

"Who do you think?"

"The Lubavitchers?"

"That's right. No more relying on the police. It was never a good idea for a Jew to depend on the *Czar's* protection in the first place. It just took us a while to figure that out here."

"Oh boy!"

"Oh boy *what*?"

"It's going to cause trouble. Hasidic community patrols in a seventy percent black neighborhood isn't going to go over very well."

She considered his point.

He looked at her. "I'm sorry I came to your home. It was probably the most idiotic thing I've ever done."

"*Probably!*"

"There's no excuse."

"But I'll just bet there's an explanation."

"Well," he said hesitantly, "there is, if you want to hear it."

"I'm dying to." Sarcasm.

"I needed to run this by you tonight; they want an answer tomorrow morning."

"And I suppose it has something to do with me?"

"It has everything to do with you; with *us*."

"*Us*," she repeated, "I don't even know what that means after tonight."

"That's good because I didn't know what it meant before tonight."

"So that's what this whole thing is about, isn't it? You had an opportunity to test the waters, to see just how far you could come into my life, and you decided, *what the hell, why not? I can't stand her silly little rules anyway!*"

He realized she was right: he had been motivated by more than simply getting her approval for the Larry Pilgrim case. He had used the case for another agenda, and why not; why not go to her home, have her mother see them together, and bring the whole damn thing out into the open at last?

"That's it, isn't it?" she continued.

"I did want to know how you felt about me taking this case."

"I'm sure you did, and I'm sure you're clever enough to have found a way to get in touch with me without involving my mother. But you *wanted* to involve my mother, didn't you?"

"I suppose," he confessed, "it's possible I got carried away with things . . ."

"*Carried away!* That's an understatement."

"Look Rachel, I'm sorry if I hurt you; that's the *last* thing I'd ever want to do, believe it or not. And maybe you're right, maybe I am tired of all your restrictions, but one thing I'm not, is ashamed. I am not now, nor will I ever be, *ashamed* of having gone to your home. If you can't understand and accept that, then there really is no *us*."

She was taken aback. Her expression changed. "I'm sorry," she said softly.

"It's okay." He was visibly shaken.

"It isn't. I haven't been fair with you; I haven't been fair with *us*."

"It's not about being fair, it's about surviving."

"Thank you for trying to get me off the hook, Joshua, but I can take responsibility for this. I'm a grown up."

"And what about the Larry Pilgrim thing?"

"You're a grown up too. You don't need my permission."

"You're absolutely right. I don't *need* your permission, but I do need to know your feelings."

"I think you should take the case."

"Huh?"

"You heard me. You should take it."

"But why?"

"*Why?*" She thought for a moment. "Well, for starters, I believe it's what you really want, and that I'm the only thing standing in the way. I don't want you to sacrifice for me, or to deprive yourself any more than you already have." She reached over, placed her hand on his cheek. "You see, I know what it is to sacrifice, to give up the things you truly want in life. We've both had enough of that, and it has to stop sometime." She moved closer, touched up against him, stood on her toes, and kissed him gently on the cheek. "I want you to take the case."

"I don't think it's a good idea," he said.

"You don't think *what's* a good idea?"

"Taking the case."

She was puzzled. "Joshua, I don't underst . . ."

"Listen, this may sound crazy, and it probably is, but I can't take the Pilgrim case. Maybe I knew it all along, or maybe I just figured it out. Either way, it's a bad idea."

"But why?"

"Because it would destroy us."

She shook her head in defiance.

"*It would*, regardless of what you think now. I know you want to believe that we're invincible, and it's true, we have survived some pretty nasty things together. *This* would break us."

"It wouldn't! Nothing can!"

"It *can* and it *would*! Listen, this Pilgrim thing is bad, a lot worse than you can imagine. It's not going to be about that rabbi and this black guy. It's going to be about race, about tensions and hatreds that have been festering for years, just waiting for a moment like this. It's going to blow up in our faces, and whether I take the case or not, it's going to drive a wedge between us."

"But this isn't about race, Joshua, it's about murder. No one condones murder, black or white."

"Rachel, *everything* is about race."

He was surprised he'd actually said that, but once he had, he realized it was what he truly believed.

He searched her face, wondering if she could see the yearning in his eyes. He reached over and stroked her cheek. She moved closer and embraced him. It felt more intimate than anything they'd shared before, yet still not quite what he had dreamed of.

CHAPTER 48

Hannah Weissman, still half asleep, stumbled into her kitchen for her morning coffee and found Rachel sitting at the table, engrossed in the newspaper. "Good morning," Rachel said, her eyes on the paper.

"Good morning," Hannah answered. "You're up early today."

Rachel glanced at the clock on the wall and saw it was seven-fifteen. She had thought it was much later. "You're right, I didn't realize."

"Couldn't sleep?"

"No, I slept fine."

"That's funny, I thought I heard you sneaking around in the middle of the night, thought I even heard you go out."

Rachel looked aghast at her mother, and found herself tongue-tied.

"You went to see him, didn't you?"

"See who?" Rachel asked defensively.

Hannah sat down at the table, looked Rachel in the eye, and said, "Joshua," as she took her first sip of coffee.

Rachel, stupefied, stared at her mother for a beat, then said, "How did you know?"

"I've known for a long time that there had to be someone; rather, I've suspected. You don't go out on *shiddoch* dates, you often come home late at night, it doesn't take a genius. So when Joshua showed up here last night; well, I put two and two together and came up with, whatever."

Rachel wondered how she could possibly have this conversation with her mother. "It's not what you think," she said.

"Oh," Hannah reacted. "And what exactly is it that I'm thinking?"

"We're friends, good friends. That's it."

"Friends, that's interesting. So why such a big secret?"

"Because . . ." Rachel stopped herself and thought about what she was going to say. "No one would understand, that's why."

"Understand? I think I understand plenty."

"You're not making this easy."

"*You* didn't make it easy. All these years, this *friendship*, keeping it from me, your father. Did you also keep it from your husband, this *friendship?*"

"Binny knew that Joshua was my friend, Joshua was at my wedding, remember?" Snide.

"I remember many things, Rucheleh, *many* things. My mind works perfectly well; too well, I'm afraid. It's my heart that I'm worried about."

"Mama."

"Don't worry, Rucheleh. You're a big girl now, divorced and all. You can make your own decisions. I always knew you were somehow different from the other girls, you and Esther. I always knew we wouldn't be able to keep you. I tried to tell your father, but he wouldn't listen. Not *you*, not his little precious Rucheleh. 'She will bear rabbis and scholars,' he used to say. Not quite, I'm afraid."

Rachel watched as her mother drifted off to another place, distant and unreachable. "Mama," she said again.

"It's okay."

"Mama, nothing has happened between Joshua and me. It's really not what you're thinking. Yes, we're something more than friends, and yes, we love each other. But we have an understanding; we've always had an understanding. We're from different worlds, and we respect that in one another. There have always been lines that neither of us would ever cross."

"Until last night."

"Last night was a mistake."

"Last night was a sign!"

Rachel didn't respond.

353

"Don't you see how naive you are? How can you possibly expect a man to love you without insisting on being with you?"

"I know." Reluctant. "It's hard for him; it's also hard for me. But we both see everything that's going on these days, and we really have no choice."

"And how long will *this* understanding last?"

Rachel considered her mother's point. "Tell me, Mama, what is it that upsets you most, that he's black, or that he's not Jewish?"

"Oh please, Rucheleh, what kind of question is that?"

"One to which I'd like an answer."

"I don't know the answer. Neither is wonderful."

"Well, let me ask you this: what if he was to convert?"

"Then God would accept him. But I can assure you, the community wouldn't, especially today."

"*Who cares about the community?*"

"I do, your father did, and you should."

"People convert all the time; blacks have converted."

"And everybody laughs at them, thinking they're crazy, saying things like, *he doesn't have a hard enough time being black, he needs to be Jewish too!* They're scoffed at and ostracized, and you know it. And what do you think happens to their children?"

Rachel realized she couldn't argue with that. "I know, Mama, that's why it could never happen. Joshua is too proud of what he is to become anything else, and I suppose I'm . . ." She hesitated, then concluded: "I'm just too weak."

Hannah watched as tears fell from Rachel's eyes. She wanted to reach out to comfort her daughter and tell her that everything would be okay. But she couldn't; it wouldn't.

"So I guess you have nothing to worry about, Mama, nothing at all."

⁂

Paul Sims sat still, waiting for Rav Schachter to start the meeting. Being summoned was a distinct privilege, a sign he was gaining prominence with the elder. He tried to hide his curiosity.

"Well, Reb Pinchas, how have you been these days?"

"*Baruch Hashem*, thank God. And how has the Rav been?"

"Good, good, except for the recent crisis, of course." Schachter was referring to the killing of Israel Turner.

"Yes, a tragedy."

"There are terrible things happening in the world around us, and we must protect ourselves."

"Yes, we must. I think it is great that we have set up our own patrols. The streets will be safer." Paul knew that Schachter was one of the driving forces behind the establishment of the community patrols.

"Have you joined the patrols?"

"No," Paul answered, embarrassed. "Not yet."

"Your participation would be most welcomed, and invaluable."

"I have been planning to join." *What does he really want?*

"Good." Schachter stared into space.

"Is there some specific reason for which the Rav has requested my presence?" In the past, Paul would have waited for Schachter to get around to it. He was feeling a bit more brazen these days.

"Yes, now that you mention it," Schachter responded. He hesitated, seeming to gather his thoughts. With him, it was always a chess game. "In addition to the patrols," he continued, "there are other ways in which we must fight to save our sacred corner of the world, ways in which a man in your position could be quite helpful."

Paul feigned curiosity, but had a sense of where this was going.

"It is my understanding that your father owns some considerable property in our neighborhood, and that you personally manage this property."

"Yes, he has three buildings, all of which I manage for him. He tried to sell them years ago, but the offers were meager."

"So he has decided not to sell?"

"For now. With my father, one never knows, but I don't think he's looking to put me out of work, or to have me go and work with him on the Island. By keeping the buildings, he gives me something to do, and keeps me away from his main business. I'm sort of an embarrassment to him, I suppose."

"It is terrible, the way these assimilated parents treat their children who come into our midst."

"Yes, it hurts to think about it," Paul said, realizing that Schachter was coaxing him. He was beginning to find their dialogue amusing.

"Anyway, I have a proposition for you."

Paul realized it was now payback time for the elder's assistance with his father when he married Chava.

"I understand that most of the tenants of your buildings are *shvartzes*," Schachter said.

Paul nodded, hiding his distaste for that particular term.

"Would you like to change that?"

"Yes, I suppose," Paul responded hesitantly. "But it isn't realistic, considering the neighborhood."

"That is something we must change too, but first things first."

Normally, Paul would have dismissed such talk, but not when it came from Rav Schachter. Schachter was a man of power and influence, and everything he said was to be taken seriously. "Does the Rav have an idea in mind?" Paul asked.

"Yes, I do. I do *indeed*." Schachter hesitated before continuing, hoping to heighten Paul's curiosity, though unbeknownst to him, Paul already had an idea of what he was about to say. It was unusual for a man of Schachter's intellect to underestimate someone, and Paul enjoyed being that someone. The elder continued, "It is simple, and perfectly legal, I might add."

Paul nodded respectfully, but wasn't convinced.

"When an apartment becomes available," Schachter continued, "you tell us, and you rent it only to one of our own. It might take years, but we do have to think in terms of the future. In the end, the values of the buildings go up. Everyone's happy."

Everyone, except the blacks, Paul thought. "And what if someone finds out? I think it *is* against the law." Paul was uncomfortable challenging Schachter, but he didn't like the plan. He hadn't forgotten Loretta, the woman who had raised him and loved him more than his own mother.

"No one will find out, I assure you. The *schvartzes* are stupid, you know that. They'll never catch on to this."

"I'll have to discuss it with my father." Paul knew his father would never go for it, not because Alfred loved blacks, but because Alfred wouldn't do anything to endanger his business or his reputation. At least nothing so blatant as this.

"If you must," Schachter responded, wearing his disappointment. He had hoped to make a secret deal with Paul, not involving Alfred.

Paul felt a tinge of relief, he had found an out, if only temporarily. He knew, however, that Schachter wouldn't fold so easily.

"There is one other thing," the rabbi said.

"Yes?"

"Another possible way for you to help our sacred cause."

"I would be honored to do what I can."

"I am starting a group whose job is to compel local real estate brokers to arrange things so that we get first opportunity at any homes that come up for sale. The group will also visit with black homeowners in the immediate area to persuade them into selling their homes to us. Would you be interested in joining, perhaps even leading, this group?"

Paul didn't like this idea any better, but felt he couldn't refuse Schachter again. To his mind, it would be the lesser of two evils. "If the Rav believes I could be of service, I would be glad to."

"Good. Excellent."

"May I ask one question?"

Schachter nodded.

"How will this group be effective?"

"With money, of course."

"Whose money?" Paul asked.

"Not yours, so don't worry. I will raise the money, it will not be a problem."

Paul appeared uncomfortable.

"Please, Reb Pinchas, don't worry so much. There will be no violence, only financial negotiations. We will offer generous incentives if need be, whatever is required. We have no choice but to do this, no choice but to succeed. In addition to the crime problem, our families are growing in leaps and bounds. We have an influx of brethren from all over the world who need to live close to the *Rebbe*, within walking distance of the synagogue, and we have a shortage of housing. The situation will soon get out of hand if we don't act. The *shvartzes* can live anywhere, and with God's help, as far away from us as possible!"

Paul understood that there was no "we." The elder would work behind the scenes, command the troops from his study, but never actually get his hands dirty. And dirty was the word, for blockbusting was a dirty business and Paul was to be smack in the middle of it. Payback time, indeed.

It occurred to Paul that Schachter had probably never even intended to succeed with his initial request, but had used it only for bait, knowing that Paul wouldn't dare deny the elder twice. Paul had been outsmarted, and with his humiliation came a tinge of respect for the elder's savvy. "When does the Rav want to start this project?" he asked.

"Immediately. There is no time to waste."

CHAPTER 49

It was six-thirty a.m. Joshua lay in bed, awake, listening to his mother preparing for work. He got up, walked into the living room, and saw her in the kitchen, standing at the table, folding her uniform. He walked in.

She looked at him. "You're up early."

"I know, didn't sleep much last night."

"I'll bet."

He wasn't surprised by the comment; he'd figured she'd heard most of what had occurred. "You were awake?"

"Who wouldn't be, all that screaming!"

"We weren't screaming, we were talking."

"Sounded like screaming to me."

He didn't argue.

"Tell me something, Joshua, why are you always picking women who are going to hurt you?"

"Good question."

She finished with her uniform, placed it in a shopping bag, picked up her pocketbook, and moved toward the door. "I best be going, don't want to be late."

"You don't have to go, Mama?"

"What?"

"You don't have to go to that job any more. I make more than enough money for us. You can stay home now and take it easy."

She gave him a strange look. "Now listen here, Joshua, it isn't your place to be telling me what to do with my life! I've been doing this job for more than twenty-five years. I don't plan on stopping now just because you're a big lawyer or something. Mrs. Sims still needs me."

"*Needs you*, for what? All these years you've been telling me how she doesn't need anyone to clean her home. Hell, you've been joking about how she probably cleans up after you leave."

"That's none of your business, Joshua!"

"But it is my business, Mama. You're tired; you've been tired for a while now, traipsing out there every day just so we could live, so you could take care of me. Now it's *my* turn to take care of you."

She approached him and ran her hand through his hair. "I'm proud of you, Joshua, prouder than I ever believed I'd be. But you should be thinking of yourself. You should be finding a woman, a *proper* woman, and having a family of your own. You don't need to be worrying about me; I'll take care of myself just fine."

He knew there was no use arguing; there never was. She hugged him, kissed him on the cheek, and left. He stood, stunned and helpless, wondering why none of the women in his life ever listened to a word he said.

~~~

Connie stampeded into his office, wearing a look that spelled trouble. "How could you?" she exclaimed.

"How could I what?" He pretended ignorance.

"You turned down the Pilgrim case, without even consulting me!"

"Who told you that?"

"Thompson, *that's who*! Who did you think?"

"He doesn't waste any time, does he?"

"What's that supposed to mean?"

"It means he's dividing us to manipulate us into taking the case."

"Oh," she said, "*he's* being manipulative. Thank you for clarifying that."

"Look, I'm sorry I didn't tell you. I *was* planning to."

"*Planning* to tell me!"

He was wordless.

"Listen, Joshua, and listen *clearly*! If we're partners, then you don't tell me about such things *after* you've decided. You *consult* me and *we* decide together."

"I'm sorry. You're right. It's just that they needed a decision this morning and . . ." He stopped himself, realizing he was about to dig a deeper hole.

"And what?"

"And I was going to say that there wasn't time to contact you, but that wasn't true. I just wasn't thinking. I did some pretty dumb things in the last twenty-four hours, and not consulting you was definitely one of them."

"What the hell are you talking about?"

He proceeded to relate his escapades of the previous evening.

"You mean," she said, "you *actually* pretended you were there to see the rabbi? That's a new low, one for the books!"

"Thanks."

"Only kidding."

"Not quite. You're still pissed."

"I'll get over it. I'm more worried about you than anything else."

"Me?"

"You don't sound like you're playing with a full deck lately."

"That's putting it mildly."

"She really gets to you."

He hesitated, then said, "She does."

"It'll work out; these things always do."

"Not for *me* they don't."

"Isn't that a double negative or something? Unbecoming for a lawyer of your stature."

"Life's a double negative."

"You'll survive." She started to leave, but stopped at the door. "About the case, you really think you made the right call?"

"The guy's guilty, Connie. Thompson wants to use us to make it into a racial thing."

"Can't see as I completely blame him; you used the situation for *your* racial thing."

"Touché, counselor."

She smiled, and left.

He tried to get busy with work, but the events of the past twenty-four hours kept intruding on his mind. Between Connie, Rachel, and his mother, it had been a memorable day. And then there was the biggest shocker, Jerome Williams, right there in his office, after all these years. He wondered about Celeste, where she might be, and was sort of relieved at not knowing. He also wondered if Thompson would actually use that dark chapter of his life against him. Either way, he knew Connie was right: he would recover. He always seemed to, though the costs were building.

⚬⚬⚬

He didn't hear much about the Pilgrim case in the following months. Either Thompson hadn't managed to find another sucker, or the media just wasn't biting. He also didn't hear anything about his history with the now Reverend Jerome Williams. *That* whole thing had merely been a bluff, though he didn't discount the possibility that it might still, one day, come back to haunt him.

Nine months after the murder of Israel Turner, on July 29, 1976, a small paragraph in the back pages of The New York Times reported that Larry Pilgrim had been sentenced the previous day to 25 years to life. Pilgrim was 24 years old at the time, and Turner would have been 55. A waste all around, Joshua thought, as he read the article over his morning coffee.

Suddenly, he realized that time was passing much more quickly these days. Nine months in a flash. It was frightening. Things had been moving along nicely, however. Business was booming. He had even had a brief fling with a nice looking paralegal who had been working for an opposing counsel on some civil suit. He'd waited for the case to conclude before calling her, naturally. Her name was Cheryl, and it had been quite pleasant for the two months it had lasted. It was his fault that it had ended; his heart was elsewhere.

He'd managed to keep the affair from Rachel, but hadn't had as much luck with Connie. Connie always knew everything, and had a crafty way of making him aware of it. Loretta also knew; it was hard to keep anything from her.

Things went along much the same with Rachel. He tried to find satisfaction in what was, rather than misery in what wasn't. On balance, he figured he was ahead of the game, considering where he'd started. His blessings would always be mixed.

In all, things had pretty much settled in. The cases in the office were fairly routine; the rest of his life was status quo. He was learning to appreciate the serenity and, oddly enough, was even getting used to it. Though he knew it wouldn't last.

BOOK V

CHAPTER 50

Mrs. Sawyer was absorbed in her work as Joshua came through the front door. She glanced up at him, then turned her eyes to the waiting area. He was late, and the office was packed with people, sitting restlessly, some with appointments, some walk-ins.

"Court ran over," Joshua said, apologetically, hoping the patrons overheard.

"Yes, I've been telling them you would be arriving *momentarily.*"

"Where's Connie?"

"In her office, on the phone. She's been on the phone for hours, *not* to be disturbed, she says."

"Who's she talking to?"

Mrs. Sawyer shrugged. "Lots of different people, one call after another. I have no idea who they are."

He detected her annoyance, and wasn't pleased to hear of his partner's obliviousness to an office full of people. He marched to the back, knocked hard on Connie's door, and stuck his head in before she could respond.

Connie was on the phone, but didn't seem to mind the intrusion. "Hold on, just a few seconds," she said to the person at the other end, before covering the mouthpiece with her hand. To Joshua: "Come in, come in, sit! You're not going to believe what just happened."

"Connie, we have an office full of . . ."

"Arthur Miller just died. No, correct that, he was killed by the cops."

"*What?*"

"I've been on the phone all afternoon, trying to find out exactly what happened. Friends, relatives in the area, anyone who knows anything. I've got Eunice Scott on the phone now."

"Eunice who?"

"Eunice Scott, she's a clerk over at the ME's office. I met her when I was with the DA. The body's being examined by the ME as we speak."

He planted himself in a seat in front of her desk. He definitely needed to sit. She went back to the call. "Listen, Eunice, I've got to go now, but promise me you'll call as soon as you know anything." She paused. "Thanks, talk soon."

She hung up the phone and looked at him. He said nothing, but his mind was thinking all kinds of things, *dreadful* things. It had been four years since the Willie Johnson case, four years of progressively declining relations between the black community and the police, and now this. A storm was brewing.

Arthur Miller wasn't a close friend of his, but no black person lived or worked around Crown Heights without having crossed Miller's path. Throughout Joshua's involvement with the Nostrand Avenue Commerce Association, he'd met Miller on more than one occasion, and had even had the pleasure of a brief conversation at a recent luncheon that Miller had organized to raise money for the association's youth program. It was a cause that was close to Joshua's heart and, as usual, Arthur Miller was at the helm.

To Joshua's mind, Miller was a man who had it all: four children, a burgeoning construction company, and a grocery store on the side. He was also champion of several local philanthropic causes, and had a robust handshake and hearty manner to boot. Miller's friends affectionately called him "Sampson," referring to his short, muscular stature, and everyone regarded him as an ambassador of the black community in Crown Heights. And now, at 35 years of age, he was dead, allegedly killed by police.

"What the hell happened?" Joshua asked.

"From what I have so far, it started as a thing between his brother and two white cops over a pile of debris in the street in front of a construction site that the Millers were working on. I think they were converting a tenement into a catering hall or something."

"I've met his brother. I think his name is Samuel."

"Yeah, Samuel, that's it. Young guy, about 21, worked with Arthur."

"What building were they converting?"

She consulted her notes. "Here it is, 748 Nostrand. You know it?"

"I've passed it. Seen the debris."

"Anyway, word is the cops were rousting Samuel about the debris, and also because he was loading it onto a truck which he'd been driving with a suspended license."

"What precinct?"

"77th."

"Why am I not surprised?"

"Wait, it gets better."

He waited.

"So Samuel claims the license isn't suspended anymore, asks the cops to escort him home, where he has the paperwork to prove it. They don't buy. At this point, Arthur comes walking down the street toward them, shouting something like, 'It's me. Cool it. Cool it. You're wrong.'"

"How do you know all this?"

"No one was whispering. It was broad daylight. There are lots of witnesses."

"But the cops all know Arthur. They should have given Samuel the benefit . . ."

"That's just it, they *didn't*!"

"Sounds like this was about more than just trash or a suspended license."

"Tell me about it. Anyway, the cops *apparently* didn't recognize Arthur, but they saw he was wearing a gun."

Joshua remembered having seen the gun himself the first time he met Miller. It was hard to forget something like that, but it was an understandable reality in a neighborhood such a this. Many businessmen carried, some of Joshua's own clients, and it was often his job to help obtain their permits.

Connie continued, "So even though Arthur has his hands up, one of the cops gets on the radio and calls for help. An argument ensues, Samuel loses it and topples a fruit stand on one of the officers."

"Good God."

"Within minutes, a sergeant and another officer arrive to supervise the arrest. At this point, the argument supposedly intensifies. Arthur loses it and pushes the sergeant, who then orders that Arthur also be arrested. A brawl breaks out, Arthur hurls one of the officers over his shoulder and drops him to the ground. The officers call a '10-13,' officer in need of assistance, on the radio, and less than five minutes later, twelve more cops swarm onto the scene."

She stopped to catch her breath. "Witnesses say Arthur's mouth was foaming as he was shoved into a patrol car, that his feet were sticking out the window as the car drove off. The cop who Arthur threw, broke his kneecap. Two other cops had back injuries, and a fourth had an injured or broken thumb or something. Next thing I hear, Arthur's DOA at St. Mary's."

"This is bad."

"That's putting it mildly."

"Do you know who the cops were?"

"Not yet."

"I don't get it. Arthur was friendly with all the cops around here. It just doesn't add up."

"Not unless, of course, there was something else going on."

"You mean the cops were asking for payoffs?"

"Makes sense. They come by, complain about the debris, looking for graft, threatening summonses. Young Miller says no, starts loading the garbage on the truck, they check his license—knowing he's had some problems with it—big brother Arthur comes on the scene, and the proverbial shit hits the fan."

He had to agree it was possible, and far from unheard of. Mrs. Sawyer stuck her head in the door. "There's a Miss Scott on the phone for Constance, *and a room full of people outside I might add.*"

Connie picked up the phone. "Hi Eunice, got anything?"

Joshua sat, and listened to Connie's end of the conversation, wondering what would happen once the news spread to the streets. Connie picked up a pen and started jotting down notes. "Uh huh . . . Uh huh . . . Uh huh . . . Wow, thanks Eunice, I owe you one. We'll get together for dinner sometime next week . . . Good . . . Thanks again . . . Take care."

"So?" Joshua asked.

"So, seems the coroner's report is going to attribute Miller's death to asphyxia." She looked down at her notes, and read, "Pressure applied to the front of the throat in a narrow area by a rod-like object, such as a forearm or a stick."

"Choked to death!"

"I suppose one could put it that way. She referred to her notes again. "Get this, the cops are saying that there's 'no evidence of excessive savage beating.' That's a laugh."

"No one's going to be laughing. Look, I suggest we tell everyone in the waiting room to go home, and that we go home ourselves."

"What are you talking about?"

"I'm talking about riots. What do *you* think's gonna happen when this news gets out?"

She considered his point. "I haven't really thought about it."

"Well, do *think* about it, and let's get moving." He stood up and headed towards the door.

"You really believe they'll riot?"

"I don't know what I believe, but I'd rather be safe than sorry, wouldn't you?"

"I suppose so," she muttered under her breath.

"Get your stuff together," he said. "I'll talk to the folks in the waiting room, then call a cab and see you and Mrs. Sawyer home."

❧

There were no riots. In fact, the immediate aftermath of Arthur Miller's death was surprisingly quiet, the community too shaken to respond. The funeral was small and uneventful, and there weren't any demonstrations until four days later, when a crowd of about a hundred people gathered at the foot of the courthouse during Samuel Miller's arraignment on charges of resisting arrest and assault.

Joshua hadn't planned on attending the rally, but he happened to be coming from the courthouse on business while it was occurring. He stopped and noticed that the crowd was rather orderly, despite the rhetoric from the podium that Miller's death had been provoked by the victim's repeated refusal to comply with police demands for payoffs. Joshua didn't want to believe that, but he couldn't deny that it did explain some things.

He looked around and wasn't the least bit surprised at seeing Professor Alvin Thompson and Reverend Jerome Williams near the podium. He was due back at the office, but something kept him there. He waited, and watched, and soon found himself trailing the crowd as they marched across the Brooklyn Bridge to City Hall. He didn't know what compelled him, only that he was drawn to follow.

They came to City Hall, stood outside, chanting and yelling, until Mayor Edward Koch emerged and spoke to the crowd. He appeared sincere, expressed his condolences, and promised a "full investigation" into the details of the case. The crowd was unimpressed; many tried to shout the mayor down. But he was tough, and at one point even admonished the crowd against making this a racial issue, pointing out that two of the police officers who escorted Arthur Miller to the police station were, in fact, black. For a brief moment, as the mayor stepped down, the shouting lulled and the crowd seemed to consider his words, but that didn't last long.

Reverend Jerome Williams climbed the steps and turned to the crowd. "First they try to extort us," the reverend exclaimed, "they try to sell us their lies."

"You tell 'em, reverend," someone in the audience yelled.

"Right on!" others joined in.

Jerome continued, "When they aren't trying to sell us, they're trying to buy us. And when we protest, they offer vain promises, false promises! For all they really want is to *buy* and *sell* us, just like they did in the old South. But we aren't for sale, and *we* aren't listening to their lies anymore! No more *buying*, no more *lying*!"

"*Right on!*"

"The truth will emerge eventually, my friends. One way or another, the truth always emerges! Either they will admit what they've done, they will repent before God and beg forgiveness, or it is going to be a *l-o-n-g, h-o-t* summer!"

"*Right on.*"

"*You tell 'em, reverend!*"

Joshua, hearing the rage in his old friend's voice, couldn't help feeling responsible and frightened. Then, suddenly, he emerged from his trance and realized that he had joined the crowd. And that was even more frightening.

❦

Regarding the actual causes of Arthur's death, Dr. Milton A. Wald, the deputy chief medical examiner, who had performed the autopsy, reported exactly what Eunice Scott had told Connie: death by asphyxiation, but "no evidence of excessive, savage beating." A police spokesman admitted that "considerable force was being used . . . violent force," and added, "A blow may have been delivered, or pressure applied by an arm or whatever resulting in injury to this area of the body (the larynx), which resulted in death." The spokesman qualified his statement, however, explaining, "When you think of someone being 'choked to death,' you get the impression of somebody with two hands around the neck. We do not have something like that here."

Reading this in the paper, Joshua wondered what exactly it was that they *did* have here, and where all this would lead. He had no answers, only the echoes of his mother's words when he had come home the night after Arthur's death: "This isn't right, Joshua, not right at all. Trouble's coming, and it's going to be bad. *Real bad!*"

CHAPTER 51

Cruising down Union Street, Paul Sims sat confidently behind the wheel of his '78 Impala, and looked over at his partner, Yossie Bloom, in the passenger seat. As usual, Yossie was oblivious to the world, his eyes glued to the book of Hasidic mysticism in his hand. Paul looked past Yossie onto the street, making sure all was safe and sound, then glanced at the blackjacks and baseball bats on the back seat. They were well prepared.

The car, compliments of Paul's father, was a business lease, tax deductible and all. If only Alfred knew exactly what sort of business his son was conducting with it. But Paul didn't worry about that; he had the streets to concern him. And his inattentive partner.

"How can you see what's going on outside if you're eyes are glued to that book?" Paul said.

"Ah, Reb Pinchas, that's why I have you. You watch for me, and I study for you; that way, we each have two *mitzvahs*."

Paul chuckled. Yossie was a sharp one, and—Paul had to admit—a solid partner in a crunch, who never had any compunction about stopping a black or even a group of blacks in the street, even just to ask for identification. And he also had a way of making them cooperate.

Paul recalled how, a year earlier, they had tangled with a big black kid who turned on a fire hydrant and refused to close it when pedestrians complained. Boy, they showed him! Paul held the kid from behind while Yossie whacked him in the gut with a blackjack. And no one had messed with any hydrants on their watch since. That Yossie was okay, Paul mused, even with his head in a book.

Comparing this with his past, when the Italian and Irish kids beat him up after school, brought a tinge of satisfaction. Now *he* was the tough guy.

He also thought about Rachel, if only she could see him now. He often fantasized about running into her, and even rescuing her from danger as Joshua had once done. Surely she wouldn't reject him after that, or so he wanted to believe. His mind turned back to the present. "Things look good tonight," he said.

"Things have been good for a while," Yossie responded, still reading.

"What about that Russian guy who got mugged last week?"

"Oh yeah, I forgot about him. But things have still been better."

"Better, but not great."

"An interesting point," Yossie said, his tone betraying a desire for his partner to just watch the streets and let him study. It was often this way when they were together.

"How do you like what the police did to that black guy, what's his name?" Paul asked.

"You mean, the *shvartze*, Miller?" Yossie gave up and closed the book.

"Yeah, Miller."

"Funny thing."

"How is it funny?"

"The police have been criticizing us for our tactics, and they go off and kill a guy that way."

"You think he deserved it?"

"He's a *shvartze*," Yossie responded. "Who cares, as long as he's gone. One less mugger to worry about."

Paul was still discomfited by such characterizations, even though such was a common sentiment in the community. For him, it was one thing to beat up criminals and trouble makers, and another to indict an entire race. But he never voiced his thoughts, not to Yossie, nor anyone, for he understood that they had never known the likes of Loretta Eubanks. Yossie had grown up in Crown Heights, a place where black crime was rampant, a place where perceptions were skewed and bigotry was pervasive. And if Paul had learned anything in his life, it was that arguing with perception was futile.

Suddenly, they heard shouting down the block. Paul scanned the area, searching for the source. "*There*, over there," he said, pointing to a group of Hasidic men chasing a black kid. He floored the gas, sped up the block, and skidded the car around in front of the black kid. He and Yossie jumped out, and trapped the kid between them and the crowd. Paul looked at the kid, who appeared no older than sixteen. There was fear in the kid's eyes; he was caught, and now he would be taught a lesson, one he would never forget.

Paul and Yossie moved in with their blackjacks, as the other Hasidim approached. The kid stood, helpless, waiting, nowhere to run. Within seconds, the group set upon him, throwing him to the ground, stomping on him, kicking him, shouting ethnic slurs.

Paul suddenly realized that there must have been at least thirty of them beating this one kid. He didn't know why, but naturally figured the kid must have done something serious to merit such reprisal. Without thinking, he joined in and started striking with his blackjack. It was a good five minutes before they heard police sirens and fled, leaving the black kid unconscious in the street, lying in a pool of his own blood.

As they sped away, one of the other Hasidim who had been on foot patrol jumped into the back seat of the car. "Good job guys, we really showed him," he said.

Paul didn't know their passenger personally, only that his name was Ari and that he was a large, stocky fellow who somehow managed to be involved in every skirmish. "What did the kid do?" Paul asked.

"He grabbed a yarmulke off the head of a yeshiva guy, and started to run," Ari answered.

"He *what?*" Paul said incredulously, starting to feel queasy.

"A group of guys were coming out of a wedding at the Brooklyn Jewish Center, and this punk runs up to one of them, grabs his yarmulke, and starts running," Ari explained, almost nonchalantly.

"And all of you chase him and beat him for *that?*"

"All of *us?* I seem to recall *you* having participated," Ari said.

Yossie glared at Paul, his expression saying, *Leave it alone!* But Paul wasn't about to. "I thought he did something terrible, otherwise I wouldn't have . . ."

"Next time, why don't you ask him what he did," Ari interrupted with a chuckle.

Paul looked at Yossie, and said nothing more.

CHAPTER 52

Joshua arrived at the restaurant on time. Rachel was already there, seated at their usual table. He walked over, kissed her cheek, and sat down.

"I can't believe what's happening," she said. "Everything is falling apart."

"It's going to get worse before it gets better," he replied.

"How so?"

"You didn't hear? Thompson and Williams are forming a black community patrol now."

"That's all we need, another patrol."

"Well, if you guys have one, maybe we should too."

"Is that what you think?"

"That's what they think; I don't know what I think."

"I don't know what I think either."

"Good, let's talk about something else."

"We're so absorbed, we didn't even say hello," she said.

"Hello."

"Hi."

"Want a drink?"

"I could certainly use one."

The only problem was, The Greenery didn't serve alcohol. "After dinner, we'll find a bar, get sloppy drunk, and forget about all this crap," he said.

"It's a date."

He wondered how serious she was being.

They ordered dinner, and resumed discussing the thing they didn't want to discuss. "Is there any news on that boy?" she asked, referring to Victor Rhodes, the kid who had been beaten up by the patrol.

"Not good. Critical in Kings County Hospital. Last I heard, he's in some kind of partial coma, drifts in and out of consciousness."

She looked nonplussed. "How could this happen?"

"Ask your boys."

"*My* boys?"

"Sorry."

She looked at him for a moment. "I'm not the enemy."

He took her hand. "I know, I shouldn't have said that."

"It's okay, it's been quite a week."

They finished eating, and found a quaint little pub on Bleecker Street. There was a good crowd, easy to get lost in. They felt comfortable.

She wasn't schooled in spirits, so she asked him to order for her. "Something sweet and fruity," she said. He was no maven either. A screw driver was all he could come up with. For himself, he ordered a scotch on the rocks, only because it seemed more manly.

The tables were occupied, so they stood at the bar. He wasn't used to hanging out in bars, especially one as white as this. He was the only black man in the place, as far as he could tell. But no one stared, no one even seemed to notice. Perhaps because he was wearing a suit and tie, or perhaps because this was *The Village*. Either way, it was a far cry from Crown Heights, and it felt good. For both of them.

Her first reaction to the drink was a bitter face, but after a few more sips, she began to like it. He also winced when he tasted his, but eventually it was just fine.

They felt like a couple of college kids. A jukebox in the corner played loud, Whitbread music, and the crowd was pretty noisy too. They could barely hear themselves think, so they just watched each other, smiled, and ordered more drinks.

The density of the crowd caused them to stand close to one another. They didn't mind; in fact, after a few drinks, they began to take advantage of the situation. Joshua wasn't sure who started it, but he suddenly found his hand resting softly on her waist, while her hand caressed his arm. Her eyes were glassy and her smile was uncontrolled, like a schoolgirl doing this for the very first time.

She snuggled in close, pushing her body against his. There was less than an inch between their lips. Neither seemed to care what was going on around them, perhaps because of the alcohol, perhaps because they had grown contemptuous of the perceptions of others. Whatever it was, they wanted this moment, and they were going to have it.

The distance faded, their mouths merged, and they clung to one another with a desperation neither had ever known. It was anguish and ecstasy, recklessness and resolution; everything they'd hoped for and feared, everything they'd craved but couldn't have. Neither could stop, pull away and snap back into reality, for this *was* their reality, the only one they had ever truly known, the sole moment of clarity in the lunacy that had otherwise defined their existence.

The kiss turned into kisses, to the point where they couldn't help becoming self conscious. They decided to leave, but weren't sure where to go. Joshua wanted to suggest a final drink, to keep the mood going, but something inside him said *no*. They left, stumbling out onto the sidewalk, as he tried holding them both up. Quite a feat for a man with a cane.

They were wasted, and tomorrow they would pay for it, physically and emotionally. But for now, they still had the evening. They grabbed each other, and began making out in the street. He used the cane to hail a cab, and pulled her tightly against him with his other hand. Next thing they knew, they heard screeching brakes followed by an obnoxious voice: "Hey, goin' somewhere or not?"

Joshua held up a finger signaling, *one minute*. The cabby appeared impatient but stayed put. Joshua turned to Rachel and said, "This is your ride."

"You aren't coming?"

"Coming where? We can't go back to the neighborhood in the same car, not with everything that's going on."

"I know that, I wasn't thinking about going there. I want to be with . . ."

He placed his forefinger over her mouth. "Look, if you don't get in that cab right now, I'm just liable to take you somewhere and do something real stupid. So go!" He tried escorting her to the taxi, but she resisted.

"It wouldn't be stupid!" she said.

"It *would*! Trust me, tomorrow, if you remember any of this, you'll thank me."

The cabby blew his horn. "Come on, now or never!"

"But Joshua . . ."

"Rachel, please, this isn't easy for me, just go!"

He practically had to drag her toward the taxi. The cabby gave him a disdainful look, one he had grown accustomed to. Rachel also caught it, and it brought her back to reality. Joshua placed a few dollars in her hand for the fare as she slipped into the back seat. Through the open window, her hand held his, and she mouthed, "Good night." He smiled, the cabby practically floored the gas, and her hand slid away.

He turned and began to walk. He needed to walk. He didn't know where he was heading, only that he would be kicking himself all the way.

⸎

The next few months were marked by more demonstrations over the Miller and Rhodes affairs, as rabble rousers labored to keep the cause alive. The crowds grew, but remained basically peaceful. Williams and Thompson were always at the helm, their names and faces frequenting the media. They had found their fight.

The NAACP also got in on the action and called for a federal inquiry into Miller's death, along with the suspension of the police officers involved. They got their inquiry, but the city held fast on the police officers, insisting that no action would take place until the investigation had been completed. The mayor and police commissioner took a lot of heat for their continued insistence that Miller's death was not a racial incident. The NAACP also issued public statements asking members of the community to keep cool throughout the summer.

A black citizens' patrol was formed, with the stated purpose of protecting blacks from crime, and the unstated purpose of policing the way Hasidic patrols dealt with black suspects. Patrol members were issued special green jackets, and marched in some of the protests as a unit, parading their presence and resolve. The first time Joshua saw them gathered outside the courthouse, he found himself feeling more worried than proud.

The Justice Department's investigation took about a year and culminated in a twenty-one page report. The results, released by the

U.S. Attorney for the Eastern District of New York, Edward Korman, on August 2, 1979, found that Arthur Miller's civil rights had not been violated by the police in whose custody he had died. This was consistent with an earlier finding by a Brooklyn grand jury that had ruled Miller's death a "tragic unforeseeable accident which occurred during a lawful arrest."

The report justified the arrest on the basis of radio transmission recordings and witness accounts. The recordings showed that the original officers were informed that Samuel Miller did have five suspensions against his license for failure to answer a summons, circumstances for which an arrest is *required* by law. According to witnesses who had overheard, Samuel claimed to have paid the summons on Schermerhorn Street in downtown Brooklyn, a location at which, the officers knew, payments for traffic summonses were not collected. Witnesses also claimed that Arthur attempted to intervene and prevent the arrest by pushing the sergeant and attempting to pull the arresting officer away from his brother. It was at this point when the sergeant ordered Arthur's arrest.

Samuel apparently tried to escape by pushing the arresting officer away and getting into his truck. He managed to back up a short distance and round a corner, but two officers pursued him and eventually got him out of the truck. At that point, witnesses say, Samuel became irate, grabbed a nearby table, threw it at one of the officers and knocked him unconscious.

Arthur, in his own struggle, heard the sound of the table crashing, a sound which all witnesses claimed had resembled a gunshot. At that point, Arthur, apparently fearing his brother had been shot, grappled to free himself from the officers who were constraining him, yelling that he wanted to see what had happened to his brother. He was wearing a short jacket, which was pulled up during the struggle, revealing a holstered gun. Seeing the gun, the police officers fought harder to restrain him, but had a rough time doing so. Arthur, apparently, wasn't called "Sampson" for nothing. It took twelve of them to finally subdue him, and some received injuries in the process. Eventually he was cuffed, placed in a patrol car, and driven away. He apparently lost consciousness in the car on route to the station house.

While the report exonerated the officers involved, it did not place the blame on Arthur for his own death. Most witnesses, in fact, claimed that what had initially transpired between Arthur and the officers was "never more serious than minor pushing and shoving," until the moment when Arthur had believed that his brother had been shot. A mistake, a tragic mishap, the death of a good man.

As for Samuel, his initial arraignment was postponed due to the prevailing atmosphere, but he did eventually plead guilty to a section 511, driving with a suspended license, for which he received a sentence of a one hundred dollar fine or thirty days in jail. Unable to pay the fine, he ended up serving the time. For the additional charges of second degree assault and possession of marijuana, he received three years probation.

Victor Rhodes lapsed in and out of a coma for over two months, but eventually recovered, returned home, and testified at the trial of two Hasidic men, whom police had managed to arrest shortly after the incident. The two men were believed to have led the attack against Rhodes, were members of the civilian patrol, and had been apprehended while driving a car nearby. Both were charged with assault and attempted murder.

At the trial, the defense lawyers contended that their clients had been falsely accused in a case of mistaken identity. The jury, which had six blacks and no Jews, eventually agreed with the defense, having been unable to sufficiently distinguish the defendants from the many other Hasidic men sitting near them during the prosecution's presentation. The judge had been criticized by black community leaders and the district attorney's office for having allowed the defendants to sit with their look-a-likes in the spectator section of the court, even though they had returned to the defense table after the prosecution had rested.

Joshua had followed the trial and, as a citizen, had been dismayed by the decision. As a lawyer, however, he couldn't help but admire the defense's brilliant strategy. As a man, he was petrified.

CHAPTER 53

Jonathan Kenon arrived on the shores of the U.S. from the Island of Trinidad on August 9,1970. His wife, Dorothy, and their three small children remained behind, while he, an uneducated auto mechanic, tried to establish a life so that they could eventually join him. He found lodging in a dilapidated SRO on Atlantic Avenue, and worked pumping gas for minimum wages at a Texaco station.

Jonathan was a punctual and reliable employee, and Martin Siegel, the Jewish owner of the station, took a liking to him. Martin was refurbishing his home in Great Neck, Long Island, and the contractor needed help, so he offered Jonathan extra work on the weekends. A few weeks later, one of the mechanics strained his back, and Martin decided to give Jonathan a chance to step in. Within two months, Jonathan was earning a full mechanic's salary at Siegel's Texaco on Atlantic Avenue, plus the weekend job.

It took three years for Jonathan to save enough for a down payment on a home, assume a mortgage, and send for his family. It hadn't been easy, but Jonathan was a disciplined, God fearing man. He never drank, womanized, or gambled. In fact, the only place he ever went besides work was to church on Sundays. His rent was cheap, he never bought clothing or much of anything, and his food preferences were simple. The only indulgence he had allowed himself during these years had been two trips back to Trinidad.

All in all, Jonathan had saved a "mint." By the time Dorothy and the children arrived, the red-brick house on Crown Street had been fully prepared. He had purchased beds and furniture for the children's rooms and master bedroom, a dining room set, living room set, and even some odds and ends for the basement. He had used the skills he acquired on his weekend job to renovate one of the bathrooms, and had done such a fine job installing carpet in the living room and master bedroom, he just had to bring Mr. Siegel over to see it.

"I would have expected nothing less," his boss said, offering the praise Jonathan had hoped for.

Jonathan was the last of ten children. His father had died of cholera shortly before his birth. Mr. Siegel was as close a substitute as Jonathan had ever encountered; kind, fair, and compassionate. Siegel's own parents had also been immigrants, and giving someone like Jonathan a break came naturally.

Jonathan's family had always been poor. His older brothers had worked from the time they were seven just to put food on the table. He had spent his youth dreaming of a better life, of coming to America and giving his children the education and opportunities he never had. And now, only ten years after his arrival on the shores of New York, Jonathan Kenon's oldest and only son was about to graduate from Brooklyn College.

Dorothy had found the perfect dress for the occasion, and was showing it off to Jonathan when the doorbell rang. It was late, ten-thirty, an unusual time for a visitor, and the sound of the bell was startling.

Jonathan descended the stairs to the front door and asked who was there. The caller identified himself as Ephraim Gross, one of Jonathan's Hasidic neighbors. Recognizing the name, Jonathan immediately opened the door. Ephraim Gross was not alone.

"Ah, Mr. Kenon, sorry to bother you this time of night," Ephraim Gross said. Jonathan looked at the three other Hasidic men with Gross, none of whom he recognized, wondering what was going on. Gross continued, "May we come in, please, there is something we would like to discuss."

Jonathan had known Gross for the past seven years, and had always found him to be a respectful, though cold neighbor. With what was happening in the neighborhood lately, even that was a blessing. He had no reason to suspect anything untoward from Gross, so he instinctively opened the door and invited the men into his living room.

Dorothy, still upstairs, called down to him, asking who was at the door. "It's our neighbor, Mr. Gross, and some other gentlemen," Jonathan answered, adding, "I'll be up soon."

The five men sat, and Ephraim Gross introduced the three Hasidim with him: Paul "Pinchas" Sims, Yossie Bloom, and Moshe Friedman. Omitting any niceties, Gross got right down to business. "We're here to talk to you about possibly selling your house," Gross said, almost casually.

Jonathan was dumbfounded. "But my house isn't for sale."

"Yes," interrupted Paul, "we are aware of that. We are here to make you an attractive offer, so that you might consider selling."

"I'm sorry, gentlemen," Jonathan said, "I don't mean to be impolite, but my house is not on the market, and if that's all, the hour is late." He glanced at his watch to emphasize the point.

His visitors stared blankly at one another before Paul turned again to Jonathan. He had a well-rehearsed script to deal with such resistance. "Look, Mr. Kenon, I intend no disrespect, but we are prepared to offer you a significant sum of money, cash, that will surely yield you a nice profit on what you originally paid, and enable you to move anywhere you like."

"I like it just fine right here!"

Dorothy called again from upstairs: "Jonathan, is everything okay?"

"Yes dear, I'll be right up." To the others: "Gentlemen, as I said, it *is* late."

"Just one more thing before we go," Paul said. "I don't know what you paid for this house, but I would imagine it was somewhere around fifty or sixty thousand." Paul actually did know the exact figure—to the penny. "That was seven years ago and, as you know, real estate hasn't exactly been booming in these parts." The others nodded. "In all, we're prepared to pay you a twenty percent profit on your initial investment, which, if you check up on things, is quite handsome."

"Only to someone who is selling," Jonathan responded adamantly.

"Will you at least think about our offer? We can come back next week to discuss it further."

"Don't bother, I'm not interested." With that, Jonathan stood, walked to the front door, and opened it.

Paul looked at his colleagues, signaling that it was indeed time to leave. Yossie Bloom and Moshe Friedman left first, passing Jonathan as if he were a fixture. Ephraim Gross stopped to shake his neighbor's hand, and Jonathan hesitantly obliged. Paul stopped and said, "I'm sorry if we offended you, Mr. Kenon. Please understand, that was not our intention. We simply have people coming to live here, to be closer to our grand rabbi, from all over the world, and we're running out of space. I assure you, this isn't racial."

"Fine," Jonathan responded, not wanting to get into any further discussion on the matter. He shook Paul's hand also, closed the door, and stared at the walls around him. His body trembled, he watched his hands shake. Twenty percent profit on his house, undoubtedly a tempting offer, all things considered. He calculated the exact amount in his mind, close to a year's salary. Tempting indeed! But he could never do it. Everything he'd ever worked for or dreamed of was under this roof, and nobody was going to take it from him. He thought about Paul's last words: *this isn't racial.* "Not much," he mused.

Outside, Paul and his cohorts licked their wounds. Jonathan Kenon had been their third prospect that evening, and thus far only one was even remotely interested. They had a list of ten homeowners to be covered before the end of the week. It was late, and they were worn from the defeat. They would meet again the next night to continue. Perhaps the break would invigorate them.

⌘

Paul decided to walk for a while before returning home, mulling over his acts, rationalizing that the Hasidim needed more housing within safe walking distance to the synagogue to accommodate growing families and new immigrants. But he knew that this was only part of the truth, for Rav Schachter had even spoken about encouraging Asians to buy up homes in the neighborhood; anything to rid the area of blacks.

Paul's contribution to this cause had certainly gained him respect and influence among his peers, but he was left uneasy, haunted by the voice of Rabbi Weissman telling him of how the Nazis sought to make Germany *Judenrein*, free of Jews. And then there was Loretta; how heartbroken she would be if she ever learned of this.

Still, he couldn't stop. Aside from his indebtedness to Rav Schachter, he simply couldn't deny himself the acceptance and admiration from others he was finally receiving.

He wandered for a while, unsure of where he was heading, mindlessly turning corners and drifting through the streets, until he found himself standing in front of the building in which Loretta and Joshua lived. He was perplexed as to how or why he'd ended up there, but after some reflection, he understood. It had been years since he'd last seen Loretta, and she was still the only person who could make him feel okay. He needed her now, more than ever.

As he approached the door, he hesitated, recalling that awful night with Rachel and wondering if she had ever told Joshua about it. He became fearful, and was about to leave, but felt himself compelled to stay. He had to see Loretta, and if that meant a confrontation with Joshua, so be it. He rang the bell.

Loretta answered the door in her bathrobe, appearing quite surprised to see him. It had been many years. She looked older, her hair mostly gray, and she'd added some weight to her still handsome figure.

Paul heard the television in the living room, and was relieved he hadn't awakened her. He apologized anyway, for appearing unannounced this time of night. She assured him it was nothing, and told him, in fact, that she wished he would visit more often. He was always welcome.

She lamented that Joshua was out at some sort of business meeting. Paul was silently thankful. She showed him into the living room and turned off the TV. He didn't have much to say, no explanation for his visit, and she didn't ask for one. She was happy just to see him, and went on and on about Joshua's fortune. He told her he had read about it in the newspaper, and watched her face come aglow with pride.

They talked some about his parents. He told her that it was silly for her to continue working for them. "That's funny, Joshua says the same thing," she commented, and then said nothing more about it. It was no time for a disagreement.

He stayed for close to half an hour, and left without any mention of his recent escapades. He had found what he had come for—someone who simply appreciated him. And yet, having gotten that, he felt even worse than before.

When he finally arrived home, it was after twelve. Chava was upstairs sleeping. He stopped in the girls' bedroom, as he did every night, to watch them sleep for a little while.

He stood quietly in the doorway, his eyes on Rifky, his youngest, now ten. "My little princess," he always called her, knowing that a cuter, more precocious child was simply nowhere to be found. A wave of sadness came over him; she was growing up, and Chava could not bear more children. The doctor had said no, the last pregnancy had been too difficult.

He then turned his attention to Sheindy, his first, now twelve. The serious, studious one, a pleasure across a chess board, or discussing biblical passages. God had been less kind with her appearance, he had to admit, but he was confident she would thrive. He was becoming an important man, and both his daughters were destined to marry scholars.

He caught himself, surprised to be thinking of his little girls and marriage. He looked at them, feeling ridiculous for considering such a thing while they were still so young. Yet, as he turned away and walked to his bedroom, the thought lingered. There was no denying it, the years were speeding by.

⤞

He tiptoed around the room, thinking Chava was asleep, but as usual, she wasn't. She pretended, as she believed a dutiful wife should. And she wondered.

He had never explained his late nights, and she had never asked. She knew he was involved in the citizens' patrol, which accounted for two, maybe three nights a week. But recently he'd been out almost every evening, and she knew he wasn't spending that time at the yeshiva. In fact, she'd heard through the neighborhood rumor mill that his presence in the yeshiva had dwindled quite a bit these past few months.

She had learned many things from the *yenta* brigade, like the stories she'd heard before they were married concerning his supposed interest in another woman, and other similar rumors that had resurfaced over the years. She had always dismissed such chatter, going about her business, and praying to God that everything would turn out well for her and her children. But now it was coming back to haunt her.

Paul was haunted too, his ceaseless battle with insomnia fueled by his recent adventures. He wanted to tell Chava what he'd been doing, perhaps merely to alleviate some of the guilt, but he was afraid of her disapproval, and also concerned she might pressure him to quit. He couldn't quit now; he had to stay the course.

So here he was, nearing thirty-two, duplicitous, weak, and sneaking around behind his family's back, all to attain an elusive sense of worth and importance. And in the end, amid the self loathing and incessant doubt, there was only one fact of which he could be certain: he was nothing more than his father's son.

CHAPTER 54

It had been years since Arthur Miller's death, but his memory still stirred the attendees of the annual Nostrand Avenue Commerce Association's dinner and dance. Joshua sat beside Connie, restlessly listening to speech after speech, award recipients and community leaders parroting the ills of local law enforcement and the preferential treatment afforded their Hasidic neighbors. The Miller incident and its aftermath had left a bitterness that would seemingly never wane. Joshua looked around. Hatred was thriving in the midst, unchecked, uncensored. The storm was closing in.

The complaints had become all too familiar: the closing down of streets and rerouting of buses on the Jewish Sabbath and holidays; the Hasidic anti-crime patrol preying on blacks, checking innocent people for identification when they walked the streets; rumors of attempted blockbusting by offering exorbitant amounts of money to buy out black residences; the Hatzalah Ambulance Service, an emergency medical group started by the Hasidim, denying services to blacks and other non-Jews; and lastly, the disproportionate influence of the Hasidim in the allocation of public funds for housing and other community needs. Joshua couldn't deny that much of it was true. The blacks were by far the majority, at least seventy percent of the community, yet their clout was meager in comparison to the Hasidim. Corrections were due. But the venom disturbed him.

Amid the applause and cheering, he scanned the room for fellow skeptics, and thought he spotted a few. He could tell that Connie was uncomfortable as well. They were on the same page about most things, and equally worried about the future.

The evening was redeemed by the food and music. Lobster bisque followed by a delectable three greens salad, and an entrée of Chateaubriand, roasted potatoes, with asparagus and Hollandaise sauce. Joshua had his steak rare, and when dessert came around—a choice of chocolate mousse, New York cheese cake, or a fruit cup—he had all three.

Connie skipped the soup, selected the salmon instead of steak, and stuck with the fruit cup. She watched her partner enviously. "Forget what the speakers have been talking about, what really is unjust in this world is how someone can eat the way you do, and stay thin," she said.

"The benefits of a fast metabolism," he replied.

She just watched in disbelief.

The six-piece band had a nice sound, and things livened up a bit after the speeches. It was time to party and forget the misery, something that seemed to come easily to the crowd.

Because of his leg, Joshua had always been shy about dancing. Connie had never coerced him to try, though they'd attended several dinner-dances together. They usually sat, watched the crowd, drank and joked some, and simply found pleasure in being together away from the office. Their bond was strong, even more so since they'd stopped messing around.

She'd recently been dating a gentleman named Marcus Sterling, a good looking local black lawyer who had been elected to the city council. Joshua was glad, for Marcus was an "up-and-coming," ambitious player who, like himself, rose from the streets and fought hard. The difference between them was that Marcus was a politician, savvy from the get-go, and a mite too radical for Connie's blood. Joshua had been encouraging her to stick with Marcus anyway. "Politics isn't everything," he had told her just a few days earlier.

"Maybe not," she had responded, "but it sure makes for strange bedfellows."

"I wouldn't know."

That had given her a good laugh.

Marcus was at the dinner, and had spent most of the evening smoking stogies and hobnobbing with cronies and constituents. He had greeted Joshua and Connie earlier, and had promised Connie a dance later in the evening. Now, Joshua saw him approaching their table, and figured the councilman was going to make good on his promise. But Joshua was wrong. Instead of asking for a dance, Marcus took a seat beside Connie, put his arm around her, and started talking with the two of them. He seemed smooth and calculated. Joshua knew something was up.

"So, you folks having a good time?" Marcus asked.

"Real good," Joshua answered.

Connie just smiled. Somehow she sensed, as Joshua had, that this was going to be a conversation between the two men.

"You know, Connie, your partner here seems to be the talk of the town these days," Marcus said.

"Really, what did he do now?"

They all chuckled.

"No, seriously," Marcus said to Joshua, "I've been speaking with people all night, and your name keeps popping up."

"For what?" Joshua asked.

"Well . . ." Marcus hesitated, looked Joshua in the eye, and said, "There's a vacancy coming up on the community board."

Joshua froze. That wasn't even close to what he'd expected to hear. He had thought Marcus might solicit some *pro bono* legal work on a lost cause case or something, but never this. Connie looked equally surprised.

"Community Board Nine?" Joshua asked.

"That's the one," Marcus replied.

There was a long moment of silence, which Marcus broke, saying, "Look, I understand you weren't prepared for this. Take some time, think about it. We'll get together in a few days for lunch, the three of us." He looked at Connie, and continued, "We'll talk it over then. For now, I'm going to steal this pretty lady away for a dance." He shook Joshua's hand, stood up, and led Connie from the table.

Joshua sat alone, contemplating what had just transpired. It was a flattering offer, no doubt, and quite perplexing, especially coming from Marcus Sterling. Joshua knew that Sterling was a close associate of both Alvin Thompson and Jerome Williams, and figured that Sterling must have been aware of his lack of cooperation with the professor in the past. He wondered why Sterling would be interested in *him*.

Community Board Nine was a hotbed, and had been since its inception eight years earlier in 1977, when Mayor Abraham Beame, under pressure from the Hasidic community, divided the Crown Heights "community advisory board" into two separate boards. The new districts were separated by Eastern Parkway, with Board Eight representing the north side, and board nine representing the south side. Since community boards were mandated with the allocation and distribution of public funds, the Hasidim sought the redistricting because of demographics. The south side of Eastern Parkway was their stronghold, and by excluding the north side, which was predominantly black, they became less of a minority, gained greater representation and, thus, more resources for themselves. Black leaders had challenged the redistricting in federal court, arguing that it was a political payoff to the Hasidic community for their electoral support of Mayor Beame. The case had been thrown out.

To Joshua's mind, Board Nine was no different from the streets, just another battleground for conflict between blacks and Jews in Crown Heights, its very existence a thorn in the side of rapprochement. Sadly, he knew it could have been a forum for community leaders to reason and resolve differences, but such dreams rarely prevailed against the opportunity to bicker and divide. Especially in Crown Heights.

And here he was, once again being asked to join the circus, his solicitor none other than a representative of those whom he'd thought had scorned him. His immediate inclination was to decline, of course, but first he needed to learn why they'd chosen *him*.

༺⊙༻

Loretta and Connie were ecstatic about the idea, but neither was surprised at Joshua's hesitance. Loretta relished the prospect of her son becoming a community leader, while Connie focused on the positive effect it would have on business. Joshua couldn't deny Connie's point, nor could he deprive his mother of yet another boost of pride. But then there was Rachel. This wasn't going to be an easy decision.

Rachel was cautious. "This would put you right in the middle of things, wouldn't it?" she asked, leaning on the table with both elbows, her face resting in her hands. It was the next evening, and the luncheon with Marcus Sterling was scheduled for the following day.

"It would. It would also give me the chance to do some good." He was trying to convince himself as much as her.

"Possibly. The latest I've been hearing is that the board spends all its time fighting over how many blacks versus how many Jews should be sitting on it. There isn't much good in that."

Joshua nodded.

The waitress brought their orders. Rachel had a large salad. Nuts, raisins, alfalfa sprouts, grated carrots, cherry-tomatoes, and cucumbers atop a bed of romaine lettuce. Joshua had a veggie-burger, the closest he could get to "real" sustenance.

He was amazed how they'd been coming to the same place, week after week, year after year, ordering the same dishes, and sitting at the same table. He had once joked that the owners should hang a picture of them on the wall above the table, or at least name a sandwich after them.

"You'd have to be famous for that," Rachel had said.

"Even in a place like this?"

"Most certainly."

"Then I guess I'll just have to become famous."

Once in a while they would get together with Esther and Stephen for dinner, both of whom Joshua had come to like over the years. He felt good about going out with another couple; it seemed almost "normal." He also enjoyed watching Rachel with Esther, the way the two women treated one another, and Rachel's implacable trust in Esther's discretion. There was much about their relationship that neither he nor Stephen would ever grasp. One thing he did see, however, was that whenever Esther or Stephen talked about their children, Rachel struggled to conceal her anguish. Joshua, too, had some regrets in this department.

Rachel was comforted that Esther had put on some weight since her pregnancies, and was looking healthy. Esther and Stephen had a seven year old girl and six year old boy. Luckily for them, Stephen's mother was available to watch the children during the days and some nights. Money was tight, and they both had to work to make ends meet. Several years back he had fallen into managing a grocery store owned by a distant relative; Esther was at the check-out counter. They still belonged to a small repertory that put on a few off-beat plays during the year, in a basement firetrap somewhere in the West Village. They rehearsed evenings and weekends. *So much for dreams.*

"I'm sure you've already decided what you're going to do," Rachel said.

"Not really."

"Seems you've got a lot to think about."

"What's your opinion?"

She threw him a serious look.

"I know, you don't want to interfere," he said.

"No, I do," she responded assuredly. "I think you *should* do it. Whatever Sterling's motivations, maybe you *can* do some good. God knows someone has to sooner or later."

"Yeah, but what if I get sucked in."

"Sucked in to what?"

"The prestige, the power."

She laughed. "That'll never happen."

He wasn't so sure.

⚜

Mario's was a quiet little Italian place at the far end of Montague Street, just off the Brooklyn Heights promenade, which overlooked Manhattan's downtown skyline. It had been Sterling's choice, an unpopular, out-of-the-way place with decent food and guaranteed privacy. He, Joshua, and Connie were the only customers, and Joshua couldn't help wondering if it had somehow been arranged that way.

Joshua and Connie walked from the courthouse together. They were already sitting at the bar and had just ordered cocktails when Marcus arrived. He was wearing a three-piece, navy pinstripe, starched white shirt, the collar of which was pinched by a gold tie-bar, and a solid red silk necktie with matching handkerchief. His cologne, which Connie knew was Aramis, was obvious, though not strong enough to extinguish the smell of tobacco. Connie had complained to Joshua, on more than one occasion, of Marcus' cigar habit.

They exchanged niceties. Marcus looked at his watch, giving the distinct impression that he hadn't much time to waste on chit chat. That was fine with Joshua. They took their table, and got down to business.

"So, have you considered our conversation the other night?" Marcus asked, not even bothering to lift a menu.

"Yes, I've thought a lot about it."

Connie's mind was on the menu. She knew she wasn't going to be participating much in the discussion, that she had been invited solely because her presence would make Marcus and Joshua more comfortable with one another.

"It's a great opportunity, for you, and for the community," Marcus said.

"I'm definitely flattered."

"You seem hesitant."

"Well, to be honest, I practice law, not politics."

"And you'll still be able to practice law. That's the great thing. The community board doesn't really require a tremendous time commitment. They meet once a month, and, of course, there are those annoying social affairs that you have to attend. Otherwise, your life is as it was. You conduct your business as usual, though you might pick up some new high-powered clients here and there."

Connie looked eagerly at Joshua, making her position clear once again. But Joshua was still reticent. It all reminded him of a psychology experiment he'd read about in college involving a rat and a piece of cheese. The rat and the cheese were in the same box, only the floor between them was electrified. *Poor rat*, Joshua thought, *nearly died just for a bite.* "Sounds tempting," he said.

"All you have to do is say the word, and the job is yours. You don't have to worry about any competition, you'll be unopposed."

"The Jews don't plan on putting anyone up for it?"

"A deal's been worked out. They realize that they're already 'over-represented,' so to speak. They don't want to make waves, times being what they are and all."

Joshua wondered what kind of deal had been struck, but it wasn't his place to ask, at least not until he decided to accept the offer. "There is *one* thing," he said, faltering, "that I have to know."

Marcus waited, his eyes saying, *Go ahead, ask anything, we have nothing to hide.*

"Why *me?*"

Marcus had anticipated the question, of course, but feigned surprise. He paused for a second, mulling over his prepared answer one last time, then said, "Well, for starters, your reputation in the community is solid."

"With some."

"Yes, with some," Marcus conceded. "Look, Joshua, you and I are a lot alike. You're from Lewis Avenue; I'm from Bedford Avenue. Your mother worked her bones as a maid; mine washed dishes at Dubrows. We both came up from the gutter and made something of ourselves, so I respect you."

Joshua was discomfited by how much Marcus knew about him, but realized he'd been foolish to have expected otherwise. Men like Marcus always did their homework.

Marcus continued, "Now, I know that you have your ways, that you haven't always seen eye to eye with some of my, let's say, 'associates,' but that doesn't mean shit in the scheme of things. Thompson and Williams are essential for what they do: making noise and making the people aware of what's happening. If you don't agree with their methods, so be it, but at least they're exposing the problem."

Joshua nodded.

"The community board is something different," Marcus continued, "or at least it should be. It needs to become a forum for discussion and negotiation, and that's where you come in. You have connections in the Hasidic community; you know those people and how to deal with them. That's why *you*."

"You give me too much credit. I only worked in the synagogue for a while as a kid."

"You underestimate yourself. I understand you single-handedly saved two Hasidic girls by fighting off a gang of Micks."

"That was a long time ago, and your account is a bit exaggerated," Joshua said, looking down at his leg, then across at Connie. She was also surprised at how much information Marcus had.

"Exaggerated or not, that's the perception. And I don't need to tell you how important *perception* is in Crown Heights."

Joshua agreed. In fact, he was starting to think that he might have rushed to judgment about Marcus. In public, Marcus seemed to be just another rabble-rouser, but in truth he was simply a politician. It was all part of the game, and Joshua was hesitant to become a player.

The waiter came and took their orders. Connie went for a salad, as usual. Joshua had been noticing how wonderfully she'd been doing on her diet, looking better and better each day. He figured she must have liked Marcus more than she let on.

Marcus went for veal scaloppini, and Joshua got the calamari. And another scotch on ice. He needed the drink, and didn't mind working up the tab for Marcus. It was the least he could do.

The waiter left, and Marcus took Connie's hand, thanking her for her "patience." She simply smiled. Joshua smiled too; there was much Marcus had to learn about his partner.

"So," Marcus said to Joshua, "you will at least think about it, won't you?"

"No," Joshua said. "I'll *do* it."

CHAPTER 55

Rachel Weissman stood in the shower, hot water raining down and easing her body's tensions. She closed her eyes, capturing the tranquility, escaping the sight of her nakedness and its subtle reminders of age and time. At thirty-five, she had a handsome and shapely figure, yet *she* couldn't see it. She focused on petty, inconsequential changes, her reality marred by disappointment, and loneliness.

Her life had amounted to selling dresses, living with her mother, and spending a few evenings each week with a man she loved but would never have. Both she and God had made quite a mess of things, she reflected.

In the beginning, just after her divorce from Binny, there had been a few suitors. Older divorcées or widowers, leftovers who had already fulfilled their obligations of having children. She had tried, but her manner had often been unpleasant. She couldn't stand them, or herself for being where she was. Soon, the *shodchin* stopped calling.

Rachel thought about her father. It had been a few years since his death, and at times like this, she thought it was just as well that he not see her this way.

Yet, despite everything, she had remained a "religious" woman. She still prayed daily, and continued to cover her hair although she was no longer married. And while the latter may have been anathema to her, it was a dictate of the community in which she had chosen to continue living, the very community from which she had so often felt rejected.

She attended the synagogue every Sabbath with her mother, and showed strength in facing the hordes of married young women with their strollers. This, despite the fact that her childlessness would always haunt her.

In truth, the only thing Rachel had to thank God for was her mother, her sole lasting companion in life. They had grown to be as sisters, and Rachel's secrets from Hannah had dwindled over the years. Hannah knew everything, including things she might have preferred not knowing. Yet, when all was said and done, Hannah didn't, and couldn't, judge her daughter.

Rachel's thoughts returned to the moment as she ran the bar of soap over her body, her eyes still closed. Her flesh was soft and supple, her mind stirred from the soap's sweet aroma. She imagined Joshua there with her, caressing her slippery skin with his hands. She had allowed herself such fantasies in the past, though not too often.

She slowly slid her hand up the inside of her thigh, dreaming it was *his* hand. She opened her mouth to gasp, as her other hand started caressing her chest. It all seemed so real, as real as it would ever be.

Her hands took over; her thoughts ran wild. The hunger and craving could no longer be contained. She began to pant, and tried to keep herself from groaning, fearing her mother or a neighbor might hear. She couldn't fight it; she needed to let go and scream. But then, suddenly, she stopped, her pleasure thwarted by a pervasive sense of dread.

She struggled to catch her breath as the pit of her stomach became flooded with a wave of anxiety unlike anything she'd ever known. She stared at her hands, then touched her left breast once again, as she had before. She rubbed and pressed, but this time not for pleasure. And then she felt it, a small but definite lump that she had never felt before.

She wondered how long it had been since the last time she touched herself this way. Maybe four months, maybe less. She couldn't recall. Her mind was dazed, consumed by fear.

Was this another punishment, she wondered, more payment for her iniquities? Or was it really nothing, a product of her imagination to assuage the guilt of this most recent indulgence? She felt herself again, kneading her hands around the breast, hoping to discover that it had all been in her mind. Only, it wasn't.

❦

The call came about two weeks later, from Doctor Marcia Schiffman. The news wasn't good. Biopsy results revealed a malignant mass. Schiffman insisted that Rachel and Hannah come in person to discuss the options.

Rachel's first reaction was disbelief. How could she have breast cancer at her age? But Schiffman explained that it wasn't so uncommon, especially among Jewish women of Eastern European origin. In truth, Rachel had already known this, and had heard of other such cases in the neighborhood. Only she didn't want to know it now.

Marcia Schiffman had long ago abandoned her Brooklyn practice for the glamour of Park Avenue and the prominence of the Mount Sinai Hospital. She had lost touch with Rachel over the years, but had made sure to send her an announcement when she first joined the new practice. Rachel had taken the card and placed it in a drawer, hoping never to need it. She had continued to see Doctor Silver, the ob-gyn who had handled her pregnancies, for her usual medical needs, which had been negligible since her final miscarriage. Yet, the moment she felt that lump, she knew that it was Marcia Schiffman, her old friend, whom she wanted.

Schiffman's practice was still internal medicine, and while she was no expert in the treatment of cancer, she was now well-connected in one of the world's finest hospitals, and would be able to guide and coordinate Rachel's care with specialists of her choosing. She was glad Rachel had come to her; she had always felt something special for Rachel. And that was what made her task all the more difficult the morning Rachel and Hannah awaited her in her office.

Schiffman stood outside her office door, Rachel's chart in hand, took a deep breath, and entered. "Sorry I kept you waiting," she said, barely looking at Rachel and Hannah as she walked behind her desk. "It's been a madhouse around here all day." She fidgeted for a moment, then settled in, looked up and tried to smile. "So, how are you?"

Rachel, assuming Schiffman was addressing her, skipped the social amenities and said, "You tell me."

Schiffman began nervously thumbing through the chart. It bothered her to see her own hands shake, to display even the slightest amount of distress in front of a patient. She was an old pro, and had dealt with thousands of sick people over the years. Yet, she couldn't deny it, there was something very different about this one. "Well, as I said on the phone, the lump is malignant, and we're concerned that it seems to have grown rather quickly."

"Quickly? How do you know that?" Hannah asked.

Schiffman looked at Rachel. "Well, you told me that you didn't feel it there at least four months earlier, maybe less, right?"

Rachel nodded.

"And suddenly, it's there. That's pretty fast, as far as things go."

"So what can we do about it?" Rachel asked.

This was the part Schiffman had been dreading. "Well, our first concern in situations like this is the possibility of the cancer spreading. Whatever we do, we have to try to contain the malignancy. I've consulted with two specialists in the hospital on your case, and they are both in agreement that the safest and most thorough course of action would be a total mastectomy." Schiffman felt her lips quiver as she spoke those final two words.

Rachel was stunned. "How could this be happening?" she heard herself ask.

Tears began falling from Hannah's eyes.

Schiffman stayed silent, thinking about what she had just said. Delivering bad news was an inevitable part of her job, yet she had never been so affected by it before. Perhaps because she had remembered Rachel as a young girl filled with passion and spirit, and had stood witness over the years as Rachel's hopes receded, one after another. The erosion of a life once so fraught with promise, and now this, the greatest blow of all—it was too much for anyone to bear.

Schiffman thought about her own life, the things she'd neglected while relentlessly pursuing her professional career. She had been divorced for years, and was certain that Rachel had noticed the missing ring, though they hadn't discussed it. She had no children, few friends, and hadn't gone out on a date for over five months. All the prestige and success in the world, yet no one with whom to share it. It was during moments such as this when she wondered if it had all been worth the price.

"Do you know what the prognosis is?" Rachel asked, using a clinical term she remembered from her days working in the hospital.

Schiffman was surprised by the question that most patients would have been afraid to ask. "It's hard to tell at this point. During the surgery, the surgeon will examine the lymph nodes and have a better idea as to what extent, if any, the cancer has metastasized. We're hoping that it hasn't, that it's self contained."

"And what are the chances of that?"

Hannah was growing uneasy with Rachel's questions, but tried not to show it. To her mind, some things were better off not known.

"It's possible," Schiffman answered. "More than that, I can't say."

Rachel lowered her head.

"I'm sorry," Schiffman offered, visibly fighting off tears.

Rachel raised her head, looked at Schiffman, and said, "Don't worry, I'll be all right." It was as if she were talking to herself and allowing the others to listen in. She took Hannah's hand. "Don't worry, Mama, everything's going to be okay."

CHAPTER 56

Joshua was packing his briefcase, preparing to leave the office for the day, when the front door buzzer rang. Mrs. Sawyer had left and locked up hours ago, and Connie was out to dinner with Marcus. He went to see who it was, and found Rachel waiting in the cold. Behind her, in the street, sat a taxi, its engine still running, the driver waiting, apparently unperturbed. Joshua admired the subtle ways in which men reacted to Rachel. Cab drivers were never so obliging with him.

Joshua opened the latch, ushered her in, and she signaled to the driver, who then departed. Her face was blanched, which Joshua attributed to the cold, but as he removed her coat, it became clear that her shivering was from more than just the weather.

"Are you all right?" he asked.

"No, not really," she answered, a tremor in her voice.

"What, what is it?"

"I'm sorry to bother you, were you on your way somewhere?"

"No, just home. *Tell me*, what's the matter?"

"Can we sit?"

He brought her into his private office, and they sat next to one another on the burgundy leather couch she had helped him pick out just a month earlier. "Still feels good," she said, as she planted herself.

"I hope so," he responded, recalling the eleven hundred dollar price tag.

He peered at her, waiting. She took his hand, stared into his eyes, and said, "I have some pretty bad news." She was fighting tears.

He squeezed her hand. "What is it?"

She waited a beat, then came the words: "I have cancer."

"Cancer!"

She nodded.

"How do you know?"

"I had a biopsy two weeks ago, and saw Dr. Schiffman this afternoon for the results." Her eyes began to water.

"Biopsy? Of what?"

Again, she faltered. "Breast."

He looked at her, dumbfounded. She began to cry. He reached out and took her in his arms. She laid her head on his shoulder.

"How bad is it?" he asked.

"They're not sure."

"Not sure?"

She picked up her head, took a deep breath, and said, "Not until they perform the mastectomy."

He couldn't believe what he was hearing. It had to be a dream, a nightmare. "Mastectomy?"

She nodded, as if she couldn't bear to verbalize the word again.

"There aren't any other options?"

"Schiffman's at Mount Sinai now. She's consulted with the best."

She started to weep again. He wanted to break down and cry with her, but he had to keep it together; he had to stay positive. He put his hands on her shoulders, and said, "Rachel, listen to me! We're going to get through this. I will be at your side. You have the best doctors. We're going to fight this and *win*."

Through her tears, she said, "*Win*? Oh, Joshua, when have we ever won?"

"We will win, we *will*," he responded, trying to reassure her as much as himself.

She melted in his arms, crying uncontrollably as he held her with desperation.

CHAPTER 57

Rachel Weissman arrived home shortly after three a.m., finding her mother awake and sitting anxiously in the living room. "Where in God's name have you been?" Hannah asked angrily. "I've been up all night worrying. I called the police and the *Shomrim*." *Shomrim* was Hebrew for "guardians," the name the Hasidim had adopted for their citizens' patrol.

"Why did you call the *Shomrim*?" Rachel asked, displaying some anger of her own.

"Because the police can't do anything unless a person's missing for twenty-four hours. By then, you could have been . . ." Hannah stopped herself, and added, "God forbid."

"I'm fine Mama."

"Yes, I can see that, but where were you?"

Rachel looked at her mother wordlessly.

"You were with *him*," Hannah stated.

"Yes, Mama."

Hannah didn't know how to react. Fourteen hours ago she had sat with Rachel, listening to Doctor Schiffman deliver the worst news possible, and now this. She should have known that Rachel would go to Joshua, and probably did know, though she hadn't wanted to believe it. There were so many things she didn't want to believe.

Whatever her feelings, she couldn't find it within herself to chastise her daughter. God had abandoned Rachel long ago, and maybe it was time for Rachel to grasp what happiness she could. "Come, let's get some sleep," she said, as she turned away and walked toward her bedroom.

"Mama," Rachel said.

Hannah turned around.

"I'm sorry."

Hannah stepped forward and took her daughter in her arms. "You have nothing to be sorry about," she said, her voice trembling from the words she dared to speak. "I'm just glad you're safe."

Just then, a knock at the door.

Hannah walked over to the door. "Who's there?"

A voice on the other side answered, "Yossie Bloom, from the *Shomrim*."

Hannah looked at Rachel and unlatched the door.

"Good evening, rather good morning *Rebbetzin* Weissman," Yossie said. "I'm here about your daughter . . ."

Hannah opened the door further and Yossie saw Rachel standing behind her mother. "Oh," Yossie said, "I was going to tell you that we were still looking for her, but I see everything is okay. Good, I'll inform the others."

"Thank you," Hannah said.

"It's nothing," Yossie responded. "That's what we're here for. It's a good thing when there's a false alarm. Good night." He smiled at Rachel.

"Good night, and thank you again," Hannah said as she closed the door. Then, to Rachel: "There, see, that wasn't so bad."

Rachel pretended to agree with her mother, but knew otherwise, for it wouldn't be long before the news disseminated throughout the entire community that she had been out *somewhere* until three in the morning. Whatever. She had dealt with the gossip mongers before, and frankly, she didn't care all that much anymore. She had bigger things to worry about.

<hr>

Yossie came out of Rachel's building and got into the car. "She's home," he said.

"*She's home?*" Paul responded.

"Probably just got home, otherwise the mother would have called us."

"Where was she?"

"How do I know?" Yossie snapped, completely unaware of his partner's personal interest in the matter. "Probably on a date or something. Nice looking lady, I'll say that."

"Yeah, I know."

Yossie looked puzzled.

"I've met her," Paul explained.

"Oh," Yossie remarked, wondering why Paul had sent him up to the apartment alone.

Paul started the engine and drove off, saying nothing else about the Weissmans, guessing, in his mind, exactly where Rachel had been.

Damn that Joshua!

CHAPTER 58

Rachel's surgery was "successful," though she still needed subsequent radiation treatments. The doctors had said that the radiation was pretty much routine in cases like hers, and that the prognosis remained "good." Initially, her spirits were positive; she had summoned the best of her resources to meet the moment. But gradually, over the months that followed, she withdrew and retreated inward.

She stopped leaving home, and saw Joshua only when he visited, which was usually every day. He often felt that she would have preferred that he not be there, but she never actually came out and said it. She was too listless to do even that.

Hannah, however, didn't seem to mind Joshua's presence. She no longer cared what the neighbors thought. Still, he made a point of scheduling his visits for the late evenings, when it was unlikely for him to be seen.

The doctors wanted to place Rachel on medication, some kind of anti-depressant, but she refused. She believed she had earned her depression, that she deserved it. Wallowing was the least she could do. There was no talking to her, no pulling her out of it. Not until she was ready.

The months turned into a year. Her hair grew back to its full length, and she regained her weight. She began using make-up again, dressing up, and even taking walks during the day. She resumed her excursions to

Joshua's office, every day around noon, always packing sandwiches and whatnot, more than enough for Connie and Mrs. Sawyer as well.

Connie had become engaged to be married to Marcus Sterling. She and Rachel were becoming good friends. Joshua found it hard to believe that things were finally getting into a groove. Even Mrs. Sawyer was mellowing.

Loretta still did her thing, and still didn't want to hear about it from Joshua. Between his practice and late night community board business, Joshua didn't see much of her anyway. Once in a while he would awaken with a strange feeling that someone had been standing in his door during the night, watching him sleep. He could swear he wasn't dreaming.

The afternoon lunches stopped when Rachel returned to work in the dress shop. It had been a year and a half since the surgery, and it felt—at last—that things were finally getting back to the way they had once been. She and Joshua resumed their dinner dates, even attending the theatre and a few movies from time to time. Sneaking around had somehow become far less important.

Joshua, of course, yearned for more. He would wait as long as it would take, and if that wasn't enough he would live with it. For he realized, all things considered, that however much time he had with her was a gift.

⤙⊷⤚

Connie and Marcus were married on October 24, 1987, and Rachel was Joshua's date for the reception. It was ironic, for he had often chided her for her feelings about being seen with him by members of her community, and now with the tables turned, he understood how she felt. He would never raise the issue again.

Having been the daughter of a rabbi, she had always been in the public eye. Now, he was too. He was surprised to find himself concerned about the perceptions of others, and realized how that concern was often legitimate. People were looking and talking.

They sat at a table with Mrs. Sawyer, her husband, Loretta, two other members of the community board and their wives. It was his fellow board members he was worried about. Tensions had been mounting, once again, between the blacks and Hasidim on the board, the blacks still arguing that the Hasidim were over—represented. It was an old story. At the last meeting, Joshua had argued for compromise, hoping to resolve the issue. After he had spoken, another board member called him a "Jew lover." And now, here he was, proving the point.

Joshua tried to ignore his anxieties and have fun. A couple of drinks and the scent of Rachel's perfume helped. There was also the pleasure of watching one of Connie's uncles, a distinguished looking widower, put the moves on Loretta. Joshua had forgotten how beautiful his mother was, how human she was, until she smiled and accepted the man's invitation to dance.

The music was stirring. Rachel and Joshua sat alone at the table. "Come," she said, "let's dance."

"Dance?"

"Yeah, *dance.*"

He pointed to his leg. "Can't."

"Yes you can," she said, pulling him from the chair.

"But I'll fall."

"Just hold onto me, you'll be fine."

"Rachel, I never . . ."

"Neither have I, at least not with a man. There's a first time for everything."

She dragged him to the dance floor, put his hand on her shoulder, and said, "There, use that as your cane." She put one of her hands on his waist, and cupped his free hand with her other hand. They started to move.

He was flustered, and didn't know what he was doing. Their pace was too slow for the music. "It seems we're dancing to our own beat," he said in her ear.

"Aren't we always?"

The band slowed its beat, playing a tune more fitting to their step. Rachel moved closer to him. He felt the entire room watching, but held her tightly. He was dancing.

At the end of the evening, on the way home in the cab, she turned to him and said, "You're going to catch a lot of flak for tonight."

"Flak? Me? Hey, that's my middle name."

Her look told him that she wasn't convinced.

"Don't worry," he said. "I'll handle it."

She took his hand and kissed him on the cheek. "I know. It's just that I wish the world were different."

"We all wish many things."

Joshua arrived at his office early the next morning, sleepless, in no mood for the day awaiting him. Connie would be honeymooning in Hawaii for two weeks, augmenting his already overloaded schedule, and Mrs. Sawyer wasn't due for another hour, forcing him to make his own coffee. He added an extra spoonful; he needed it strong.

He emptied his briefcase, except for the newspaper, and started working on the mail he'd neglected yesterday. When the coffee was ready, he got up to pour a cup, returned to his desk, pushed the mail aside, and grabbed *The New York Times* from his briefcase.

He leaned back and began thumbing through the pages. There wasn't anything out of the ordinary, so he skipped to the Matrimonials, and there, staring at him, was a photo of Connie and Marcus, a headline announcing their wedding, and a small write-up. Connie had known it would appear, and asked him to save a copy for her. He figured she had probably asked all her friends to do the same, just to make sure everyone saw it.

He took a scissors from his desk drawer, cut out the article, and returned to the news. A few minutes passed, he became antsy and realized there were a thousand other things he should be doing at that moment. He was about to put it aside, when something suddenly jumped up at him, a small, inconsequential paragraph, with the heading: *Black Underworld Figure Slain In Bed-Stuy.*

The paragraph read:

> A fifty-two year old black man, Robert Franklin, of 201 Van Buren Street, was found dead yesterday in the back alley of an abandoned building on the corner of Ralph Avenue and Madison Street. The coroner said the victim had sustained multiple stab wounds in the chest and abdomen, and that at least one of the wounds had pierced the victim's heart. Police sources claim that Franklin was a local crime boss, dealing in drugs, numbers, and prostitution, and had been called "Big Bob" by the many neighborhood residents who knew him. It is speculated that Franklin's killing was the result of a local turf war, or an insurgence within his own organization. The victim is survived by an estranged sister, who was contacted but refused comment.

He put the paper down and closed his eyes, trying to picture Big Bob's body lying bloodied on the ground. All he felt was numbness. And an embarrassing but satisfying sense that at last there was some justice in his otherwise twisted universe.

CHAPTER 59

It was a blustering, dreary, February day with remnants of a recent snow on the streets and walkways. Chava Sims, in full winter ensemble, trudged to the local market just three blocks from her home, the wind assaulting her face. She berated herself for not having called for a delivery.

She had been home alone—the girls were in school and Pinchas was at work—and had needed to get out. The weather had kept her indoors for days, and though the house was large, richly decorated, and comfortable, to her it was confining.

It was a new home for them, purchased just the previous year, after Alfred had given Pinchas a sizable raise. It seemed Alfred was becoming more generous with age, or perhaps more penitent. Either way, it was a perfect dwelling for their needs, a one-family limestone row-house, primely located on the south side of Eastern Parkway, just two blocks east of the Lubavitcher main headquarters and synagogue. It was a dream-house, one any woman in the neighborhood would be happy to live in, yet Chava was miserable.

Once she turned southward from Eastern Parkway onto Kingston Avenue, the buildings shielded her from the easterly gusts. She was winded, but had only one short block to her destination. She passed a row of stores, each under Lubavitcher proprietorship, noticing the posters hanging in virtually every window, pictures of the *Rebbe* smiling and waving, with bold lettering underneath, *Moshiach Is Coming!*

She recalled how a year earlier she had gone to the *Rebbe* for a blessing, and had stood in line for hours with hundreds of others, waiting to encounter the leader's magical presence. And when her turn had finally come, she was quickly ushered past him, people standing both in front and behind her, as he held up his hand, mumbled some words she couldn't hear, smiled, and handed her a dollar bill.

The dollar bill, which the *Rebbe* personally handed everyone who came before him, was a token of God's beneficence, a reminder that the *Rebbe* was God's messenger on earth. Chava had taken hers, and had placed it in her jewelry box for safe keeping, and for hope. Yet, a year had passed since that day, and the blessing still eluded her.

Her marriage a sham, her parents practically impoverished, and her mother's manic depression worse than ever, Chava was finding it impossible to maintain her faith. She wasn't merely having misgivings, nor was she in a state of disbelief; she simply stopped trusting God. She no longer relied on Him, or harbored any pretense that the future held even the slightest promise. Her world was destitute, and any chance of salvation seemed dubious.

She entered the market, and was surprised—though she shouldn't have been—to find it crowded with young women. The neighborhood was inundated with new families, lots of children needing milk, diapers, and whatnot; lots of mothers unable to wait for a delivery. Chava took a hand-basket and went about her business.

It was a small grocery, but well-stocked with essentials. The owner, a large, overweight, balding Hasid, stood behind the checkout counter, listening to Hasidic tunes being played on WEVD, an AM radio station with afternoon Jewish programming. He seemed a happy sort, appreciative to have a store filled with customers on a day such as this.

Suddenly the man yelled out, "Oh my God, Oh my God," and all the women turned to see what was happening. His face was red, he signaled for quiet, and raised the volume on the radio. An emergency report came over the air: Chaya Schneerson, the 86-year-old wife of the *Rebbe*, had just died at New York Hospital.

The man began to weep, and one of the women near Chava gasped and fainted. Chava rushed to the woman's side to help, as did some of the others. It had all happened so quickly, it was too much to fathom. The *Rebbetzin* was dead.

The woman regained consciousness. Chava helped her sit up, and offered her some juice. The woman was grateful, but still distraught and breathing heavily. Chava continued to try and calm her.

The *Rebbe* and *Rebbetzin* had no children, which was one of the reasons many believed the *Rebbe* to be the Messiah. Since there was no heir to his position, he must *surely* be the last and, ipso facto, the *Moshiach*. Now, with the *Rebbetzin's* death, the final redemption was undoubtedly at hand, and Chava Sims, tears rolling down her cheeks, felt flames of remorse for ever having doubted.

⤫

Rachel Weissman removed her coat from the hallway closet and glanced at herself in the mirror on the inside of the door. She had been in for days with what had seemed to be the worst cold ever, and she looked haggard. The coughing and fatigue were unrelenting, but the *Rebbetzin's* funeral was not to be missed.

"I still say you shouldn't go," Hannah said, putting on her own coat. "You need to stay home and rest."

"I'll be okay," Rachel insisted, coughing with the words. "It only happens when I talk," she added.

Hannah looked at her, knowing nothing would change her mind.

Rachel feigned a smile. "Please, Mama, don't worry so much. I'm a big girl."

"A big girl who doesn't take care of herself. At least promise me you'll go to the doctor if that cough doesn't clear up in the next few days."

"I promise," Rachel said, hoping it wouldn't come to that. Hannah had been *noodging* her to see a doctor since the "cold" had started, but Rachel had been resistant. "It's just a bug," she had insisted. "I'll get over it." She'd had enough of doctors.

They got downstairs, and stepped out into the chilling wind. Rachel placed her scarf over her mouth and walked silently with her mother. She tried to suppress her coughing so as not to alarm Hannah, but she couldn't. Hannah, feeling helpless, put her arm around her, trying to warm her.

They turned on Kingston Avenue, and were joined by a parade of hundreds walking towards the *Rebbetzin's* home on President Street, where the funeral procession would start. As they drew closer to their destination, they noticed the streets teeming with thousands of mourners. The crowd was at a standstill; this was as far as they would get. They stood and waited.

Many of the mourners were reciting *Tehillim*, Psalms, as was customary in such situations. Trying to forget the cold, Rachel reached into her pocket for the small leather-bound book her father had given her when she was a child. She opened it to what she considered an appropriate passage for the circumstances, Psalm 130, and began reciting softly, *"A song of ascendance, from the depths I called out to You, God. Lord, listen to my voice, may your ears be attentive to the voice of my pleas. If you preserve iniquities, God, my God, who could endure . . ."* It was a prayer of desperation, one with which she had become all too familiar.

She tried concentrating on the words, despite her coughing, and was managing until she suddenly began to feel breathless. She tried to relax, but it didn't work. She was gasping, and became frightened. Hannah noticed, and asked if she was okay.

"Yes, but I think you were right. It's too cold for me to be out. I'm going back home."

"Come, I'll help you," Hannah said, taking her arm.

"That's okay, I'll be fine. You stay here." She didn't want to worry her mother, and she was hoping she'd feel better as soon as she got in from the cold.

"Are you sure?"

"Yes, I just need to rest. I'll be all right."

Hannah was reluctant to let her go on her own, but Rachel insisted that at least one of them should attend the funeral. She reassured Hannah again, then went on her way. Although she walked the few blocks slowly, she had to stop twice to catch her breath. When she finally got home, she went directly to her room to lie down on the bed. She rested for an hour until she felt a bit better, got out of bed to go to the bathroom, and as soon as she took a few steps, she found herself short of breath again. There was no denying it, something was wrong.

Marcia Schiffman stood pensively, scrutinizing the X-ray for the umpteenth time, knowing in her mind and heart that the diagnosis was inescapable. She had already delivered the news to Rachel a few hours earlier, yet she kept looking and searching, hoping that she'd misread something. It was late at night and the office was empty, but she couldn't go home. She couldn't budge, couldn't take her eyes from the film.

She was never one for helplessness or desperation, but at this moment both were all she could feel. She had done her best to remain upbeat and positive when she'd explained it to Rachel and Hannah. "It's a cancerous nodule in a lobe of the left lung, but it's operable. The mammogram shows no changes in the right breast, the blood work is fine, so we have good reason to believe it's contained to this area."

It was always important to hold out hope for the patient. But it was also important to tell the truth, especially to a friend. So in response to Rachel's question about the possibility of future metastases to other places, she had responded, "We don't know," adding, "I wish I could tell you more than that, but I can't."

It had been the most trying dialogue she'd ever had with a patient, yet whatever she was experiencing, it was nothing compared to what lay ahead for Rachel. That much, she knew for certain. She also knew there was little she could do to protect her friend, beyond the usual medical treatment, the efficacy of which was equivocal, to say the least.

Marcia Schiffman thought about the future as she stared at the X-ray, and began to quiver. For the first time in many years, she felt a vulnerability she had thought she had overcome back in her childhood. And for the first time ever, she began to pray.

CHAPTER 60

Although on the other side of Brooklyn, the neighborhood of Bensonhurst might just as well have been a million miles from Crown Heights. Bordering the Belt Parkway and Gravesend Bay on the southern edge of the county, its spotless, tree-lined streets were protected by an unwritten code, prohibiting "undesirables," and levying harsh penalties for even the slightest infraction. A final stronghold of mostly Italians, resisting the swells of integration hitting other neighborhoods, nothing occurring within its borders could bear the slightest relevance to the tempestuous happenings around it. Not until the night of August 23, 1989.

Joshua didn't learn of the incident until the following morning on his way to the office. It was a pleasant start to a summer day, mild but unusually dry; a welcome reprieve from the heat wave that had been plaguing the city for almost a week; more than enough reason to feel good.

He stopped at a newsstand, grabbed a paper, handed the proprietor a dollar bill and waited for change. Always with a smile and a hearty "good morning," the proprietor was a pleasant old black man—tall, thin, and gray. Joshua had patronized the same stand every morning for at least ten years, and hadn't spoken more than four words to the man. Today, it was different.

"You're really gonna like that one," the man said sarcastically, pointing to the front page. "Gonna like it a lot."

Joshua looked down at the headline: *Black Youth Killed by Whites; Brooklyn Attack is Called Racial.* "Holy shit," he said, just loud enough for the man to hear. He started reading the article:

> A sixteen year old black youth was shot to death Wednesday night in an attack by 10 to 30 white teenagers in Bensonhurst, Brooklyn, the police said.

"I told you, you were gonna like it," the man said.

"Yeah, sure," Joshua reacted, not even realizing what he was saying. He was in a daze and began to walk away, his eyes still on the article. He bumped into one of the magazine piles, turned back, and said, "Sorry."

"It's okay, nothing fell."

"Yeah, thanks. Catch you later," Joshua muttered, continuing on his way, still trying to read and walk.

"I told you, you would like it," the man repeated again, this time louder.

Joshua stopped, turned around, and looked at the man, who held his hands up, as if saying, *Hey, what can I tell you?* Then, the man said, "I think its gonna get bad."

"It already is," Joshua said to himself.

❧

By the time he arrived at the office, Joshua had read most of the article. Apparently, the white teenagers had been looking for trouble, hiding and waiting for a black youth they believed had been dating a neighborhood girl. The victim, Yusuf Hawkins, had been in the neighborhood with three friends, reportedly to look at a used car. He was shot twice in the chest, and died shortly thereafter in the hospital. The police had already rounded up four suspects and were actively searching for others.

The article was provocative, comparing this incident to another racial fracas back in 1986, in Howard Beach, Queens, in which a black youth had been killed in oncoming traffic, while being chased by a gang of Italian teens. Already, politicians were out in full force, criticizing the Koch administration for not having been able to gain a handle on racially motivated crime. It was, after all, an election year.

Joshua knew this was going to be a field day for Thompson and Williams, who had been in the forefront of the string of protests that had followed the Howard Beach slaying. He had gotten used to seeing their faces on TV, and would, once again, in just a matter of hours. He dropped the paper on his desk, opened his briefcase, and began organizing himself for the morning. Mrs. Sawyer came into his office with a thick handful of phone messages.

"These are all from today?" he asked. "We're open barely an hour."

"The phone hasn't stopped. It's that Bensonhurst thing."

"What does Bensonhurst have to do with us? We have enough of our own problems."

"Mr. Eubanks," she said with her usual austerity, "you are a member of the community board, a leader in the community . . ." She stopped herself, seeing that he wasn't listening, and in a most uncharacteristic manner, said, "Look, Joshua, you're a player." She placed the stack of messages on his desk, and added, "So play!"

She marched out of his office, leaving him flabbergasted. He looked at the stack of messages. The top one was from Marcus Sterling, and was marked, "URGENT!" He wasn't in the mood to talk to Marcus just yet, so he looked at some of the others. There were a few from members of the community board and the commerce association, some from local newspapers, radio stations, and even one from a CBS-TV reporter.

He got about halfway through, when he landed on one from none other than Alvin Thompson, and another from Reverend Jerome Williams. He would never have expected a call from either of them again, *not for any reason*. The waters were indeed stirring.

Then, at the bottom of the pile, no doubt strategically placed by his dutiful secretary, was the one he was looking for, his daily message from Rachel, stating the usual "when you get a chance." He picked up the phone, and dialed her number.

She came on the line sounding strong and upbeat.

"How are you?" he asked.

"Today's a good day, so far," she answered.

She had concluded her chemotherapy treatments six months earlier, and was still regaining her strength. The lung operation had been successful, and so far the cancer hadn't reappeared. No one knew anything about the future.

"That's great," he said, trying to sound enthusiastic.

"What's wrong?"

"Wrong? What makes you think something's wrong?"

"I can always tell from your voice."

He knew she was certain to learn about it eventually. "Have you seen the paper this morning?"

"Not yet. Why?"

He proceeded to fill her in.

"Joshua, it's a terrible thing, but Bensonhurst is on the other side of Brooklyn. I really don't think anything's going to happen here."

"Rachel, this place is a seething cauldron, just waiting for a chance to explode. It has been for years. Things on the community board have been bad, tensions are higher than ever."

She was silent for a moment. "You're really worried."

"More than you can imagine."

"What are you going to do?"

"I don't know. I have about a million phone messages from the press, other board members, you name it. Seems a lot of folks share my concerns. And get this, both Thompson and Williams called."

"Oh boy."

"Oh boy's right. Look, glad you're feeling good, sorry to spoil your day. I'll try and stop by later tonight. Right now, I'm going to see what I can do to avert another world war."

❧

The meeting had been called for seven-thirty, and went till past two in the morning. It was held in Jerome Williams' storefront church which, due to the pastor's fire, brimstone, and all-around dynamism, had become one of the most well-attended in the area. In fact, the congregation had recently started looking for a bigger building.

And they needed one. The place held, at maximum, slightly under a hundred people, though the usual crowds were almost twice that. The fire marshal had apparently been turning a blind eye.

It was Joshua's first time inside, and he immediately noticed the peeling wallpaper, worn linoleum floors, and rickety pews. Yet, there was a distinct aura of sanctity. It reminded him, ironically, of the synagogue in which he used to work.

All eight black members of the community board were present, several members of the clergy, as well as a few key members of the various block and commerce associations in the neighborhood. In total, about thirty who could potentially sway the sentiments of thousands. Marcus Sterling, the senior official, chaired; Jerome, the host, sat by his side, and Thompson was right up there with them.

For the most part, there was a lot of bantering about perceived injustices in their neighborhood. As Joshua had feared, the Bensonhurst incident was being used as an excuse to rile up the locals. He sat, watched, and listened to calls for protests in the streets, boycotts of Italian owned businesses, and lots of yelling. One board member, the one who had called Joshua a "Jew lover," even suggested boycotting Jewish and Korean owned businesses, while others applauded.

Joshua finally raised his hand, and was recognized by Marcus Sterling. "Yes, Joshua Eubanks, we are anxious to have your input." The room quieted. Just as Joshua was about to begin, he saw Thompson lean over and whisper something in Jerome's ear.

"Mr. Chairman, I've been sitting here for over four hours, listening to my colleagues voice concerns that are both legitimate and troubling. There is, no doubt, tremendous need for change and development in our community, and there are many here this evening who labor tirelessly toward that end. But tonight, *tonight* we have gathered for a different purpose. We haven't gathered for our own needs, but rather for the needs of the family of Yusuf Hawkins and the other young men who were with him. We must support those families, and *yes*, we must protest the injustice, but we shouldn't do anything that would detract from that cause.

"Mr. Chairman, we here in this room are the leaders of a large community. The decisions we make, and the tenor of those decisions, can have a profound influence. We must forever be diligent and mindful of that fact.

"I fear, Mr. Chairman, that protesting on *our* streets, addressing *our* issues, will only serve to detract from this great tragedy; namely, the racial attack that occurred in *Bensonhurst*, not in Crown Heights. And I also fear that such protests would lead to needless, useless violence. We owe it to Yusuf Hawkins to not allow *his* memory or *his* cause to become confused. For too long, we have attacked our own neighborhoods in battles that should have been waged on other fronts. We have protested in, burnt, and looted our own streets, and where has it ever gotten us? *Where?*

"I agree we *must* respond, but we must respond with clarity of purpose and objective. We must respond in a way that sets an example, not in a way that further fuels the flames of hatred . . ."

He was about finished when Thompson jumped out of his seat, and yelled, "Tell me, Mr. Eubanks, will *you* go to Bensonhurst to protest?"

Joshua had anticipated this. "Yes," he yelled back. "I *will* go to Bensonhurst, and I *will* protest against violence and hatred! But I *will not participate* in violence or hatred, neither in Bensonhurst, and certainly not here!"

The room was quiet for a few seconds. Then came the responses to Joshua. The discussion went back and forth for a long while, until a somewhat less than unanimous decision was reached. Joshua won; there would be no official protests in Crown Heights. Everyone would encourage friends and neighbors to join the already scheduled protests in Bensonhurst. The problems in Crown Heights would be tabled "for now."

At the conclusion of the meeting, Thompson approached Joshua. "So, Mr. Eubanks, you shall be joining us on the streets after all," he said gleefully, as if victory was actually his.

"Yes I will," Joshua answered firmly, cloaking any hint of ambivalence. "By the way," he added, "it won't be the first time. I was at the march to city hall the day after Arthur Miller died."

"Were you now?" he asked, his grin sobered.

"Indeed. You know, Professor, there *are* times a man must stand up for what he believes."

"Yes, seems I taught you something, didn't I?"

"More than you know."

Joshua was about to leave, when Jerome caught up with him. "Did you get my phone message?" he asked.

"Yes," Joshua said, appearing embarrassed at not having returned the call. "I had so many messages about this meeting, I didn't think it was necessary to . . ."

"It wasn't only about the meeting." His expression was somber.

Joshua looked at him curiously.

"It was also about Celeste."

"Celeste?"

"I heard from her recently, and thought you might want to know."

"Know what?"

Jerome's eyes watered. "She has AIDS," he answered.

"AIDS? My God!"

Joshua suddenly felt connected to Jerome in a way that he would have sworn had died long ago. Jerome was telling *him* because there was no one else who would understand. "Where is she?" he asked.

"She wouldn't say. I think she's still on the streets." Jerome took a handkerchief from his back pocket to wipe his eyes. "I think she'll call again; she sounded in a bad way."

"Call me if she does, please!"

"I will."

Joshua placed his hand on his old friend's arm. "Jerome, you know my feelings for Celeste. If there's anything you or she needs, I'm there."

Jerome looked into Joshua's eyes. "Let's just get through this Bensonhurst mess, then we'll see."

"Good." Joshua released Jerome's arm and held out his hand for Jerome to shake. Jerome took it, as always, but this time Joshua sensed something beyond mere civility, something more akin to desperation. Or maybe even forgiveness.

⌘

They marched, three hundred strong, through the streets of Bensonhurst, only to be jeered by an equal number of white spectators, many holding up watermelons and chanting obscenities. It reminded Joshua of the protests in the deep south during the sixties, scenes he had watched on film, distant events and places in which he had never imagined finding himself. Yet here he was, almost thirty years later, inextricably tied to this legacy of indignity and defilement, wondering if he could ever have truly escaped it.

There were more protests over the following weeks, smaller in number, targeting the Brooklyn courts and City Hall. The Koch administration came under attack from black leaders, contending that the mayor had a longstanding history of insensitivity to the minority community, and had demonstrated a lack of leadership in quelling racial conflicts.

❦

On November 7, 1989, David Dinkins defeated Rudolph Giuliani, and became the first black mayor of New York City. Pundits speculated that the election came on the heels of the Bensonhurst incident, bringing flocks of minorities and liberals to the voting booths to right some recent wrongs. They finally achieved victory; the largest city in the world now had a black man in City Hall. There was great jubilation in the community. The Hawkins incident was at rest, at least for a while.

Six months later, when the trials began, the protests and marches returned, and Thompson and Williams were once again grabbing headlines. Joshua observed their adventures through the press, seeing mostly youthful protestors struggling to balance rage with the struggle for dignity. And while he stayed away from the frontlines, he somehow always saw himself in the pictures.

Eventually, only one of a total of eight defendants was convicted of second degree murder, and sentenced to thirty-two years to life imprisonment. Two others were acquitted of murder and manslaughter, but found guilty of lesser charges and also sentenced to prison. Another two were acquitted of all major charges, but found guilty to lesser charges and sentenced to probation and community service. The remaining three were acquitted of all charges.

The jubilation was over.

CHAPTER 61

A spring day, the beginning of May, 1991. Rachel Weissman exited her apartment building and sauntered down the block, absorbing the scents of budding trees and early flowers. It was good to be up and about.

Aside from a recent backache keeping her from work for the past two days, she had been maintaining her health. It had been almost three years since the nodule in her lung had been removed. The radiation and chemotherapy had been extensive, and as horrible a memory as it was, she was determined to put it behind her. Her subsequent checkups, most recently five months ago, had all been promising. No signs of metastases. Still, no one would guarantee she was out of the woods.

But she *was* out of the house, and the sky was bright. Two days in bed with her back was more than enough for her. She still had some mild discomfort, but the muscle relaxant Dr. Schiffman had prescribed seemed to be doing the trick. Rachel loved these early morning walks to the dress shop. Nothing was going to spoil her day. Years earlier, she hadn't realized how precious a simple walk could be.

She arrived at the store, and immediately got busy. She had been working on the inventory the afternoon of her last day in the store, and wondered for a moment where she had left the notebook. She tried to think, but couldn't remember. "Have either of you seen the inventory book," she asked her boss, Mrs. Rosenberg, and the other woman who worked with her.

"Sure, it's right here," her boss said, opening a drawer under the counter. "Exactly where you put it yesterday."

Rachel felt funny for an instant; *how could I have forgotten that?* "It must be spring fever," she said, feigning a smile.

❧

Chava Sims peeked through the window of Rosenberg's dress shop and found what she was looking for. Inside, assisting a customer with a fitting, was *the* woman. Chava had seen her many times before, on the avenue and in the synagogue, but had never actually spoken with her. Now, that was going to change.

For years, Chava had endured rumors of her husband's interest in this woman. For years, she had tried to ignore them, or forget. But not today. She just had to learn more about what it was that so enthralled her husband.

Chava grew anxious at the sight of Rachel, and for a moment considered turning back. But she couldn't. She had obsessed over this for weeks, and was going to go through with it. She grasped her pocketbook tightly, took a deep breath, and entered the store.

The bell above the door rang as she entered. It was noontime and Rachel was alone while the others were at lunch. She turned toward the door to see who it was, and thought the face familiar. She offered her saleswoman smile, and held up a finger, indicating she would be right over. Just then, it hit her: the face belonged to the wife of Pinchas Sims. She felt a lump in her throat, turned to glance at the woman once again, and their eyes met.

Rachel nervously finished with the fitting. "Looks great," she said to the woman who was trying on the dress.

"You think so?" the woman asked.

"Stunning," Rachel replied.

"Okay, I'll take it," the woman said.

Chava was browsing through the racks. She hadn't come to buy, but one never knew for certain, especially with such nice things and a healthy bank account.

"I'll be right with you," Rachel called to Chava as she rang up the cash register.

"You're really sure?" the woman asked again.

"Positive. It's to die for; your husband's going to love it."

Rachel bagged the dress, handed the woman back her credit card, and assured that everything was returnable. The woman thanked Rachel and went on her way, leaving Rachel and Chava alone in the store. Rachel walked over to Chava, trying to conceal her uneasiness. "Is there anything I can help you with?" she asked.

"No, not really. I'm just looking." Chava was equally uncomfortable; she hadn't really planned on what to say.

"Okay, well I'll be over there," Rachel said, pointing to the register. "If you need me, just call."

"Yes," Chava said hesitantly, "I will."

Rachel walked behind the counter and Chava continued perusing the dresses. The silence was cold, broken only by the screeching of hangers against the metal racks, as Chava moved the dresses, and by the turning of pages as Rachel thumbed through the inventory book. Rachel looked at the clock. About five minutes until the others were to return from lunch—an eternity.

"You're Rachel Weissman, aren't you?" Chava said from across the store.

"Yes, I am. How did you know?"

"Oh, I've seen you around," Chava answered, her eyes on the dresses. "Your father, may his soul rest in peace, was a pious man. It's hard having a father like that and not having people know who you are."

"I guess so," Rachel responded, observing Chava, as if challenging her to reveal the purpose of her visit.

"Do *you* know who *I* am?"

"I think I do. Your husband is Pinchas Sims?"

"Yes. I'm Chava." Hesitation. "You know Pinchas?"

"I remember him from years ago. He used to come to our home for *Shabbos*."

Chava contemplated what to say next. Nothing was coming to her. "Well, I don't think I've found anything here."

"I'm sorry. We're getting in a shipment of summer dresses in about a week. Why don't you check back then?"

"I suppose I might." Chava moved toward the door. "It was nice meeting you."

"Yes, same here."

"I'll send Pinchas your regards."

"Please do."

The door closed behind Chava. Rachel shuddered, and couldn't recall the last time she'd been so unnerved. She was completely puzzled, wondering what it was that Chava could possibly have wanted. The sound of the bell distracted her; Mrs. Rosenberg was back. It was time for her lunch break, only she wasn't very hungry.

⁓

Chava Sims walked up the block, feeling like she had made a fool of herself, and regretting having ever set foot in the store. She hadn't found Rachel distasteful in any way; on the contrary, she'd found her rather pleasant in both appearance and manner, the kind of woman for whom most men would probably do anything. Chava didn't see herself as that kind of woman; it was hard for her to feel anything positive about herself during times such as these.

⁓

The day passed quickly, something Rachel usually resented. Since her illness, she coveted every minute, but this day had been one she would just as soon forget. She was still shaken by its events. She would be okay, she knew, especially since tonight was one of those nights for escaping and forgetting the world. It was what she had come to call a "Joshua-night."

She tidied up the store, tallied the cash register, and was on her way out, when she felt a sharp pain in her back. Her legs weakened and she needed to find a seat. Mrs. Rosenberg noticed and came to her assistance.

"Are you okay, dear?" Mrs. Rosenberg asked.

"I think so. It's just my back; a spasm, I suppose. I've been taking medication, but it doesn't seem to be working so well right now."

Mrs. Rosenberg could see that Rachel was still uncomfortable in the chair. "Come, let me help you to the back room, you can lie down on the couch there."

Rachel got up slowly and, with the woman's assistance, managed to make it to the couch.

"I think I'll call your mother," Mrs. Rosenberg said.

"*No!*" Rachel said. "I don't want to worry her. It's only a backache; it will pass."

"My dear, you can't even walk. How are we going to get you home?"

Rachel thought for a moment. She couldn't ask Mrs. Rosenberg to call Joshua. "Call me a cab. The driver will help me home."

～

Paul Sims observed the sights of black children playing on the sidewalks, as he drove down Eastern Parkway, recalling his own childhood in Hewlett Harbor, when summer was a time for camp or the beach club. What he now saw—the stark reality of life in these parts—saddened him. Camps and beach clubs didn't exist for these kids, only the street.

His mind turned to the task at hand. He and Yossie had recently been invited to join the *Rebbe's* motorcade, a weekly entourage to the graves of the *Rebbe's* wife and father-in-law in the Old Montefiore cemetery in Springfield Gardens, Queens. It was a great honor to escort the *Rebbe*, a reward for their dedicated service in the citizens' patrol.

It was a modest motorcade, usually three or four vehicles led by a police car. Not quite the retinue for a head of state, but the *Rebbe* didn't require grand displays of his importance, for in the eyes of his followers he was more than a mortal leader. To them, he was the messiah, the savior of humankind. And Paul, for one, was absolutely certain of this. The *Rebbe* would bring peace to the world, and elevate the Jewish people to their rightful position of prominence. It would happen soon, any day.

～

Once in the taxi, Rachel instructed the driver to take her to Joshua's office. "But Ma'am," the driver said, "the lady gave me this address." He showed her the paper in his hand.

"I just need to make one quick stop on the way," she said. It was difficult for her to talk. She thought about taking another pill, but she had taken the prescribed dose about an hour earlier.

The ride went quickly. The cab pulled up in front of Joshua's office. Rachel tried to get out on her own, but couldn't. The driver came around to help her.

Joshua was in his office and heard the bell as the front door opened. He looked at his watch. Knowing it was Rachel, he quickly straightened his tie. He came out to greet her and was shocked when he saw the driver holding her up.

"Rachel," he exclaimed as he rushed to her side.

The two men sat her in a chair. The pain was so excruciating, she was finding it hard to breath.

"I think we should go to the hospital," Joshua said reluctantly.

"No. Please, no hospitals. It's just a back spasm."

"But you can't walk! You can't even sit!"

"Maybe I just need to take another pill."

She took her pills out from her bag, and Joshua got her some water. The driver stood by, waiting for instructions.

"We're going to take you home," Joshua said.

She didn't argue.

⥽⥼

"Have you been having any other symptoms?" Schiffman asked. "Any numbing, tingling, or weakness in your arms or hands? Pain any other place?"

Rachel shook her head.

"How about your vision? Headaches? Memory loss? Bowel problems? Stomach problems?"

Rachel thought for a second. "Not really," she said tentatively.

Schiffman looked at her. "What do you mean?"

"Well, yesterday morning I forgot where I had put the inventory book at work. But people always forget things like that."

"Do *you* always forget things like that?" the doctor asked, already knowing the answer.

"No." Rachel moved uncomfortably in her chair.

Schiffman ordered a bone scan and a CAT scan of the entire body, as well as mammography of the remaining breast. Both scans revealed the presence of metastases to the brain and spine, and the mammogram revealed metastases to the right breast, which had been undetected on routine examination. Rachel was hospitalized that same day, and started on an immediate and aggressive course of chemotherapy. Joshua and Hannah spent the night at her bedside. Schiffman described the prognosis as "guarded."

The "medicine" made Rachel sicker than the disease. She was in and out of the hospital for the next three months; a week of treatment, three weeks home recuperating, then back to the hospital for another dose. A grueling cycle of unrelenting torture.

By mid-August, she had endured four treatments. She was tired, close to giving up, yet something kept her going. Perhaps it was her faith, the very same faith that had sustained her through all else. Or maybe it was her stubbornness.

❧

Joshua stood aside as Hannah helped Rachel get dressed to go home. Schiffman came through the door, a dreary expression on her face. Rachel noticed, and asked, "What? What is it?"

Schiffman looked at Hannah, then at Joshua. To Rachel: "Your tests are back. The news isn't great."

Silence.

Schiffman continued, "It seems the cancer is still growing. Last month the results were inconclusive, but the recent scans and blood work are fairly clear."

Hannah sat down on the bed. Joshua felt a surge of dread in his stomach. Only Rachel remained calm.

"What does that mean?" Rachel asked.

Schiffman: "We're not sure. All we know at this point is that the chemo isn't stopping the cancer completely. What we don't know is whether it's slowing the growth, or if it's totally ineffective."

Rachel: "How do we find out?"

Schiffman: "We continue with a few more treatments, and hope for the best."

"That doesn't sound too promising," Hannah interjected.

"It's the best we can do," Schiffman answered.

Joshua looked at Rachel, knowing she wasn't finished with her questions. "What if it doesn't work?" Rachel asked, almost impassively.

Schiffman: "Why don't we worry about that later . . ."

"*No!* I want to know *now*," Rachel reacted.

"Rachel," Schiffman said softly, "we don't have anything else to offer you."

"So I'm going to die."

"I didn't say that."

"But I am, aren't I?"

Joshua was wordless, paralyzed.

"*Stop it!*" Hannah yelled.

"No Mama, I can't stop it. I'm going to die, and I know it!"

434

Schiffman: "With a few more treatments . . ."

"*What?*" Rachel interrupted. "*What*, with a few more treatments? I'll get even sicker than I am now from that poison you're giving me, if *that's* even possible, and then *what?* I'm going to die anyway!"

Joshua reached out for Rachel, but she threw her arms up to stop him. "*Don't!*" she ordered. "Please, I don't want to be touched."

Hannah began crying hysterically.

"Rachel," Joshua said, "Let's go home now. We can talk about this later."

"Talk about *what*, Joshua? I'm going to die, that's it, isn't it?" She looked at Schiffman, who didn't respond.

"*Isn't it?*" she repeated.

"We need to try a few more treatments," Schiffman asserted.

"No! *No more treatments!* I've had enough of your poison, enough nausea, enough aches all over my body. *Look at me!* I'm almost dead now, why not just get it over with."

"*Please stop!*" Hannah shouted. "*Just stop!*"

Rachel's outburst suddenly abated. She walked back to her bed and fell into a sitting position. "I'm tired now," she said. "I want to go home."

Schiffman simply looked at Rachel, tears welling in her eyes, then turned away and left the room without a word.

"I want to go home," Rachel repeated.

CHAPTER 63

Paul Sims marveled at the voice of Hasidic music's great superstar, Mordechai Ben David, and sang along while he followed the Rebbe's motorcade. The stereo in the new Lincoln made the music seem live. Paul was proud of the car. His father had always driven Lincolns, and now he had one. He drove at a good speed, keeping pace with the entourage, lost in the melodies, and in his elation from being among the chosen.

Yossie, as usual, fixated on his book. He was exhausted and anxious to get home to his family. They had spent the entire afternoon at the cemetery, frying under the torrid August sun, while the *Rebbe* prayed for his beloved wife and father-in-law. For Yossie, being among the chosen was more a burden than anything else.

It was about eight-twenty in the evening. They were the fourth and last car in the motorcade, immediately behind a 1984 Mercury Grand Marquis station wagon carrying some of the *Rebbe's* secretaries and other dignitaries. The station wagon followed directly behind the *Rebbe's* car, which in turn was led by a police car from the 71st precinct.

Paul followed the cars in front of him, turning from Eastern Parkway onto Rochester Avenue, and then right onto President Street, continuing west at a speed set by the police car. They were just a few blocks from home.

Suddenly, as they approached the intersection at President Street and Utica Avenue, Paul and Yossie watched as a 1981 Chevrolet Malibu, traveling north, somehow entered the intersection and crashed with the station wagon in front of them. "Oh God!" Paul exclaimed, jamming on the brakes. Luckily, the Lincoln stopped without incident. Things were not so fortunate for the station wagon.

They sat helpless, horrified at the sight of the station wagon veering out of control as it spun onto the northwest sidewalk and struck what appeared to be two black children. Neither was certain of what they had seen; it had all happened in a flash. The Malibu also spun around, but came to rest on the street, without hitting any pedestrians.

"Let's go," Yossie screamed, as he sprang from the car. But Paul was paralyzed, afraid to move. "Come on, let's go," Yossie yelled, pointing to the crowd forming around the station wagon. "We have to help."

Paul hesitantly opened his door, got out of the car, and followed. He had a bad feeling about all this. They ran across the street, pushed through the crowd, and saw that the children were pinned beneath the station wagon. Paul knew the driver of the station wagon, Yosef Lifsch, as a gentle and righteous man, one who would never intentionally harm anyone. He saw that Lifsch was distraught, attempting to extricate the children. The crowd was angry and began attacking Lifsch and the passengers in his car. Paul and Yossie approached with trepidation, each wondering what good they could possibly do, but it was too late to turn back.

The crowd was growing by the second. Some of the bystanders endeavored to free the children, but most joined in the attack against Lifsch and the others. Paul and Yossie struggled to break through the commotion, as the crowd began to turn on them as well.

Within minutes, a Hatzalah ambulance, having overheard an EMS call, appeared on the scene, and also attempted to assist. Seconds later, two police officers and an EMS ambulance arrived. The crowd had grown to more than one hundred and fifty within less than five minutes, and was out of hand. The officers tried to contain the crowd, and called for emergency assistance.

Additional officers arrived instantaneously, and instructed the Hatzalah ambulance to take Lifsch and two other injured Hasidim to the hospital. The police continued their efforts to contain the mob, while the EMS workers succeeded in extricating the children. But the crowd quickly grew larger and angrier. The sight of the Jewish ambulance leaving with its own didn't help.

Paul and Yossie managed to escape, and returned to the Lincoln. Yossie had a bloodied lip, and Paul had a few superficial scratches on his arms and face. Both were pretty shaken up. Paul nervously started the engine and pulled away, his arms and legs unsteady. He looked over at Yossie, who was gazing silently through the window at the angry mob. Neither of them could believe what had just happened, yet each knew that this was only the beginning.

⌖

Hannah Weissman walked to the bedroom window. She had been resting in a chair beside the bed, watching Rachel sleep, when she suddenly heard strange noises coming from the street. The window was open, the sounds loud enough to awaken Rachel. "Mama, what is it?" she asked.

"I don't know," Hannah answered, peering out the window. "I thought it was some kind of screaming or yelling." She looked up and down the block. Nothing. Silence. She turned from the window. "I guess whatever it is, it's over," she said, holding her hands up empty. "Why don't you go back to sleep."

Rachel had been refusing air conditioning, because the chemo had made her feel cold all the time. On most nights, a cracked window did the trick, except for periodic annoyances from the street. But what they had just heard had sounded like more than an annoyance.

Hannah moved from the window, when suddenly the screaming recurred. Her body jolted. This time it was unmistakable.

"What was that?" Rachel exclaimed.

"Shouting," Hannah replied, turning back to the window. "People shouting." She looked outside again, and still saw nothing. But the clamor was now unrelenting, coming from somewhere else, another street, getting louder by the second, as if it were coming closer.

"Can you see anything?" Rachel asked.

"No. It sounds like it's from around the corner."

Rachel struggled to get out of bed to see for herself, but Hannah rushed to her side. "What are you doing?"

"I want to see what's happening." Fear.

"There isn't anything *to* see," Hannah said as she helped Rachel back to bed.

Rachel complied, and allowed her mother to cover her with the quilt. Hannah returned to the window, looked out, and finally saw something: a group of men coming down the street, shouting. At first she wasn't sure who they were, or what they were yelling; she wasn't sure, or couldn't accept what her eyes and ears told her. And then there was no denying it. Hannah Weissman was staring at a mob of about twenty black men, storming the street, rocks and bottles in their hands, anti-Semitic epithets flowing from their mouths.

"*Mama!*" Rachel screamed, having heard shouts of *Heil Hitler*.

"Stay in bed!"

"What's happening?"

"I don't know." Panic.

Suddenly, a loud blast and flash of light. Hannah watched as a car across the street burst into flames. "*What's happening?*" Rachel shouted again.

"We have to call the police," Hannah answered, as she moved to the nightstand and picked up the phone.

She dialed 911. A female voice came on the other end. "Police operator, what is your emergency?"

Hannah tried to remain calm. "I live on Montgomery Street, just off Albany Avenue. There's a gang of men outside on the street. They're yelling things and they just blew up a car."

"What is your name?"

Just then, a sound of crashing glass.

"Mama!" Rachel called.

"Don't worry," Hannah said to Rachel, covering the phone, "the police will be here soon." She returned to the phone. "They're throwing stones and bottles, breaking windows . . ."

"Ma'am, could you please tell me your name and exact address."

Hannah was reluctant, fearful to give her name. "Look, I can't tell you my name. All I can tell you is that there is some kind of riot on Montgomery Street. It's a Jewish area, and a gang of men are shouting terrible things and throwing things."

"Are these men black, white, or Hispanic?"

"Black, okay. They're black."

"Can you give me an exact address on Montgomery Street."

Again, Hannah didn't want to give any identifying information. "I told you, off Albany Avenue. Get the police! *Right now*! Get the Police!"

"How many men did you say there are?"

"I don't know. At least twenty. Look, my daughter is sick, she's bedridden. We can't go anywhere. We need the police. *Now!*"

"You don't want to give me your name or address?"

"I already told you where it is. Just send the police." With that, Hannah slammed the phone down, walked over to Rachel's bed, sat and ran her hand through Rachel's hair. "They'll be here soon," she told Rachel in as reassuring a voice as she could muster. "Don't worry, it will all be over soon."

⌘

Yankel Rosenbaum walked alone, as he often did, nearing the corner of President Street and Brooklyn Avenue. He was returning to the house where he had been staying, after having visited with some friends. The hour was late, eleven-fifteen to be exact, but Yankel was not concerned. He was always safe on the streets of Crown Heights.

Yankel was a tall, lanky fellow, regarded by his friends as "happy-go-lucky." Blessed with a sharp Australian wit, he was fun to be around, and always managed to fit in, despite the fact that he was far from home. Yet, he also had a somber side. He was a student of history, with a master's degree from the University of Melbourne in Australia, and had come to New York to do research for his doctoral dissertation on the persecution of Jews in Poland during the Holocaust. He was the twenty-nine year old son of Jews who had survived the Holocaust in Poland before emigrating to Australia, and his work was more than just a vocation, it was his life's blood, his search for his heritage. Days and nights he toiled through archives, probing for material that most of his professors believed didn't even exist.

First it had been Poland, where he interviewed survivors and witnesses, visiting small towns, libraries, and anyplace else he could gather new information. Then, it was New York, home of the world's largest Jewish community, haven of capacious archives, and the sanctified residence of his revered Grand Rabbi. He had gathered much in his travels, had grown intellectually and spiritually, and he had made many new friends. And now, it was time to wrap things up, to return to his position of lecturer at the university, and complete his thesis. Three more weeks, and he would be back in Australia, back with his beloved parents and brother, in the home he missed.

Bigotry and hatred were the things that had fascinated Yankel, the things to which he had dedicated his life to analyzing and understanding. Had he found his answers? Had he achieved any profound insight into the untamed evils of the human condition? Or had he wasted his time, preoccupied with a history of antipathy and desolation that would forever recur because there were no answers? In the end it didn't matter, for whatever his quest had unveiled, no one would ever know. And however inspired the lessons he may have learned, none could compare to the one he was about to receive.

Yankel approached the corner, and suddenly heard someone shout, "There's a Jew! Get the Jew!" He looked around, not believing what he had heard, and immediately realized that *he* was "the Jew." A group of about fifteen black men emerged from nowhere, came upon him and attacked him. He didn't have a chance.

Seconds later, Yankel Rosenbaum lay on the hood of a car, beaten and stabbed four times in the back, left helpless, yelling, "Cowards! Cowards!" as his assailants ran, searching for other victims. Three hours later, at Kings County Hospital, he died.

Yankel Rosenbaum's education was now complete.

❦

Hannah and Rachel Weissman heard the sirens in the distance. Hannah walked to the window. It was now eleven-thirty, about five minutes since she had called 911. She looked outside. The street was empty, except for the rioters, who seemed to have at least doubled in number. Their shouting had grown louder. *Get the Jews! Kill the Jews! Heil Hitler!* The hurling of stones and bottles at cars and buildings intensified. The approaching sirens didn't seem to deter them.

Then, finally, flashing lights from two patrol cars shone down the block. The cars moved slowly, announcing over their loudspeakers for the rioters to stand clear and desist. No one listened.

The patrol cars moved in closer toward the rioters, attempting to intimidate them. A few Hasidic men emerged from their homes, feeling safe to be on the streets now, since the police had at last arrived. Hannah was certain it would all be over soon.

And then, anarchy. Pandemonium. Incredible and disturbing things appeared before Hannah's eyes as some of the rioters turned on the police cars with clubs and bricks, while others pummeled the Hasidic men. The furor exploded, the mob attacked the patrol cars, jumping on top of them, yelling, *"Kill the pigs,"* breaking their windows, and pulling the officers out. The few Hasidic men who had dared venture the street didn't stand a chance, their fate joined with that of their supposed protectors.

Hannah gasped with horror as she watched members of the mob overturn one of the patrol cars and set it ablaze, while others trounced the four police officers and the Hasidic men. She ran for the phone, and dialed 911 again. Rachel was hysterically crying, lying helplessly in bed.

"Police operator, what is your emergency?" This time it was a man.

"It's the police, they're being attacked and beaten, and the men . . ."

"I'm sorry Ma'am, I can't understand you. Where are you calling from?"

"Crown Heights! Where else? Don't you know what's happening here? The police are getting beaten up and . . ."

"Ma'am, may I have your address."

"It's Montgomery Street, between Albany and Kingston Avenues. The police tried to stop the mob, but they're getting beaten. Some Jewish men are getting beaten also. You have to send more police!"

"Can you describe the perpetrators?"

"They're black men. It's a riot!"

"Okay Ma'am, I understand. Can you please give me your name and exact address?"

"What the hell is the matter with you people? I told you where it is. Just send help! Please, send help!"

Hannah hung up the phone again, and tried to comfort Rachel. "Don't worry, it will all be over soon." She knew she was repeating herself. What else could she say? She lay down next to Rachel and put her arms around her daughter, cuddling her as she had when Rachel was an infant. She began to pray, *"V'hu Rachum . . . And He, the merciful One, will forgive iniquity, and will not destroy; and often He withdraws His anger, and restrains all His rage. You, God, do not withhold Your mercy from me; may Your kindness and Your truth always protect me . . ."*

Rachel, trembling and frail, joined in her mother's chanting, fervently reciting the words by heart; words of her youth and ancestry; words her blessed father had recited each day of his life, through despair and ecstasy; words that were surely upon the lips of each and every Hasid in Crown Heights, and would soon be echoed by others around the globe. And as she prayed, her head nestled on her mother's breast, she wondered, "Was any*One* listening?"

Then, more sirens. This time louder, piercing. Whistles, and voices shouting over megaphones. Hannah rushed back to the window, and saw what must have been fifty police officers in riot gear, walking up the block, accompanied by five cars.

This is the police. Stand clear and retreat!

The mob complied in part, withdrawing only enough to allow the police to retrieve their battered and unconscious comrades in the middle of the street and three Hasidic men lying on the sidewalk. The police, outnumbered by about four to one, formed a line, and an ambulance quickly came in. The crowd grew restless behind the line, shouting, throwing rocks and bottles towards the police, but the police held fast, at least for the time being. Another two ambulances arrived within seconds, picked up the remaining wounded, and hastened off.

Hannah waited for the police to take control, move against the crowd, make arrests and haul them away, but that wasn't what was happening. What she saw, instead, frightened her to death. Once again, she couldn't believe her eyes as she watched the crowd break through the police line, attacking with clubs and bats, forcing the police to retreat. A few members of the mob got bludgeoned by nightsticks as the cops got a few licks in, but in the end it was all the same. The street belonged to the mob.

Hannah related what she saw to Rachel, unable to hide her dread and hopelessness. What could they do now? There was no one left to call.

"Joshua, Mama, call Joshua!" Rachel insisted.

"*Joshua?* What could Joshua possibly do?"

"He'll help us, Mama, I know he will. He'll get us out of here."

❧

Gaven Cato was seven years old, and had just finished the first grade. He lived in a two bedroom apartment with his family, and spent summer days riding his bicycle and playing with friends. His parents had relocated the family from Guyana to Brooklyn only a year earlier, with hopes of finding a more prosperous life.

Gavin and his cousin, Angela, also seven, were the two children who had been pinned beneath Yosef Lifsch's station wagon on that tragic August night. Lifsch, a twenty-two year old rabbinical student from Israel, was a devoted follower of the Rebbe, and had never been in any trouble of any sort. He was a man who prayed to God three times a day, gave ten percent of his income to charity and, like the Catos, lived in hope for a better world.

Gaven and Angela Cato were playing on a street corner, Yosef Lifsch was performing his duties to his Rebbe, and in one brief instant the fates of these three people collided. For Gaven, life ended within a few minutes. He would never have a chance at the things for which his parents so ardently labored. He would never sit behind that second grade desk, and neighbors would never again see him pedaling through the streets. For Angela, there were traumatic physical injuries from which she would eventually recover, but the emotional impact would last a lifetime. She would forever be scarred by reminders of her childhood playmate and cousin, of innocence shattered and lost one summer night on a Brooklyn corner. For Yosef, there would be an existence of grief and anguish, of the inescapable knowledge that he was the one behind the wheel of the vehicle that had marred so many lives.

For the rest of the inhabitants of Crown Heights, there was the storm; it had finally arrived.

CHAPTER 64

It was just past eleven-thirty. Joshua's phone hadn't stopped ringing for the past two hours; it seemed the entire neighborhood had his private number. He was about to go out and take a look for himself—against his mother's better judgment—when it rang again.

"You get it, Mama. Tell them I'm out-of-town or something."

"Wait! Joshua," she called from the kitchen as he was nearing the door. "It's Hannah Weissman. She sounds bad."

He picked up in the living room. "Hannah?"

He listened to the panic in Hannah's voice as she related what was happening. His heart began to race; he hadn't realized how bad it actually was. The previous calls had described some degree of unrest, but nothing like what he was hearing now.

"What should we do?" Hannah asked desperately. "We have no police protection. They can just come in here and kill us if they want to. My God, what can we do?"

"How is Rachel?"

"Scared. She barely has strength to speak, and can't even get out of bed."

"Listen Hannah, please try to be calm, and try to calm Rachel too. I'll be there. I'll get you both out, I promise. Just hold on!"

Joshua hung up. Loretta stood behind him, her expression bewildered. "How are you going to help them?" she asked.

"I don't know."

He took a circuitous route to his office, avoiding the streets where the violence was concentrated. He opened the front door, flicked on the light, rushed to his private office, and began searching through an old file cabinet. He'd defended a lot of clients in his time, but only one who truly owed him. He found the file, pulled it, and looked for the phone number. He prayed that Willie Johnson would still be living in the same place, would be at home, would remember him after seventeen years, and would be willing to help.

A voice came on the line, but Joshua wasn't sure. "I'm looking for Willie Johnson," he said.

"Yeah?"

"Is this him?"

"Who's asking?" Suspicious.

"Joshua Eubanks."

"*Joshua Eubanks*! I'll be! How you been, Mr Eubanks?"

"I'm okay, Willie. Sorry to be calling this time of night."

"Oh no! It's okay. You can call me anytime."

"I'm glad you feel that way, Willie, because I need to ask you a favor, and I don't have a lot of time for chit chat."

"What do you need, Mr. Eubanks?" Willie said as if he were ready to fill any request. Joshua felt good hearing it.

Joshua explained the situation, and what he wanted to do.

"That'll take a few men, four maybe five." Willie responded.

"The more, the better."

There was a brief pause, then: "No problem. I know just the guys. You tell me where you're at, we'll be there within an hour."

Joshua phoned Hannah from his office, told her to sit tight, and waited.

Willie showed on time, with four associates, two of whom Joshua recognized as having been among his alibis that infamous night seventeen years earlier. The men were large and ominous looking, exactly what was needed.

Willie looked pretty much the same, though a bit older and fatter. He embraced Joshua fiercely and introduced Joshua to the others, saying, "This here is my man, Mr. Eubanks. He believed in me when nobody else did, defended me because he knew I was innocent. Now, he's got a problem and we're here to help." He didn't have to say anything more. The others were obviously with him. Joshua didn't want to know exactly what enterprise Willie was currently mixed up in, he was glad enough just to see the man.

Joshua explained the plan. Getting to the Weissmans' building wouldn't be a problem; unless, of course, someone from the street recognized him. That was where Willie's men came in. It was their job to keep Joshua surrounded and shielded from view.

Getting Rachel and Hannah out was another matter. Joshua hadn't completely figured that one out yet. He suggested avoiding the streets, and taking the back alleys.

"We're going to have to hit the street sooner or later," Willie said.

"I know," Joshua responded, not having much else to offer.

"Look, don't worry," Willie said. "We'll do what we got to do. No one in the streets is going to mess with us." He pointed to his cohorts with pride.

"I don't know, Willie," Joshua said. "Those folks are angry. They've already scared the cops, and they think they've won. They're all hyped up, and just aching for another showdown."

Willie held back a smile, as if he were enjoying this. Two of his cohorts chuckled. "We ain't no cops," he said as he leaned in closer to Joshua and pulled his jacket open just enough to reveal a very large handgun hanging from a shoulder holster.

"Willie, I'm not sure I'm comfortable with . . ."

"No need to worry. I never use it. Just keep it for security.

His friends nodded in agreement.

Joshua then realized that they were all packing, but he was desperate and had no other options. He looked at Willie's crew and knew that they were his best shot at getting Rachel and Hannah out. "Good," he said. "Let's go!"

<hr />

They made it into the thick of things, and were on Rachel's block just a few hundred feet from the entrance to her building. The crowd was yelling and breaking windows, while Willie's crew did a good job camouflaging Joshua, who held his head down just to make sure. Then it happened, the loudest noise Joshua had ever heard—two cars blowing up in the street. He couldn't help but straighten up to see. He'd heard about riots his entire life, and had watched them happening on TV in other cities, but being in the middle of one was unlike anything he'd imagined.

The flames illuminated the entire block, and for a split second his eyes locked with someone else's, a familiar face not more than fifty feet from where he stood—Professor Alvin Thompson. Joshua instantly knew that Thompson recognized him by the stare and grin of satisfaction on the man's face. Thompson had waited for this night his entire life—the uprising of the streets, the launching of the revolution. It was the crowning culmination of all his teachings and yearnings. And now it was his to lead.

Joshua realized his plan had hit a snag. He expected Thompson to use the mob to stop them, discredit him, and prove once and for all that he was the Jew-loving, Uncle-Tom others had claimed him to be. It was only a matter of seconds.

Joshua was fearful of a confrontation, especially considering the artillery that Willie's crew had. He placed his hand on Willie's shoulder, about to abort the plan, when suddenly to his utter bewilderment Alvin Thompson turned away. It was as if the professor hadn't seen anything at all.

※

Hannah rushed to the door, opened it, and gazed strangely at Joshua's colleagues. "They're friends. They've come to help," Joshua said.

"How can anyone help, even the police ran away," she said, panic still in her voice.

"Don't worry," Joshua answered, "we have a plan."

Joshua went into Rachel's room, and found her lying in bed. She looked at him. "I knew you'd come," she said. "You always come when I need you." It was difficult for her to talk. She took his hand.

"We don't have much time," he said. "We have to get you and your mother out of here."

"How?"

"With God's help."

She smiled, he could still do that to her.

Willie and company entered the room.

Rachel: "Joshua, who's . . ."

Joshua: "Rachel, this here is Willie Johnson, and these are some of his business associates. They're here to lend God a hand."

Rachel: "Willie Johnson?" Hesitation. "I remember, he's the one you . . ."

Willie: "One and only, Ma'am, at your service."

Rachel: "Joshua, how can we possibly get out?"

He told her the plan.

"I can't," she said.

"What do you mean, you can't? You have to!"

"Joshua, I can barely get out of bed without falling. How do you expect me to go running through the streets and alleys?"

"I'll carry you."

"You can't! Not that far. You won't be able to move fast enough."

"A bunch of us will carry you."

"Joshua." she squeezed his hand. "I'm too weak. Too much pain. I can't." It was getting more difficult for her to speak.

"Rachel . . ."

"Please, I don't want to leave my bed. Please! Just take Mama and go!"

"*No!* I'm not going anywhere without you," Hannah insisted.

Willie held his hands up in surrender. His eyes said, *What now?* Joshua didn't have an answer.

Joshua: "Rachel, you're talking crazy. We can't just leave you!"

Rachel: "I'm not crazy, Joshua; I'm dying. There's not much left. I'm scared for Mama. You have to help her get out of here."

Hannah: "Stop talking nonsense! I'm not leaving! Joshua, I appreciate what you're trying to do, but Rachel's right; she can't go anywhere, and neither can *I*. We'll be okay. God will help us." She didn't sound too convincing. "Thank you," she said, looking at Willie and his friends, "but we'll be okay."

Joshua noticed that Hannah sounded weak and frail herself. Rachel looked at him, and repeated, "Joshua, please, take her with you. For me."

"I have an idea," Joshua said. He took Hannah by the hand and ushered her to a corner of the room. "I can stay here with Rachel. I'll take care of her, keep her safe."

"*You?* What can you do?"

"Look, Hannah, if someone decides to come in here, I have a better shot at bringing the situation under control than you."

"*Control?* You can bring the situation under control? Then why not go out on the street and do just that?"

"She's safer with me."

"I'm not going anywhere, but if you insist on staying also, you're always welcome."

"Mama, *please!* Stop arguing. Do you want me to leave this world knowing that you were harmed because of me? Is that what you want?"

"*Rucheleh! Stop!*" Hannah's breathing was labored. She began swaying, and seemed to be losing consciousness. Joshua caught her in his arms and carried her to the bed. She was out.

"*Mama!*" Rachel screamed.

"It's okay," Joshua said, trying to sound reassuring. "I think she just fainted."

"Mama," Rachel called again.

"She's unconscious," Willie confirmed, trying to revive her.

"No don't!" Joshua said to Willie, stopping him. "Let her be. It's the only way we're going to get her out of here."

"And how's that?" Willie asked.

"Carrying her."

"And what about your friend?"

"I'll stay with her. She's too sick to go anywhere, and we wouldn't be able to carry both of them anyway."

"Who says we can even carry one?" Willie asked. "If she wakes up, she's going to put up a hell of a fight."

"You'll just have to make it happen. And get her to a hospital right away," Joshua said.

Willie responded with a reluctant, but conceding expression. "Okay, let's do it before she wakes up."

"Joshua," Rachel said.

"What?"

"It could be serious," she said. "We need an ambulance."

"We do, but we don't have one, and by the looks of things outside, there aren't going to be any. Willie's our best bet. They'll get her through the mob and to the emergency room. I promise."

"Don't you worry, Ma'am," Willie added.

"Joshua," Rachel said.

He looked at her.

"You're staying?"

"Of course I am." He brushed her forehead with his hand.

"It's not safe."

"We'll be fine."

She didn't argue. All the fight had gone out of her.

Willie and the others picked Hannah up and carried her from the room. "Don't you worry, Ma'am. We'll keep her safe and get her to a doctor right away."

"Thank you," Rachel said, but Willie didn't hear. He was already out of the room with Hannah and the others. Three seconds later, the front door slammed. Rachel and Joshua were alone.

CHAPTER 65

The riots in Crown Heights began on Monday evening, August 19, 1991. It took more than three days for the police to regain control of the streets. The official word from City Hall was that Mayor David Dinkins had been uninformed about the full extent of the unrest until the third day, due to a breakdown in communication. This, despite the fact that the mayor, Police Commissioner Lee Brown, and various other aides, had all visited the 71st precinct at about one o'clock Tuesday morning, for an emergency meeting with police brass. The mayor's office argued that, notwithstanding the emergency meeting, the mayor hadn't actually visited the streets until Wednesday morning and, thus, could not have had a true grasp of the situation until that time.

Investigations into the riots revealed that police were instructed by their superiors to exercise restraint and not make arrests. The department's explanation was that they were concerned that their officers not escalate the situation and become targets themselves, which, in fact, had occurred in more than one instance. The department also claimed that arrests were made. There were six disturbance-related arrests on Monday, twelve on Tuesday, and thirty on Wednesday. However, on Thursday, after a firm arrest policy was finally issued, sixty-one arrests were made, almost twice as many as the previous day.

Challenged by the media, accused of ineptitude, the department eventually admitted that there was too much ambiguity, and a breakdown in the chain of command in the field. Until Thursday, when they received specific orders, *many officers weren't sure about how to handle the situation. The department, however, has never assigned accountability for the breakdown.*

There was additional controversy, particularly relating to the handling of 911 emergency calls. For unexplained reasons, many response times were far in excess of the norms for that area. Some critics have suggested anti-Semitism as a factor. Whatever the reasons, one thing remains clear: along with City Hall, the New York City Police Department, and 911, all of Greater New York, and the country at large, watched news reports for three nights before any significant action was taken to quell the unrest.

CHAPTER 66

A mid November chill filled the air; the sky was overcast, and the humidity was high. Joshua got out of the passenger seat of the ambulette and helped the driver pull the gurney out from the back. Rachel lay still upon the gurney, tired from the trip, eager for the warmth of her house.

It had been a gruesome week, but now she was home. For Good. She had consented to these last two treatments, more for Joshua and Hannah than for herself, but now it was over. There would be no more treatments; they had proved ineffective, and there was nothing else to be done.

Hannah greeted them at the door in her wheelchair. She was still recovering from her stroke, but was making good progress. With continued therapy, she would soon be using a walker and, perhaps, eventually a cane. She was eternally grateful that Joshua's friends had gotten her to the hospital that night, for things could have turned out much worse.

Behind Hannah stood Loretta, who had finally quit her job, and would now be helping Hannah and Rachel full-time. Next to Loretta was a young Philippine woman, a nurse from a local hospice, who would set up and monitor some of Rachel's medications.

Loretta started putting away Rachel's things, while Joshua, the driver, and the nurse transferred Rachel to her bed. Rachel's fatigue was evident, her breathing labored. Hannah made some tea; she'd become quite adept at getting around the kitchen in the wheelchair. She offered the driver a cup, but he had to be on his way.

Rachel fell asleep quickly, the benefits of a morphine drip. The nurse left, and would return later that evening to check on things. Joshua, Loretta, and Hannah sat in the kitchen, sipping tea, making small talk, and waiting. All that was left to do was wait.

⁓

Joshua entered Rachel's room. It was almost ten o'clock at night, and he'd just come from a community board meeting. The situation in the neighborhood remained dire, the wounds from the riots still fresh. Rachel's condition wasn't much better.

"How'd it go?" she asked, barely able to speak.

"Same old shit."

"Don't be so negative."

"Who's being negative?"

It hurt her to laugh.

"How are *you*?" he asked.

"Same old . . . whatever."

He touched her cheek and smiled. Her breathing was loud, her eyes glossed, her face listless. Her body had become ravaged by the cancer, emaciated to the point where he could see tumors beneath her skin. To him, she was still beautiful. "You don't have to talk," he said.

She offered a faint smile of her own, the best she could do.

Hannah and Loretta came in from the living room. They had overheard the conversation. Rachel had barely spoken during the five days since she'd returned from the hospital, and Hannah didn't want to miss a moment of it.

"Mama," Rachel whispered.

"I'm here," Hannah said as she maneuvered the wheelchair around to the side of the bed.

"You okay?" Rachel asked.

"I'm fine," Hannah answered. "The doctor says I'll be walking in no time. You're going to be fine too!"

"No." Rachel hesitated, she needed to swallow. It was hard to do even that. "I'm not."

"But you will be. The *Rebbe* has been praying for you."

Rachel looked at her mother. She had neither the heart nor the strength to reply.

"You should rest," Hannah said.

"Can't rest . . . afraid."

"There's nothing to be afraid of. God is with you."

"God is waiting for me. Papa is . . ."

"Don't say such things, Rucheleh." Hannah was desperately trying not to cry.

"Mama."

Hannah looked at her.

"I'm sorry."

"Sorry, for what?"

"For leaving you." Rachel was getting weaker with every word.

Hannah burst into tears. She was beyond words. Joshua was on the other side of the bed, and took Rachel's hand. "It's okay," Joshua said, trying to smile.

"Oh Joshua," Rachel said, tears falling. "My Joshua." She tried to lift her hand to touch his face, but couldn't. He lifted it for her.

"God has been unkind to us," she said. "Life has been unkind."

"There's been some good," he responded.

"Not enough."

"Just being with you has been enough."

"Has it?"

Their eyes met, communicating that it hadn't. She coughed and gasped for breath. He put his hand on her shoulder to relax her. "It's okay," he said.

"I'm so tired," she said.

"Then rest," Hannah said.

Rachel looked at Joshua.

"Rest," he said. "It's okay."

"Is it?"

"It is. I promise."

"I'm afraid."

"Don't be. We're right here."

She surrendered and closed her eyes. A few seconds later, she stopped breathing.

Joshua stood in a daze, as Hannah put both her hands on Rachel, shaking her, yelling, "No! No!" When Rachel didn't respond, Hannah began hitting herself.

Joshua gently restrained her, as Loretta knelt down and took hold of her. "Come, Hannah," Loretta said, "you should lie down."

"No! I can't leave her!"

"She's gone," Loretta said, looking Hannah in the eye. "Let me take you to your bed so you can lie down. You need to, or else you'll get sick again. Joshua will take care of everything."

Hannah buried her head in her hands as Loretta wheeled her out. Her wails echoed through the house: "*Rucheleh, Rucheleh, Rucheleh . . .*"

Joshua stood alone in the room with Rachel. He reached out and put his hand on her cheek. "Goodbye, my love," he whispered. He took the sheet and covered her, thinking that at least one of them was finally at peace.

⸻

Rachel Weissman was buried the following morning. It was a small gathering as Hasidic funerals go, the final scorn she would have to endure from her community. The service was held at the grave site; there were no long speeches. Among the less than twenty attendees were Hannah, Joshua, Loretta, Esther and Steven Butler, Esther's parents, and a few neighbors and family friends. And Paul Sims.

Joshua wondered what Paul was doing there, and figured that Paul must have been wondering the same about him. It was Joshua's first Jewish funeral. He'd never before seen a group of men actually bury a person till the ground was leveled, and wasn't surprised when they didn't allow him to help.

One of the rabbis started chanting the memorial prayer. The mourners bellowed in anguish. Joshua was deaf to all of it. He didn't cry, he was beyond crying. And he wasn't angry either. His anger had been spent long ago. He stood, holding his mother's hand, like a small child grasping onto the only person left in his life. The only one he'd ever truly had.

CHAPTER 67

Paul Sims sat in his living room, staring at the walls. It was past twelve; Chava and the girls were asleep. He was trying to study the weekly Torah portion, but couldn't concentrate. He couldn't take his mind off Rachel's funeral.

Between Rachel's death and the recent riots, Paul found himself contemplating his life. His participation in the neighborhood patrol, the blockbusting, and his obsession with Rachel all these years—he didn't have a lot to be proud of. He hadn't told Chava that he'd attended the funeral, but he was sure she suspected as much. She wasn't stupid, and had her own way of learning things. He wondered if he could ever mend his relationship with her, turn it around and start over.

There was a knock at the door. He wondered who it could be so late at night. He got up, walked to the door, and looked through the peephole. He was shocked when he saw the face of Joshua Eubanks.

Paul's hands trembled as he opened the door. He was apprehensive, wondering if Joshua had come to get even with him or something, but then he saw that Joshua was nervous too. It had been close to thirty years since the two of them had stood face to face.

Neither seemed to know what to say. They observed one another in silence for a moment, until Joshua broke the ice: "You going to invite me in?"

"Sure, of course," Paul said, holding the door open, feeling his own awkwardness.

Joshua walked in. "Nice digs," he said, trying to be nonchalant. His tie was loosened; he appeared to have come from a long day, but still he looked the part of a lawyer.

Paul found it hard to imagine that this was the same person who had grown up wearing his hand-me-downs. He wondered if Joshua was reading his thoughts. More than that, he wondered what Joshua wanted.

"Sorry to bother you this late," Joshua said. "I know it's been a rough day."

"For all of us."

"Yes, I suppose so," Joshua reacted, reflecting on the comment. "I needed to talk to you about some things. Is it a bad time?"

"No, no. Please," Paul said. He took Joshua's coat, showed him into the living room, and offered him a drink.

"Some scotch would be fine," Joshua said.

"Great. I happen to have some good stuff." Paul wasn't sure why he offered the good stuff, but something about Joshua made him want to. He opened the liquor cabinet and took out a bottle of Glenlivet 18 Year Old. He wasn't from the fancy single malt drinkers, but kept the stuff around for his father's occasional visits to see the girls. He took out two glasses. "Ice?" he asked.

"Neat, please."

Paul put some ice in a glass for himself, poured the drinks, sat down, and waited for Joshua to start.

Joshua sipped his drink. "Very smooth," he said.

"I wouldn't know the difference; my father's the connoisseur."

"Yes," Joshua responded contemplatively. "So I've heard."

"It was good seeing your mother today. I wish only that it had been under different circumstances."

"She was glad to see you, too. She's always been very fond of you."

"I know."

Joshua hesitated a moment, then continued, "Speaking of my mother and your father, *that's* what I came here to talk about. That, and some other things." He stopped, took another sip, then added, "*A lot* of other things."

Paul squirmed a bit in his chair, at once both uncertain of, and dreading what was coming.

It ended up being a long night, close to five hours for Joshua to tell a story that was as difficult for him to reveal as it was for Paul to hear. And in the end, shaken by what he had learned, Paul still couldn't understand why Joshua had chosen to bring this to him now, after all these years. He was inclined to ask, but opted not to, figuring that Joshua probably didn't completely know the reason either. Perhaps it was Rachel's death, Paul mused, or maybe it was simply that the time had come.

Paul did, however, ask if Joshua was planning on telling Loretta what he knew, and Joshua answered, plainly, "No."

"Why not?"

"I don't want to hurt her."

Paul wasn't surprised by the answer; he believed that Joshua hadn't intended to hurt him either.

"Will *you* tell your father?" Joshua asked.

"No."

"Why?"

"Same reason."

It seemed they had some things in common.

By the time Paul showed Joshua out, the sun was rising. They shook hands and promised to keep in touch, a promise that, for some inexplicable reason, they both knew they would keep.

EPILOGUE

Joshua had thought that the cancer ward at Mount Sinai hospital was the most wretched place he'd ever been, until he stood in the hallway of the AIDS unit at Kings County Hospital. The lighting was dim, the institutional-green walls hadn't been painted in years, and linoleum floor panels were chipped and lifting from their base. The smell of death permeated the air, and moans of torment echoed from the rooms.

He walked into her room. It was barely large enough for four patients, but it held six. No one noticed his presence. The patients seemed lost. Coughing. Groaning. Gasping. He looked at their faces, and moved slowly until he recognized the one he'd come to see.

He stood by the foot of her bed for a few minutes, watching her sleep. She looked different. Sickly, emaciated, but he would have known her anywhere.

She opened her eyes as if she knew someone was there, and for a moment she thought she was dreaming. "Joshua?" she said.

He smiled.

"Is that you?"

"Yes, it's me."

She smiled broadly, a tear fell from her eye. He moved closer to wipe it, feeling the weathered flesh of her cheek. "I'm here, Celeste."

"I knew you'd come. Sooner or later, I knew it."

"So did I."

She coughed, took some water and drank. "Jerome told you where I was?"

"Yeah."

"Good old Jerome."

"He tries. He loves you."

She thought about his words. "He says he's going to take care of me from now on."

"You going to let him?"

"Suppose I should. I'm tired of the streets. Need to get healthy. The doctor says I could live a long time if I cleaned up and took my medicine. Says I wouldn't be in the hospital so much."

"Sounds like a plan to me."

She coughed again. "Damn pneumonia. Third time this year."

He was wordless.

"You know," she said, "my mama's in a nursing home, feeble minded. Sad thing."

"Yes, Jerome told me."

"Your mama's okay?"

"Like the day I was born."

She stared off in silence. "Let me touch you," she said as she took his hand. "Feels good to touch you."

"For me too."

"You been okay?"

"Up and down."

"Yeah, I heard. Jerome told me about that lady friend of yours. Sorry thing, real sorry."

"Sure is."

She saw the glimmer in his eye. "You loved her?"

"Very much."

"Just like you, Joshua, going off, loving the wrong people."

"That's true enough."

"Guess you can't help who you love."

"Never could."

"Neither could I." She squeezed his hand.

"Strong grasp for a sick lady."

"Not as sick as you think; I'll be out of here in no time!"

He smiled again. She was always able to make him smile.

"Jerome also tells me you're a big lawyer now."

"A lawyer, yes. Big?" He looked himself over. "Not really."

She laughed, and coughed some more.

He watched her.

"So you here to save me again?" she asked.

"You need saving?"

"Probably."

"Then I'm your man."

"Good. Cause when I get out of here, I'd like to have you around."

"You'll have to get an army to keep me away."

They laughed together.

"There's something I need to tell you," she said, sounding serious.

"Yeah?"

"It's something bad. Real bad."

He looked at her curiously.

Her tone turned to a faint whisper. "If you're my lawyer, I can tell you anything, right?"

"You could tell me anything even if I wasn't your lawyer."

"I know, but this is *real* bad."

"Doesn't matter how bad it is."

She pulled him closer. "You hear 'bout Big Bob?"

"I read about it in the papers. He was killed."

"He sure was."

"You know something about that?"

She looked him in the eye. "I was the one."

"The what?"

"I was the one who killed him."

Joshua swallowed hard. "Why?"

"He found me and beat me bad. Sent me back into the streets, his streets, demanding all kinds of money. Made a habit of beating me when I came up short. One night, he met me in an alley. I was real sick then, and he still wants his money and all. I didn't have anything. He came at me like he was going to kill me, only he didn't know I had a knife. I Finished it there and then."

Joshua stared at her.

She waited for a response, tears fell from her eyes.

"It's okay," he said. He wiped her tears again.

"It's not okay," she replied, "but it *is* over."

"Yes, that it is. Over and done. So leave it be; you've got more important things to worry about. You have to get healthy."

"Yes, I do, and I will."

"I know."

They talked a little more, and he promised to return the next day. She would be out of the hospital in another week, and would be staying with Jerome. Joshua assured her he would come by often, spend as much time as possible with her, as much time as she had.

"That could be a while," she said. "I plan on sticking around for a long time."

"I plan on it too," he said as he kissed her good-by. "See you tomorrow."

"Yeah, see you tomorrow."

He came out of the hospital to a bright, crispy afternoon. He breathed deeply; the air was as fresh as it ever got in Brooklyn. He started toward the street, when he saw Jerome Williams walking in his direction. Jerome spotted him.

"So you came to see her," Jerome said.

"You knew I would."

"Yes, I did."

"Thanks for telling me where she was," Joshua said.

"She asked for you."

Joshua smiled at his old friend. "She seems like she's going to be okay."

"The doc says she has some time if she lives right."

"She's in good hands with you."

"I'll do what I can."

"I'd like to come around," Joshua said.

"Hope you do."

The two men looked at one another, each feeling the things that would forever remain unspoken between them. "I'm sorry about Rachel Weissman," Jerome said.

Joshua appreciated that Jerome knew her name. "Thanks," he said.

"Well, don't want to keep Celeste waiting," Jerome said.

"Right."

"See you around."

"You will."

They shook hands, and started to part when Joshua said, "Jerome."

Jerome turned around to him.

"I just wanted to say that . . . I'm sorry too."

Jerome appeared curious, unsure of what Joshua was alluding to.

"For your father. I'm sorry. If it means anything."

Jerome contemplated for a moment, looked at Joshua, and said, "That was a long time ago."

"Yes it was. But sometimes it seems like yesterday."

"I suppose so. Maybe you need to make your peace with God about it."

"God's easy; you're the tough one."

"Not as tough as you think."

"Good to hear."

Jerome put his hand on Joshua's shoulder. "Come around the house when Celeste's there. We'll talk more."

"Look forward to it. Maybe we could even solve some of the world's problems while we're at it."

"Pretty tall order," Jerome said.

"One never knows."

"That's for sure."

They said good-bye, and went their separate ways. Joshua had planned to catch a cab back to the office, but had decided to walk.

It was a good day for walking.

POSTSCRIPT

The twenty years since the Crown Heights riots have witnessed significant efforts by the African American and Hasidic communities to promote dialogue and heal tensions. Notwithstanding, there is still much to be done towards enhancing understanding and sensitivity in a broad and meaningful way. I hope this book contributes to those endeavors.

Made in the USA
Lexington, KY
16 June 2014